To sleep, perchance to kill

A Lilbury Murders Mystery

James Quentin

To Alasdair,

For being nothing like Simon, Ollie, or any other man in this book.

Chapter 1

There once was a small church that sat on a small hill in a small village.

Except, the small church that sat upon the small hill in the small village was actually not that small.

The hill – a rise, really – was also a decent height, and the village was actually average-sized.

Right, let us start again. The church, which, to be fair, was larger than several others in a ten-mile radius, was on a slight (yes, let's go with that) rise in a village of indeterminate size.

Its vicar, however, we can describe with much more precision. He was around his early-to-mid-forties, which made him a baby compared to the usual ages of Church of England vicars – and was not unattractive. He had curly strawberry-blond hair that he wore a little too long and had a face that was a little too unevenly textured to be classically handsome. His body was strong from years of half marathons for charity and abstemious avoidance of Mildred from the Women's Institute's ever-present scones at parish council meetings.

This aforementioned vicar made his way out of the rectory on a sunny spring morning, whistled as he walked down the path, stopped at the gate, and in a flight of fancy (making sure no one saw him), vaulted the gate instead of opening it, landing gracefully on the other side. "Still got it," he whispered to himself while also running a hand along the arse of his trousers to make sure he hadn't ripped his second-best chinos in the process.

The walk to the church was about fifty yards, and the vicar continued to whistle tunelessly as he made his way across the grass. He stopped at the door to the nave, next to where the glass-fronted bulletin board for parish announcements was catching the sun, and checked his own reflection. He fastidiously manoeuvred his hair into place. The vicar was a vain man, something vicars were not supposed to be, what with the being all up in God's business thing and vows to do good and the like. But no vicar was perfect; even members of the clergy had to delete 'hot-babe-on-babe-action.com' from their web browser histories occasionally.

Our vicar, who was christened Jethro, went by Jed, and was nicknamed JedRev by the local village, was one such man. He had cultivated an air about himself – he could be seen in the organic shop in Sittingston ruminating over which type of quinoa was less harmful to Bolivian peasants or completing one of his aforementioned half marathons to raise money for dyslexic Azerbaijani orphans.

He was also occasionally seen in Davey's – a less than salubrious drinking establishment in Sittingston (across the road from the organic shop, to be precise) where he had downed four vodkas. He'd have his hand on a fellow customer's knee, slurring that they should come back to his place, and he'd help them see God.

But back to today. He opened the door, ceased his out-of-tune whistling finally, and instead turned on the little radio that sat on the windowsill. Out came the tunes of 98.1 FM, Dorset's easy listening station with Jonny T and Marla in the mornings. JedRev had once been given a medal by Marla after coming third in a half marathon. She'd eyed his muscular thighs.

JedRev wandered through the back of the church, noticing where Mrs Crocker, the cleaning lady, had not poked her hoover and cloth into, so he could inform her she needed to do a bit better. He had inherited Mrs Crocker from the previous vicar, and frankly, much like his selection of brandy in the drawer of his desk, Jed wouldn't mind her being poured out.

With these thoughts occupying his rather small brain, he didn't hear the door open again. He didn't hear the soft footsteps on the stone floor, nor the sound of a candleholder being picked up off a table in the back room. And, as the person holding it was good at silences, he didn't hear them turning it over in their hands to check its weight and give a few whacks to the air to see if it had good aerodynamics before they decided they were satisfied with it. He did, however, hear a tiny creak as whoever it was stepped off the stone flooring and onto a wooden step. "Mrs Crocker, is that you? You're early today!"

There was a dull thud and then a groan. The sound of footsteps, and then JedRev sank to the floor, a pool of blood emanating from the wound on his head. The attacker looked at the body lying on the floor, and then down to their glove-clad hand, where they still held the candleholder. They gave a small shrug and decided to give him a few more whacks for good measure.

Chapter 2

I have never been sporty.

The act of physical exertion is not something I have ever thought *Gee whiz, getting out of breath and sweaty, that's something I wish my life had more of* about.

And yet … yet, here I am. Running. Running through a field. "Oh, Jesus," I cried as I reached the crest of the hill.

"Two minutes to go, you're doing great!" said the American-accented woman in my pocket.

"Fuck off, Brenda, or whatever your name is," I snapped. Beside me, Kenny ran along, happily oblivious to my near death.

This was torture. But I kept going. That's when I saw them – and what a sight they got to see in return: me in a sleeveless T-shirt and running shorts, red as a tomato, sweating profusely as I jogged (very slowly) up a hill with my dog running rings around me.

"Hi, Arden!" Rita Parkinson called out from the cab of her tractor. She swung out of the open compartment door, while her husband, John, drove. "You're doing so well. We've been watching you. Remember last month, you had to stop and walk up this bit!"

As neighbours, I loved the Parkinsons. They were calm, peaceful people who looked out for you. Rita's actions as my number one exercise fan, however, were not the best part of my day.

I waved back and then ducked through a hole in the hedge. "Kennedy, come, we're going this way now!"

Kennedy, my rescue dog, a half Dobermann and half black Alsatian, didn't even bother to slow down as he bounded through the hedge. He was basically a panzer tank and could have made his way through the Ardennes and into Normandy in less time than it took you to say, "Please stop humping my leg."

I was never sure I was a dog person, but after the things that had happened over the last few months, I decided that a big beast of a guard dog was probably not the worst idea.

The only flaw in this plan was that Kennedy was more likely to lick things to death than anything else.

I'd also been against the idea of having to train a puppy and deal with their overly energetic chaos. My naturally bleeding heart had told me to try and adopt an older dog who might not be as popular as a younger one.

Kennedy was five and had a little bit of grey around his muzzle, but aside from that, he was as fit as a fiddle, and my plan to get a dog who didn't have enough energy to run the Iditarod on a daily basis had not been picked up by him.

On the very slim plus side, this meant his need to burn energy had driven me to start running. On the negative side, I now had a dog that was eating me out of house and home, chased the cats if I even thought about taking a day off from exercise and worst of all – did I mention this yet? – made me have to go running.

"That's it for today. Wow, you did so well," Becky with the good hair or whatever her name was told me from the app in my pocket.

"Piss off and die, you little bitch troll from hell!" I yelled at her but deep down I was glad I'd made my daily target. "Come on, Kenny. No, put that down. Don't eat it! For fuck's sake!"

I walked through my front door ten minutes later and promptly collapsed my sweaty body onto the floor of my kitchen. Kenny licked the sweat off me. "Kenny, stop," I said, weakly. I knew if I didn't tell him off, he'd start licking in some private areas, and I didn't want to be up on a bestiality charge.

From inside my pocket, my phone began to buzz. Christ, why did people insist on calling me? Had I not given off enough of an *I hate you, leave me alone* vibe?

I saw the name of the person calling. It was only 9 a.m., and already my day was turning out horribly.

"Hi Ollie," I said and rolled over onto my front, pushing Kennedy's exploring nose from my shorts.

"Hello? Why do you sound like that?"

"I've been running."

"Really?"

"Do not sound incredulous or I will hang up on you," I warned.

"Ooh, touchy-touchy. Anyway, I'm calling to see if you're free for lunch?"

I perked up, slightly panicked. "You're in the neighbourhood? Or am I supposed to be in London?"

"No, I'm in Bristol. Stayed over last night after a client meeting that ran into the small hours. I've been up and working again since six this morning and am knackered. I'm taking the afternoon off as a quasi-long weekend."

"Is it Friday?" I asked. I'd lost all track of time. All I did was run and edit my latest book to the sadistic wishes of Verity, my agent, and my editor, Hortensia. Verity would dangle news of a possible TV adaptation deal of my books in front of me whenever my mood darkened, which was, frankly, becoming a joke. We'd had one meeting with some executives months ago and then never heard from them again.

"Yes, of course, it is. Have you been drinking?" he said.

"No." I pushed Kennedy's investigating nose away again and got up to open the fridge to find him some food. Mostly so he'd stop sniffing me in places I normally only let people into after the third date. "Just busy."

"Ha. Well, anyway, I'll be done in about an hour or so here, and then my self-declared half-day begins. How would you feel if I took the long way back to London and stopped in to see you? We could have lunch at the pub in your village."

"Pub's closed," I blurted out.

"It's not," Ollie said.

"I live here, I think I know it's closed."

"Then how come it had a 'grand reopening' party last weekend, which was on Twitter?"

"Because the internet is fake news."

"Come on, it's a beautiful day. Going to be a scorcher apparently, with this heatwave. Why not spend it in the beer garden with me? I'll pay and everything."

"I don't know, I've got loads to do." It was a lie.

"That's a lie. Arden Forrest has never been too busy for anything. Dropping everything to focus on something new is your preferred way to live."

"Fine. But let's not go to the pub, I could meet you halfway? Oh, why don't we go to Bath? Bath's nice and has loads of restaurants."

"Because you don't live in Bath, and I want to see your village."

"No, you don't. It's a shithole. Right awful dump. Potholes, casual racism, horse shit all over the street. It's feudal."

"Can't be worse than south London," he said.

"I—"

"Great. I'll be there soon. Can't wait!" He hung up.

"He hung up on me," I informed Kennedy, who was staring at the tin of dog food in my hand and wagging his tail in a sly *if I play my cards right, there could be food* manner.

"I can't believe he hung up on me," I told him as I forked some pieces into his bowl. Within seconds, it was out of the bowl, and he was eating it on the floor and making a mess. I sighed. "Do I want Ollie to come here? I should clean."

Two hours later, post me showering, post Kennedy getting a bath, post the bathroom being put back together and Kennedy sulking under my bed when I tried to dry him, post the rest of the house getting a frantic cleaning (which mostly consisted of me throwing paper in cupboards), I deemed us acceptable for guests.

"Kennedy, sit still. Try and look calm and demure."

He was parked in front of the fridge licking his bollocks. "*Demure*, Kenny." I eyed the cats, who were asleep on the sofa. "Good. Stay like that. Don't move a whisker."

I heard a car in the driveway. Ollie, because he was a prick, drove a Jaguar. Sorry – let me expand that properly – because he was a prick with too much money, Ollie drove a Jag. A 1983 V12 XJS. It was supposedly sleek and powerful and sexy and lots of other words.

The only thing I could tell you about it was that it was a nice maroon colour.

I'd had to stand in field after field, after industrial brownfield site, after driveway on cul-de-sacs in Essex, after used car lots in Walthamstow, after motorway service centres, while Ollie searched for his dream car the year before we'd split up. He'd always wanted a classic Jag, and he was at a time in his life when he could afford it (i.e. no longer subsidising me), so he was going after his heart's desire.

"Isn't it beautiful, Ard?" he said about the car on the driveway of a particularly BNP-looking man's house in suburban Essex one Sunday afternoon, which had also been the hottest day of the year.

"It's a nice colour," I offered as I fanned my T-shirt, trying not to show how it was sticking to my sweat-slicked torso.

They had gone back to discussing prices, and the man's wife had come out and offered me a drink and told me how nice it was that I had accompanied my friend on his journey. "Making sure that it's not a bad decision and he doesn't get in trouble with the missus," she'd said, giving me a wink.

"Lady, I am the missus" was what I absolutely did not say. Instead, I laughed blithely and silently wished he'd fucking buy it or not so we could leave. It was his money; he could do what he liked with it. As long as it didn't affect the week in Portugal we had booked as a holiday, he could buy a gold-plated shredder to stick £50 notes in.

Back in the present day, Ollie emerged from that same car. "Hello!" he called as he got out. I hadn't seen him in about three months. Not since we'd run into each other at a cocktail party where my boyfr … the person I was with had threatened to have him ejected in a coke-fuelled temper tantrum. Previous to that, we'd had dinner in London in the weeks after I'd moved down here. He'd asked me to come back to London, and, more importantly, take him back. I'd said no.

Let's say, considering we had dated for five years, lived together for four-and-a-half years and been in love for somewhere in between those two amounts of time, our last few meetings had been strained.

It was his fault, I told myself. He was the one who'd slept with the twenty-two-year-old from his work. Who'd sent dick pics and lied to me and brought him to our flat to have sex with in our bed while I was away.

What had I done wrong? Oh, there'd be something – most people cheat for a reason, even if that reason is as shallow and callous as *I was bored*, instead of something deeper like *I had met my soulmate*, *the sex was mind-alteringly good*, *they made me feel alive*, or my mother's preferred reason with all of my stepdads: "He was a drunk who got a bit punchy-punchy when he'd had a few."

He'd told me I hadn't seemed to need him any longer. I had hated that. What was I, some fledgling who'd fallen from the nest and needed Oliver Ross, Lord of CrossFit, Vice-Captain of the Durham University Rowing Team, Head Boy of Dumfries Grammar School, Patron Saint of Protein Powder and Tough Mudders, to look after him?

When I met Ollie, I'd gone from being a broke waiter to getting my first job as a reporter at a finance magazine. Verity had got me the job, and even though I was earning shit money, I had business cards and could claim expenses. I was on my way.

Ollie in his swish suits, with his £100 holdall for his gym kit that went everywhere with him; with his uni friends who booked a villa in Nice every August; with their country pub Sunday lunches, and visits to Royal Ascot; his parents in their big house who commuted to Edinburgh and stayed at their pied-à-terre during the week; he was never the right fit for me.

His parents could tell – "Oliver told us you were from Poland, but your English is very good. We'd even looked up a few phrases in case, hadn't we, dear?" – his friends could tell – "Ollie said you worked in finance … oh, you report on finance. Well, all the same, right? Except for the size of your pay! Hahaha!" The only person who didn't seem to realise we were doomed from day one was Ollie.

"Hello, stranger," he said, whipping off his sunglasses and grinning at me.

He stood in the May sunshine at the bottom of the path, wearing his boat shoes, blue chinos, light blue dress shirt, and with his tousled light brown hair catching the light. His confident smile made my heart soften a bit. I did love him for much of those five years. Perhaps from the moment that we sat down on our first date.

He hadn't been to my house before, so I gave him the tour. The living room was deemed "very nice".

"It hasn't been decorated since World War One," I replied.

"Yes, but it's … homely?" he offered.

The kitchen was next. "Is this finished?"

"Mostly. There is a bloke from one village over, but I'm bottom of his list. He's due to come back again in a few weeks and do the last bits."

"Weren't you getting this done over the winter? How is it still going on?"

There was a story I didn't want to tell him. "And, these are the animals," I said, changing the subject. Oliver liked animals – in theory – so I all but threw the cats at him and let Kennedy go wild. "What's upstairs?" he asked as Kennedy sniffed his crotch and tried to get his nose into the pockets of his trousers.

"More house."

"Am I allowed to see it?"

I sighed. "It's just the bedrooms and the loo."

"Good. Busting for a whizz. Had way too much coffee this morning."

So, we went upstairs. He poked his nose in my bedroom, and I made sure the visit was brief. I pointed at the bathroom and said I'd wait in the lounge.

When he came down, I handed him Kenny's lead. "Consider this your workout for the day."

He seemed amiable enough, and so we made our way outside and started down the lane. Ollie pointed at the field to our left. "Is that the path you can cut through to the village?"

I nodded.

"We don't take that because it's where …"

"Yes."

"Understood."

A few months earlier, just a week after moving here, I had found the body of a barmaid, Arabella Sweet, near the pub. Her murder was pinned on her boyfriend. But it was my new boyfriend, Tarquin, who had killed her. Then he tried to kill me and another person when we figured it out. I tried not to think about it.

I thought for a second. “Sorry, I’m being a mardy git. You’ve caught me in a mood.”

“Doesn’t matter,” Ollie said, lying, as he strained to keep Kenny from running off. “I assumed you’d be in an odd mood with me for just turning up and … the last few months.”

“It’s okay,” I said. More needed to be said, but I couldn’t face it.

He smiled at me in that way that spoke of unconditional love, so I quickly turned away from him and started pointing out local landmarks. “Church, pub, old manor house – Honningtons, home to Lady Georgiana Frobisher,” I said. There weren’t a lot of other landmarks.

Ollie nodded away as I nattered to distract myself, and we made our way into the village. I felt a shiver go down my spine as we neared the pub. I had been here once since I’d found Arabella’s body.

“You alright?” he said, as once more Kennedy tried his best to strangle himself with his lead as he took in every smell around him.

“Yup.” I pushed open the door to the pub. Inside, it was dead. Well, not completely, but there was a grand total of one other customer. An old man with a copy of the *Daily Express* sat in the corner with a Guinness.

In front of me, though, was Cytrine Hughes, the landlady of the Fox and Lamprey. She was a large French Caribbean woman who wore bangles and a lot of leopard print. “Arden!” she said in surprise and stopped wiping down the bar. “Goodness, me.” She dropped the cloth she’d been using and came around with her arms open wide. “It’s been too long.” She gave me a bear hug, which I awkwardly received.

“And who’s this?” she asked, meaning Kennedy.

"This is my rescue mutt, Kenny."

"Ah, yes, Rita mentioned," she said. "I'll get him a bowl of water." She stood up from where she'd crouched down to give him a scratch behind the ears.

"Cytrine, this is my friend, Ollie, from London. He's visiting."

"Lovely to meet you," said Cytrine, and they shook hands. "I thought you were never going to come and visit us ever again, Arden," she added, turning back to me.

"Oh, you know …" I mumbled. "Where's Alan?"

Her face darkened. "At the bottom of *La Manche*, for all I care. That lying, cheating, no good— Twenty-five years of my life I wasted on that man! And all the time …" She caught herself and took a deep breath. "Excuse me. I mean, Alan and I have agreed to separate. And the brewery has let me take over the licence of the pub as sole operator. They warned me this is my last chance after … you know, but I assured them it'd be fine; that the pub would make more money than ever now that he wasn't here drinking half the profits when he should be working."

She beamed at us. "Sounds great, congratulations," I said.

Her smile widened. "Go outside and find a table, everyone's out back in the garden enjoying this very non-English weather. Two pints, I assume?"

We made our way outside, where half the village was congregated. All but a couple of tables had a family or a group around them. Ollie burst out laughing. "So, this is where everyone is. Out boozing. When they say it's five o'clock somewhere, they clearly mean here."

"There are lots of retirees in this village," I said, but most of the people in the garden were our age or slightly older.

Cytrine brought us a menu and our pints. She waved at someone. "Woohoo, look at who it is!" she said and pointed at me. Within seconds, several people were headed towards us.

"Oh, God."

"Who are all they?" Ollie asked as Kennedy tried to drink his pint.

"Arden, what a surprise to see you in a pub, not!" said Odette Douglas as she came over.

"I mean, you're literally in a pub as well – I mean, hi Odette! Hi Tatiana!" I said to her daughter who was walking beside her.

"Did you hear?" Odette said before she'd even got near our table and turned to show us her profile. She cupped her belly in the long flowy maxi dress she wore and leaned back so her tummy protruded ever so slightly.

I stared at her for a second, before it clicked. "Oh! Oh, wow. Congratulations."

"I'm nine weeks!"

I cocked my head. "Isn't that very early to tell people?"

"Mummy's very happy to be pregnant," said the weird Victorian child that Odette swore blind was her actual daughter and not some orphaned ghost that haunted her. "She told Daddy to lie on top of her and wrestle a lot, or she would divorce him after he lay on Arabella Sweet a lot and wrestled with her."

Ollie choked on his pint.

"And now I'm having a baby sister, and we will call her Eurydice," Tatiana informed us.

Odette laughed gaily and yanked Tatiana away, but not before her husband – Tommy, the aforementioned wrestling enthusiast – came up to join his wife and child. And his soon-to-be second child, who, despite Tatiana having already named, was far more likely to be christened 'Daddy's Last Chance'.

"Hello, Arden," he said. Tommy was a smug man with a severe Napoleon complex. He was about five foot six, and this bothered him. He worked as a GP in Sittingston and had been one of the many, many men to enjoy Arabella's company. A fan of mine, he was not.

He saw Ollie. "Friend?" he said. He was also a homophobe.

"Oliver Ross," Ollie said. Ollie had a knack for knowing when people were twerps and trying to puff themselves up. He stood up when he introduced himself, as he was taller than me he had at least six inches on Tommy, and deepened his voice to really draw on that Lowland burr. It usually worked on annoying Englishmen.

Tommy looked him up and down and smiled. "Tommy Douglas. *Dr* Tommy Douglas," he said and put out his hand for a shake. Ollie gripped it, and I saw Tommy wince.

"Pleasure," Ollie said, locking eyes. To add to the scene, Kennedy stuck his nose in Tommy's crotch.

"Well, we must be off. We just came in for some fish and chips, as I'm not much of a drinker, not like you, Arden," Odette said. "Come along, Tatiana, mummy needs a lie-down. I shouldn't be on my feet for such lengthy periods in my condition, and Arden's kept me talking too long."

They toddled off, and Tommy threw us a filthy look as they left.

Ollie stared at me.

"What?" I asked, stopping Kennedy from getting up on the table.

He was still staring at me.

"I wasn't exaggerating about the people around here," I said.

"Yes, I'm seeing that now."

At that moment, Kennedy escaped my grip and made a beeline for Cytrine, who was bringing out some banana sundaes that were about to make a child's day. She squealed and tried to hold them as high as she could out of Kenny's way. Both Ollie and I rushed over. "Cytrine, I'm so sorry. Bad, Kennedy. Very bad dog!" I yelled.

I looked up to see a slightly taller woman take the two sundaes out of Cytrine's hands. She yelled "Heel!" at Kennedy, and he did exactly what he was told. He sat on the ground and waited obediently for his next command.

"Good boy," said Nigella. She whistled, and her two sons, Archie and Luca, ran over to us and each grabbed a sundae. "And what do we say?" she asked them.

In unison, the two little dark-haired boys recited in perfect RP: "Thank you, Mummy, thank you, Mrs Hughes, hello Mr Forrest, hello Mr Forrest's friend."

"Good boys, now go back to the table and eat them – slowly!" She turned to Cytrine, who was glaring at Kennedy. "Are you alright, darling?"

"Train him, Arden!" Cytrine said and returned inside.

Nigella laughed and turned to me and Ollie. She walked between us and looped an arm around each of our elbows, and led us back to our table. "Well, well, well. You must be the ex," she said to Ollie.

Ollie blushed. "Um …"

"I was going to come over the moment you walked in, but then I saw you being accosted by Odette. I would've come to save you, but I'd just had half an hour of her telling me about remedies for morning sickness she's found from a group on Facebook, and I had lost the will to live." As she said this, Cytrine came to our table and deposited a large glass of wine in front of her.

"Ah, my will to live has returned," she said, and we clinked glasses.

She took a sip and continued talking. "Darling, it's wonderful to have you back out and about once more. We were all very worried you were going to sell up and move back to London after, er, you know, what happened."

"I needed some time."

"He fell off the face of the earth," Ollie said to Nigella. "I almost drove down here several times to see if he was still alive."

"I ..." I decided not to say any more.

Nigella gave me a long look. "Whatever you needed to do, let that be the end of your self-imposed exile. No one around here is blaming you; I want you to know that. The only conversation topic in the shop was how worried we all were about you. The Hetheringtons wanted to give you a medal for saving Ellie."

I blushed. I had been trying not to think of Ellie. Because it led to thoughts of that night. I traced the scar on my head where there was a bump from the tyre iron Tarquin had bashed me with.

"Anyway, you're not even the biggest conversation topic anymore because of Sheridan," said Nigella.

"Mmm, big drama there," Ollie said, nodding along as he supped his pint.

"What or who is Sheridan?"

They both stared at me in confusion. "Arden, did you crawl out from under a rock?" Ollie asked.

"Macauley Sheridan," Nigella said to me slowly.

I shook my head. Was I supposed to recognise that name?

"The MP. Our MP," she added.

Oh. "Did he get caught doing something?"

"No, he died," Ollie said. "In Parliament. His secretary found him in his office one morning a couple of months ago. He'd had a heart attack while working late."

"How did you not hear about this? It was in the news for weeks," Nigella said. "The tabloids had a field day with their puns."

"He was a hardcore Brexiteer Conservative, so they've been celebrating his life," Ollie added.

"The *Daily Star* even tried to say it was murder for a hot second," Nigella said, rolling her eyes.

Cytrine brought us our meals. A ploughman's lunch for me, a steak for Ollie.

"Yes, and now we're going to have a by-election," Cytrine said as she placed the dishes down. She gave Kennedy a withering look. "Enjoy!"

"I hadn't heard any of this," I said, admitting my ignorance.

"Oh, Arden," Nigella said in a matronly manner. She looked over to her children, and my eyes followed hers. At her table, Archie and Luca were tucking into their sundaes while Nigella's husband, Matteo, sat on his phone looking bored. His eyes met Nigella's, and he mouthed something to her before gesturing at the children.

"I think I'm due back," she said. "But, on a side note, the first hustings for the election campaign are tomorrow at the Sittingston village hall. There are going to be a few surprises, let me tell you." She eyed me. "Come with?"

"I'm not political."

Ollie rolled his eyes. "He'll be there," he said. "Because he needs to leave the house more."

I glared at him. "Fine," I said, as Nigella stood up and made to go back to her family. "I'll join."

"Great! I'll text you the details."

She placed a hand on Ollie's shoulder. "Lovely to finally meet you." Then turned to Kennedy – "Good boy, no – stay."

As she departed, I moaned at Ollie. "What did you do that for?"

"Stop being a sulky git," he said. "You're at risk of becoming an asocial hermit. One of those men who hoards newspapers and keeps boxes of milk bottles."

Those men were very sensible if you asked me.

"You seem popular down here," he said after a minute.

I shrugged. "I've been welcomed."

The truth was, I *had* been made to feel welcome. In the beginning. But after Tarquin, I'd seized up. I couldn't do it anymore.

"Just as long as not too welcome," he said with a wink. Ah, there it was.

In the past few months, I'd slept with two men. One of whom I couldn't bear to think about, and the other, well, he was an enigma.

Then there was Guy Frobisher, who had once asked me out.

There were three of them. Three men who seemed keen on me at one point. Three men with whom I could see myself being content. Oliver – with his perfect light brown hair. Gym-built muscles. His middle-class values. His job in law. Brimming with effervescence and self-confidence.

Then there was Guy. The upper-iest crust of the crust. Old money. Blond hair, a lean body, a craggy face from a love of the outdoors. The country gent. Slightly awkward. Slightly bewildered. But always in charge and always treated with deference.

And then there was Simon Anson. The man who had used my body like a glove. Sent me to heaven and back on my living room floor and had me seeing stars and panting. Big. Bulky. Arms so broad you couldn't get your hands around. Ginger hair and blue eyes. Some kind of Celtic outdoorsman. An educated man from a good family who slummed it as the village handyman, drove a pickup truck, and wore a toolbelt over practical clothes.

Surly and unrefined. True, he didn't seem to like me very much, but his sweetness that day, after he'd rocked my world, couldn't have been faked. I was sure of it.

Three so very different men. I didn't understand any of them.

And if you asked me to pick one, I couldn't.

I tore my mind away from such matters and focused back on Ollie. We talked for another hour or so. We finished our meal. Ollie asked for a tour of the church. We walked in the sunshine. I briefly considered taking his hand. The lubrication of a pint or two in the sun, a nice meal. Being out of the house.

"Why do I do it to myself?" I asked.

"Hmm?" He glanced over as we made our way back up the hill.

"Hide away when anything goes wrong."

"Babe, I wish I knew. You're far too entertaining and smart to take yourself off into the corner when it all gets too much."

Maybe I should try a different strategy? My life seemed to be in a constant ebb and flow. Hell, it was mostly ebb.

We arrived back at my house, and Ollie looked up at it expectantly. I leaned over and kissed his cheek. He clung to me for a hug. "It was good to see you," I whispered.

"Please don't be a stranger." He let me go but leaned forward again to brush an eyelash from my cheek.

"I won't. I promise."

Ollie sighed and then got back into his car. He gave me a long, searching look. For a brief second, I changed my mind and wanted him to come inside. To lie in my bed with me and never leave. But instead, I waved.

He pulled away. As he did, he rolled down his window. "Be sociable!" he yelled and drove off.

Sociable. I could be sociable. It wasn't that hard.

Chapter 3

Early the next day, I drove into Compney Parva to see probably my only friend in this part of the world.

Sonia Bliss had been my estate agent when I purchased the cottage. We'd moved on since then to breaking and entering, and I felt a kindred spirit in her. Someone else who was able to force a smile for the outside world when they didn't really feel it on the inside.

I parked my faithful Green Mobile on the high street and walked into Bliss Real Estate.

The office was two shops knocked into one. The larger had been a butcher's and retained some of the old tiling and ornate Edwardian designs of the former business. Halfway down the internal wall was an opening with a step down to the smaller of the two former shops, reflecting Compney's steep high street.

The larger of the two rooms had a handful of desks but was mostly taken up by a reception and sitting area.

In the room, I was greeted by the sight of Dhapinder Bliss, Sonia's sister-in-law, and a much fiercer estate agent who had parked herself at the semi-circle sofa that took up half the room. She had lacquered nails, a full blowout of her long black hair, and an expensive jacket over a well-fitted blouse.

"Mr Forrest," she called out, standing up. "What a pleasure. What can we do for you?" She had the carefully considered glance of a salesperson; would I be buying? Did she need to have the charm on, or would surface-level politeness be okay in this instance?

I smiled back. "Hi, Dhapinder. I'm here to see Sonia." I glanced around. There were several more staff in the next room. As I looked through, I saw Dhapinder's excruciatingly attractive husband, Trevor, sitting at one of the desks, showing a middle-aged couple some houses on his laptop.

Dhapinder tracked my eyeline. All too aware of her husband's aesthetically pleasing disposition. She gave me a shark's smile. "I'm afraid Sonia's out at the moment, showing a potential buyer around a farm building near Winterborne Minster, but she should be back any second. Is there anything wrong with the property?"

Property. That most annoying of estate agent words. It's a house, or a home, not a property. It's somewhere to live, not a commodity. Of course, even I didn't say this and instead smiled back. "Not a problem, I'll go get a coffee," I said.

"You're more than welcome to wait here," she said with a flourish and directed me to the enormous sofa in the 'waiting area'. I felt torn. "Uhhh ..." I failed to think of a reason why not and instead meekly walked over and took a seat on the faux-velvet (polyblend) sofa in an art deco style.

I was glad, despite the hot weather, that I hadn't opted for shorts and flip flops today, but instead chinos and plimsolls. "Coffee?" Dhapinder asked, gesturing towards their Nespresso machine.

"That'd be lovely."

"You look like a man who likes an espresso?" she said, fiddling with the pods.

I was a man who liked his coffee weak, milky, and sweet, but I smiled instead. "Perfect." I leaned forward and looked through the alcove to the next room and saw several staff tapping away on keyboards. A phone rang, and a thick Dorset accent belonging to one of the keyboard-tappers answered it. "Bliss Real Estate, how can I help?"

"Business is good then, I take it?" I said, benignly.

"More than good. We're too busy to know what to do with ourselves. Can barely keep up with demand."

I smiled graciously as she brought me a coffee and set it on the table. "Good to hear," I said. "I suppose Trevor and Sonia's dad must be glad his legacy is thriving?"

"The business is ours now," Dhapinder said with a forced smile. Oh, touchy subject.

"Of course," I stuttered. "Got to put your mark on it."

"Quite," she replied and took a seat at a desk, where she gave me a look that could lose you a finger.

"Arden!" came a voice from outside. I turned and saw Sonia peering through the glass of the front window. "What are you doing here?" she called.

Dhapinder rolled her eyes and beckoned Sonia in. "For goodness' sake, Son, don't stand at the window like a twit, come inside." She tried to not shake her head at her overenthusiastic sister-in-law but failed.

Sonia entered with a clattering of bags, heels, paper, and dumped it all on another desk. Dhapinder winced slightly at the damage to her pristine aesthetics.

Wearing a short, tight skirt and a low-cut blouse with her jacket sitting heavily on her shoulder, she was clearly ruffled by the warm weather. Her face was red, her blonde bob slightly tousled and not helped by the large sunglasses she'd perched haphazardly on her head.

She cracked open a can of Diet Coke and fanned herself. "Scorching outside. Lovely – but scorching." Her face searched mine for why I was here.

"Arden's been waiting for you, Son," Dhapinder said, offering the information when no other conversation was forthcoming.

If truth be told, I hadn't spoken to Sonia in weeks and was starting to feel awkward.

"I was hoping we could grab lunch?" I said, rather lamely.

Sonia instantly brightened. "Yeah, sounds great. I'll go freshen up." She hopped across the room to a door at the back, which I assumed led to the staffroom and toilets. "Hope you're taking me somewhere fancy."

Just as she disappeared, the bell above the door in the room next to us chimed as Trevor led his customers out. "I'll be in touch about the house on Stinkbottom Lane. In the meantime, do give our website a peruse, okay, bye for now." The door closed, and Trevor's very fine form walked up the steps to the room we were in. He saw me and gave a big smile.

"Mr Forrest," he said, offering a huge hand. I took it and felt a guilty twinge in my nether regions. "How nice to see you, I was saying to Son the other day, 'We haven't seen your mate Arden in a while, how's he keepin' on?', wasn't I, Dhaps, love?"

His accent was as strong as his sister's, and somehow the deepness of his voice meant it had a bit more aplomb.

"You were indeed," she said, folding her arms and leaning forward in her chair.

"Dhapinder has been telling me how busy you've been," I said. *Too busy for early morning shagfests on your runs, I bet*, I thought. She must have you on a tight leash these days.

Thinking of Trevor on a tight leash did nothing for my suddenly too-small boxer shorts, and I wiped the thought from my mind.

"Very," he said. "But who complains about business being good, eh?" He gave me a twinkly smile that lit up his perfectly shaped, perfectly clean-shaven face.

"Right," said Sonia, bustling back in. "I'm off for lunch, back in an hour." She came over to me, grabbing her bag as she passed her desk and barging Trevor out of the way.

"Take all the time you need," her brother said.

Sonia was taken aback by this. "Oh, no, I've a million and seven things to do this afternoon."

"No, no, take your time," Dhapinder agreed. "Bye, Arden, lovely to see you again." She gave a small wave.

I meekly offered a wave back, and with a final surreptitious (at least I hope it was) glance at Trevor's crotch, I dragged a confused Sonia outside.

Once we were in my car, I started in on them. "Good God, those two are like being interrogated by the Gestapo."

It was nothing they said – quite the opposite. But it felt like being circled by sharks. First sign of blood, and they would have you.

Sonia gulped the last of her Coke. "I know, Trevor's gone from being a laugh to dead serious the last couple of months. Him and Dhaps have all sorts of plans for the business they've been working on. Never mind that I own half the company, and Dhaps doesn't own a thing; they act like it's theirs."

"I see," I said. "But you wanted out anyway, right?"

She shrugged. "I don't know. It's the family business. I don't want to leave. Just felt like I was never any good at it. But those two … they're being dead secretive. All – what's the word – furtive."

She shook her head and shrugged again. "Right, where are we going for lunch?"

I hesitated. "So, I may have lied."

"Arden!" she said, her tone severe. "I am not breaking and entering again."

I laughed. "No, nothing like that, this is all legal," I explained the situation.

"Politics?" she said in disgust as I drove the short distance from Compney Parva to Sittingston. The view across the land was of parched fields that desperately needed rain, but even the farmers had shut up for once and were keen to enjoy the once-in-a-generation summer.

"Look, we both need to socialise more," I said firmly.

"Speak for yourself." She folded her arms.

"Fine, I need to socialise more, and I'm dragging you along for moral support."

She gave a small nod at this.

"Please?"

"Well," she said. "You've already kidnapped me, so I can hardly say no, can I?"

The church hall was packed when we got there. Sonia took off her sunglasses as we emerged from the car. "People actually care about politics?" she said.

"I know, it's a crazy concept, Son," I said. We would educate Sonia about a citizen's responsibility and civic duty another time.

We walked into the hall, probably tipping the scales from none to more than one in ten people without grey hair. The room was full, with little white heads floating about in sensible pantsuits across the space. At the front – difficult not to see – was a woman whose naturally jet-black hair reflected in the summer sunshine that was streaming in from the windows.

"There's Gella," I said.

"Is she going to be nice to me this time?" Sonia asked.

Gella clearly decided she would be as she gave Sonia a kiss on the cheek when we arrived.

Nigella was, of course, a keen follower of politics. She'd worked in Westminster in some advisory capacity back in her high-flying career woman days, along with several other impressive jobs in PR and think tanks that painted a picture of some late-Thatcherite feminist revolutionary against the boys' club. "Sonia, you look lovely, darling," she said with a wry smile.

Not sure if she was being insulted, Sonia looked herself up and down to make sure her outfit was presentable and then gave a tight smile in response, taking her seat.

"Oh, Arden, it's so nice of you to bring a friend. But she's not even a voter here," said a familiar voice. Nigella had been leaning forward to give me a kiss on the cheek when the comment was made, but paused and then gave a small sigh.

"Odette," she said, turning to the woman. "Just because Sonia doesn't live in Lilbury doesn't mean she isn't in the constituency. The area is quite large, yes?"

Odette appeared shocked by this. I honestly wouldn't have been surprised if she really had thought her MP was so hyper-local that they just represented Lilbury.

"Also, anyone can come to a husting, Odette," I added. "They don't have to be a constituent."

She laughed. "Arden, it's so nice of you to act like you know about these things." She waved her hand at me in an "Oh, you!" manner.

I gave Nigella a look only to discover she was already giving me the same one. "I'm sorry, she jumped in my car when I was leaving. I thought it was a stray dog for a minute."

Nigella shifted to the end of the row. I sat next to her, with Sonia following me. Odette took the last seat in the row and leaned over Sonia to speak to me. "So nice to see you out and about again. No one is even talking about you harbouring a murderer anymore."

I shrank in my seat.

"Odette, you bloody muppet, would you shut your gob?" Nigella snapped, sounding more Dagenham than Dorset for a second.

She went to respond – presumably in outrage – but a woman with a haircut that would make the 1980s cry banged a gavel on the table set up on the stage. "Ladies and gents, it is my pleasure, as the head of the Compney Parva Small Business Association, to welcome you to this, the first hustings for the by-election of the Central Dorset constituency."

There was a polite smattering of applause.

Nigella leaned over. "Hetty Carter-Bowles. Owns the haberdashery with her husband on Compney Parva High Street. Rumour is they run a BDSM club in the backroom every second Thursday."

Hetty was still talking. "Now, please join me in giving a round of applause for our five candidates." She shuffled her cards and cleared her throat. "In alphabetical order by party name, please welcome: the candidate for the Conservative Party, Guy Frobisher."

There was a solid amount of applause, and my jaw dropped to the floor.

Nigella nudged me. "Told you that you'd want to be here."

Guy walked out onto the stage in a light blue suit, with his blond hair flattened more than usual. He wasn't wearing a tie. Looking very much the part of a gentleman farmer who had put on his only suit for a special occasion. Except the suit was tailored and must have cost well over £1,000.

The last time I'd seen him, I had just shot someone.

I gulped. "You knew?" I whispered to Nigella.

"Darling, of course, they don't keep their candidacies a secret … would rather defeat the purpose. And Guy has always had ambitions for Parliament. We all thought he'd be another ten years or so, but apparently, this was his shot."

"God, I can't believe a Tory asked me out."

Guy took his seat at the far end of the table and poured himself a glass of water.

"Next up, the candidate for the Green Party of England and Wales is Marjorie Potsdam," Hetty said, barely able to hold the disdain from her voice. A less enthusiastic level of applause welcomed a woman in her late forties onto the stage. Guy jumped up to shake her hand.

Marjorie had short hair with a blue streak in her fringe. She wore linen trousers and clogs, with a peasant-style shirt and knitted waistcoat over it.

"I can smell the hemp from here," Nigella muttered. "She's lovely, though. She and her wife run an organic strawberry farm out the back of Brimborne Upon Wylde. They've adopted two dyslexic Azerbaijani orphan girls."

Marjorie gave a polite wave.

"Our next candidate is for the Labour Party, Dr Riz Patel," Hetty said. If she had disdain in her voice for the Greens, she basically threw the card away that announced this guy.

"An Indian doctor, ground-breaking," Nigella whispered, and I snorted despite myself.

Guy once again jumped up to greet the latest candidate. Dr Patel was … oh, actually … Dr Patel was pretty alright looking. In his late thirties with a surprisingly muscular build underneath his linen dress shirt and blue chinos. He bounded onto the stage with a sharp beard and dazzling smile.

"Well, I'd do him," Sonia said to no one in particular.

There was a rustling beside me, and suddenly, I felt Nigella's weight change as she turned in her seat. "You made it!" she said.

I turned to see who she was talking to and felt my lip curl out of instinct. My mortal enemy slash former lover, Simon Anson, slightly flushed from having to rush here, was taking his seat beside her at the end of our row.

"Wouldn't miss it," he answered. He gave me a look. "Arden," he said in a tone that was devoid of emotion.

"Simon," I replied, keeping my eyes looking forward.

"You're here, Simon. I was so worried you'd miss it, now that you're off spying on people again," Odette said, piping up.

"For fuck's sake," Nigella muttered and rolled her eyes.

"I don't spy on people," Simon said, giving a laugh.

Odette nodded and tapped her nose. "Course not."

Sonia looked at me in want of an explanation. I shrugged. Posh people. Ain't like I understand them either.

Nigella was in a matchmaking mood. "I wish you two would try being friends again," she said to me and Simon. "If you got to know each other properly, I'm sure this … tension would break."

Little did Nigella know we'd broken quite a lot of tension on my living room floor a few months back. The kind that involved me having carpet burns on my knees afterwards.

We both gave a non-committal noise in response.

Hetty was shuffling her cards on stage. "Our penultimate candidate is from the Liberal Democrat party, please welcome Ms Suzy Rabbit."

Once again, there was applause as Ms Rabbit joined the others on stage. I saw Simon grimace as Guy did his recurrent jump up to greet her. Suzy Rabbit was a busty woman of about fifty with sandy blonde hair. She wore a sensible dress and court shoes with a chunky beaded necklace that showed she was toning down her normally more acerbic style for today's baby boomer audience.

"She's good, she is." Odette leaned over to tell us. "Her daughter was head girl at Tatiana's school a few years ago. And she worked at the hospital in Warminster as an administrator, before that a nurse. She has that inside knowledge. So she's very good at whipping those other lazy nurses into shape from what I hear – they're so overpaid and spoiled—"

"The Lib Dems have come second in every election in this area since the end of the SDP," Nigella informed me, speaking over Odette, thankfully. "But the gap has been narrowing every election. Last time they came within five points."

"She's in with a solid chance if Frobisher screws it up," Simon said.

"But Guy will do well," Odette said. "He's so smart and is the natural choice."

"Yeah, people around here will vote Tory rain or shine," Sonia added.

"Our final candidate," Hetty was saying, "is from the UKIP Party" – there were cheers and a few boos – "Mr Bob Thrall."

Bob Thrall was a red-faced man in a pinstriped suit who shook Guy's hand heartily as he stepped up and then instantly whipped out a hankie to wipe his perspiring brow. He hesitated before shaking Riz's hand.

"Yikes," I whispered.

"Runs a construction company in Blandford," Nigella said. "Small bit of trouble with the taxman a few years ago, but I think he's got used to living in the caravan now."

The hustings began with Hetty asking each candidate to introduce themselves fully.

Guy went first: "I am passionate about the community, that's why I sit on the parish council, the Chamber of Commerce and volunteer. My family has lived in this area for hundreds of years. I intend to go to Westminster and get them to listen to real, honest people."

I applauded politely. Simon didn't. Nigella elbowed him sharply, and he gave a few half-hearted claps.

Marjorie Potsdam went next. "THE BEES ARE DYING!" she yelled at the top of her lungs. "DORSET COUNTY COUNCIL WANT TO BUILD A NEW DUAL CARRIAGEWAY. JOIN ME, AND WE'LL LIE IN FRONT OF THE BULLDOZERS."

There was shocked silence. This was the most public emotion shown in Dorset in years.

"Are the bees really dying?" Sonia whispered to me.

"Yes," I answered.

"Oh my God, I swatted one the other day. Wait, no, it was definitely a wasp. Are they dying too?"

I shushed her.

Riz stood up to introduce himself. "I was born in this country to immigrants who came here for a better life, so I understand what it is to want to help your family. I'm an anaesthetist at the Royal Salisbury Hospital, so I know what challenges our NHS is under and I have ideas for how to fix them. Send me to Westminster to fix the country, not the guy from the party who actually created them." There were a few jeers at this and some polite applause. Simon clapped for him.

Suzy Rabbit gave the most polished introduction; she cracked a joke, asked the audience how they were, complimented Hetty, and did so well that you could see Guy and Riz rebuking themselves for not doing better.

Bob Thrall stood up. "No more red tape! No more immigrants! No more lefties bleating on about bees! No more French people! No more Poles taking English jobs! No more members of the homosexual community asking for pronouns and to be referred to as a goat, no more—"

"And time for the first question," Hetty said, cutting him off. This question is from Mr Grant A. Wish, the editor of the *Sittingston Citizen*, who wants to know about improving train connections to Bristol."

The next hour, let me tell you, reader, flew by. There's barely a moment I've been happier to lose than that one in the swelteringly hot church hall listening to racism and conspiracy theories (and those were just the questions), while Sonia asked me questions such as "Do the Greens like other colours?" and "Why don't Labour call themselves 'Work!'?".

There was some proper discussion: what to do about the comprehensive in Sittingston needing more funding to renovate its crumbling buildings, the need for a bypass through some of the villages, whether enough was being done to attract people of working age to live here, and what opportunities there were to keep those from the area from moving away.

A screaming match between Bob Thrall and Marjorie's wife was the highlight, though. "Fascist demagogue!" she yelled as she was asked to leave. "Commie pinkeye!" he shouted back.

"I think he meant 'pinko'," Nigella whispered as Marjorie's wife was escorted out.

The meeting broke up, and most people began to leave, while some made a beeline for the candidates for overtime. Riz, however, jumped off the stage and made his way to our group.

"How'd I do, babe?" he said.

"You were great," Simon answered and planted a kiss on him.

Nigella's eyebrows going heavenwards informed me she had been unaware of this development, too. Odette went bright red and began to make a "hhhmm" noise.

"Everyone," Simon said, turning away from Riz, but holding his hand, "this is Riz. My … uh … well, shall we tell 'em?" he asked Riz.

"Fiancé!" Riz answered for him.

"Guess we're telling them," Simon said.

"Oh my … Oh my goodness!" Nigella exclaimed. "Come here and give me a hug, both of you." She turned to me over the shoulders of both Simon and Riz and mouthed, "Oh my God."

A woman came over to our group. She was forty-ish with dark hair that had patches of red in the sun and a pinched face.

"Riz, I thought we agreed to keep it under wraps."

"Everyone, this is Marina Holt, my campaign manager. Normally, she's not quite so strict and boring," Riz said, gesturing to the woman like she was the bane of his existence. Marina tried to arrange her face in a friendly smile. She gave up and looked at her phone instead. Nigella managed to give a greeting. But I was unable. I felt like the world was spinning a bit too fast.

"Sonia, we should go," I said.

But she was busy congratulating them as well. "What lovely news! How long have you been together?"

"About a year," Riz answered. Was I imagining it, or was Simon staring straight at me? Wait, a year. That meant …

"Yeah, we had a brief break-up over Christmas, but Simon came pounding on my door to win me back," Riz said, continuing his explanation.

"We didn't even know you were seeing anyone!" Odette said.

"Sorry, you broke up at Christmas?" I asked.

"Uh, yeah," Riz said falteringly. "I was working too much; Simon was working too much." He gave me a look. Simon, however, was definitely not looking in my direction.

Oh, Christ.

"And when did you get back together?" Sonia said, as if this was the most natural question in the world.

"It was sadly after Simon's friend Arabella died. I understand you all knew her, too? Yeah, what was it you said, sweetheart? That 'life was too short for regrets'?"

"Something like that," Simon said stiffly.

Oh my God. I was a whore. I was everything I'd broken up with Ollie because of. I was a homewrecking slut.

"Sorry to intrude, but I couldn't help but overhear, Riz, are you getting married?"

Everyone looked to me as Suzy Rabbit appeared at my shoulder.

"Yes, I am. Everyone, this is Sooz. She may be a filthy radical centrist, but she's also a dear friend," Riz told us.

She shook everyone's hands and then hugged Riz and Simon.

A man came up and stood next to me. Apparently, we were attracting all sorts. "He's getting hitched? Damn, that's a good backstory. But to a man, that might cancel out any goodwill from that around here."

I looked at the man and then looked again. "Oh."

He was a tall Black man who appeared to be somewhere in his late thirties but was probably well into his forties. He was dressed in a nice suit and even nicer shoes, and held all the easy charm that Marina Holt did not.

"Errol Mottley," he said, holding out his hand to me. "Suzy's campaign manager."

I shook his hand. "Arden Forrest, local swing voter."

"Oh, I think that's a lie."

"Sorry?" I asked.

He laughed. "I don't mean to offend, but I think Mr Patel can safely count on your vote. C'mon, you're clearly one of those London types who've moved down to the countryside."

"I'm not sure if I should be offended."

"I mean no offence," he said, holding up his hands. "Just stating the obvious."

"Is that so? And what about you – that suit tells me you stepped off the train from London about fifteen minutes before this kicked off and you're racing back to the station now."

Errol laughed – it was a nice sound – but shook his head. "I'm based in Bristol; I manage our campaigns here in the South West."

I nodded. "Right, right, I stand corrected."

A photographer from the local paper called out to the candidates, and both Suzy and Riz made their apologies to join the others. Riz gave Simon a kiss before he was dragged back by an anxious Marina. Errol nodded towards the assembling potential-MPs. "I need to babysit; she only photographs well from her right. A pleasure to meet you, Arden. Hopefully, I'll see more of you on the campaign trail." He left to join Suzy, and I felt myself flush.

Nigella and Sonia were preoccupied with Odette, who was convinced the baby was kicking. Simon took his opportunity while they were busy and grabbed my elbow. "Can I have a word outside?"

"You're not giving me much of an option."

We went out into the blazing sunshine where, thankfully, most of the crowd had dispersed.

"You're getting married?" I yelled as soon as we were outside.

"Please don't make a scene." As always, it was someone else's fault with Simon.

"We slept together when you had a boyfriend."

"No! No, that's not right, we had broken up, we only got back together after—"

"So, sleeping with me convinced you to go back to your ex, and then you proposed?"

"Listen—"

"No, you listen," I snapped. "I don't care what you're up to, you've made it clear you don't like me, and I was just a tumble in the hay, but don't act like you're innocent-Mr-High-and-Mighty like you always do."

"Just don't tell Riz, okay? That's all I ask."

I scoffed. "I'm not getting involved in your life any more than I have to."

There was a silence. "You promise you won't say anything?" he asked.

"Promise. None of my business, besides, you're adamant that we did nothing wrong, so why would I?" *Look at me being brave*. Usually, when it came to being accused of wrongdoing, I panicked and worried I'd be made the suspect regardless of any guilt.

"That's right. I got back in touch with Riz the day of Arabella's funeral." He paused and looked at me for a moment. "I was drunk and upset, and I wanted someone to talk to. And one thing led to another, and now three months later, we're engaged."

“How romantic.”

Before Simon could answer – or deck me – Sonia joined us outside. “Odette is crying because Nigella said she’s a stupid cow for going on about the baby kicking when it’s too soon for it to be doing that. She’s locked herself in the toilets.”

Chapter 4

An hour later, after dropping Sonia off at the office and – thank Jesus – depositing a hysterical Odette at her doorstep, Nigella and I were having a G & T in her garden and discussing the day's events.

I'd never seen her garden in hot weather before, and I'm sure she was doing her best to keep her flowers from wilting, but in this heat, even a green thumb like Nigella's had to admit defeat; parched brown grass and droopy flowers abounded.

"So, you shagged Simon on that filthy carpet in your living room?"

"It's clean!" I said, protesting.

"Fine. Not filthy. Threadbare."

"It wasn't planned."

"No," she said, and sipped her drink. "Your conquests never are. I'm beginning to see the pattern."

"Rude."

"And he won't tell Riz? Gosh, even Matteo and I didn't start on that bad a foot when we got married."

I cocked my head. "Problem? Where is the mister, anyway?"

"Milan. As always. Mamma clicked her fingers and off he flew. Some minor manufacturing hiccup that a middle manager could have fixed in two hours, but off Matteo went. Even though he made all sorts of promises to help Guy with his campaign, and not to mention help with the boys."

"Oh, Gella, I'm sorry."

"Ah!" She waved it away. "Marriage. It's a marathon, not a sprint."

The doorbell dinged from the other side of the house.

"That's good timing. I have a surprise for you."

"Noooo," I whined. "I've already had surprises today. No more until next year."

"It's a good surprise. It's the woman who bought the Sweet's house. She moved in a couple of weeks ago. You'll like her. I was thinking about inviting her to the book club. I lent her some bits on local history and promised some of my back catalogue of *Which?* Magazine."

I reluctantly got up, followed Nigella inside, and waited in her oversized extension. Her kitchen was so painfully chic I felt like I was taking money off the asking price of her house just by being there.

"Come in, come in!" I heard her say.

"I hope I'm not intruding," the woman said as she followed Nigella back into the house.

"Not at all. Arden, this is Katrina Pettigrew, Lilbury's newest resident. Katrina, this is Arden. Local gadabout and whoremonger," Nigella said before I could say anything. I proffered a hand – glaring at Nigella – which Katrina took briefly.

Katrina laughed. She was a well-kempt woman of sixty-ish with short, light blonde hair that was being kept from grey by expensive dye jobs. Her clothes and subtle jewellery spoke of money. Also, she'd bought Arabella's old house, which would've cost a bomb. "Nice to meet you," she said with a light burr.

"Ah, another Scot?" I asked. Just what my day needed.

"Is there more of us here? Oh, that bloke from Aberdeen you introduced me to in the pub, aye?" Katrina said to Nigella.

"Yes, Simon. Who is, we've found out today, about to be off the market, possibly to our next MP," she said.

Katrina took this information in. She showed a similar reaction of pretending to care that I would expect anyone to have. "Wow, quite the bunch of movers and shakers in

Lilbury, aren't you? Gosh, I'll have to up my game if I want to fit in."

There was a small pause in the conversation, so I jumped in. "And what brought you to Lilbury, Katrina? Is it just you?"

"Yes, my husband died last year. Stomach cancer."

"Oh."

"So, I sold up and moved away for a fresh start."

I didn't really know what to say to that. Nigella did, though. "Arden's pretty new here as well. He moved to the village because he found his ex-boyfriend screwing an intern in their bed."

"He's Scottish too," I said. "The ex. Not the intern."

Katrina didn't blink at this. "Right. Right, okay. So, Lilbury attracts all sorts, then?"

Nigella was about to say something when the sounds of sirens outside distracted us all. "God, those are loud," she said. The three of us went out to the street where we saw a police car following an ambulance, both belting towards the church.

"Goodness, what's going on?" Katrina asked. Most people had come out of their houses.

An elderly woman stumbled down the street wiping away tears. She was being half-led, half-carried by the local shopkeeper, Roz.

"Mrs Crocker?" Nigella called out. "What on earth has happened?"

Roz shook her head and answered for her as the three of us gaped. "Gella, it's awful, poor Delia here is terribly shook up. I'm taking her back to mine to wait for the police."

"What's happened?" Nigella called out again this time with a lot more panic in her voice.

"The vicar," Delia Crocker said in a strong Dorset accent. "It's the vicar, Mr Fulford. He's … he's dead."

Chapter 5

He wasn't dead. But he was as good as. Apparently, there was a flicker of life in him, hence why half the Dorset ambulance service turned up. Nigella rang me the next morning to tell me he was on life support in Bournemouth Royal Infirmary.

"It's fifty-fifty whether he'll ever wake up," Nigella said down the phone as she sniffled.

"God, I'm so sorry, Gella. I know he's a friend."

"It's a lot to take in," she said. "Thank God that Mrs Crocker forgot her reading glasses at the church the day before and went to look for them. Otherwise, he'd have died on the floor there all alone."

I told Nigella not to think like that. I was sitting at my breakfast bar, idly pretending to work. It was a sunny Sunday morning that promised to turn sweltering later in the day. Kennedy was half-heartedly chewing one of his toys at my feet, and the cats were nowhere to be seen. Off pillaging and murdering, I assumed.

My laptop in front of me dinged with a new message update.

Ollie: And now the vicar is dead? You didn't half choose a wild place to live.

I chose to ignore the tone of the message and replied that he wasn't dead, merely just *nearly* dead.

Ollie: Have the police got any leads?

Not as I know of. But they don't often tell me those things.

Ollie: I saw your man on TV this morning talking about it.

This grabbed my attention. Which man?

Ollie: Posho I met at the party back a few months. The blond.

The irony of Ollie calling others posh.

"Apparently, Guy was on TV this morning talking about it?" I blurted out to Nigella, interrupting her telling me about Delia Crocker's cataracts.

"Oh, yes, of course he was. *BBC South West.*"

I found the page and opened it.

VICAR LEFT FOR DEAD read the headline. There was a short blurb underneath: Dorset Police are investigating the motive of an attack at St Candida Church in Lilbury, which has left one man in hospital with critical injuries that are thought to be life-threatening. Local sources have confirmed the man as Jethro Fulford, 44, who has been the parish vicar in the local area for several years.

I pressed play on the video. Scenes of the cordoned-off church were followed, naturally, by a mention that this was where Arabella was murdered a few months previously.

"Arabella Sweet was a barmaid at a local pub and daughter of the businessman Miles Sweet. Her alleged killer, Tarquin Scott, is imprisoned awaiting trial after being caught while he was trying to kill two people who were witnesses to his purported crime."

At least they didn't mention me by name. Odette popped up on screen. "Local residents are shocked," said the voiceover from the reporter.

"This isn't the sort of place where this happens," said Odette. "It's because we have lots of people from London moving down here, and they're bringing their drugs and crime connections with them. There's Arden Forrest, for instance; he was dating the man who killed Arabella, and some around here think he was in on it."

"Arden Forrest, the writer?" the reporter asked.

"Yes, Arden Forrest. That's F-O-R-R—"

Guy popped up on screen alongside Riz. "Local resident and Conservative Party candidate in the Central Dorset by-election, Guy Frobisher, agrees. He was joined by

Labour Party candidate Riz Patel to call for more community policing in the area."

"Riz and I both agree that swinging cuts to rural policing has seen crime rise in these areas, and we want this to be looked at," Guy said.

Riz nodded. "Both Guy and I are fully agreed on this. Robust community policing must be in place to stop tragedies like these from being allowed to occur."

I shut the laptop. Well, at least the near death of our vicar had brought the Left and Right together again. Nigella was still talking.

"Riz and Guy are running a meeting tonight outside the church, a sort of vigil cum community watch thing. I think Roz is making sandwiches."

My doorbell rang. "Gotta go, Gella."

"Come tonight. I'm heading over with the boys about seven."

"I'll be there."

I hung up and made my way to the door, unsure of who I'd meet. But it definitely wasn't the person I got.

"Guy, how nice to see you."

Guy Frobisher was a very handsome man. He had a slightly lined face from too much sun and not enough interbreeding with other social classes, but if you were looking for good hair and symmetry in face shape, he was that.

He stood in a crisp white shirt with the sleeves rolled up and a pair of light green chinos and brogues. Summer election wear for the modern hug-a-hoodie Tory.

"May I come in?"

"Of course." I stood aside to let him pass.

"Hello, boy. Who's this?" he asked as Kennedy jumped on him.

"My ferocious guard dog, Kenny." Said dog licked Guy's face and then tried to stick his nose in his crotch.

Guy made an inscrutable facial expression at my guard dog comment, but said nothing. "Coffee?" I asked.

"Please, God, no," he said. "I'm having thirty cups a day at the moment. Campaigning is basically caffeine addiction writ large."

I stood awkwardly then, unsure of what to do. Guy picked up on this, stopped stroking Kennedy to stand up fully again, and looked at me.

"I'm sure you're aware that Tarquin is planning on pleading not guilty."

"Yes," I said, my voice doing an involuntary crack. "I was aware. God only knows how he thinks he can."

"Because he's a narcissistic sociopath who thinks he can bring others down with him if he has a trial. He's hoping for some eleventh-hour reprieve."

"You've spoken to him?" I asked.

"Lawyers," he said, calmly. "Anyway, as family we get informed of all the developments, but I wanted to let you know what was going on. It looks like it's all going ahead to trial. They are going to start calling witnesses, the whole shebang."

"Shit," I said.

"Yeah," said Guy. "Yeah, it's all a bit shit, isn't it?"

I sighed. "I'm sorry he's dragging this out for you and your family."

Guy shrugged. Wary resignation washed over his face. "I'm trying not to think about it."

"Is that the reason you're running?" I asked.

He shrugged again. "Some of it." He made to leave. "I wanted to let you know … Anyway, er, will I see you at the vigil tonight? For JedRev?"

"Yes, I'll be there."

He made his way to the door. "Oh, um, Arden." He had gone bright red.

"Yes?"

"Everything that's gone on the past few months …"

I stood very still, waiting for him to continue.

"My feelings haven't changed," he said.

"As in your feelings for …" I said, stumbling over the words, my brain not quite working.

"For you," he said. "When I asked you out a few months ago, I said I liked you. I still do."

"Guy, I'm not really sure this is the right time—"

"I know," he said. "It's shit timing. But you dated Tarquin and Tarquin murdered Arabella, and he was my best friend, and now I'm trying to be an MP. The timing is never going to get better. The timing is going to be as shit now as it is in a year or five years' time. That's why I have to tell you this. Because if I don't, I'll keep on finding excuses not to."

I didn't really know what to say.

"Right," is what I eventually managed to come out with.

"Would you like to go to dinner?" he asked after a pause. "One night next week? There's an Italian place in Sittingston that's very nice."

I thought for a few seconds – the cons went through my head. A) My ex's best friend. B) My ex that I shot. C) Who murdered Guy's cousin.

But also, he's really hot, and it'd been a few months.

"Um, sure. I mean, it's just dinner, it can't hurt."

Guy's face changed into a large grin. "Great. I'll text you about it. I'll see you later at the vigil."

He left, and I closed the door after him. "Kennedy, Daddy has a date with a very posh man. Do you think I should go read some Mitford sisters' novels to learn how his people act?"

I sat back at my laptop and worked for a few hours. I was just managing to make some headway on a part of the novel that had been causing me headaches for several days when Verity called.

"Bloody hell, it's like Piccadilly Circus in here today," I said as a greeting.

"How is your village like *Midsomer Murders*? They've killed a priest now?"
"Vicar."
"That's not a difference."
"Can I help you, Verity? I'm terribly busy writing the book you want from me."
"Your priest is on the front page of the *Mail Online*."
"Am I mentioned?"
"Why? Why would you be mentioned?" Verity had gone into agent = panic voice.
"You know, that whole 'my ex tried to kill everyone' thing that happened a few months ago."
She scoffed. "People won't put two and two together. Oh, wait, I've scrolled down. It has a big section about it."
I put my head in my hands. "Is it bad?"
"I mean, it's not great," Verity said. "Unless the publicity makes you sell more books. In which case, yes, it's great!"
Verity was a capitalist at her core. My oldest, dearest, friend was also my agent. She'd quit her job as an editor at the finance magazine I'd been a reporter at to go back to her first career as a publishing agent and then opened her own agency. "I'll sign you," she'd told me when I showed her my scribbles when we first met. "As soon as I have my own agency, you'll be my first client." I'd scoffed at the time. She'd kept her promise, and I'd been her first author.
Our working relationship was sometimes clouded by our personal friendship, and vice versa, yes, it was true. However, in the near five years since I'd published the first novel, we had never had a sizeable falling out and had limited our emotions to the odd eyeroll and cross word with each other.
"Did you know him well?"
"'Do', not did, Vee. He's alive." Just.

"Yeah, yeah. Do you know him?"

"We've met socially a handful of times. He knows Nigella well and Guy, too. I think he might even be friends with Simon."

"Posh lady, posh guy MP… guy who you fucked on the floor, right?"

"Oh, yeah, I forget you haven't met any of these people. You really should come down for the weekend."

"By all means, invite me to the pheasant hunt, or whatever it is you all do down there."

"The landlady of our local pub is Black, so you can't pull that card."

"I can pull multiple cards. I'm a casino card dealer."

"A croupier?"

"There's an actual word for that?"

"I feel we're getting off track. Anyway, I'm going to some … vigil-type thing tonight for him," I said.

"Sounds awful. If you ever need a break from all this rural intrigue, I can offer you a place to work, you know."

"Canary Wharf? No thanks."

"The house in Surrey is nearly done," she said. "Just waiting on the final touches. Should be in by autumn. If ever you need a place to escape in the country from the country."

"This was my escape in the country."

"The offer is there. Right, now I'll leave you to your murder-fest village. Do some fucking work."

Chapter 6

I arrived at Nigella's front door just before 7pm wearing a light black jumper matched with a pair of black jeans. I worried my outfit was too gothy, but how was one supposed to dress appropriately for a vigil when it was thirty degrees C outside? It was only when I knocked on the door that the realisation hit me I was wearing all black to an event designed to provide hope that someone would pull through from their injuries. Fuck.

This faux pas became even more apparent when Nigella opened the door wearing an off-white-coloured sundress with a cornflower blue cardigan over it. On her feet were light brown flats in some velvety soft leather, which were sure to have been horrendously expensive.

"How … um, artistically you've dressed, Arden," she said as she made her way out. "Boys!" she yelled.

I glared at her. "I realise my mistake," I said.

Archie and Luca came bounding up to us and then straight past to where Kennedy was waiting beside me. "Puppy!" they squealed.

"Doggy, doggy, doggy!" chanted … er, Luca, I think.

I looked down. Clearly, in a moment of inspiration, Nigella had dressed them in matching T-shirts, which had been monogrammed with their initials. It was "A.P." who was chanting doggy, while "L.P." was trying to hug Kenny.

"Boys, be gentle with Kenny. He's a living creature, not a toy," said Nigella.

"We won't hurt him, Mummy! We love him!" Archie said. "Can we take his lead, Mr Forrest, pleeeeeeease?"

"Of course, you can, but hold it firmly. He gets excited, and we don't want him anywhere near the road."

They grabbed the lead in both hands. I was expecting a tantrum to start about just one of them holding it, but they quickly figured out a way they could both grasp at the same time. They made their way down the path and turned left towards the church when they hit the street.

We hung back a few metres to give them their air of independence as well as have the chance of a private conversation.

"Any word on his condition?"

Nigella shook her head. "But his parents are over from France now – they retired to the Dordogne, *such* a lovely region – anyway, they made it over this afternoon. So at least if the worst happens …"

"And the police have no leads," I said, summing up for us before she had to dig deep to admit it. She nodded tightly.

"Christ," I muttered. And then, as we turned the corner, I said it again much louder. "Christ!"

In front of us was a media scrum beside an impromptu political rally with some sort of vigil wedged in between it.

"Good God, there must be two hundred people. I was expecting a couple dozen," Nigella said. "Boys! Come here, stay with us."

We approached as a foursome (plus dog) and soon found ourselves beside several villagers. A familiar blonde woman turned and glared at me. Nigella *mwah mwah*-ed her friend. The woman, Margo Cadbury-Smythe, gave me a filthy look. Somehow, I'm sure, this was my fault in her eyes.

"Margo, you remember Arden," Nigella said diplomatically.

She gave a short sniff as an answer. Without paying me any more notice, she began to fill Gella in on the current lay of the land. "There's the girl who does the politics reports on *BBC South West Tonight*. Too much blush. The ITV one is around here somewhere, too. I saw him earlier. Awful tie. There's some local news, not any national newspapers, though."

Looking around, I noted Katrina Pettigrew a few metres away from us. She seemed stressed from the number of people around her. I waved, but she looked past me as she focused on what was happening at the front of the crowd.

Ahead of us, several members of the press were trying to grab Guy and Riz's attention. Simon was standing nearby but off to the side. Guy approached the raft of microphones. "Good evening, everyone. Thank you all for coming. It means so much to us here in Lilbury that so many of Jed's friends have come out to pray for his swift recovery—"

Before he could say more, a reporter interrupted. "Jenny Begood-Toomey, *Bournemouth Times* – Mr Frobisher, are you and Mr Patel suspending your campaigns?"

Guy was annoyed but plastered on a smile. "Of course not, Riz and I agree on certain actions for this, but we will not be suspending the campaign—"

Another reporter perked up. "Terry Cloth, *Bristol Online* – Mr Patel, does the Labour leadership approve of you running campaign events with the Tory candidate?"

Riz plastered on his own smile and joined Guy, but you could tell he was suppressing a sigh. "This isn't a campaign event. We're both here to send good wishes to Jed and urge anyone who might have information to contact the police—"

The impromptu press conference carried on in this vein for several more minutes. Both candidates fielding increasingly bizarre claims of what not jointly laughing over the body of a man left for dead meant for British democracy.

That's when I noticed the evening was about to turn to real shit. A plain car, which screamed *driven by the coppers*, pulled up nearby and out hopped two officers.

“Shit,” I said too loudly, and several people turned around to glare at me. Archie and Luca giggled at the swearing.

Getting out of the car was DI Gary Neuberger. The man who had been happy to try and pin Arabella’s murder on me.

“What’s he doing here?” I whispered to Nigella.

“He’s leading the investigation, I assume,” she said giving him a glare as well.

The detective walked over with the other officer. Neuberger was middle-aged with short spiky grey hair. He dressed a little too cool to be a policeman in my view. The man beside him … wait, man? A few months ago, he’d had a different partner, a woman, the perma-sour-faced DS Wales.

“She must have had the baby,” Nigella said, reading my mind. “Mat leave. I wonder if the baby was born with a face like a smacked arse, too.”

I sniggered as I took in the man. He was … not unattractive. A big bruiser would have been an accurate description. He was wearing a shiny suit, which did nothing to make him look less like a gorilla. He was forty-ish and had short brown hair combed down in a Caesar cut and a square jaw. He wasn’t ugly, but you wouldn’t call him handsome. The kind of man one went to when one wanted a brutal encounter.

They made a beeline for me.

“Oh, come on, I barely know Jed,” I muttered. I grabbed Kenny’s lead off the boys. “Here, gimme. I need him more than you two.”

“Mr Forrest, what a surprise to see you here,” said Neuberger as they came up to us. We were quite far back, and the journalists’ flurry of questions were sucking all attention away from any conversations in the crowd.

"I live here, detective. So, is it, really?" I could be a sarky bastard to them now. I was completely clear of any suspicion. There was nothing they could pin on me.

Neuberger turned to Nigella: "Mrs Pettoni, how nice to see you." Nigella bared her teeth in an approximation of a smile.

"Are you working on the vicar's case?" she asked. "I do hope you'll do better this time. Arden can't solve all your crimes for you." And with that, she turned back to the scene in front of us, dismissing the men.

Neuberger ignored the snub. "This is my new partner, DS Jack Maslin, recently transferred from the Met."

Maslin gave me the once-over and then the most perfunctory smile I'd ever received.

"Pleasure," I said.

"DS Maslin will be working with me on the Fulford case. I do hope we won't be seeing too much of you." He nodded his head, and they took their leave. Maslin gave a look over his shoulder as they made their way through the crowd.

"Ugh," Nigella muttered in my ear. "What ghastly men."

I couldn't agree more. Just Neuberger being near me made my skin crawl. Alright, I hadn't been completely innocent towards the end of the … shall we say … Arabella/Tarquin debacle, but I was when it started, and Neuberger had still decided I was a person of interest.

Even when I'd stopped Tarquin from killing both myself and Eleanor Hetherington, and given a wealth of evidence to convict him for Arabella's murder, Neuberger had spent a day in a police interview room trying to find a way to pin some sort of obstruction of justice or aiding and abetting charge on me. The duty solicitor had been flabbergasted by his attempts to spin my relationship with Tarquin into some sort of murderous partnership. Something she had basically told him to knock off unless he wanted an official write-up of his conduct to be made when the interview concluded. Which it did, not long after she'd threatened that. I really should have sent her some flowers.

I put the man out of my mind and returned to the press conference.

"I'd like us all to take a minute of silence to send thoughts and prayers to Jed," Guy was saying. "For those who aren't religious, please take this time to reflect, and if you know Jed personally, focus on those moments where you saw him at his best."

A reporter tried to ask something else, but Guy had called time on questions. It was quite masterful, actually. He had a knack for handling the press. His authoritative nature and well-cut suits were beginning to make me look forward to that date we had scheduled. I found myself picturing a life as a political spouse. Would I be more of a Cherie Blair or a latter-day Bill Clinton? I caught Guy's eye before we both lowered our heads in solemnity, and he gave me what can only be described as a look of pure lust. He winked and licked his lips. I felt filthy knowing a man had given me those eyes in a public place. In front of a church, no less. A part of me was horrified I'd basically eye-fucked a Tory in public as well.

As the moment of silence began, I could feel my cheeks flushing. Archie and Luca leaned in between me and Nigella and one of the boys casually took my hand and held it as they copied all the adults in silence.

It was a nice feeling, being given a seven-year-old's trust in a moment of reflection. I just wish I wasn't having impure thoughts about a man they called "Uncle Guy" while it was happening.

There was the normal rustling and coughing as the minute progressed. Someone's phone beeped, and there was another rustle as they quickly reached to turn it off. A muttered "Sorry."

Then a second phone went off.

"People have no respect," Margo said.

Another phone. Then another. By now, people were looking up.

Then my phone buzzed in my pocket.

I heard Nigella's phone too.

The sound was near constant.

I looked up and saw Guy, Riz, and Simon all pulling their phones out as well.

One by one, people around me started to gasp, to go bug-eyed, and form Os with their mouths in shock.

Then a flurry of journalists began to press forward. To Guy, who stood in front of them, with his face completely drained of all colour. He seemed frozen.

"What's happening?" I asked.

Nigella turned to me, her phone in her hand, her face mirroring Guy's. On it, she had an email open. It showed a picture of – oh dear – a naked man taken on what looked to be an old-fashioned digital camera. I squinted to get a better look. He was young and attractive. It was Guy.

Chapter 7

I'd never actually seen anyone flee before. But that's what Guy did. And to their credit, Simon and Riz stood in as he hot-footed it off with his campaign team to take the barrage of questions from the reporters.

Riz did his best, but there was no way he could handle that. His own campaign manager came over to shut it down as quickly as she could. A particularly eager journalist tried to shove a mic in Riz's face and found a red-haired Scotsman less than politely removing it from their hand and handing it to a cameraman with a deep growl.

It was the most menacing act I'd ever seen, and the reporter shrank back like they'd seen their own death.

"We should leave. Boys! Home! Now!" Nigella called before I even had a chance to answer.

Archie and Luca knew when to whine and when to do exactly what their mother ordered. They raced after her. It was only when I felt myself being dragged along that I realised I was still being held by one of them.

Kenny bounded along beside us with a confused look on his face as we left the melee.

"I need to get to Lady F and try and do some damage control," Nigella said as we ran to her house. "Christ, this is bad. She can't find out about this kind of thing from the papers. Guy will need all the help he can get."

Nigella had worked in PR for a large chunk of her pre-twins career and probably knew what she was talking about.

We reached her gate. "What can I do?" I asked. I could help. I had no idea how. Make tea?

Nigella's eyebrows raised. "Oh, Arden. Darling. No, you need to get the hell out of dodge. Like, now."

"What?" I was confused. No one even knew I'd been asked out by Guy …

Nigella saw my expression and took her phone out again and scrolled down, hiding the screen from the prying eyes of children. There wasn't one photo of Guy but dozens. And he wasn't alone. She scrolled down to an image and held it up for me to see. In the photo, a handsome young Guy was naked, looking at the camera, with a … oh shit … an even more handsome and young man next to him. Also fully naked. His dark brown hair and square jaw accentuated in the soft light. Tarquin.

"Those reporters are about to click who that is and beat a path to your door. If I were you, I'd get out of the village tonight. Do you have somewhere you can go? If not, I have a friend with a house near the coast, I can see if she—"

"I have somewhere I can go." To hide.

"This is a dream come true for tabloids, Arden. This is going to be a shitstorm. You need to keep your head down and disappear until it's all over. Do not say a word unless I tell you to, okay? I've dealt with this stuff before. I beg you, disappear off to a hotel or to France or somewhere – stay out of London – and wait until it's all blown over. I'll keep you updated." With that, she hugged me tight, then hurried inside with the boys, already calling someone on her phone.

I looked around in a daze. I didn't know what was happening.

A whine alerted me to Kenny. He was staring up at me with what was probably hunger, but right now it felt like concern. "C'mon, lad, we need to get home," I said.

Ten minutes later, I slammed the door to the cottage and let Kenny run off for some food. I stood in shock. What the hell had just happened? What do I do? Should I run like Nigella said to?

Yes. Yes, that made perfect sense. But where? I couldn't go to a hotel. I couldn't leave Kenny in some kennel, and so few places took dogs. Oh, God, and the cats. Where would I put them? Fuck. The only place I could think of was Verity's. But Nigella said stay out of London.

Oh.

I rang her as I ran upstairs and began throwing things in a bag.

"My love, I'm watching the *EastEnders* omnibus, so make it snappy."

"Need to stay in your Surrey house. Is there a key?"

"Aha! Knew you'd come around and wanna flee murder village—"

"Verity, is there a key?!" I shouted.

"Alright, Ar—"

"No, it's not alright," I said, panicking. "Look, in about half an hour, or an hour, there's gonna be a news story that breaks. It's … it's not good."

There was a pause. I heard the distinct sound of a wine glass being put down.

"Do I want to know what you did?"

"I didn't do anything, it's … it's a Tarquin thing. It's starting all over again. There's gonna be a field day."

I needed her to not make a "good for sales" joke right now. I really needed her not to.

She came through. My best friend in the whole world. "Okay, babes, I can meet you tonight. I'll change and make my way over there. I'll try and get to the house for" – she paused, I assumed doing some mental calculations on traffic and distance and how sober she was – "10 p.m. probably? I'll wait there for you."

"Thank you, Vee." I was so relieved I almost cried. "Sorry about yelling. I'll explain it all when I get there."

I hung up before anything else could be said and threw a few more T-shirts in a bag, and tried to concentrate. What else? Pants, laptop, toothbrush, chargers … shit, where was the cats' carrier case? How was I gonna get Kenny to stay still in a car for two hours?

The panic was on me in waves. I was sweating buckets. I felt sick. So, I did the only thing I could do – I made it worse.

I took out my phone and opened the email. The address was truth4you@truth2power.co.uk and the title: *Guy Frobisher TRUTH*. Christ.

There must be forty-odd photos, and I waited for them to load. They were taken on a digital camera – the date was emblazoned in orange in the bottom right-hand corner, like it was on a million photos from that era.

7 Nov 2002. Guy and Tarquin would have been twenty-ish, in their second year at Oxford.

I knew they'd gone to different schools. Tarquin went to Stowe, Guy to Harrow, but they had vaguely known each other through loose acquaintances and sporting events during their teens. They'd been mates from day one at Oxford, in the same college, the same floor of their halls, doing the same degree. Both applying to be on the same sports teams.

Tarquin came out straight away – he'd already been open about his sexuality in school, whereas Guy had only taken tentative steps out of the closet and hung back in case of repercussions. Tarquin told me all this one night during pillow talk. They'd dated very briefly in their first few weeks of knowing one another and discovered there was zero romantic spark between them, but they were happy to be mates. "We hooked up a few more times through uni and in our twenties," Tarquin had explained in a matter-of-fact tone. "Does that bother you?" It hadn't at the time.

I scrolled through. The photos were … well, they didn't leave much to the imagination.

Guy naked on a bed, his erection cupped in his hand, and several more photos of other acts, which Guy had clearly enjoyed to their inevitable climaxes.

There was a whole show here.

I zoomed in on one of the final photos. It was Tarquin, lying on the bed on his stomach, naked, his legs bent at the knee with his feet swinging. He casually smoked a spliff and grinned at Guy taking the photo. My last shred of hope disappeared. There was no chance they had been faked – the small mole in the centre of Tarquin's arse cheek was there. The patch of hair on the back of his right thigh that grew out in a different angle to the rest of his leg hair because of some old scar underneath. If there was one thing that I knew well, it was Tarquin Scott's naked body. I recognised those marks. Seeing him in Speedos would let you know about the scar, but you'd have to have seen him naked to know to add a small mole on his right bum cheek if you wanted to fake this with Photoshop.

Not to mention Tarquin's dick looked exactly as I remembered from my many, many, intimate acquaintances with it. These photos were real.

I breathed out deeply. In theory, it was two lads who'd, as horny not-quite-still-teenagers, taken some dirty photos when they were at uni. It meant nothing. But of course, these two faces had been splashed over every newspaper for the past three months. The man whose best friend had murdered his cousin. The culprit in the millionaire murder. The soon-to-be MP and his murderous pal. And now they had the gay sex angle. And tabloids only loved gay sex when it was licentious and tawdry.

Pull yourself together, Arden, I thought. I cleared my throat as if I was about to speak, but nothing came out. I put my phone away and took another deep, steadying breath. This was not the end of the world. I wasn't even in the photos. They would have to recognise who the person with Guy was. Then they would have to care enough to go and find that man's ex-boyfriend. That guy who was awaiting trial for murder. And his ex, who was a famous novelist with a big grinning picture on my Wikipedia profile.

Shit. Okay, get packing.

Twenty minutes later, I emerged from the house with Kenny's things. The cats were in the car already, hissing and spitting their way to an early death at the indignity of being put in their carry case. There were a couple of bags of clothes, a laptop, and some snacks. Beside them was a huge pile of dog food and assorted toys. The house was locked up. Now it was a case of driving over a hundred miles with a dog who could barely sit still for ten seconds.

It was almost certain to end with me driving us into the back of a truck while I yelled at Kenny to stop trying to chew the gearstick.

Oh, well. The only way to know for certain was to try. Kenny sat in the back seat and wagged his tail. "Please, stay. Please. Please," I said, begging. "There's your blanket on the seat. Just curl up and go to sleep, be a good boy. Please?"

Kenny gave me his happiest, stupidest, tongue lolling-out-est look. "Okay, well, as long as you are stationary."

He had been in the car a few times, but never very far. We had tried the boot, which was attached to the main part of the car and had no top to separate it. He could stick his head out and look into the front of the car. He could even jump over the seats. Instead, he had howled and cried like I was murdering him the entire way back from the pound on the day I brought him to Lilbury. "Okay, okay," I'd yelled halfway home as I pulled over and let him out. "Not the boot, I get it."

We pulled out of the drive, and I had managed to get almost half a mile before the whining started.

"Kenny," I said plaintively. I needed to concentrate. My mind was racing, and I was upset and not a great driver of long distances at the best of times.

Silence.

More whining.

"Keeeeeenny," I begged.

There was a rustling, and then the car jolted.

"Kenny!"

I glanced over my shoulder and saw the back seat was empty. I felt a pressure on my hand and looked down. Kenny was sitting in the passenger seat, curled up in a ball. His head resting on my left hand, where I was holding the gearstick.

He sat perfectly still and looked up at me with his huge brown eyes. His tail gave some furtive wags.

"Good boy," I said softly.

He stayed still after that. Every so often, I fed him one of the treats from the bag I had hidden in the glove compartment. Thankfully, he was well-behaved enough for once to not obsessively whine and scratch for them.

As I drove through the rapidly approaching darkness, heading east, I began to think. Who could have sent that email? Why would someone do that to Guy? Was it because they had wanted whichever Tory candidate was in the running to lose, or was it about him specifically?

The Conservative Party had been in power for several years and hadn't exactly gone out of their way to rake up support from outside their core backers. From austerity to anti-immigration stances, to the Scottish referendum to Brexit, there were a lot of people – including myself, if I was honest – who wouldn't have pissed on the cabinet if they'd been on fire.

Was it homophobia? Guy had been out in his private life for years, but if his business associates in London had known he was gay, I couldn't have told you. He was somewhat well-known before the Arabella murder. His family lineage and wealth had made him a prized member of the society set. And then there was his rapid fortune-building a couple of years ago, when he had earned a massive windfall that enabled him to leave the financial world at thirty-five. It probably had been in a trade mag interview somewhere – a casual mention that he was unmarried and supported a certain charity. People could have put two and two together. However, in the early days of his campaign (I'd done some reading up on his media coverage over the past two days) he mentioned it often in interviews. Using his preferences to bridge the gap between the metropolitan images of a thirty-something out and proud man – which the Tory HQ probably wanted – and trying to toe the line in a constituency where the average voter was in their mid-sixties.

As I approached the intersection to join the A303, which would take me past Stonehenge and onto the M3 eventually and into Surrey, my mind raced.

A horrible thing to happen. Targeted. Awful. A smear campaign. And on top of the issue with Jed. At his vigil no less…

At his vigil…which might not have been a coincidence.

I had a thought that made my hand jerk the wheel to the side it hit me with such ferocity. What if the attack on Jed and the photos were linked? I almost pulled over to the side of the road.

Christ, could they possibly be related? No, they couldn't be. The photos had come through to countless people in the village who knew Guy personally, and to members of the press at the same time.

But the thought stayed with me. It made me feel sick.

I much preferred assuming it was a political rival. Maybe an attack from a foreign power trying to destabilise British democracy. Yeah, the Russians. Must be the Russians.

The road lay out ahead of me and I drove on. Eventually, the gnawing in my stomach got too much, and I stopped at a service centre to grab a greasy McDonald's. Maybe I'd even manage to eat some of it before I got back to the car and had to give the rest to Kenny. As I returned, paper bags in hand, I heard a howling. Oh, no. A woman passing by my car turned to her companion and tutted. "Imagine leaving that poor animal in a car. Probably been in there for hours."

"He's been in there twelve minutes!" I muttered angrily as I sped up to a run.

"You are such a shit," I snapped at Kenny as I opened the door, and the howling ceased immediately. "Fucking drama queen."

He gave me a look. "Yes, I got you a burger too." I pulled out a Big Mac and watched in disgust as he ate it in three bites, but somehow managed to make a mess all over the car.

I sighed. "Right, everyone ready? Let's go. Aunty Vee is waiting."

Forty minutes later, I crept into the grounds of the racecourse in deepest, darkest suburban Surrey, where Verity and her husband's country folly was located. The house they had bought was in the middle of the track. It had been owned by a stable manager or something before falling into rack and ruin decades earlier.

They had found it at an auction and, after years of jumping through endless bureaucratic hoops, had their plans approved for purchase and remodelling. All they had to do was run an equine-related business on its vast grounds.

It shouldn't be too difficult. Verity's husband Gravz grew up on a farm in South Africa and had spent most of his youth bow-legged from riding horses … and whatever else people did in South Africa on farms. I don't know, hunt hyenas.

I drove around the grounds and found the entrance to their personal driveway. The house sat off to the side of the track in a copse of trees. It was dark by the time I made my way up to the buildings. The lights of the giant home were all on, and in the doorway was the diminutive shape of Verity waiting for me.

Kenny jumped out and made his way around the house, sniffing enthusiastically. "God, you really have turned into some sort of gay Dr Dolittle," Verity joked as I approached, holding the cats' carry case.

"We can put them in the adventure room," Vee said and swept inside.

"Adventure room?" I asked. "If there's a sex swing in there …"

Verity rolled her eyes and opened the door off the foyer to a tiled room with plain white walls. It was a vast space with nothing in it except a cardboard box with some old paint sheets around it.

"What in serial killer hell is this?"

"This," she said, "is what happens when childless people buy a six-bedroom house. What the hell am I supposed to put in here? Honestly, I'm asking. I haven't got a clue what to use it for. I could rent it out to a family of four, I suppose. Anyway, dump the moggies in here. They'll be safe. There are the sheets for them to curl up in."

I did that. Eisenhower and Roosevelt both growled and prowled at their new abode as Verity went out to the car and collected the rest of their stuff for me. "Oh, shut up," I told them.

Verity arrived back and upturned the box with their toys and treats onto the floor with little care. "There. They're sorted. Right, time for wine."

I followed her out into the kitchen, which was bigger than my house and full of space-age cabinetry and appliances that one had to rub in odd places to open them. "If you need to open the fridge, be warned, it's as awkward as a teenage boy trying to find a clitoris. The memories it brings back," she said as she deposited a bottle of Pinot Grigio in front of us.

I fidgeted nervously.

She softened as she looked at me. "Babes, I saw. How are you? Apart from more than a tad manic."

"Oh, you know. It's currently the most read story on *BBC News*, *The Guardian*, and number one trending on Twitter. So, I've been better." At my feet, Kenny whined from his new spot on the kitchen rug.

"That rug was expensive," Verity told him in case he got ideas. She turned back to me. "Listen, I think your friend Nigella had the best idea. No statements, we keep our noses clean. I'll reach out to a couple of PR friends I have in the morning to get some proper advice."

I nodded and got out my phone. Her own pinged on the counter. "I sent you Nigella's number, you two can see if we can co-ordinate anything. I've texted her to tell her to expect your call in the morning."

She nodded. "Good thinking." She took a long sip of her wine. "I'll stay here tonight and drive back in the morning."

I sighed and put my head in my hands. "God's sake, I can't believe this is my life." Up until a couple of days ago, things had been going swimmingly. And now …

"Christ, the memes on Twitter," Verity said, looking at her phone. "Some of them are ingenious." She cackled away at them with, frankly, no regard for my feelings, then gave me a look. "On the bright side, I must say, Tarquin actually got better looking with age. He's packed on the muscle as he's got older."

I glared at her. "What?" she said. "I'm only human."

Unfortunately, I agreed. "And who knew Guy Frobisher was putting away some serious heat in the underwear department?" I said. I had come this close to being able to take a stab at that. It was very unlikely our date would go ahead. Even Guy's 'never good timing' rule couldn't compete with this.

Verity nodded. "Right, let's finish these and try and get a proper night's sleep. I'm going to leave early to try and do some damage control with Donal and Ffion—"

"Why? What have they said?" Verity's partners in the agency weren't my biggest fans.

"The usual. But don't worry, we'll never drop you. You make up half the agency's profits. Your contract is quite safe despite their complaints."

"They want you to drop me?" My throat suddenly stopped working, and it became hard to swallow. If they took away my career, which let's be honest, was all I had …

"Only a little, and it's not happening," Verity said, meeting my eye with an expression that told me *Don't worry, I got this*.

"If you're certain it'll be fine."

"They wouldn't dare. Appolina and Gracie would eat them alive if they tried some sort of coup," Verity said, name-checking her finance and operations managers respectively, both of whom had a soft spot for me.

After that, she shooed me up to bed with Kenny following me. "Pick a bedroom," she told me when we got upstairs.

"Door number three," I said and opened it. Inside was a massive room painted white with soft furnishings to match (straight out of some showroom) and a gauzy netting over the plush queen-sized bed. "Good God."

"I know, I know," Verity said. "The interior decorator turned out to be a basic bitch. But she was efficient." She turned her nose up at the wall art and shook her head.

"Bathroom is next door. On either side. There are about twenty, so no shortage. My room is at the end of the hall with the double doors that look like Marie Antoinette's sex grotto. I'll knock in the morn."

She departed, leaving me and Kenny. I sat on the bed and tried not to feel lost and alone. Kenny laid his head on my knee and whined. "I agree, mate."

Chapter 8

I slept like a baby despite my misgivings. After a long shower, I'd headed for bed with Kenny forming a protective, restrictive ring around me. It had taken no time at all to fall asleep, which was odd as usually I would have spent the night tossing and turning.

In fact, I slept so late that I awoke to find it nearly lunchtime. A message from Verity on my phone told me she'd opened the door and seen me conked out at a much earlier hour and left me to sleep. You looked done in last night, so you seemed to need it. I'll ring you tonight and catch you up on what everyone has said today xx.

It was another scorching hot day, and the curtains were blocking out neither light nor heat. I could hear movement in the house. Christ, if there was a burglar, then they could take anything they wanted. I decided to send Kenny down to investigate what the noise was, only to discover my shadow was gone.

"Kenny?" I called, sitting up in bed in a panic. "Kenny, boy, where are you? Kenny!?" I hopped out of bed and raced to the door. The noises in the house grew louder. Maybe it was a builder? I ignored that I was careening around Verity's house in nothing but an old pair of blue boxers and ran to the end of the corridor and down the stairs, calling out Kenny's name the whole way. I raced through the foyer and into the massive kitchen, where I found the source of all the noise.

Which was unexpected to say the least.

Kenny was being dragged around the room on the kitchen mat, clinging on with his teeth and claws. His tail wagged at a million miles an hour as he play-fought with the person pulling him, who was laughing uproariously at his huffing and barking.

"Ollie?" I asked. Shocked.

Ollie let the rug go, and Kenny came to a halt. Both dog and man looked up at me, and it felt weird to see two faces so pleased to see me. Kenny ran over and stuck his head in my crotch. "No, off, no, naughty," I said. "What are you doing here?" I asked Ollie.

"Getting vaguely jealous of a dog, if I'm totally honest," he answered, his eyes looking south. I clasped my hand over my underwear.

Ollie pointed at them. "I think I bought you those boxers … about four years ago."

"May I reiterate my earlier question?" I asked peevishly.

He grinned. "Verity rang me first thing this morning. Telling me his lordship was out for the count, and would I be a doll and bring him some supplies for his confinement in Surrey," he said, and then his smile faded. "Then I saw the news and figured out what had happened. I'm so sorry, Arden."

"So, you're here to …" I ignored his second statement.

"I've taken today off," he said brightly. "And told them I'll work from home all this week. I think they can cope without me. I have Court on Thursday, but other than that, I can be here all week."

"You don't need to do that. In fact—"

"Stop," Ollie said, holding up his hand. "First, you should eat. I've made shakshuka."

I rolled my eyes. Of course he had. And we needed to discuss his staying here, not eat. But my stomach betrayed me and grumbled loudly as he took the lid off the sauté pan on the hob to give it a stir. "Needs another minute. You can save any formal complaints about me being here until we've sat down to eat."

"Well" – I tried to pull myself up to stand taller and straighter – "I will … um, well I'll go and get dressed then."

"No need on my account. That's my favourite view." He grinned.

"Yeah, I'm gonna go find my turtleneck," I muttered. I heard Ollie cooing over Kennedy the moment I left the room.

I quickly changed – and put on deodorant, ran a comb through my hair, brushed my teeth, and – what was wrong with me? – spritzed on some aftershave – and came back downstairs in a pair of running shorts and a T-shirt (it was simply too hot for anything else).

Ollie smirked as I entered; he was wearing his traditional light blue shirt and dark blue chinos. His uniform when not wearing one of his endless blue suits. We'd been dating for nearly a month before I saw him in a different colour.

He brought the pan over to the table and placed it in the middle. "Looks good," I commented as evenly as I could.

"So, going commando, eh?" he said as he sat down opposite me with the biggest grin on his face.

I went as red as the shakshuka. "How did you—"

"I bought you those shorts as well." Another grin came over his face. "I remember you demonstrating how well they fit. I also remember running behind you several times after you started wearing them and almost drooling at the sight."

I was a tomato. I was a beetroot.

It was true. I had deliberately worn these shorts without any underwear on when Ollie dragged me out running – officially because it was more comfortable, unofficially because our runs always got shortened on those days and we'd go back to the flat and spend the next hour doing ungodly things to one another.

I'd gotten used to wearing them commando, so I never even thought to put on underwear.

"It wasn't meant to be indicative of anything," I said, spooning out some food onto my plate through my embarrassment.

"Never mind, I won't mention it again." Ollie was unable to hide his amusement.

I was silent for a moment. "What's um … you know." I stumbled for words.

He cleared his throat and turned serious. "Do you want the long or short version?"

"Short."

"Front page of every newspaper. Number one story on every website. All over Twitter. Your name is everywhere, too." He checked his watch. "And starting any minute now is an emergency debate in Parliament with MPs standing up to condemn the invasion of privacy and demand an investigation."

I put my head in my hands.

"Hey, hey," he said and held his own out. It was what he always did. Laid his hand, palm up on the table, for me to take it in my own time. It was a gesture that used to make me melt.

I put my hand in his and he squeezed it for all he was worth. "Ninety-nine per cent of the coverage is sympathetic. A lot of people think it's horrible. Yes, they've all gone and searched on Twitter for the photos, but in public they've condemned it," he said.

"I expect Guy will have to drop out of the race."

Ollie nodded. "I can't see a way he can claw anything back from this. But, like I said, everyone is sympathetic. Owen Jones was on *Sky News* saying how bad he felt for him. Owen Jones!"

I rolled my eyes. Owen Jones, one of the UK's most strident left-wing commentators, was sticking up for my centre-right love interest. "Do I dare open my phone?"

"If you want. Just remember—" He took his own out of his pocket, swiped it to unlock the screen. "Oh, look, someone is being a prick on the internet – you know the solution for that? Swipe, swipe, and back in the pocket," he said and did just that.

I opened my phone and began to scroll. Tory HQ releases statement in support of candidate, Prime Minister to make statement on Truth2power photos controversy, Guy Frobisher makes statement.

"What's Guy said?" Ollie gave a pained expression.

"I wouldn't read that particular statement."

"What? Why— oh." Guy's statement was defending himself – not from having his nudes leaked but from the fact that they featured a man who was awaiting trial for murder.

I had no knowledge of Tarquin's true nature at the time. He was my friend, and I cared deeply for him. It was my choice to introduce him to members of my family and let them take him into their trust, which he would betray so gravely. I will have to live with that for the rest of my life, I read out loud.

Ollie tried to give a reassuring smile, but none came.

I did the worst part and searched my own name on Twitter.

"Don't torture yourself," Ollie said, putting some toast on my plate to try and distract me. It usually worked with carbs.

I began to read the tweets and felt my stomach drop. I used to be a fan of his, but this is sick, said one. Can't believe my favourite writer is caught up in all this shit, said another. How could he have been with that fucker? asked a commenter. He can claim he didn't have a clue, but I bet he knew all about it.

Ollie took my phone out of my hand. "Hey!" I snapped.

"That's enough now, Arden." He had upped the Scottishness in his voice. Not the Dumfries accent that was mocked by other Scots for the way they talked at a million miles a minute. No, this was his serious barrister voice with a pronounced sonorous burr. A voice that gave gravitas to everything he said. “Torturing yourself is not the best idea.”

Not to be dramatic or anything but I started crying. “Oh, no, babe. Come on, hey, hey, this will all blow over.” He held both my hands in his before coming around the table to crouch down in front of me.

“I’m never gonna be free of him, am I? It’s always gonna come back up. I only …” I tried to avoid Ollie’s eye. “I only started dating him to try and get over you.” I didn’t know why I’d told him that, because the look on Ollie’s face was one of undeniable hurt. I wasn’t even sure if it was true. Yes, I’d jumped in with both feet into a relationship with Tarquin much faster than I might have normally. Partly because he was charming and gorgeous and we clicked, but because I was in my thirties now and I thought that was how it worked when you were a bit older. You didn’t have all the jittery angst of your twenties. You were surer.

I didn’t have a lot of time left of being passably attractive if I wanted to meet someone, so best grab the first one that comes along. Everyone knew the lay of the land, and if you liked someone, you went for it.

Ollie had been silent for a while.

“I’m sorry, I shouldn’t have said that.”

He gave me a wan smile. “Yeah, but you did, and it’s not an unfair comment to make.”

I sniffed and wiped my eyes. “Okay, new strategy. How about I try not to throw everything back in your face and blame you for all my fuck ups, and you keep my phone away from me when I start to obsess?” I was trying for levity but probably failing. “I’m not sure what you get from the next week, but you’d be helping me immensely.”

He looked up at me, and slowly a grin crept over his face. "I get to hang out for a week with my best friend. Sounds like a win to me."

He returned to his seat and tapped my plate with his fork. "Eat. I did not spend I-don't-want-to-admit-how-long trying to figure out the buttons on Verity's oven, which is like something out of fucking *Star Trek*, to have you ignore my very fashionable brunch."

I sniffled a bit more. "True. You could charge £20 for this in Shoreditch."

"Right?" he said.

I sighed. Perhaps this was the worst of it.

It was not the worst of it. In fact, Tuesday was much worse as several other MPs and public figures had their nudes leaked in what the media called 'copycat attacks'.

"I have never seen Laura Kuenssberg look so awkward," Ollie said from beside me on the sofa on Tuesday night as we finished off the bottle of wine we'd opened with dinner.

"She did have to say the word 'frottage' on the ten o'clock news," I countered.

Ollie grunted in agreement. "Honestly, I thought that Yorkshire MP's pegging habits being exposed was much worse. His wife doesn't look the sort."

"How do we know it was the wife doing it?" I asked.

"They issued a statement this afternoon saying it was an invasion of their privacy. If he'd been getting pegged by busty Britney from down the Coach & Horses, I think she'd have been less inclined to use 'we' all the way through the statement."

"Good point," I said. "Maybe she watches him and Britney going at it?"

Ollie cringed. "I think I just lost the ability to ever sustain an erection at the thought."

Monday had been dire. I'd spent most of it in a daze, wandering about in the garden with Kenny while Ollie cooked various dishes for us to have over the week. In the evening, Verity called. "I've spoken to your girl Nigella, she's ace by the way. Anyway, we've drafted a statement. I'm gonna run it by a few more PR people I know tonight and release it tomorrow. But we're still on lockdown."

Nigella texted me later to ask how I was. Your cottage was inundated all day, sadly. Crowd of reporters outside. Village crawling with them. Horrible. Honningtons is inaccessible unless you know paths in from the back through the woods.

How's Guy? I texted back.

About as well as you can expect she'd answered. All this and Jed. Hopefully just some random and not a homicidal maniac running around the place. Again.

Sonia had called and expressed sympathy, and, weirdly, this morning I'd had a text from Simon. Heard you got out in time. Riz and I wanted to check you were okay?

I ignored the text. Instead, for the past several hours, I'd been trying to think of something to write to Guy. Currently, the cursor in the empty message box was flashing at me in a garish manner, reminding me of its lack of sympathetic words.

"Who are you texting?" Ollie asked as he looked over.

"No one." I fumbled to hide my phone. He looked as if he was going to say something, but at that moment, there was a crash somewhere in the house and we both yelled in unison, "Cats!"

I got up to check what they'd destroyed and was joined by Kenny for the walk. In the darkness of the middle of the house, I brought up the message app again, and my finger hovered. I hope you're okay I wrote. No, too blasé. I couldn't rely on trite concern. This was someone

I'd been hoping would pin me up against a wall and convince me of the merits of the trickle-down effect mere seconds before this had all been blown open. This is shit I typed. Can't begin to imagine how you feel. Let me know if there's anything I can do. I hit send.

No, no, that was a terrible text. I fumbled to undo it and delete the message, but it was too late. The two ticks appeared in the corner. Sent. Received.

My phone started ringing, and in shock, I answered it. "Hello?"

"Mr Forrest! Arden! Please don't hang up!" said a man's voice down the line. A Brummie accent. "My name's Dominic Grundy, I work for the *Daily*—"

"I'm not speaking to journalists," I snapped.

"Wait, I want to help you!" he said, but I hung up.

Ollie's head appeared around the door frame, and I nearly screamed in surprise. "Did you find what they've broken?"

"Oh, what?" My heart was racing. "No, not yet."

"What's got you all distracted tonight?" His eyes narrowed. "You're not on Twitter again, are you?"

I scoffed and went looking for the cats instead of answering.

Wednesday dawned as the hottest day of the year. The radio was blaring out the weather as I entered to find Ollie cooking again and feeding Kenny all the scraps.

The weather presenter was telling us that this was expected to be the hottest day in fifty years. "That is, until tomorrow when it's expected to be even hotter. London and parts of the home counties could see temperatures of nearly forty degrees," the manic sounding presenter chuntered on.

"This is awful," I said.

Ollie looked up from where he was doing something fiddly with cheese. "It'll blow over. The weather is the lead story this morning. They've barely even mentioned that Macauley Sheridan once got caught with rent boys in his office, which was trending all over Twitter last night."

"No, I meant the weather. I'm not built for heat."

"I think it's glorious!" Ollie shouted as he threw whatever he'd made in the oven and departed off to another room in the house. "I have loads of work to catch up on today," he said coming back into the kitchen. "I'm going to sit in the garden and answer my four million emails. I wish Verity had thought to put a pool in."

The last thing I needed was to see Ollie in tiny swimming shorts.

I decided to do some work myself. And once I had purposely not connected my laptop to the Wi-Fi, I began to get down to the matter at hand. It was easy to lose myself in the process, and thankfully, when I next looked up, it was lunchtime. I was just writing a scene where my main character jumps off a waterfall into the viscous lakes of Planet Zzxx IV chased by its native carnivorous crocodile people, while also feeling guilty for missing her boyfriend's big football game, when I heard a door close and looked down to the floor to see I'd been deserted by Kenny.

I shrugged and ate a plate of the cheesy concoction Ollie had made earlier. It was some sort of pasta; whatever it was, it was incredibly calorific, so I was doing him a favour by eating it.

Half an hour later, the door banged again, and in came Kennedy, who went straight to his water bowl in the corner and began to lap like his life depended on it. Ollie, at a much slower pace, followed him in. I did a double take. "You did *not* go running in this weather?" I asked.

Ollie was bright red with sweat coming off him in rivulets. His hair, which was the exact shade where blond turned to brown, was much darker than usual and slicked back with moisture. His sweat-wicking T-shirt was plastered to his body from his perspiration. His arms below the sleeve were baby pink from their exposure to the sun.

"Please tell me you were wearing sunscreen?" I asked, looking at his arms and then down at his legs, which were surely the same.

"Like I mentioned earlier, I love this weather."

"Ollie – you're Scottish," I said. "Your people were not designed for summer. You shouldn't be outside, and if you do go, you should hide under a sheet and run from shady patch to shady patch."

Ollie scoffed, the effort of which seemed to nearly do him in. He leaned on the counter and gulped a pint of water down.

"Remember Valencia?" I told him. Our first anniversary had been around the same time as Ollie's thirtieth birthday, and when my book was going to get its first big print run in the US market. We'd celebrated with a fortnight in July at a luxury villa in Spain, where we sat by the pool all day, ate carbs, and tried our best to destroy the four-poster bed in the master bedroom every night.

Well, we had, until the mercury kept going up every day, and Ollie had taken against it and become a walking lobster person. Even when he took ice-cold showers, he was bright red and looked like he'd run a marathon. People came up to him in restaurants and asked if he needed to lie down. Spanish grandmothers approached him as we toured beautiful old churches and tried to make him take their seats in the shade and force him to drink lemonade.

To make Ollie's mood worse, my Slavic genes discovered a lost Mediterranean side, and I never burnt nor had a moment of discomfort the whole time, instead I got darker and darker, until by our last night I was basically mahogany. Ollie sulkily accused me of doing it on purpose. I'd crawled up him as he sat stoney faced on the bed and tried to entice him with my newly discovered ability to tan to place his hands all over me. It had worked. Eventually. I don't think he properly stopped sulking until months later, when he saw me looking at myself in the mirror and smirked over my now completely faded tan.

"I can handle heat," he said and walked to the utility room next door, where he deposited his top in the washing machine and came back in shirtless. My eyes roamed to his large, hairy pecs, which were damp and shiny with sweat …

I apologise, reader, I got a little distracted there. I cleared my throat. Ollie knew exactly what he was doing. We both knew it. So, when he came up behind me while I sat at the table, we both knew it as well. He put his hand on my shoulder to read my screen.

"Making progress?" he asked casually.

I looked a smidge to my left. His crotch was beside my face. The outline of what was in his shorts would be obvious from space.

I cleared my throat a second time and bent down further to peer determinedly at my screen. "Yup, got through some thorny bits," I said. "Hortensia should be pleased with the edits. Think I'll be ahead of the deadline too."

I dared to dart a look back over my shoulder. Still there. Neither of us mentioned that Ollie seemed to be sporting a semi, which I could have sketched in thorough detail through the gossamer fabric of his running shorts.

"Your shoulders are tight," Ollie said in his low gravitas voice. "Do you want me to rub them?"

Oh, God, I wanted him to break me in half. But no, he was an ex for a reason. This domestic routine may have been lovely – a parody of how well we had got along when we lived together – we had never been this nice to each other.

I was about to answer when there was another crash. Oh, thank God! The cats. I jumped up and nearly hit Ollie in the dick with my shoulder as I did. “Gotta go see what they’ve broken now!” I said and departed the room.

That night, Nigella rang and gave some much-needed good news. “Jed’s been taken off life support and is breathing unaided!”

“Sweet baby Jesus, what a relief,” I said. Ollie came in from the kitchen, where he was making … something … involving salmon and looked inquisitively at me. “Jed,” I mouthed.

He gave a thumbs up and walked back into the kitchen.

“Yes, he’s obviously not out of the woods yet, but the immediate danger has passed. There are all sorts that can go wrong, and we won’t know about long-term damage until he’s more stable,” she added.

“I’m so glad he’ll be okay.” Truth be told, I’d completely forgotten about Jed, but no one needed to know what a selfish prick I was.

“Have the police made any progress yet?”

She gave a disgruntled sigh. “Not a lick, in my opinion. Roz said they’ve spoken to Doris but it’s not like they’ve been going door-to-door.”

“Do you not think they are taking it seriously?”

“It seems to me they’re treating it as some sort of robbery gone wrong,” she said.

There was a noise from the kitchen. Ollie swore loudly, and a pair of little furry fluffballs both scarpered into the room across the hall. “Cats!” he yelled.

“Who’s there with you?” Nigella asked a little too casually. “I spoke to Verity today – congratulated her on a very well-worded statement – and she said you were at her house in Surrey.”

“Just, um, Ollie,” I said equally as casually.

I could hear her eyebrows going up from here. “Oh, shut up. He’s my friend.”

“Your friend who dumped you for a twenty-two-year-old rather than try and properly work on your problems.”

"That wasn't what … Nigella," I asked, "everything okay with your relationship?"

She scoffed. "Of course, Matteo came back as soon as he heard about Jed."

There was a very pregnant pause as I waited for her to say more, but she didn't.

"Uh-huh. Okay, well, my ear is always available to be talked off if there is something."

"Not at all changing the subject," she said, obviously, changing the subject. "But the number of reporters at your place has thinned out. There was only a couple today. I think – barring any disasters – you'll be all clear to come back by the weekend. All these copycat leaks have taken the focus off us and poor Guy. Did you see what that Northern Irish MP has been getting up to? Honestly, I can't work out how it's pleasurable, but if the washing machine isn't going to electrocute him, who are we to judge?"

Ollie came into the room holding a bowl of food in each hand.

"Gotta go. Dinner is served." I hung up.

He handed me a bowl and turned on the TV to watch the news. I plonked down beside him on the sofa and drew up my feet to sit cross-legged to better hold steady my bowl of salmon on a bed of … "Is this barley?" I asked. "It's delicious."

"Great recipe I found on a shredding diet website."

I rolled my eyes. Ollie caught me and gave my knee a slap. "Oi, you liked it until I said it was healthy."

I smirked at him and took an extra big bite to show my appreciation.

Fiona Bruce was telling us about the updates in 'TruthGate' and said their reporters had been back to the place of the first leak to check the ramifications.

"Four days is barely long enough to judge the effects," Ollie said, frowning. "Hey, look, it's your village."

I groaned as the Fox and Lamprey came up on screen. The reporter was speaking, and then Riz appeared. He was sitting casually on a bench on the village green, looking relaxed in an open-necked linen shirt, his hair gently tousled in the breeze.

"He's the one you said was getting hitched to the Aberdonian bloke who did your kitchen, right?" Ollie asked. I nodded and hoped he didn't need any further clarification on how I knew Simon.

I turned the volume up to properly hear the interview. "… But you're twenty points behind," the reporter was saying to him. "Labour have never won this seat; your chances of winning are slim-to-none."

Riz smiled. "Look, I'm not saying the Tory party brought this on themselves, but they have fostered a culture of disunity in the country. We now have people crowing about which party has more leaks about their MPs. This culture comes from the top."

"That sounds like victim blaming?" the reporter asked.

"I'm merely saying that sometimes the people who have been complaining the loudest have the most responsibility to take."

Both Ollie and I turned to each other, frowning. "That's an odd route to take," I said.

Ollie shrugged. "He's Labour, they are snakes."

I rolled my eyes. "I forgot you were Thatcherite to the core."

"Am not. I'm not pro-Tory. I'm anti-Labour. If there was a viable alternative—"

"The Lib Dems—"

"Pfft," Ollie snorted.

"The Greens?"

"May as well use my ballot paper to wipe my arse with for all the good it'd do to vote for them."

"Of course," I scoffed. "You're politically homeless."

"I am! I'm fiscally conservative but socially liberal."

"You were against Scottish independence," I reminded him. He'd been furious that he couldn't vote as he was registered in London.

"So were most of Dumfries!" he said. "I'm proud to be Scottish. In my heart, I wanted an independent Scotland, but my head said no. Too much of a risk."

"You also want trickle-down effect, benefit cuts, a flat tax rate, and zero checks and balances on the City, not to mention free trade deals with any and every tinpot dictatorship," I needled him in the way we used to bicker over politics.

"Yeah," he said through a mouthful of salmon. "But I'm also pro-LGBT rights – and not only gay marriage but the proper stuff that doesn't affect me as a middle-class white guy – mental health services, AIDS research, homeless shelters for queer youth, trans healthcare."

I gave him props for finally listening to me talk about all those problems over the years. "Okay, fine."

"I'm very woke these days. I'm up on all the issues. I read up all about how Black history isn't taught in schools, and it blew my mind how we get brainwashed into thinking the British Empire was such a great thing and ignore the slavery and the genocide." He turned to me with a big grin on his annoying face. "I've got some great articles on the topic I could share with you if you want to know more about it."

I pulled a face. "You did not just comment on how woke you are."

He was still smirking.

I looked back at the TV. "Wonder why he did that interview?" I asked the room.

Ollie shrugged. "Probably saw an opportunity to make a name for himself. He's not going to win the seat even though Frobisher has now withdrawn – Lib Dems will take it, but he needs the top dogs at Labour to see he made a fight of it and tried his best, so they'll give him a seat he can win when the next general election comes about."

I turned my nose up. Ollie noticed. "Politics ain't a clean business, babe."

I stared at Riz's handsome face on the TV as he continued to drive his point home. "Ain't that the truth?"

The next morning did indeed turn out to be hotter than the last. From midday onwards, I had simply given up trying to do anything and instead lain on the floor in the main living room with the curtains drawn and the windows open, and tried not to die from the heat. Kenny was having the same issue. He was sitting on the tiled floor in the kitchen, huffing to himself in his sleep.

Ollie had caught an early train into London but was due back soon. He'd said his case was in the morning. I pictured him strutting around Temple in his gown and wig. It took my mind back to the time on, maybe it was our third or fourth date, when I'd been given the grand tour of the Temple grounds, which had turned into an extremely hot session in Ollie's tiny office, where we had to try not to knock over his desk while we went at it with people in rooms on either side. "Don't make a sound," he'd pleaded with me as I'd got close. His eyes bulged, terrified that I was about to scream the place down, but more concerned with the fact that he was about to blow his own load.

The door slammed, and I heard his whistling as he came in. A pair of shoes appeared in my eyeline. "Is the floor comfortable?" he asked, grinning at me as I raised my eyes to meet his.

"Hot air rises," I answered. "The floor is the only place I can bear to be."

He laughed and took off his jacket. "I can assure you this house is ten degrees cooler than London and about twenty degrees cooler than the courtroom I've been in. I thought at one stage I was going to faint." I looked up at him and saw a thick dark patch of sweat down the back of his shirt. It was clinging to his skin.

"You should have gone naked under your bar gown," I said.

"The judge would have loved that. 'Mr Ross, please approach the bench, and tuck your willy away while you're at it.'"

I laughed as he came to lie on the floor next to me. "Oh, this *is* nice and cold," he said. "I get the appeal."

"See? My madness has meaning."

He undid his cuffs and rolled up his sleeves as I spoke. His tie got discarded. "Can I take off my shoes, or will you complain?"

"You have smelly feet!"

"Yes, which you reminded me of all the time. Fuck it, I'm taking my shoes off."

A sock was thrown in my direction. "Bleurrgh!" I said and held it away. "I bought you these," I commented. They were blue socks with a pattern of pineapples, but only around the foot. The neck of the sock was plain. "Party on the foot, business up the leg," I remembered.

"They're my favourite socks," he said, resting on an elbow. "I smile every time I put them on."

"Do you?" I asked, rolling over.

"Of course. They're from you." He was staring at me intently. I looked down and noticed that this time I was the one wearing running shorts and a thin T-shirt.

He was gazing at me still. "Ollie," I said in what I hoped was a warning tone.

I'd barely moved when he was on top of me, his mouth finding mine. I wanted to resist and thought, for a second, that I could, that I could push him off and we could pretend it hadn't happened. But then his tongue was in my mouth, and I gave in and kissed him back as hard as I could. He rolled over on top of me fully and held my wrists above my head as his mouth moved along my jaw line and down my neck.

"This is a bad idea, Ollie," I whispered.

"Shut up and let me fuck you, like I know you want me to," was the answer I got.

I groaned and tried – very weakly – to move away, but instead Ollie opened his legs. He used them to bring mine together and trap them in between. He propped himself up and took off his shirt. I was helpless. Almost instinctively, I reached up and grabbed his pecs, my favourite body part of his, and ground my palms against them as hard as I could. I leaned up and my mouth found one of his nipples. "Oh, God, Arden!" he whispered. "Fuck, babe, I have missed this!"

Somehow over the next few minutes, all my clothes vanished, and I found myself lying naked on the floor with a half-dressed Ollie on top of me. His hands sliding all over and touching every part of me, exploring every nook and cranny that he already knew in exact detail. "You look great," he whispered as he kissed me somewhere around my navel.

He stood suddenly and grabbed my arm. I jerked up and found myself being pushed against the fireplace. "Face the wall," he said. I didn't argue. My mind was racing. Oh, God, this was a disaster. This was a huge mistake, this was … oh God. Ollie was kissing the back of my neck as he pinned me against the wall, and it was all I could do not to dissolve into a puddle on the floor. He kissed every vertebra on my spine as he slowly, slowly made his way down to … wow.

"You hate doing that, stop, you don't have to, we can do other things," I whispered hoarsely.

"Shut up unless I tell you to talk," he said and gripped my knees to force my legs apart.

Ahem. Dear reader. Well, it appears we know each other a little better now. So, skip ahead if you want.

After several minutes of eye-popping tongue movements, Ollie came up for air, and I honestly couldn't have formed words if he'd said anything. I was a wreck. It had been years since anyone had done that to me with such skill and attention to detail. I hovered in a dreamlike state somewhere on the edge of consciousness.

Ollie departed the room, which brought me back to earth. I called out his name. Oh no, he'd always hated doing that, and it had been a ridiculously hot day – I wasn't exactly shower fresh down there. He was probably desperately swishing mouthwash – but then he came back into the room, his trousers pitched into a tent in the front. He was holding condoms and lube. "It's unbearably hot upstairs. I thought we'd stay down here," he said and grinned. He pulled me down onto the floor and began to kiss me all over again.

"What's wrong?" he said.

"Nothing, I … I thought you'd left because you were having second thoughts."

He brushed the hair off my face. "This is all I've thought about for eight months, Ard. If you think I'm giving up on my chance, you're a madman." And with that, his head disappeared between my legs, and I let out a yell of such animalistic intensity and volume that we had to scramble to shut the door before Kennedy made it into the room to try and join in.

Just as I couldn't take any more, Ollie let me go and finally took off his trousers and underwear. He stood above me, letting me look at him. His slightly sunburnt arms and legs and the smooth skin of his thighs, the firm stomach, and the perfect dick that I had considered my second home for five years. He lay down again and rolled on top of me, ripping the condom out of its wrapper and pausing to stare at it.

"What?"

"It's weird to use one with you, that's all. I can't remember when we even stopped buying them."

"Yeah, that's not a 'right now' conversation. Just like how we'll also discuss why you brought condoms and lube with you in the first place."

He grinned.

"Budge up, dear, and open your legs, there's a good lad."

He thrust straight in, but it wasn't painful. It felt perfect. Like no time had ever elapsed, like it had only been a few days since we'd last done this. Like we were back in our flat in Bermondsey, in the bed we'd picked out, in the expensive sheets I'd bought for us from Heals, in the bedroom we had spent ages finding the right arty print to go above the headboard for. That the fights and the heartbreak and the name-calling and the crying and the screaming had never happened. That I'd never found the texts, that I'd never snuck home from my book tour a week early when I should have been in Newcastle and found him with Jamie the pupil from his barristers chambers in our bed.

That he'd never acted like it wasn't even a big deal, like he'd never been smug about it and tried to laugh it off and claim I was overreacting, like he didn't say I was acting crazy. Like, a few days later, I hadn't been sitting alone in a hotel room crying so hard I thought I was going to make myself sick when I started getting voicemails from him where he sounded hoarse. "Arden, I don't know what the fuck I was thinking. Jesus, I'm an idiot. I'm sorry, where are you? I'm sorry, please tell me where you are, and I'll come to you, and we can try and make this right. I'll do anything." Message after message.

I still to this day don't know what flipped the switch in his mind, why he'd acted so awfully those first few days and laughed in my face and then turned into a snivelling wreck, begging me to take him back days later. Maybe it was bravado. Maybe he'd been so shaken I'd figured it out that he'd doubled down to try and save face. It was the only reason that I'd been able to think of. Because for those few days, I was convinced that he'd never loved me, and that I'd imagined everything between us for those past five years.

But then he'd told me again and again how much he loved me. That he'd never loved anyone else. That he could never love anyone else.

By then, it was too late.

"Arden? Baby, are you okay?"

I jerked back to see him looking at me, his face flushed, his mouth opened a touch, concern in his eyes. "Is it too much? Am I hurting you?"

"No, it's good. It's great in fact."

He grinned and bent down to kiss me and then pushed in deeper. "Oh, Oliver."

"Arden, Arden! Oh, Arden!" he yelled. He buried his face in my hair as his hips pushed forward and every muscle in his body tensed. I couldn't work out what was his and what was mine, what was pain and what was pleasure. We were enmeshed completely. His hot breath in my ear. His hands gripping me, his body cemented to mine.

"Arden," he said into my hair in a choked whisper. "I never stopped loving you. Not for a second, baby."

I gripped one of his arse cheeks in each of my hands and held on for dear life. "I'm not going to last much longer," I said, or he said, I couldn't tell.

"I'm close," he called out, and we both finished in a crescendo of yelling and grunting, sweat and tears and God only knows what else.

He lay on top of me afterwards, his head on my chest while I stroked his hair, and maybe it was the heat, or the length of time since we'd last been intimate, but the most peculiar sensation was flooding my body. I couldn't identify it. I'd never felt anything like it in my life.

Chapter 9

I awoke with a shudder. My chest heaving as if I'd forgotten how to breathe.

Where was I? What house was this? What room was I in? What day was it?

Panic began to envelop me. Sunlight was streaming in through an open window, and the room was dazzlingly bright. I didn't recognise anything. I was in a huge four-poster bed with a canopy above me. There was no other furniture in the room. Wooden floors stretched for miles on either side of me before they reached the walls.

The bed was empty except for me. I looked around for any clues. I was naked and had no clothes to hand. Grabbing a blanket off the bed, I slowly made my way over to the door and opened it.

Oh.

I remembered now. I was at Verity's house. I closed the door to the Marie Antoinette Sex Grotto behind me. Ollie had suggested we try that room last night. "What about my room?" I'd said.

"That room gets the sun all day and is boiling," Ollie answered.

"What about the room you've been sleeping in all week?"

"The bed creaks like it's possessed. I had a wank last night and thought it was going to wake the dead."

"Why were you wanking?" I'd asked as he dragged me up the stairs.

He gave me a look. "I was thinking what we might have got up to on that kitchen table if you'd let me massage your shoulders."

Where was Ollie now? I called his name out.

"Down here, babe," he yelled.

I made my way to the kitchen, where he was standing in his boxers making coffee.

"What time is it?" I asked, wrapping the throw from the bed around me.

"A bit before eight. Coffee? Oh, and your clothes are on the chair."

My shorts and T-shirt from yesterday were folded nicely beside my laptop. I went to pick them up and realised to put them on I was gonna have to drop trou – well, drop throw – in the middle of the room. Anything else would have Ollie questioning why I'd gone shy suddenly.

A wolf whistle informed me that he was pleased with the view.

"You are a sex pest, you know that?" I muttered. I felt his arms around me the moment I finished pulling on my T-shirt.

"Only for you, love. Only for you." He leaned in and nuzzled my neck. "Mmm, you smell terrible."

"Thanks." God, he felt nice. He felt like home.

"Like sex and sweat and loads of nice things."

I sniffed his hair. "You smell like coconut shampoo."

"Correct, I've already had a shower."

"Oh?" At least if he was clean, he might be less likely to want round two. Well, technically, like, round five, but semantics. Anyway, it might help de-complicate the situation if he didn't try and bend me over the table before breakfast.

"Yeah," he said slowly. "Things turned to shit yesterday. I have to go straight from here into the office, I'm afraid."

"Oh." My voice wavered only slightly.

"It would have been lovely to stay here all day and fuck in increasingly bizarre places around this truly ugly house, but I can't."

Without thinking, I told him, "I was planning on leaving today," in, I hoped, an even tone of voice.

Ollie's face fell. "I thought you … maybe … might come to London for the weekend? I've made some changes to the flat. I wondered if you'd want to see them. I think you'll like them."

"That might not be a good idea for Kenny and the cats. I think it best I face the music and head home."

Ollie sighed and turned me to face him. He pressed his forehead against mine. "Do you regret last night? Please be honest. I need to know if it was anything. Because I can't build my hopes up if it was nothing."

"Last night was … perfect," I said.

"But there is a but isn't there?"

"Ollie," I started – my phone began buzzing with an incoming call. I looked at it. "It's Nigella, I should take it."

He sighed again and walked back to the coffee, running his hands over his face. "I'll go get dressed and give you some privacy."

As he left, Kenny came up to me and leaned on my leg. "Hello, boy," I said, stroking his velvety ear and then pressed answer.

"Good morning." I tried to sound cheery.

"Is it?" Nigella asked.

"Someone not enjoying the heat?"

"Is it hot? I hadn't noticed." She sounded sincere.

"Everything alright?"

"Guy's asked everyone around to Honningtons tomorrow night. He wants to clear the air and move forward."

"Wow," I said. "That's … I don't have a message from him …"

"No, I'm doing that. He said it's my discretion who I invite. It'll be just a few of us."

"I'm coming home today, anyway."

"Great. Come to my place for seven. There are a few reporters, so I'll have to take you the back way. I think you're the only one who doesn't know the route."

"Sounds awful. Can't wait." I hung up.

I looked down at Kenny. "Today is going to be shit."

Ollie left not long afterwards. He gave me a timid kiss on the cheek as he got ready to depart, once again, suited and booted for the city life.

His £100 holdall was in his hand. The Jag awaited. The week-long reprieve from Real Life was over.

"Shall I call you?" I knew he was seeking clarity on where we stood. I should let him down gently. Or I should be firm and direct. Any route would be better than the one I took, which was to give a wan smile and nod slightly.

He cupped my cheek for a second and then made his departure.

After a final inspection of the house to make sure I hadn't left a cat behind and there weren't condom wrappers flung around the bedroom, I hit the road back to Lilbury. Kenny behaved himself on the journey, which was twice in a row, so I assumed he now knew car etiquette, and I could take him with me anywhere.

I arrived in Lilbury a little after midday and realised there would be nothing in the fridge except for things that by now had grown friends. I pulled over at the Co-op at the northern end of the village and walked in. It was less risky here, as most of the residents used the shop owned by Roz at the other end of the high street. This was purely for passing traffic.

Making my way around, throwing my odds and sods in a basket, I walked smack bang into Katrina Pettigrew. She looked as startled as I did, and we both clutched our chests like we were having a heart attack.

"Goodness, you're stealthy," she remarked, trying to smile.

"Sorry, my fault," I stuttered.

She finally settled her nerves enough to give me a hundred-watt smile. "I'm so sorry to hear what's been going on. I've been helping Nigella all week with the fallout."

"Oh. Oh, thanks. Are you a PR person too?" I asked. Or a Tory?

"Gosh, no. I worked at a hospital in Scotland, so I've a bit of experience in the IT side of things, which poor Nigella doesn't understand at all. It's been dreadful this week – what they've put Guy through. It makes me so mad."

I gave my now practised wan smile.

"Will I see you tomorrow at the … meeting, shall we call it?" she asked.

"Of course," I said. For reasons unknown to me, I was desperate for an escape. The last time I'd met Katrina, she'd barely have said boo to a goose, and now she was Chatty Kathy while my Ben & Jerry's was melting.

"Have you been away this week?" she asked. "I thought I'd see you helping out, but you never appeared."

"I was … uh, in Surrey. Staying with a friend." How could she not know?

It seemed to click as soon as I said that because her eyes went wider than should be humanly possible, and she fumbled to find the words in a garbled apology.

"It's fine. I'd rather not dwell. On any of it."

After several more minutes of awkward chit-chat where she deliberately didn't bring it up again, we parted ways.

Kenny and the cats were delirious to be home and showed that by doing laps of the house at high speed and having a rare spat. Normally, the cats ignored Kenny, and he ignored them. Eisenhower tolerated his presence slightly more, but Roosevelt wouldn't even acknowledge him. That is, until I came into the living room in the evening and found the three of them curled up together on the armchair, all looking happy. "Is this an *I can't see you if you can't see me* situation?" I asked as I backtracked out of the room with three sets of eyes glaring daggers at me.

After separating them all and giving everyone a telling off, I took a long shower to scrub away the drive and the lingering smell of Ollie on my skin. Under the water, though, a new issue occurred as I remembered every touch and squeeze and kiss he'd given me yesterday, and I struggled to convince myself to leave the shower again.

I decided to take Kenny for the longest walk of his life. "Come on," I said as we made our way out the door. With this attitude I'd definitely be able to convince everyone else and possibly myself that I was *fine*.

"How are you, Arden?" they would ask.

"I'm *fine*," I would say with almost no hysterical high-pitched inflection. I had chosen a pair of upmarket chinos with tapered legs and my most non-awkward thirty-something dad plimsolls and a lightweight polo shirt for the evening. I instinctively turned right to take the lane down the hill to the village, but looked out over the meadow across the road, which was a yellow haze melding into the light blue of the sky. It was another fine day, and I breathed in deeply. I took a step, and instead we walked across the lane and into the field, taking the path down the hill to where it met the pond around the back of the Fox and Lamprey. The place I had found Arabella's body.

The evening was extremely warm, and this way Kenny could run as I held my head up to meet the sun, instead of watching for cars. I felt almost relieved as the heat coursed through my body. Yes, sun, come fix all my problems. Soon – too soon – I was at the bottom, feeling very self-congratulatory for my feat – and determinedly looked at the pond as I walked past it, taking in its details. See, no corpses there today. There were voices, from the pub's beer garden several metres away, of happy families and couples enjoying a Friday night in the hottest summer of a generation. Not a care in the world. For once, I wasn't even jealous.

I don't know why my mood was improving – maybe it felt good to be home? Maybe it was that despite the crisis, everyone I knew and cared for had acted impeccably and with my best interests at heart. Nigella had been an angel, Verity my stalwart, Ollie my … unexpected protector, and my trusty steed, Kenny, still thought I was God's gift.

We walked further, trailing around the village before coming home an hour later.

That night I slept like a baby. I knew I'd pay for it later, but right now it was a joy.

On Saturday, I got up and worked for a few hours, then I took Kenny running before the heat built too much.

I dozed in the garden in the afternoon, and before I knew what had happened to the day, it was time to go to Honningtons.

There was a missed call from Verity when I got out of the shower, but I didn't have time to ring her back. She could wait until later.

My phone buzzed again as I made my way down the alley between the pub and the next house to the high street. Ollie's name flashed. I declined the call. I wasn't in the mood for any emotionally taxing conversations right now. Verity had called a second time, I noticed.

No, would deal with that later. I'd get through what was going to happen with Guy and then we could go into whatever else had cropped up.

I made my way to Nigella's to find her standing on the doorstep with one of her neighbours. "Arden, there you are! You remember Betty from the tea shop? She's watching the boys for me tonight." She spoke up much louder as she addressed the woman. "Which is so nice of her! Thank you, Betty. I'll see you in a couple of hours."

She waved and made her way down the path and took my arm. "Deaf as a post, but the boys are terrified of her, so it's a win in my books."

"Is Matteo meeting us there then?" I asked, puzzled as to why they needed a babysitter.

Her hand on my arm tensed. "No, he's back in Milan."

"Wasn't he—"

"Emergency. Couldn't be helped." She began to walk quicker. "Anyway, glad to see you back."

My phone buzzed again. "Sorry, I'll switch it off, I'm popular for some reason tonight."

She laughed. "Come, the back path is this way, you can fill me in on your week as we walk."

We skirted around the north side of the village and found ourselves in a line of trees that opened to a field. We walked through these, then past some farm buildings before we doubled back on ourselves via another set of trees. We hopped a stile and in front of us was the grounds of Honningtons. The back of the house was to the right, and we made our way slowly to the impressive terraces that ran along its rear.

Ewa, Lady F's housekeeper, greeted us. She was standing on the terrace holding a tray of elderflower pressé. "*Cześć*, Ewa." I leaned forward to kiss her cheek.

She gave a smile. "You look well," she said in English, conscious of Nigella. "You're the last to arrive; they're in the Red Room."

We took our glasses and made our way in. Nigella, knowing the house better, walked slightly ahead and led me to a different room from any I had been into on my several prior visits. It was a smaller, brighter room at the back of the house. There were open windows all along one side, which enabled a lovely breeze. The room was covered in knick-knacks and chintzy tables. Rose-pink and white swirling wallpaper covered the walls. I suppose in certain lights you could call it red.

Everyone turned to look at us as we entered, and the expressions on their faces told me my good mood had been as misplaced as I expected it to be. Lady F wasn't there, which surprised me. Perhaps her nephew's genitals making it onto the internet was too tawdry for her to deal with.

"Oh, Arden," said Rita Parkinson from where she sat on a sofa, twisting her hands together. "I'm so sorry."

Riz came up to me before she could elaborate and held my shoulder in a firm grip, leading me forward. "The most important thing to do now is to not panic, if you want to sue them into oblivion, you've got to be calm and not say anything that could exacerbate it or be misconstrued."

I looked around the room. As well as Riz, Simon stood in the corner, looking furious. Beside Rita was her husband, John, giving me a sympathetic look. Eleanor Hetherington and her parents sat across from them. Surprisingly, Suzy Rabbit, the Lib Dem candidate and her campaign manager, Errol Mottley, were also there. On the other side of the room was Odette and Tommy Hughes with Marina Holt – I was surprised she'd let Riz in the same room as me. Standing beside her was Katrina Pettigrew.

"What's happened?" I asked. Simon came over to me, and for the second time in a week, someone else's phone blew up my life.

"I'm so sorry, Arden," he said. His voice was choked.

He handed over the phone. On it was a news article.

THE TRUTH ABOUT ARDEN FORREST – The openly GAY author who changed his name to hide his FOREIGN past and CRIMINAL family.

I froze.

"When did … when did this …"

Simon spoke up after an awkward silence. "It went up online about an hour ago. It'll be published tomorrow in the Sunday edition."

Behind us, the door opened, and Guy came in. "Ah, good, everyone is here. Arden, are you okay? You look like you've seen a ghost."

He stood there, handsome and smiling and wearing his hug-a-hoodie outfit he'd had on the other day, even though he'd dropped out of the race.

"I have to go," I said and brushed past him, dropping Simon's phone on the table by the door as I exited. Behind me, followed a chorus of my name and the clatter of footsteps as people raced out of the room after me, but I can be quick when I want to be, and escaping through a part of the house I remembered from my last visit, I found my way to the tiny toilet at the back of the stairs, where I had once run into Miles Sweet.

I locked myself inside and leaned against the door, trying not to make a sound. Chest heaving, I fought to even my breath enough not to puke.

There were voices outside and heavy footsteps. Occasionally, my name would be called.

"He must've legged it back over the stile and through the village," I heard Riz say from near the door.

"No, because Tommy and John would have caught up to him by now," said Nigella. "He doesn't know the route, and everyone always gets lost the first few times they use it."

"So, he's still here?" came Guy's voice from further away. "He must be out in the gardens then. Keep looking!"

Footsteps departed, and I breathed again. There was the tiniest of knocks on the door.

"Arden," came a familiar voice in a reassuring accent. "I know you're in there. If you wanna make a break for it, let me know and I'll distract them. But don't go out the front. There are still reporters there."

I didn't say anything. Eventually, I heard Simon move away.

As his footsteps receded, I put the lid down and sat heavily on the toilet. I took my phone out. Missed call after missed call. I opened Google and searched my name. Up it came.

The smoke and mirrors man who has been trending on Twitter all week. Despite not being in the TruthGate photos, which have kicked off one of the biggest scandals in British political history, Forrest was front and centre in the case.

Forrest, 35, ("I'm thirty-two, you arseholes," I said to no one.) was the 'boyfriend' of alleged murderer Tarquin Scott when Scott committed the heinous act, and is a close personal friend of Guy Frobisher. The handsome multimillionaire was seen days before the photos were leaked at one of Frobisher's campaign events, smiling and even hugging the prospective MP.

"I didn't hug him," I muttered. "But I'll take handsome multimillionaire."

FRACTURED FAMILY

Arden Forrest, or Arkadiusz 'Arek' Puszcza, as he was originally known before changing his name to the current Anglicised version, came to the UK from Poland when he was eight to escape the horrors of post-Soviet life.

He was born in the impoverished village of Skymr on the country's eastern border with Belarus. His mother, Julia, brought her three children to England after leaving Forrest's biological father, Tomek, who had several previous convictions for violence-related offences.

Old friends of Tomek's in the village say he was involved with smuggling goods over the border from the former Soviet Union. "In those days it was the wild west, you could get anything across. Guns, cars, women," they told this newspaper.

Attempts to reach Forrest for comment have been unsuccessful. His literary agent also refused to comment for this article, as did his publisher.

Forrest's father disappeared not long after his wife left him. It is unclear where he is now. It is also unclear whether he is the father to Julia's two eldest children, Jakub, and Gosia.

Julia took her children to the Lincolnshire village of Skirting, where she found a job picking strawberries. Within six months, she had remarried to the publican of the village pub, Gary Hearst. The marriage lasted two years before Julia packed up and left in the middle of the night.

The family resettled in Eggleton, outside Grimsby, where Julia once again moved in with a publican. Tony Devizes, the manager of the village's British Legion, left his wife for Julia. She stayed with him for five years before his drinking and infidelity became too much for her. Relocating out of Lincolnshire, she settled in the Norfolk village of Tattishall and gained her own pub for the first time.

The Beggar's Cup was a run-down flat-roof pub that had been partially burned down the previous year and needed extensive work and remodelling. Rumours at the time were of an insurance job. The family's luck began to change. Soon Julia was making a tidy profit, but as her fortunes improved, her children's turbulent lives began to get worse.

Forrest's older brother, Jakub, who went by the nickname Kuba, was first arrested at sixteen. By age twenty, he had already served a 30-day stretch for theft. But then the problems got worse when he was discovered in possession of a hard drive full of indecent images.

I put my phone back in my pocket. I didn't need to read anymore. I'd lived it. I stood up and looked at myself in the mirror. Tears were running down my face. Most of the time, I'd have instantly brushed them away, determined to try and make myself look less soft, but … I couldn't face the mirror, and I was too exhausted to even raise my hand.

Everything I'd done to change my life was for nothing. People wanted me back where I'd come from. No one wanted to celebrate my success. They wanted to tear me down because I'd made the mistake of falling for Tarquin.

I have no idea how long I stood at the sink and stared at the mirror before I was able to summon up the energy – or was it the courage? – to exit the bathroom. I put my ear to the door and listened for sounds, but heard nothing. Everyone must have either left or gone to a different room to regroup.

Wondering if I should text Simon and take him up on his offer, I instead made my way out. I saw a door to what I assumed was the kitchen and decided to leave that way. The room was dark, despite dusk being upon us outside. The half-light gave the world a menacing vibe despite the heat.

Outside the kitchen door, an orange dot glowed. I froze.

"Arden, there you are." Katrina Pettigrew puffed on her cigarette. "Don't worry, I'm not going to tell anyone I saw you."

I came up to her and blinked in the small amount of light at the doorway from the dusk outside. Katrina swatted her ciggie smoke away; but I gave a dismissive wave for her not to bother.

"I'm sorry that happened to you," she said honestly.

"You're probably the only one. Lots of people will think they did a public service."

"People never get what they deserve," she said. "The innocent suffer and the guilty prosper."

"And I thought I was a cynic."

"Oh, I'm sure you are. You shouldn't let this ruin your life, Arden. You've got happiness ahead of you. You're young."

"I feel a hundred years old."

"Hey." She turned serious. "Listen to me. I've been there …" Her voice was somewhere far away. "It wasn't just my husband I lost. My son died a few years before him. I thought I'd never see the light again. I honestly thought I'd never recover. But I did. And if I can make it out of that, then I believe you can make it out of this."

I was shocked. "I'm sorry. Did-did he …"

"He was a soldier. Twenty-five. Someone didn't do their job properly, and he suffered the consequences."

"Where was he posted?"

She laughed. "That's the worst thing. This happened here in the UK. On base. Anyway, I say this to remind you that life is precious, Arden. You can revel in the misery, or you can keep fighting, and eventually it'll get better."

She touched me lightly on the arm. "They're all in the drawing room listening to Frobisher apologise still. If you want to escape, now is your chance. Do you know the way back from the stile?"

"I think so." I smiled. "Thanks, Katrina. Have a good evening."

I walked away from her, heading back towards the stile, lost in my own mind. Behind me the door opened behind me and voices emanated from it. I'd just passed the side of the house with the terraces to my right. It was light enough that everyone could see me. Before I could move, Tommy and Odette were upon me.

"Hello, Arden, where have you been?" Tommy smirked. "Or should I say Arkadiusz?"

"Tommy!" his wife exclaimed and came towards me. "Are you okay?" she asked with genuine concern.

"Arden!" a voice rang out from above us on the terrace. I looked up to see Simon coming towards me, with Riz and Marina behind him.

"We shouldn't be seen with him," Marina said bluntly.

Simon glared.

Marina gave me a dirty look. I was besmirching her candidate by being near him.

"You can stay back then," Simon spat at her. "But I'll check in on my friend." He came down the stairs to join me and the Douglases.

Instinctively, I took a step back.

"I think she's got the right idea, actually, Anson," said Tommy. "Maybe none of us should be near him. Can't believe you've been near Tatiana. If we'd known you had family history for it ..."

Odette gasped, and Simon gripped Tommy by the arm and yanked him back.

But none of them met my eye. Maybe they were right. I probably shouldn't be near them.

"I ... I have to go," I said and began to retrace my steps towards the kitchen.

"Arden, no, go the back way! The reporters!" Odette shouted. "Simon, do something!"

But I was walking faster. "Ah, leave him!" I heard Tommy's voice. "He wants to sulk."

I walked as fast as I could around to the front of the house. The door to the kitchen was closed, Katrina had finished her smoke, so instead I started to make my way down the driveway. So what if there were reporters? Hell, maybe it'd be a good thing to try and say something. Yeah, I could give a statement. I could say—

"There he is! Forrest! Arden!" I heard a voice in front of me. The gates to Honningtons were about twenty metres away. I stumbled. A flash of lights put spots in my eyes. "Oi, over here, Arden! Any comment on the piece?"

My voice lodged in my throat. I had a speech planned … but I— I couldn't think of anything to say. I had to defend myself, but I couldn't think of any way to.

There was the rev of an engine behind me, and I jerked away. A sleek, dark car pulled up, and the window wound down.

Errol Mottley looked at me evenly from inside the vehicle. "Get in, Arden. Don't even think about speaking to them."

I didn't have much of a choice. I got in and Errol floored it towards the gates. They were on an electronic sensor and opened metres from us, sending the reporters out of the way as they swung outwards.

There was a flash of bulbs from the few reporters who hadn't been pushed back, but Errol drove too fast for them to get much of a look.

I stared back but felt his hand on my shoulder. "Don't give them the satisfaction, mate." I nodded and pulled myself around in my seat to look forward.

"Thank you."

"Not a problem." He grinned at me. "I was leaving anyway. Where should I drop you?"

"My house is up on the hill."

"Your house? Surely it'll be better to stay away tonight."

"I can't … I—"

"Tell you what, it's early yet, let's go get a drink in Sittingston and we'll discuss what you can do when you've cleared your head."

I was gonna say no, but he was already pulling onto the High Street and turning north, away from my house, before I could answer.

"I'm not sure, I should. My dog will need me."
"Does the dog have food and water?" I nodded. "Then it'll be fine for a few hours."
I felt guilty at abandoning Kenny, but the thought of going home was less than enticing. Would there be crowds of reporters waiting for me?
We lapsed into silence as darkness fell over the countryside outside. Errol's car, I noticed finally, was a nice late model with plush interiors.
"How—"
"I know what you're gonna ask, and no, the party doesn't pay for the car. This is mine. I used to be a consultant for the private sector. All very money, money. Now I'm a pauper living on donations from Brenda in Wells."
"It's a nice car. Very … sensible. German."
He laughed. It was a nice laugh.
I tried to be sociable. "Did I miss much in Guy's meeting?"
He shook his head. "Not really, he wanted to say thank you to everyone who'd helped him. To acknowledge Suzy and Riz for being gentlemanly about the whole thing and not using it to score points."
"You guys have pretty much got it in the bag then, eh?" I said. "Whoever Guy's party chooses has two weeks to try and build a new campaign."
"The Tories will do what the Tories always do." Errol shrugged. "They'll find an old white bloke and trot him out. He'll have stood as cannon fodder in thirty-seven previous elections in unwinnable seats, or they'll get some local councillor to step in at the last minute. It's not that uncommon."
I nodded. Errol kept a constant flow of conversation as we drove. He had an easy air about him. He kept the chat to purely superfluous matters and the amount of replies I had to make to a minimum. By the time we entered the

village, I had begun to feel slightly more human. Sittingston was in a happening mood for a Saturday night. By which I mean there were at least two pubs open.

"Where are you staying?"

"The Cock and Feather. You know it?"

"The pub? No. The bondage bar in Vauxhall? Very well."

He laughed again. "Is that the one next to the sauna? The door charge is extortionate."

Errol pulled up outside a less than charming looking pub at the south end of the High Street and we got out. It felt nice to not be in my house. "Come on, I'll get you a drink." Errol led the way.

Inside, the Cock and Feather was – as Sonia once described it to me – an old man pub. A few fruit machines in the corner, some sport on the flatscreen above the bar. An upmarket gastropub it was not, a friendly village local it was neither. It was decidedly middle of the road. The kind of pub I'd grown up in.

"This is the cheapest place in Sittingston to get accommodation," Errol said in an almost apologetic tone.

"Don't worry, not judging the surrounds. I'll grab a table."

A minute later, after the surly barmaid had been thoroughly won over by Errol's charm, (or his arse in the tight suit trousers he was wearing) he came over to the table I'd nabbed in the corner with two pints and a packet of salt and vinegar crisps.

"So," he said, settling himself on a stool. "Would you like to talk about the article, or would you like to talk about literally anything else?"

"The latter, please." I tipped my beer at him. "Cheers, by the way."

"Cheers." He took a sip of his own. "What can we discuss instead? Oh, I know. You can tell me about all the hot nightlife in Sittingston. Or is Lilbury where the real late-night action happens?"

I snorted. "Late-night action? Everyone goes to bed at nine thirty."

"They don't even stay up to watch *Newsnight*?" he said aghast. "But I thought posh white people fucking loved *Newsnight*."

"Oh, no, darling. They only watch that liberal propaganda in Islington."

"So it's endless *Countryfile* and Radio 4, then?"

I nodded. "There is literally an *Archers* fan club in the village. They meet in the Tea Rooms on Thursdays."

Errol's face went still. "You're … you're joking, right?"

Shaking my head, I said, "White people don't joke about *The Archers*, Errol. We take it very seriously."

His face was a picture, whether he was playing it up, I didn't know nor care because I needed a laugh.

He grinned at me. "You're much better looking when you laugh. Not that it's an unattractive view when you're serious, but your eyes light up when you laugh."

I blushed so hard I'm surprised I lived to tell the tale.

He leaned forward on his elbows. "I must admit, I rescued you from the reporters with not … completely innocent aims. I thought I'd grab you and take you for a drink and see if I could have my wicked way with you."

I rolled my eyes. "Really?"

He shrugged. "I've been in this place for a month. A guy has needs, and the only offer I've had on Grindr is this couple called Leon and Levi asking for a third. And I had the distinct feeling they were a bit *too* into Black guys."

"I know them," I said. It was Errol's turn to roll his eyes.

"Of course you do."

"They helped remodel my kitchen."

His eyes nearly rolled out of his head.

"Does that happen a lot, by the way?" I asked.

He frowned and cocked his head, wanting me to elaborate.

"You know, white guys just wanting a Black guy and not really caring about the type of man the appendage is attached to?"

"You're thinking about my appendage?"

"How could I not when you're in those trousers?"

He gripped the fabric and pulled at it. "What? These are my baggiest ones." He grinned. "To answer your question, yes, and sometimes it gets very frustrating. I'll chat to a nice guy and think, wow, this is a proper connection, and then he'll have a few more drinks and start saying he wants me to put on a gold chain and backwards cap and just ruin him."

I gave a mock pout. "That must be really hard. Guys offering you sex without even bothering to talk to you."

He laughed. "What about you? Do you rely on stereotypes for your sex life?"

"I'm Polish, so yeah, we're hung like carthorses. If some guy happens to think he's getting more bang for his buck, I'm not gonna stop him."

"Oh, I know the stereotypes of Polish men. I used to live in west London before I came home to Brizzle. You couldn't move for Slavic builders sending pictures of their footlong subway sandwiches to you on Grindr."

"Ah, well, when I was young, I lived in east London, so I had a fair amount of Jamaican meat in my diet."

He took a swig of his pint. "Racist. I'm Antiguan."

I shrugged. "I'm one-eighth Slovakian."

"What's the deal with you and Simon?" Errol grinned as I choked on my pint. "Gotcha."

"What do you mean?" I asked, trying to stop hacking up cheap lager.

"He couldn't take his eyes off you at the hustings last week. All week, he's been talking to Frobisher about you.

This evening, he raced after you when you left. If I was a nosey parker—"

"It seems you are."

"—I'd swear Riz was seething with jealousy. So, what is it between you two?"

I frowned. "There's nothing."

Errol gave me a look that said he didn't believe me.

"We shagged a few months ago. When he and Riz were broken up. I had no idea about the guy. It was one night. Since then, Simon has been a dick to me. We've literally not spoken."

Errol nodded as he took this in. Over his shoulder, the barmaid yelled for last orders for the night. I hadn't realised it had got so late. "Then there's no one at home pining for you?"

I thought of Ollie. "Nope," I said.

"So, would you like to finish these and come up to my room and have some fun?"

I grinned. "Thought you'd never ask."

Chapter 10

I know what you're thinking. I can hear your judgement from here. But listen … I don't care. I was having a crap evening, and Errol was hot. And unlike the last time I got any action, I had no close connection to him. In a fortnight, Suzy would probably win the election, and Errol would be off to do whatever dark political arts he did somewhere else.

I'd never have to see him again.

Did I mention he was hot?

He took me up to the second floor, where his room was located. "This is their deluxe suite," he said.

"Suite?"

"I think they're including a bathroom to make it a suite. I don't know, it's the countryside. I'm glad there's electricity."

He opened the door to a small but pleasant room. A floral bedspread drew in the eye – away from the pine furniture and beige carpet. It was, also, swelteringly hot. Just walking inside made me break out in a sweat.

"Functional," I offered, wiping my brow.

"I'm hardly ever here. Suzy has her first campaign event in" – he checked his watch – "Christ, nine hours. You don't mind if I sneak out early?" he asked.

"You're letting me stay the night?"

He sat on the bed and opened his arms wide. "I'm a gent, bruv."

I walked up to him and stepped in between his open legs. "Hopefully not that much of one."

He grinned and pulled me down on the bed. His kisses were sweet and tasted of beer. His body was like iron underneath me. "Jesus, how much do you work out?" I asked as I made my way down his stomach with my mouth, slowly undoing buttons.

"I … uh, I'm incredibly vain and self-involved."
I looked up at his face. "You work in politics. You didn't need to tell me this."
He gave me a shove. "Get back to it, writer-boy."
I grinned and began to undo his belt. His trousers came off and out sprung all of Errol's equipment.
"Bloody hell," I yelped as I leaned back so as not to lose an eye. "You weren't joking."
"Were you?" he said, palming his enormous dick and giving it a terrifying *thwack* against his hand.
I shrugged. "I'm happy with what genetics gave me."
He grinned and gave his head a flick to tell me to keep removing clothes.
I shouldn't be doing this. I should be home with my dog, listening to all those messages from Verity and Ollie. I should not be doing this. Should not be. Should—ooh, he was good at that.
I rolled over, and Errol took off the rest of my clothes. After some perfunctory foreplay, we got down to the main event.
"Would you be keen to …" He flicked his eyes up.
It took me a second to click. Oh. "Sure thing."
He grinned and grabbed a condom from the side and passed it to me. Then lay on the bed and waited for me with an eager expression.
I rubbed up against him, and apparently, I was making more noise than I realised. "I'll put some music on," he said, easing out from under me to grab his phone and turn on a playlist.
"Sorry, people tell me I'm loud. I always forget," I said. He returned to his original spot.
"Just try not to wake half the county—"
"What about you, are you loud? Especially when …"
"When what?"
"When I do this—"

He gave a deep guttural yell and arched his back so hard I thought he was gonna bend in half. I grinned and pushed in deeper.

"Good?" I asked.

"So, so good," he mumbled in a language I think was English.

I gripped the headboard above me and, for several minutes, went to town. I took the grin on his face as proof that I was doing a half-decent job.

When I let my mind drift, all those emotions of the past week came back to me. So instead, I drove my hips down to get closer to him, and he wrapped his arms around my chest. I used the headboard to leverage myself up for some traction. We both dripped with sweat in the hot little room; the bedspread underneath Errol was going to be soaked, but right then, it didn't matter.

All that mattered was keeping my pelvis bucking in the perfect rhythm so that the expression of absolute pleasure stayed on Errol's face.

Too soon, that rhythm faltered, and I let out a gasp. Errol had seconds to finish before I did. He managed to achieve his goal as I let out a long shuddering sigh and rammed it home one last time.

I fell forward and rested my head on my arm atop the headboard above him. Panting for dear life.

He ran his fingers down my damp body and laughed.

"Good?" he asked.

"Bloody excellent."

"Pretty sure all of Dorset heard."

"Lucky them," I said sincerely. "That was a ten-out-of-ten effort."

"You weren't bad either," he said as I dislodged myself. He stood up and went to the fridge in the minute kitchenette.

"Drink?" he asked.

"Only if it's alcoholic."

He passed me a beer. “Luckily, this campaign drove me to the booze weeks ago.” He took a swig. “Do you wanna grab a shower?”

“If I’m allowed.” I jumped off the bed and swigged my beer.

“Take it in with you, I’m not gonna judge.”

I shrugged and did that. Drinking beer in the shower always makes one feel rebellious, but tonight it felt extra so. Ten minutes later and a lot of sweat lighter, I exited the bathroom, fully nude. Owning the point of a one-night stand was making me feel liberated.

Errol looked up from where he lay on the bed, reading Twitter, and grinned. He was in the nude, too. But more importantly, there was a breeze. “Where did you get a fan from?” I asked while air-drying a few certain body parts in front of it.

“Last week, when I realised this weather wasn’t going anywhere. It’s the only way to sleep in this furnace.” He departed into the bathroom, giving my bum a squeeze on the way.

I finished my beer and resisted the urge to check my phone.

Errol finished up in the shower and switched off the light. “Shall I wake you in the morning for a quickie before I leave?”

“If I’m not too sore to move, sure,” I said.

He reached over and gave me a kiss, and then the light went out.

Obviously, I didn’t sleep. Long after Errol’s breathing turned to a regular chorus of soft snores, I stared at the ceiling, wondering what life would bring in the morning.

The night began to give way to light, and Errol stirred. His eyes opened, and I grinned. He was instantly on me, and a perfectly credible blowjob later, he was in the shower while I lay dozing.

He sauntered out and started to dress. "You're welcome to stay until a more sociable hour," he said. "I'm aware leaving first thing in the morning is a bit unbecoming, but I've got to be in Compney Parva for 7 a.m. and I need coffee by the bucketload."

"No worries, I promise to stay an appropriate amount of time and not be here when you get back."

He grinned and gave me a quick kiss. "This was fun." He left, and I slumped back down. My eyes had just closed when my heart gave a thump.

Kenny.

He'd been on his own for ten hours. He'd have torn the house to shreds. I hadn't taken him out for his night-time pre-bed wee in the garden. Oh, no, he must have been so confused.

I was up and dressed and closing the door to Errol's room in thirty seconds.

There was cash in my wallet. The taxi firm by the station was slow, but I knew it was officially twenty-four hours. Hopefully, there would be someone who could get me to Lilbury before lunchtime. Maybe I could call Nigella if they took ages?

It wasn't even 6 a.m., yet already there was blazing sunshine, and the heat was building. It was going to be another scorcher. "How is this England?" I asked, looking up at the unspoilt shade of Morning Blue sky.

Sittingston was deserted. I walked for several minutes before I saw another person. A teenager tottering down the street in the opposite direction to me, swigging from a bottle of cider, his own vomit on his shirt. We nodded as we passed.

Having lived in the area for a few months now, I knew the shortcut across to the station parade where the taxi office was located. You had to hang a right at an intersection and then cut through the car park at the back of the High Street, which went through to a green space, and then up the hill to the station.

I turned right after a small café, meandered past a travel agency, and entered the car park. It was a large, unkempt space of empty concrete with shabby back doors to shops and the entrances of flats above. There were derelict-looking garages on the other side. Weeds grew out of the cracks in the slabs of concrete.

It was bereft of life. Except for one car parked exactly in the middle. It was a late model SUV in black. A more generic car you couldn't think of. The engine was running. But it wasn't moving. And why was it parked in the middle? Parking along the edge would be more practical.

My gut instinct was to cling to the edge of the space and walk as close as I could to the walls of the shops.

But a voice was telling me that there was something wrong. Something very wrong. I had to check.

I made my way forward. Every step akin to walking through molasses. If I turned back now, it wouldn't happen again. If I walked in the opposite direction I'd be okay.

Reaching the driver's side of the car, I could see the window was wound down. Adrenaline coursing, sweat poured from me and my guts churned. Light-headed from an empty stomach, beer, and no sleep. It was all catching up on me.

I looked in the car window.

His body was slumped sideways, leaning over the gearstick. Hair flopped over his face, a line of blood from the bullet hole in the side of his head. All his black hair steeped in red.

Riz was very, very dead.

Chapter 11

It didn't take long for the police to arrive.

While I waited, I did the logical thing and spewed my guts up in the weeds. I managed to do it as far from the car as I could run in three seconds. That was all the time my body gave me as a warning that it was not happy with the situation.

When the cops arrived, I was sitting with my arms clasped around my knees. I didn't look up. I didn't want to.

A vehicle crawled into the car park and made the long, slow procession over to me. The doors on both sides slammed, and a shadow blocked out the already hot sun.

"Arden," a voice said gently, and PC Adebayo Oduwole took my hands apart to help me stand. "What on earth happened to you?" His face was a picture of concern. We weren't friends or anything. But he was currently dating Sonia in an on/off capacity and had been eager to keep himself in my good books.

"Jesus, look at the state of you," he said, brushing some of the dirt off me. Where had that come from?

"Go wait in the car and I'll come see you in a minute." He beckoned for his fellow officer, PC Lauren Trescothick, to let me in. Lauren opened the door silently and then did a double take when she recognised me.

A few minutes later they returned to the car where I sat in the back staring into space.

I have no idea what they said or what they were asking me. Ade called my name several times and even waved his hand in front of my face before eventually giving up.

I couldn't speak. The idea of making conversation, of answering questions, was too much.

Riz was dead. Dead. Simon's Riz was dead. His fiancé.

Bullet to the side of the head.

There was the sound of more cars arriving. An ambulance. Another police car. More vehicles. Tape went up, tents were erected. Radios were spoken into. All the time I sat there staring into space. Eventually, the door opened, and Ade appeared with a bottle of water. He crouched beside me. "Drink," he commanded.

"I …"

"Drink."

I guzzled it and then managed to swallow half down the wrong tube and coughed violently. Ade patted my back. "Who should I call for you?" he asked.

"No one," I said a little mournfully. *It's happening again. Maybe this time Tarquin will finish the job.*

Ade pursed his lips. "C'mon, mate," he said.

"I wanna go home. My dog needs me."

"Okay. Well, I think they're gonna want to speak with you down the station." He drummed his fingers on his knee for a second and then took his phone out. He dialled a number.

"Hi, babe, it's me. Listen, sorry to wake you on your day off. I know, I know. Yeah, it's a bit of a situation." He covered the phone with his hand and addressed me. "Do you have a spare key to your place?"

I nodded. "In the shed on the windowsill."

"Hey, can you go to Arden's place and see if his dog is okay? On the windowsill in the shed. Yeah. I'll explain later. We'll drop him off in a while."

He hung up and gave me a weak smile. I stared into the distance.

"Does Simon know yet?"

Ade shook his head. "Don't worry about all that. We'll sort it."

Another car pulled up beside us. Out hopped the person I wanted to see least in the world. DI Neuberger glared at everything in front of him as he made his way over to another officer and got the lay of the land. DS Maslin followed him from the car.

Neuberger beckoned for Lauren to come towards him. She spoke for a second before pointing me out. He gave me a look of pure venom.

Ade stood and patted me on the shoulder. “Everything’ll be alright, Arden,” he said. As he departed, he gave a nod to Neuberger.

“Mr Forrest. We meet again,” the DI said as he approached.

He and Maslin stood beside the car and glowered down at me.

“Quite the habit you’re making of this,” he continued. “One could become suspicious.”

They both stood waiting for me to speak.

“I’d like to go home, please,” I said eventually. A bit more plaintively than I would have hoped.

“Yes, I think we can see to that. But first, why don’t we have a chat down at the station? Sound good? Jack.” He flicked his hand at Maslin and walked off to inspect the scene.

Maslin gestured for me to join him in the unmarked car they had arrived in, and I meekly followed. The man was so broad and tall that he created not just a shadow as he walked but a small eclipse. He opened the door to the back seat for me.

After I got in, he shut it with an almost imperceptible click.

His giant dinner plate hands were capable of subtlety.

He got in the driver’s seat and reversed around the cars and tents, and then turned and drove out of the car park.

We said nothing. Maslin gave me filthy looks in the rear-view mirror as he drove, his big hands sitting lazily on the steering wheel. I stared out the window and slumped down in my seat.

How was this happening again? Why hadn't I kept walking?

Sittingston Police Station was no more than a third of a mile away, and we were there in a few minutes. It was a small and phenomenally ugly prefab beige building sitting in the middle of a car park that never seemed to get sun. It was behind a large church off the High Street, with the only block of flats in the town to the other side.

We pulled into a space in the dark, cool car park, and Maslin went through the same rigmarole of letting me out like we were in *Downton Abbey* and I was the duke. Wait, was he a duke in that show? A lord? I laughed to myself. Maslin gave me a look like I was insane.

I probably was.

He led me into an interview room. I sat and waited. He brought me a glass of water. I waited some more.

Then I waited more. How long was I in there? Who knew. I could've reached for my phone; it had a few per cent battery left, but if I did that, then the rest of the world was invited back into my little palace of quiet, and I would have to deal with everything.

The last time I found a body, at least I got laid. Wait, I just got laid. God, what was wrong with me? Did sex mean death in my world? Was I a sex addict? Did someone die every time I got another notch on my bedpost?

After what seemed like days of solitude, where my thoughts began to take increasingly bizarre turns, the door opened, and Neuberger and Maslin entered.

"Mr Forrest," Neuberger said. "I've brought you a sandwich. Thought you might appreciate it as we're assuming it's your breakfast that we found a few metres away from the crime scene?"

I nodded and accepted the sandwich. It hadn't been my breakfast. When did I last eat?

"Please go through the specific details of this morning. All in your own time."

I breathed out shakily and took a bite of my sandwich – egg and cress – and chewed slowly, then gave them the short spiel of my walk across Sittingston.

"And where did you spend the night?"

"Cock and Feather. They have rooms for rent above."

Maslin noted this, presumably to check out later.

"And can anyone corroborate that?"

I swallowed. "The barmaid served me a few times. If they have cameras, then I'll be on them."

Neuberger paused. "Anyone else confirm this?"

I eyed him.

"C'mon, Arden, not like you're short of companionship."

I closed my eyes to stop from screaming at him. After a long pause, I spoke again. "Errol Mottley."

Maslin wrote that down, then paused. "The bloke managing Suzy Rabbit's campaign?" he asked in a proper cockney accent. Not a hint of estuary or mockney. No, he was old-school Bow Bells.

I nodded.

Neuberger eyed me steadily. "Are you dating?"

I startled. "Is that relevant?"

They both shrugged. I shook my head and ate more of my sandwich.

"Do we have a number for Mottley?" Neuberger asked Maslin.

"With all the Frobisher stuff." Maslin looked at me.

"Oh, yes. The Frobisher stuff," Neuberger said. "So sorry to see your private life splashed over the papers, Mr Forrest. Can't imagine. Now, you were with Mr Mottley from when to when?"

Twenty minutes later, it was all over. Neuberger whistled as he exited the room. Maslin grabbed my empty sandwich wrapper and gave me a nod. "A uniformed officer will drive you home," he said.

I followed him out but hesitated by the gents. "Can I?" He waved me on.

The bathrooms were a truly vile shade of beige with little in the way of space. I checked the place was empty, then went to the sink and ran the tap. I scrubbed my face vigorously and splashed enough water over my cheeks to drown a small elephant. My hair and the top of my shirt were sopping. A stinging sensation travelled over my skin as I scrubbed with my hands. Suddenly, my shoulders gave in, and I slumped down, resting my forehead on the mirror in front of me. The cool glass felt amazing on my skin.

The door opened and I scrambled to stand up straight.

Simon stood before me in the doorway. His burly frame taking up most of the space and red hair standing out at all angles over his pale face. He took in the sight of me and then slowly closed the door.

I tried to speak, but nothing came out. "I'm … so sorry," I managed eventually. He nodded tersely. Like the act caused him pain.

"I …" I had nothing to say.

"Are you okay?" he asked me through gritted teeth. His voice sounded choked, like the idea of my well-being sickened him. But he was polite.

"Fine," I answered. "I'm fine."

He did the nod again. "I need to know—" He faltered. His head cocked, and a second later, he walked into a cubicle and shut the door behind him, his feet disappearing.

I had no time to react prior to the door opening again and Jack Maslin walking in. He whistled as he did. He'd started unbuckling his belt before he'd even opened the door and was turning to the urinal when he saw me and stopped.

"Sorry, I forgot you'd be in here still."

"I … I needed to wash my face … I—"

He gave a grim smile. "Perfectly understandable," he said. "First time I saw a dead body, I had the shakes for a week."

I shuddered at Simon hearing that. Not my first dead body, I wanted to correct.

"Listen," he said, reaching into his blazer pocket and pulling out a card. "We were a bit rough on you in there, but you know how it is, people don't always remember what they actually remember if you don't push them to get the facts straight. But if you think of anything else, don't call the station or Neuberger, gimme a bell, alright? I'll go easy on you. I've no bad blood over that nonsense with the Sweet murder. I'm a friendly ear if you need one."

He smiled.

I pocketed the card and returned the smile as best I could.

He cocked his head. "I'll go get that lift sorted for you." He departed before I could react.

Instantly, the cubicle door opened. Simon stood there giving me a filthy look. "Why did you hide?" I asked.

Simon came forward and gripped my arm. "Is there anything you're not telling the police? Please, Arden, be honest. Any dodgy shit you've been up to doesn't matter to me."

"What? No, of course not. Jesus, dodgy shit? What do you think I do?"

His face fell. "Sorry," he said gently. "I should choose my words better. I apologise." He turned and paced the room. "But there's nothing?" he asked again after a few seconds.

"Simon, no. Why?"

Simon shook his head. He tapped Maslin's card and gave a rictus grin. "Only you could pull in a police station." He shook his head again and departed the room.

Wait, what?

In the end, it was Maslin himself who drove me home. An officer who had the conversation skills of a mannequin escorted me out to the car. In fact, I was fairly sure, from his oddly sallow skin, that he *was* a mannequin. A crash-test dummy come to life.

Maslin was waiting by the car. "I thought you were finding a uniformed officer?" I asked.

My crash-test dummy friend did too because he seemed perplexed by Maslin's appearance, lounging on the side of the car. His enormous arms folded across his enormous chest.

"Orders from Top Dog," Maslin said in a voice with zero inflection.

In my mind, a Top Dog was something quite different to what Maslin probably imagined. Whichever East End pub he did his womanising in was probably not to my tastes. It made me wonder if the Red Wagon on Bow Road was still around. A guy from the dodgy pub I'd worked in as a student would go there after his shift to pick up divorced women in their forties.

'Top Dog', I assumed, was Neuberger. *Keep an eye on the Foreign Homosexual Criminal. His eyes are too close together.*

Maslin gestured for me to get in the front seat, which I did. Bone tiredness overtook me the moment I sat down. Home. Feed Kenny. Sleep.

He pulled out of the car park and onto the street, speeding up quickly. I forgot that police officers, particularly plain-clothes ones, got special training for defensive driving and therefore were all speed-demon maniacs behind the wheel.

"So, you knew Patel, you said?"

The question took me by surprise. Had I not spent twenty minutes in an interview room?

"Not well."

"But you know his fiancé better, right?"

An image of the top of Simon's head between my legs entered my mind. "He renovated my kitchen a few months ago."

"Did you get a feel for him?"

Yeah, about six-and-a-half inches and thick as a bedpost. "In what way do you mean?" If he was probing for insights into Simon's psyche, I could safely tell him honestly that I hadn't the fucking foggiest. He'd slammed the door on that pathway sharpish.

Maslin gave me a look. Suddenly, I clicked what he meant. And why he was driving me home. I'm gay – Simon's gay – ergo we must know each other, and ergo does he strike me as the type to kill his boyfriend?

My snooping around Arabella's murder had resulted in one statistic coming up again and again. In an overwhelming percentage of murders, it was the person's partner who did it.

Ollie had told me this at a candlelit French restaurant in London. I could see it with said ex. He was one of the few people I'd met that I could imagine battering to death with a kitchen implement.

"Simon's very good at controlling his temper."

We passed through fields and intersections and turned into the narrow lane down the back of Compney that ran to Winterborne Minster. For a man who'd just moved here, Maslin sure knew the shortcuts.

"Did you ever see him and Patel fight?"

"Nope."

"Get an uncomfortable vibe off them? Like they were mad with each other?"

"I saw them together twice. And like I said, Simon is very good at controlling his temper."

"How do you know that?"

Shit. Whatever I said would be too much. "He was around me when the Sweet case was happening. He was … calm."

Maslin nodded.

"I can't see Simon killing his boyfriend. Especially can't see him shooting him in a car park," I said.

"Because he's calm?"

"Because Simon isn't a psychopath."

He shrugged. I had to concede that if the stats were right, very few murderers were psychopaths. They snapped and had a moment of madness. Tarquin was that. Well, his later actions rather undermined that theory, but the original premise stuck.

"Can I give some unsolicited advice?" I said. Whatever I was doing was the opposite of my usual plan with the police, which was to shut the fuck up as much as possible.

Maslin made a hand gesture indicating for me to proceed.

"Simon's job. It's complicated. Don't expect co-operation or to be allowed to haul him over the coals. Cops or no cops. Murder or no. Some things are above even you lot."

For the first time, Maslin looked at me with something other than anthropological curiosity. We were stopped at the intersection of Winterborne village green, waiting to turn right for the lane to my house. A tractor rattled past at the speed of anti-sound. I shrugged. "You'll see."

Even if he was the murderer, the establishment was not gonna let it be known. Maslin had swapped tower blocks for hay bales, but it was just as messy, this country idyll.

Conversation ended after that, for which I was grateful. Maslin was lost in his thoughts. Probably tossing up stats on partners killing their spouses versus whatever faction of Her Majesty's Most Secret Service Simon fixed the IT systems for.

What I wasn't grateful for was the photographers outside my house blocking the path. They didn't even make room for the police car. One banged on the window as we passed. "Oi, Arden! Your brother a paedo then?"

Maslin parked as close as he could. "Do you want me to escort you? Knock some heads together?"

Last thing I needed. Though Maslin looked like he'd enjoy kicking the paps. His application form to the police probably listed 'waylaying bunches of yobs' under 'Special Skills'. I shook my head. "Thanks for the lift."

"Good luck," he said as I made a run for it. About half a dozen photographers tried to accost me as I hot-footed it up the path to my house and slammed the door shut. Kenny came bounding towards me.

"Oh, I'm so sorry, boy. I'm such a bad dog owner." I put my head onto the thick fur around his neck and let him lick me. "Do you forgive me?" I asked and took further licking as a good sign.

"He was fine," Sonia came in from the kitchen, drying her hands on a tea towel. All the curtains were closed, I noticed. Clearly, Sonia had been accosted earlier. "Bit hungry and whiney, but he'd been a good boy and only done one very small wee on the kitchen floor, so at least it was easy to clean."

"You didn't pee on the carpet for once? Good boy," I said and kissed his fur. I stood up. Which was an effort.

Sonia noticed. "Mum sent me round with enough food to feed an army. Go shower and I'll have a chilli con carne ready for you when you're done."

Ten minutes later, I was shovelling rice and beans into my mouth without tasting anything. "When was the last time you ate?" Sonia asked.

Did a sandwich count? I stopped to think. "I wanna say yesterday? Lunchtime?"

"Arden, that's twenty-four hours without food. No wonder you always look like you're about to collapse. That's terrible for you."

"I know, I know, but I'm never hungry so I … forget."

"Christ, you should bottle that and sell it. You'd make a fortune."

"I thought you said it was terrible."

"And so is society. A pill to make you forget to eat would sadly sell a million on the first day."

She nodded at my phone. "You gonna charge that?" It had died during the interview.

I spun the phone in a circle with my finger.

She looked at me. "Do you wanna talk about it?"

I shook my head. "Anything else, please."

"Okay, well, Mum gave me about twenty portions of this and an entire chicken and leek pie, and a nice apple crumble. So, don't even think about not eating this week."

"Thanks, Son."

She smiled at me. "We all worry about you, Arden."

"We?"

"Do you know how many calls I got last night about where you were? Nigella wanted hourly updates in case you turned up on my doorstep. I told her that you'd never even been to my house."

I stopped eating and glanced at her. She gave me a look I couldn't read. "Are you sure you don't want to talk about it? No one saw you for months. Nigella was sending news on whether you were dead or alive based on your neighbours seeing you out for a run. No one even knew you'd got a dog. And then this all happened, and you've run away every time."

I sat still for a long time. "S'just easier to get out of the way when shit hits the fan. Force of habit. I'm not good with …" I took a long breath. This was agonising. "Not good with … being exposed to things." I gestured at the room, my life. "You can probably work out why. It's easier to leave and start again. Or at least hide until it all blows over."

"You don't need to do either. People care about you, Arden. I've been sitting here for months holding out my hand to be a friend and you never took it."

I looked up at her from where I'd been staring at the table. "I'd like to be your friend."

She grinned. "I'd love to be proper friends." Her face darkened. "But don't ever ask me to break into any more houses."

She was never gonna let go of that, was she?

I went upstairs to sleep for a few hours, and Sonia said she'd give the house a quick spruce up ("It's very obvious a single man lives here.") and then depart. I was asleep when she left. I woke up mid-afternoon cocooned in a sweaty mess with Kenny, my perma-guard.

I had put off the inevitable long enough. I switched on my phone.

And instant barrage. No less than eleven voicemails, which I think was a record. I deleted all of them without listening. Some were from unrecognised numbers, which I didn't want to know about. Numerous texts and WhatsApps from everyone at the meeting last night were read and then left un-replied. Once again, unrecognised numbers were deleted instantly.

Ollie had left three voicemails and numerous messages. I ignored them. If I replied, he'd jump all over me and want answers to questions that I barely knew.

There was a message from Guy. Arden, thank you for your text during the week. It meant a lot. I'm sorry this is happening to you. You don't deserve it. X

"I don't think my date's happening," I told Kenny. It looked like Guy and I had missed our shot.

The last person to contact me was Verity. Her last message was at 9 a.m. today. Call me when you can. Urgent.

A deep sigh emanated from me of its own accord.

I dialled her number.

"Arden, thank God. Are you okay?"

"Yes, I'm fine."

"Listen, good, okay. Look, I know this is bad, but we can fix it."

"It's a story, Vee. What happened to the 'all publicity is good publicity' mantra?"

There was a pause. "What are you talking about – did you listen to any of my messages?"

"There were so many."

"Jesus, Arden, I am doing everything I can to stop this, and you're swanning about in a sulk!"

I leaned up. "What? I—"

"Donal and Ffion called a meeting for the first available moment this week. I've managed to hold them off until Tuesday so I can spend tomorrow seeing how things are sitting with the publishers, at least. They're on the warpath. Arden, they want to cancel your contract. They think you're bringing the agency into disrepute."

"What? They can't do that!" I jumped off my bed and paced the room. "Verity, they can't do that!"

"They can. They're equity partners; equal and joint owners of the business. We make decisions together."

They were going to take my career away. I was going to be dropped. I didn't have anything else. No matter what had happened over the past year, at least I'd had my bizarre fluke of a career to rely on to keep me occupied and well paid. "What do I do? Should I come to London? Do they want me to beg? Do I have to grovel? I'm not proud, I'll do it."

They couldn't cancel my contract. If I lost Verity … would another agent even take me with the publicity I'd garnered over the past few months? Would anyone else put up with my reticence on social media and my standoffishness in the face of trying to market the books?

"Look, not all hope is lost. They're not stupid. They know the business needs you. But … you know, there might be changes, stipulations. New clauses in your contract."

"Do they want more money?"

"No, maybe, I don't know. Arden, I'm going to bat for you, I promise. I'll do everything I can, but for God's sake, keep your head down and don't do anything stupid. Maybe try and calm down a bit. Less manic."

She hung up.

I was going to lose everything. I had rejected Ollie. Tarquin was a psychopath. Verity had clearly had enough of me. And everyone else was basing their assumptions about me on a tabloid article.

Did I have enough in savings to pay my mortgage for a while, at least? I had lost track of my money over the past few months. I think I was fine, in fact, I knew I had more than enough to live on for a few years, but the deep dread was crawling up my skin. *You were a poor, lonely little boy with no friends once. You'll be that boy again.*

I crawled up beside Kenny and waited for the night to come.

Chapter 12

I woke to my phone buzzing and with no idea how long I'd slept. I had gone from never sleeping to always sleeping. Neither seemed to have improved how I felt.

After a lengthy search in the covers (and the dog), I found the device. Nigella's name looked at me from the screen. It was Monday morning. I'd been dead to the world for half a day.

"Hello?" I croaked.

"Darling," she said. I nearly started crying. "I've heard everything. You poor thing. Are you decent for visitors? The boys are at school, thankfully, so I'm free for the day. Be over in twenty."

After putting the phone down, I dragged my sorry, lifeless arse to the bathroom where I tried to make myself look human. Did everyone else jump in fright when they saw themselves in the mirror? No, just me?

I sat on my back step, drinking coffee, and hoped Kenny didn't decide to run around the front of the house where several photographers waited for me. Thankfully, he sniffed about the back happily.

Nigella crested the hill above the garden. She waved as she made her way down through the field, and I clambered to help her hop over the ancient stone wall. "That took an age," she said. "Had to wander halfway to Winterborne and then get up this hill to avoid those bloody reporters."

She arranged her summer dress in a more becoming manner and smiled serenely. "I've brought muffins," she said and led me indoors, stopping to give Kenny a pat on the head.

We sat at the breakfast bar, and encouraged by the magic of her soothing middle-class tones, I was able to give the full rundown of everything since I'd fled the room at Honningtons.

"Darling." She rubbed my arm. "You've been in the wars, I mean, obviously others have it a bit worse – we'll speak about that in a minute – but you poor thing. Do you really think they'll cancel your contract?"

"Your guess is as good as mine."

She rubbed my arm again. "Do you want to discuss finding … you know."

I shook my head. "What was this other thing you wanted to speak about?"

"Oh. The village is rallying around Simon. I'm going to his place later to offer some moral support. I spoke to him last night." She checked her watch. "He said his parents were driving down to Edinburgh to get a flight. They should be getting in soon. I've got a shepherd's pie in here." She patted the reusable canvas shopping bag she'd brought. "Do you have a speciality you can whip up?"

I went cold. "Apple crumble?"

"Oh, that'd be perfect. Everyone will need a treat. I didn't know you baked."

I remained silent and instead took a big bite of my muffin. Nigella continued to witter on for a while. She folded a tea towel for the seventh time.

My eyes narrowed. "Gella, is everything alright with you?"

"Silly really," she said in a small voice, looking away.

"Go on, spill. You've heard my latest self-induced crisis."

She kept folding the tea towel. Eventually, however, she began to speak. "Ahhh, um – well … Matteo – and I – have decided to separate," she said quietly.

She looked at me, and I instantly went to her. Her eyes were glistening with tears. "Gella, I'm so sorry."

"It's so bloody hard, Arden. This is not how I thought it'd be." She paused, shocked at her own candour. "Kids, house, jobs. We've been married for twenty years. I thought we'd last forever. We just … are. We've been together most of my adult life. I can't remember who I was before I knew him."

I guided her to the table and sat across from her. She looked pale and tired. I held her hand.

"It's … it hasn't been working for a couple of years. He's never bloody there, and when he is, he's always emailing and dealing with work. Never even looks at the boys. Then he says I'm not interested in him, that I'm turning into a gossipy old woman. That he misses the old me. What old me?" she scoffed and reached up to wipe tears from her eyes.

"Is he back in Milan now?" I asked as gently as I could.

"Yes, of course, where else would he be? Back with *mamma* in the bloody palazzo. I have an appointment with a lawyer booked for a few days from now."

My face must've given off my surprise.

"He says there's no need, but how many times have you heard this situation and wondered why the woman let herself not get a lawyer."

"Do the boys know?"

She shook her head. "Not yet. God, Arden. I don't know how to do this. I've been half of a couple for so long that I can't remember how to be on my own. Nigella and Matteo. Mrs Pettoni."

I hugged her, and she hugged me back and sniffled into my shirt. "Oh, no, I've gone and cried all over your polyblend. Darling, why don't you go up and change into that lovely green one you have, and we'll make a move down to Simon's?"

We both knew I was being told to wear something nicer, and I didn't argue. Feeling guilty, I spoke up: "Can you do some magic with the apple crumble? It's still in the dish. There are some old plates in the cupboard beside the sink to put it on." The last thing I needed was to lose Mrs Bliss' favourite pie dish.

"Of course, I've a knack for it."

I left her in the kitchen wittering to herself about how surprised she was at my baking acumen.

Upstairs, as I changed into my nice green shirt (it was more olive) and a pair of black chinos, I wondered if it was appropriate for me to be at Simon's. Don't get me wrong, I wanted to offer my support on what was probably the worst day of his life, but whether he wanted me there was another thing. We were hardly friends.

This isn't about you, Arden, I told myself. Other people have problems too. Turn up and do the dishes or something, keep your head down and stay in the kitchen.

I thundered down the stairs, where a happy Kenny met me. "Sorry, lad, not really a dog-friendly environment, you're gonna have to stay here and keep an eye on Roosevelt and Eisenhower. But I promise we'll go on a big walk tonight when I get back."

Kenny walked off into the living room without a second glance. "I'm getting the silent treatment," I told Nigella.

"It's to be expected. Right, sensible shoes, I'm afraid. That trek halfway across the county round the hill is not ankle friendly."

I grimaced but waved her on. She grabbed her canvas bag, which had my plastic-wrapped apple crumble on top, and we made our way to the top of the garden.

The walk back around the edge of the village required some subterfuge in order to make it up the hill without being seen. We made a sharp left and walked parallel to the main road going south out of the village before swinging into a bank of trees that emerged into the field at the back of Simon's street.

The cul-de-sac he lived on was full of 1960s houses that sat on the southern side of Lilbury, on the opposite side of the main road to the rest of the village. Lilbury was shaped like a pregnant woman's belly – Simon's road was a tail pinned on at the bottom.

The street was well kempt, though. Unlike the child-centric residences around the church and school, old-age pensioners almost exclusively inhabited this area. A lot of the houses were split into maisonettes, like Simon's, which was a two-bedroom flat on the first floor with access to a long, thin garden out the back. The intersection, where a tiny lane took you up the hill to my cottage, was a few hundred yards to the north of us. Beyond that were the backs of the few shops on the high street and then the pub.

A copse of trees ran along the fences at the back of the houses. There was a vague dirt path connecting each garden gate to the trees. Outside were many piles of firewood, wheelbarrows, and other outdoor supplies, showing that most of the residents here used the area as an extension of their gardens. Nigella let go of my arm, which she'd been holding on to since we left my house and opened a white gate to one of the better-kept gardens, which I assumed was Simon's. I'd only ever visited the front of his house and couldn't remember which one it was.

The door to the house opened as she did so, and a pleasant-looking woman with sandy blond-grey hair stood at the back door and spread her arms out to Nigella.

"Marion," Nigella walked to her. "How is he? How are *you*?" They embraced, and when they parted, Marion gave a shuddering exhale.

"About as well as you can imagine," she said in a Scottish accent. She looked me over.

"My manners. Marion, this is Arden Forrest, a friend. Arden, this is Marion, Simon's mum."

Great. The mother. But instead of glaring at me, like I usually got from mothers, she beamed at me. "The famous Arden! Gosh, it's lovely to put a face to the name. Simon's told us all about you. I've been looking forward to meeting you. I'd hoped it'd be in slightly different circumstances!"

I struggled to arrange my face in a way that hid my surprise. Simon … talked about me? To his mum? In positive tones?

She grabbed my arm and dragged me inside. "So sorry about all that business with you in the paper. How awful for you. I'm sure you didn't need that dragged up. But what can you do? We don't choose our family."

Inside was a small landing and then a steep staircase that led up to the flat on the first floor. A door at the top opened into a surprisingly spacious kitchen, which was freshly decorated in greys and whites.

A man stood at the sink and looked like he was struggling with several dishes, most of which seemed to be filled with various kinds of pasta.

"What are you doing? Back away." Marion swatted the man and shooed him from the counter so she could look at the scene. He grinned at me and held his hands up in defeat as he took a place on the other side of the kitchen.

"Eleventy billion pasta bakes, and nowhere to put them," Marion muttered. She remembered the rest of us. "George, you remember Nigella. And this is Arden."

George gave Nigella a kiss on the cheek and then turned to me. "Arden! I feel like I know you already. Simon's told us all about you. We even went and bought some of your books so we could know what he was talking about."

He shook my hand and gave me a clap on the arm as he did so. George Anson was a burly, but slightly short man in his mid-sixties. He was bald but handsome with a roguish smile and bright eyes. His arms were like rocks, and his hands were callused. He wore a simple white shirt over practical trousers. Completely unassuming, but I bet he was as fit as an ox. I could see some of Simon's face in his. The line of the jaw, the curve of the lip. But it seemed the red hair came from Marion's side, as in the sunlight streaming through the kitchen windows, her freckled arms and a vague hint of strawberry blonde in her hair were more apparent.

This pleasant middle-class couple that probably enjoyed National Trust properties and bought all their clothes from Marks and Spencer were not the sort of people I'd imagined raising a scowling wall of anger like Simon. "It's a pleasure to meet you both."

They beamed back. "Would've been nicer in different circumstances," George said. We all nodded.

"How is he?" Nigella began divesting her bag of food onto the counter.

"He's in the lounge," said Marion. "And your guess is as good as ours. Barely two words since we got here."

Nigella embraced her, while I stood there like a chump. I spotted some coffee cups and nabbed them. When in doubt, do the dishes. It's how I got through everything.

I ran the tap and washed up the cups. Oh, good, there were some bowls over there. Ah! Jackpot, some empty plates from where Marion must've combined dishes to fit them all in the fridge. There was at least ten minutes of washing up to be done. I looked around and saw the others had departed for the living room. I finished up the remaining dishes and decided I, too, should go through to see the person I'd come to help. But first, the counter had some crumbs on it. I'd grab something to wipe it with. But also, the recycling needed tidying up. And when was the last time someone had run a cloth over this kitchen windowsill? There were some serious cobwebs in there.

Some half an hour later, with Simon's kitchen noticeably tidier, I edged my way into the living room to find it full of people. The flat had been redecorated recently, judging by the décor. A charcoal L-shaped sofa took up the left-hand wall of the living/dining room with a TV on the wall opposite. At the front of the room was a small bistro-style dining table and chairs.

On the mantlepiece was a photo of Simon and what must be the rest of his family. They looked loving.

Simon sat on the sofa with his mum and Nigella on each side. George stood at the window speaking softly to Guy Frobisher.

They noticed me first. I gulped and made my way over.

"Arden," said a voice from the sofa before I took a second step. I looked over to see Simon staring at me. His eyes were red, and he was as pale as a ghost. Worst day of his life.

After a second, he gave me a small smile. "Thanks for coming."

I returned the smile. "Of course, and if there's anything you need."

He nodded and lowered his head again. I made my way over to George and Guy, who were glaring out the bay window at the front of the room.

"Vultures," George said as I arrived beside him. In the street were several photographers, all sitting around various cars looking bored.

"Have they been there all morning?" Now I understood why we'd come around the back way. See, Arden, other people have problems too.

Guy nodded. "Luckily, Doris and Betty have been making their lives hell. A few have already left. And old Frank at number 37 has been out there banging on to them about the BBC licence fee, so I'm sure some are near the end of their tether."

As we stood there, a car pulled up on the street and out got the woman from Honningtons. Riz's campaign manager, Marina Holt. Instantly, the reporters mobbed her, despite Doris yelling at them that they were causing an obstruction.

"I shall call the council!" Doris said, giving a literal wave of her fist.

"What does she want?" Guy snarled, looking at Marina. His tone shocked both George and me, and we stared at him. "Sorry," he said, composing himself. "Last week, she and I had a few words. Things got a bit heated. But it's not the time."

George clapped him on the back. "Nae worry, lad," he said, sounding very Scottish. "I'll go tell Simon she's here."

He departed over to the other side. Simon's face fell when his dad told him who was outside. I looked down to where Marina was giving an impromptu press conference on the front step.

Guy nudged me. I looked up at the handsome face. "Hey," I said softly.

"Are you okay?" he asked. "Sorry, I went AWOL last week. Everything … well, you know what happened. But I'm sorry I didn't reach out and check in on you. I felt terrible, but I didn't know what to say."

Guy had been worried about me? "I was fine. I had people to help me."

"Do you want to talk about the article?" he asked gently, his hand on my elbow. "It was cruel, and half of it was pure conjecture. You should sue."

I shook my head. "I want it to be forgotten about."

He nodded. "Still. I didn't believe a word of it." He looked over at the sofa and then turned back to me with a sly smile. "Apart from when they called you handsome."

I reddened. "Guy …" I said after a second.

"I know, I know. Not appropriate. And, yeah, I know I asked you out …" He sighed. "But, it's not going to happen, is it?"

"Probably not."

"Ah, well. Anyway, not what we're here for today." He looked over at the sofa again. "I can't imagine what Simon is going through right now."

"Yeah, poor Riz."

Guy was silent and didn't share my sympathies for the dearly departed, but I chose to ignore that. George led Marina Holt into the room, and she politely nodded at everyone. Well, she nodded at Guy. She and Simon made eye contact, and he stood. She followed him through the kitchen, and the door outside closed with a firm click.

"What does she want?" Guy didn't bother to mask his tone.

"Probably wants his answer on whether he'll do a press conference with Riz's parents," Marion said. "She wants it done as soon as possible. She rang him twice about it yesterday."

We all sat in silence.

After an age, I broke. "So … do the police have any leads?"

George puffed out his cheeks. "Take your pick. Politically motivated, hate crime, robbery gone wrong."

"That awful policeman this morning asked if Riz went cursing—" Marion said.

"Cursing?" Guy mouthed at me.

"Do you mean 'cruising'?" I asked gingerly.

"Oh, do I? I think I do, yes," she said, going pink. "But I told them, Simon's not into that sort of thing and he wouldn't be with someone who was."

I met Guy's eyes. Yes, because all gay men told their mums about their sex lives. Nigella caught us and sent a warning look.

The silence stretched on. All of us trying not to look out the back window to see what was happening. Eventually, Marina Holt came back upstairs and glared at everyone before remembering her manners. "Good afternoon, I hope you're all coping under the circumstances. Guy." She nodded at him.

"You've perfect timing, Marina. I must get going, and you can be my cover. Come, come," he said and stood. He shook mine and George's hands and then kissed Marion and Nigella on the cheek. "Tell Si that I'm sorry I couldn't stay any longer," he whispered to Nigella.

They took their leave – Marina clearly furious – and the shouts of the photographers briefly filled the room before the front door closed. George and Marion went into the kitchen and looked out the window, and we followed. In the back garden, Simon stood in the middle of the lawn staring out over the trees. His back to us. "Should I go?" George asked.

"Maybe we should give him a minute," Nigella said.

Simon was rubbing his face, and I could see how tense his massive shoulders were under his T-shirt. I walked to the fridge, instinct guiding me that what I was looking for would be inside it. Yup, there they were. I grabbed two. "You guys take it easy for a bit, I'll see what I can do," I said and departed.

Downstairs, I opened the door, making enough noise to alert him to my arrival. I moved to stand beside him and handed over the bottle of beer I'd taken from the fridge. "It's five o'clock somewhere," I said when he hesitated.

He took the bottle. "I've been trying to avoid the stuff while ..."

While you're upset and emotional.

I gulped my own down. "I don't think one will have you living on the streets pissing yourself."

He took a swig.

"Do you wanna talk about it?" I tempted a glance over my shoulder to the kitchen window and saw three faces there. I cocked my eyebrow and Nigella put her hands up in defeat and began to usher the Ansons away.

"Not really." His voice was hoarse.

"Then do you want to tell me why you and Marina Holt hate each other so much?"

He snorted. "You know, usual reasons. I'm not political candidate boyfriend material."

My eyebrow returned to cocked position.

"They couldn't even say what I do for a living in any blurbs. 'Riz's fiancé works for the government' was as much as we could offer."

Oh.

"Wow, you actually are a spy?" I asked, feeling a bit stupid.

He gave me a look.

"Can you answer that?"

He was giving me the look still.

"Can we sit?" His voice seemed small. He pointed towards a tree stump that was repurposed as a seat. I followed him.

"Did you make this?"

He nodded and swigged his beer. He purposely sat faced away from me, staring at the trees, and sniffed loudly. I looked at him in surprise; there were tears running down his face.

"Sorry, I was trying not to cry in front of anyone." He cleared his throat in the way men do when their embarrassment has caught up with their other emotions.

"Don't do that," I said. "You loved him."

"Why?" he said sharply. "Why has this happened? There's no rhyme nor reason to it. Riz wasn't going to win the seat. Not even with Guy dropping out. He … he was a doctor, for God's sake."

No rhyme nor reason.

"I know." I put my hand on his shoulder.

He slumped forward, tears on his face. We sat there for several minutes, maybe longer. It could have been an hour. The only sound was Simon's occasional sniffs. He angled himself so I couldn't see his face.

"I need to find out who did this, Arden," he said eventually.

That snapped me back to attention. "Let the police do that, you focus on you."

He shook his head. "No, I need to know who did this. I need to make them pay."

"Simon."

He spun around to me. "You caught Tarquin. You could show me what you did."

Ah. "It wasn't really a case of me catching him, per se." I'd thought Tommy Douglas had done it.

He shook his head again. "But the police have nothing. They told me this morning. Neuberger said they found no physical evidence at the scene."

"The killer will make a mistake," I said, trying to ease his fears. "They'll catch him. He'll try and sell something he stole from Riz's wallet or—"

"It wasn't a robbery, Arden. He wasn't carjacked," he snapped. "This is Dorset, not Johannesburg."

I was saved from this going further by Marion opening the door and coming out into the garden. "Darling, there are some more people here. Lady F."

Simon grimaced but stood up and wiped his face. "I need a minute to fix myself up," he told his mum and went inside.

She came over to me and sighed. "Who could do such a thing?" Behind the kind face was a look of abject terror.

We were silent a minute. "I'm so glad Simon has so many friends in the village. It's reassuring. He can be a grumpy sod. Even when he was a wean."

She sat beside me, and I took the opportunity to look at her properly. I could see her son's face in her own. A face that was usually full of laughter and fun but was now marred with concern and stress.

“I’ve read your books, you know,” she said after a minute of silence. “They were very good. I enjoyed them.”

“Thank you,” I said. “I’m finishing the next one, it’ll be out for Christmas.”

“Lovely. Simon encouraged me to read them. He loved sci-fi as a teenager, always with a book in his hand.”

I couldn’t help but snort. We’d been the same. Nerdy boys with our noses buried in a book.

She went quiet again, but eventually spoke. “Could – could you keep an eye on him? We won’t be able to stay forever, and—” She twisted her hands in her lap. “He used to tell us everything. It’s like there’s a wall up between us now. He rings every Sunday, but I can feel that for every detail of his life he does tell us about, there’s ten more he doesn’t.”

I should have told Marion that he and I weren’t as close as she imagined. We were no great friends. But I couldn’t.

“I worry he’ll do something silly,” she said. “Or that he won’t do anything at all. That he won’t process it.”

No one knows what grief will do to you. I hadn’t predicted it’d drive me to amateur sleuthing. Or that catching Tarquin would turn me into a shut-in for months.

Instead, I smiled, and I gave her assurance. I soothed her tired nerves with trite words about a fictitious friendship with her son. I ignored the comments he’d made earlier. The vehemence.

We played a dance of social niceties. Marion looked at me with her kind eyes – the sort of eyes my mother never looked at me with – and she smiled. “You’re a good man, Arden.”

I departed not long after. Sharing pleasantries with Lady F, and a brief flicker of a smile to Simon. Back home, drained, I stared at the ceiling. One day, I told myself, one day you'll know how this is supposed to work.

Chapter 13

After a restless night of tossing and turning in the heat, I gave up at about 5 a.m. on Tuesday and rose from my pit.

Every time I'd managed to close my eyes, Riz's face appeared in front of my eyelids. Except he was holding a gun to my head and spoke in Tarquin's voice.

Together, Kenny and I beat the paps for a nice run in the opposite direction across the fields towards Winterborne Minster.

Forty-five minutes later, I nodded at a man about the same age as me, waiting near the village green, as we arrived.

I kept my distance. But I already knew it was too late. He'd been smoking a fag but dropped it on the ground as I approached. "Arden?"

I froze.

"Don't worry, I won't make trouble. Dominic Grundy, you answered my call last week?" he said in his Brummie accent. He was late twenties, with a scraggly beard and thin, sloping shoulders. Not a looker by any stretch of the imagination. "I saw you running off in this direction while all the others were busy scratching their arses. I'm not paparazzi, I'm a reporter."

"No comment," I said.

"You were a reporter once; you know what it's like. Trying to get through to someone."

My career in journalism was a distant memory. I was mostly in it for the evening canapé receptions.

"I don't care. I have no comment to make. On anything."

"Listen," he said, looking around. "I'm working on a story about Macauley Sheridan. Nothing to do with you. But this is tangentially involved."

Kennedy seemed intrigued by him, and I had to hold him back.

"See, your dog trusts me."

"My dog eats fox shit," I snapped. Kennedy looked up at me. An expression on his face that I could have sworn was telling me *Hey! I thought that was our secret. Like when you kick me out of the bedroom for twenty minutes after viewing certain websites.*

"Look, I'm warning you. There might be more shit heading your way. Be prepared. And if you do want to get ahead of it—" He held out a business card. I took it and grunted when I saw which tabloid he worked for. "As I said, you're not my primary interest. I want some answers on other topics. Your name – it cropped up, is all. If you ever want to talk, let me know." He backed away, his hands up to show he meant no harm.

As he walked off, I nodded at him and made a show of pocketing his card. "Probably not, but thanks anyway."

"Your choice," he said. I watched him depart. He walked across the village green to a shabby hatchback and lit another cigarette before getting in and driving off.

I made a push to get back to the safety of home quickly. We returned before the day had even fully begun. I made myself a healthy breakfast, put Dominic Grundy to the back of my mind, and then tried to figure out what to do with my time.

About 9 a.m., Nigella texted me: Turn on your TV now.

I switched it on and saw that a press conference was about to get underway. The backdrop read *Dorset Police* – the reporter was nervously over-explaining every facet of the investigation of the case.

"And we're a few minutes away from the family coming out. Sources in the police have told us they hope the press conference from the family will jog the memory of those in the local area on Saturday night—"

I sat on the floor in front of my TV with Kenny wrapping himself around me like a comfort blanket. I scratched his head in an absent-minded manner, and he licked my other hand.

The reporter broke off as several people arrived. A police officer in full uniform, followed by a man and woman in late middle age, as well as Marina Holt and … Simon.

"Good morning," the officer started. "I'm Bryn Fordham, chief constable of Dorset Police. I welcome you all to this press conference today. We all wish it were under better circumstances, but unfortunately, we are not that lucky. I am joined by Mr and Mrs Patel, Riz Patel's parents, Marina Holt, his campaign manager, and his fiancé, Simon Anson."

Simon's jaw was locked, and his eyes were focused on the middle distance. Marina gave a tight smile while Mrs Patel let out a sniffle and leaned into her husband.

"The murder of Mr Patel has shocked not just the local community but the UK, and even the world. For a political candidate to be killed in such a way is almost unprecedented in the UK. There have been almost no cases like this in the past forty years, not since the days of IRA terrorist action on the British mainland," he said solemnly. "We understand that there has been chatter about similarities of this to the killing of Jo Cox MP in 2016 in Yorkshire, but as we have so far been able to ascertain, with help from other forces in the UK, there are no links between these murders.

"I will give a full briefing in due course, but now I would like to pass to Marina Holt, who was Mr Patel's campaign manager for his race in the Central Dorset seat."

Marina's dark red hair was pulled back in a severe ponytail, and her mouth was a slit of red lipstick. She wore a rather expensive-looking cream suit with a pussy bow blouse underneath. I felt my lip curl against her.

She took the microphone on a stand in front of her and arranged it awkwardly closer to her face and began to speak. She had a plummy accent that turned her Rs into Ws in the most infuriating manner.

"Riz was not just a colleague, but also a *fwend*," she said. I could see the insincerity dripping off her. "We, and the Labour Party, want justice for him and his loved ones."

Chief constable Fordham stood again as the endless flashes and clicks of off-screen cameras from the press on the other side continued.

"We will now recount the last few hours of Mr Patel's known movements on Saturday night." He clicked a button on a remote in his hand, and a monitor behind him showed a Google Earth image of the area. "Dr Patel had been, along with Ms Holt and his fiancé, Mr Anson, at a campaign event in Borrington Upwild." He named a village about two miles north of Sittingston that had a pretty green and not a lot else.

"The event lasted from around 13:00 until just before 14:30 when Dr Patel and Ms Holt travelled to a nearby café, the Cupcake Rooms, for a late lunch, which they departed from around 15:30. Dr Patel went outside for several moments to take a phone call around 14:55.

"From there they travelled to Bournemouth for a 17:00 interview with Marla Dickens, on her Saturday afternoon politics and talkback show on Smooth 98.1 FM." Fordham clicked the remote, and a map of Bournemouth popped up on the monitor.

"Smooth's offices are in the Hinton Road area of the city. Dr Patel drove separately from Ms Holt and arrived there at about 16:40. He was in the building until around 17:25. Phone records confirm he took another call about this time, which lasted around ten minutes. After this, he made his way back to his fiancé's home in Lilbury.

"Dr Patel arrived at his fiancé's home on Rosebud Gardens in Lilbury around 19:00. This is unusual as the journey is only around fifty minutes, and traffic was light. Dr Patel grew up in the Bournemouth area; he'd made this journey several times and knew the route well. We are sure that with his local knowledge, he could have reached it in just over forty minutes. Ms Holt travelled separately and made her way back to her home for several minutes to change her clothes.

"This means we have around thirty minutes unaccounted for between him leaving the station and arriving in Lilbury." The chief constable looked at the crowd over the top of his glasses and enunciated each word carefully. "We need anyone who saw a black late model SUV on the A341 between the aforementioned times to contact police.

"We have several CCTV images of Dr Patel driving through Bournemouth, through the Winton and West Howe areas of the city, which matches a route that he should have taken. However, the GPS appears to have been switched off in both his car and the location data for his phone. Unusually, Dr Patel seems to have switched these off several weeks ago. We are yet to understand why. We have no further CCTV images of Dr Patel's vehicle until much later on in the evening.

"Dr Patel was wearing light brown chinos, brown lace-up shoes, a blue linen shirt with the sleeves rolled up. He was five foot nine, weighed eleven stone, and was British Asian. He had medium-length black hair and a short beard with no piercings or tattoos.

"At around 19:00, Dr Patel arrived at his partner's home, where he appeared agitated and stressed and took several more phone calls throughout the evening. At approximately 19:30, he and his partner were joined by

Ms Holt and made their way to the home of Guy Frobisher at Honningtons manor house on the other side of the village of Lilbury." Fordham clicked the remote again, showing another satellite image.

"They arrived around 19:40 and were present with several other people until around 21:30 when they left. Ms Holt accompanied them home and left around 21:50.

"Dr Patel and his partner were at home until around 23:00 when Dr Patel had another phone call and said he would instead spend the night at his own home in Salisbury, a forty-minute drive away. This was not uncommon, according to Mr Anson. Mr Patel frequently became anxious about his workload and campaigning and preferred sleeping at his own house.

"Around 03:00 on Sunday, we have CCTV images of Dr Patel's SUV arriving in Sittingston from the western side of the town, which is unusual as Lilbury is to the south and Salisbury to the east. Dr Patel has no acquaintances in the village and, until this campaign, had reportedly no connections to it. He travelled up White Ball Road to the corner of the High Street, where he was captured on the CCTV of a local bank. He spent several minutes idling in the town centre before being captured on a separate camera at the entrance of the St Margaret's Road Car Park, where he was later discovered by a member of the public at approximately 06:00.

"We urge any members of the public who saw his car travelling between the hours of 17:00 Saturday and 03:00 Sunday morning to contact Dorset Police immediately. No detail is too small."

The chief constable took off his glasses and shuffled his papers. I held Kennedy a little closer. Behind me, I heard one of the cats jump up on the sofa and purr contentedly as they settled in for a nap. "I will now open the floor to questions from the media," he added.

There was a clamour. He pointed to someone off-screen.

"Chief constable, do you think this was politically motivated?"

"We have no evidence of a motive yet."

"Chief constable, do you think this was a hate crime?"

"We have no evidence of a motive yet."

"Chief constable, what do you think of the rumour that Riz Patel was the one who leaked images of Guy Frobisher's sex tape?"

My head snapped up, and I saw Simon's do the same on screen. The chief constable huffed. "We have absolutely no evidence of that. We understand certain websites have been uploading theories around this scenario, but we have no basis on which these could be verified."

"Mr Patel," yelled a journalist. "Is it true that you and your wife hadn't spoken to your son for several years? Is it because Riz was gay?"

Riz's father hugged his wife a little tighter. "We loved our son," he said.

"Simon! Simon!" yelled another reporter. "What do you say to the person who killed your fiancé?"

Simon remained silent. He stared at the camera, his eyes unblinking. Worst day of his life #2.

"That's quite enough questions," the chief constable said. With that, he led the Patels, Marina, and Simon from the room.

"That was the live scene from Dorset Police headquarters," said the TV reporter as the feed was cut and the view returned to the studio. "No closer to discovering those responsible for the death of political candidate Riz Patel, now forty-eight hours after his body was found."

My phone started buzzing, and I nearly broke an ankle scrambling for it when I saw Verity's name on the screen. Kennedy was most put out as I splayed myself across the living room floor to grab it.

"Hello!" I said, jabbing the remote to mute the TV.

"Arden, morning," she said stiffly.

"How's the meeting? Surely you've barely started."

"Listen," she said, continuing with the stiff tone. "Arden, I know this is going to be difficult. Donal and Ffion are here with me. You're on speaker. We're all in agreement."

She paused, presumably so Donal and Ffion could greet me, but there was nothing but silence down the line. "Anyway," she carried on. "Arden, we're advising you that … We … the agency, that is, would like to assess your contract. The terms of which have now become untenable with current circumstances. We'd like to approach this as amicably—"

"You're cancelling my contract?"

"No, but we're going to have to change it, Arden. We can't continue to represent you with the current headlines swirling. We have no choice but to work with legal representation to seek out our options to protect the agency and our other clients." Her voice was robotic.

My world was falling apart. I was going to lose my career. And Verity sounded like she didn't even care.

"Do you understand, Arden?" came Donal's voice.

"Yes," I said quietly.

"We advise you to get your own lawyer," Verity said. "When our legal team have worked with us on options, we'll send it to you, and we hope we can get this all worked out as soon as possible."

"Great," Donal's voice came down the line again. "Good to speak to you as always, Arden. We'll be in touch when our lawyers have worked up a new contract."

Verity started to say something, but I cut her off. "Sounds good. Talk later." I hung up.

I sat on the floor for some time with my brain reeling. I'd lost my career.

No, don't be silly. How bad could they make it? What kind of caveats and retroactive stipulations could they put in my contract? A morality clause? Not to bring the agency into disrepute?

But … that really wasn't the worst thing. It was barely 10 a.m. The meeting would've just started before the call was made. Donal and Ffion were in complete agreement and had railroaded Verity into whatever was done. She hadn't put up much of a fight by the sound of things. Sounded like she didn't care very much. Maybe she was glad to be rid of me, if that was to be the way things were.

Donal and Ffion would arrange a contract that would keep me at the agency but rewrite the terms to bleed me dry. Their cut could double or triple to keep up with any 'reputational damages' they incurred by keeping me on their books.

I should leave before I was pushed. I should reach out to other agents and try to staunch my losses before …

But no, I made millions for Verity's agency. Literally, millions. It was my books that were keeping the lights on over there. Surely, they wouldn't want to lose me, no matter how deranged my life seemed to them.

I'd been approached by several other agents since my books hit the big time. I had a swathe of business cards in a box somewhere and a good dozen emails from other agents in London and abroad who had deemed me an attractive option at one stage or another.

There was Bryce, the handsome Californian with a big agency out in LA, who had invited me for drinks when I was in New York last year. Just before I'd come back to England to find Ollie in bed with flexible Jamie.

He'd rolled out the welcome mat for me. Which was a polite way of saying he basically invited me to sit on his face in the middle of a Midtown Manhattan cocktail bar. He said his agency was very keen to sign me.

Then there was Camilla, who worked for a posh agency in London. We'd met at a launch or something before

Christmas last year. She had shoved her mobile number into my pocket with a wink. "If you ever want to ditch Jones and her cute little, ah, start-up, give me a bell. I'd drop everything."

But I'd vowed always to stay with Verity. Yes, her agency was tiny and sometimes it limited what we could do, but dammit, ten years of friendship were more important than more bloody marketing opportunities or adding another zero to our bank balances. She'd been with me through thick and thin – mostly thin and then very recently a huge chunk of sudden thickness.

It'd always been smooth sailing until now … Maybe it was the case that Verity had no real experience with my profile or the magnitude of coverage I seemed to garner.

Perhaps that was cruel to think, but Verity was acting like this was just business. No, this was my life.

I could rely on her … couldn't I? She'd always have my back. Just like I'd always have hers.

It hadn't felt like it over the past few days, but for God's sake, Arden, she let you stay a week at her house and hasn't said a word about leaving puddles of lube on her living room floor.

Through the wisdom of the universe, my phone started ringing again. I looked down at it, hoping it was Verity ringing back to tell me she'd solved everything, or that, Jesus, what twats were Donal and Ffion, right? Anyway, never mind about that, what was going on with your life?

Instead, Ollie's name flashed up on my phone. Did I want to answer it? No. Did I? Yes. I'd felt bad for not returning any of his messages for days.

"Hi," I offered.

"Bloody hell, he lives." There was a pause. "Sorry, poor choice of words considering what's been going on." He stopped talking and waited for me to say more but I had nothing to add. I could hear the sounds of the city down the line. He'd be walking between his chambers and the

High Court or to some meeting. He always made his calls on these walks. The number of times we arranged what we wanted for dinner with him cutting me off halfway through with a "Sounds lovely, babe, gotta go, bye" were too numerous to count.

"You alright?" he asked softly.

"Sorry I haven't rung or anything," I said. My voice sounded faint. I'd suddenly become very tired.

"No, no, I understand. How awful for that bloke you know. It all sounds unreal. Can't imagine what it was like for the poor guy who found him. Imagine stumbling on that when you were coming home from a night at the pub."

Oh, you have no idea.

"How are you?" he asked.

"I need your help," I said, changing the subject. "You remember when you read over my contract with the agency when I started?" I gave him a rundown of the situation. As quick as possible, actually, because I found out when I started speaking that it was quite painful to talk about.

"I can do that for you. I'll take a look, or I can find you someone who works in that field. I know a couple of entertainment lawyers."

"Thank you."

"Babe, are you okay? Really? Don't give me the pat answer."

Was I? How do you define okay? Having friends who you trusted to have your back, I suppose, was a good sign. Having a boyfriend who didn't cheat on you or try to kill you. I'm sure most people thought that was quite essential. Having a family that … knew you were alive and vice versa. Yeah, I'd imagine nine in ten respondents would put that near the top. Well, I had a needy German shepherd and two antisocial cats. It wasn't much, but it was more than some.

“I’ll be fine. I need to sleep now,” I said and hung up.

I went upstairs and crawled back into bed – switching my phone very much off. “Let sleep take me,” I whispered under my breath, and by some miracle it did.

Bang. Bang. Bang.

Jake Gyllenhaal was about to take off his loincloth in the Colosseum.

“Yeah, c’mon, Jakey, show us the goods,” I said.

Mm, it was so lovely and warm on this summer’s day in Rome. I should have come on this trip years ago.

Bang bang bang.

“Quick, Jakey, before the Visigoths attack the city,” I said, basking in the warmth on my skin.

Bang bang bang.

“Arden! OPEN UP! I know you’re in there!”

Hmm. Those Visigoths had strange accents, best to run back towards Jakey and that nice warm sun … Wait, why was the sun going away? Why? Why was it suddenly cold?

“Arrrooooo!” came the Visigoths.

Bang bang bang.

I opened an eye. There were no Visigoths. I was in my room. The sun – well, my source of heat, which was an emotionally traumatised Alsatian-cross, had departed his position spooning me and was now barking and clawing at the bedroom window. He was more interested in whoever was downstairs banging on my front door.

And Jake Gyllenhaal was nowhere to be seen. It was that last part that smarted the most.

“Alright, al-fucking-right!” I grumbled as I stood up and then almost fell back on the bed again. A huge rush to the head saw me stagger around the room for a few seconds. Yikes. Okay, been asleep for some time then.

It was daylight, still morning, if the sky was to be believed, so it couldn’t have been more than an hour or so since I went for my nap. God, I needed a piss so badly I thought I was gonna rupture something.

I staggered out the door and managed to make it to the stairs. The banging persisted. "I am fucking coming!" I yelled. Well, tried to, but my voice came out as a strangled choke.

"Ahem," I said and tried to clear my throat. I peered outside the window and saw thankfully that the paps had gone. That was weird, they were there an hour ago.

I opened the door, and a belligerent Scotsman looked at me.

"Simon, hi, to what do I owe the pleasure?" I kept the door ajar, trying to block out the ball of melting hot yellow hate-fire in the sky that was trying to singe my retinas.

"Do you ever answer your fucking phone?" Simon barked and pushed past me to come into the house.

"Erm, usually, well, kind of. Sometimes. There are a lot of people I avoid if I'm being honest."

"I've been ringing you and you've not answered.

"How? You were in the press conference."

"A—" He stopped and looked at me with his head askew. "Arden, what day is it?"

"Tuesday," I answered.

"It's Wednesday."

"Wait, no it's not. I just got up. I went for a run, I watched the press conference, and then I had a nap. I—Are you sure?"

He held up his phone with the date on his lock screen. It clearly said Wednesday. It was also 7 a.m., so at least I hadn't … Jesus, I hadn't quite slept twenty-four hours. Just twenty or so.

Oh.

The pain in my bladder was getting worse. "Excuse me," I said and ducked into the toilet under the stairs. "Can you hum or something?"

"What?" came his voice. Aggressive.

"I need to pee, and you're standing right there. I get shy."

"Oh, for God's sake. Fine. I'll take your dog out. C'mon, boy." I heard the door slam. A second later, sweet relief began. I let out a contented sigh. And then looked down … Jesus, there was a lot of it. I really had been asleep for a day. How had I managed that? And how the hell was I still weeing? Oh my God, I was still going. I heard the door open again, and Simon muttering under his breath.

"You're still pissing? I can hear you!"

"I … I don't know. I'm quite concerned. I think I'm a medical miracle."

"Whatever, I'll feed your dog."

"His name's Kennedy!" I yelled, turning slightly, and driving my persistent stream up the wall. "Shit!"

"What did you say? Don't tell me you need to take a shit as well. If that's the case, then I'm going. You'll be in there until next month!"

"I …" He had a point. "Don't be vulgar!" was all I could summon up. Eventually, through the grace of God, I finished. "I think I've lost weight," I muttered. I washed my hands and left the toilet a new man.

Simon was standing in my kitchen – glaring.

"Good morning," I offered meekly.

He pointed to a Tupperware container. "Do you want a blueberry muffin?"

"You brought me muffins?"

"No, Mrs Hetherington brought *me* muffins, and I have no room in my house, so I brought them to you. You're skin and bone."

"Am not," I said.

"Then take a bloody muffin, so my kitchen stops resembling a refugee collection centre."

I took a muffin. "Um, not to be rude, but why …" I cleared my throat and changed tack. "How are you?" I remembered how bad he'd looked on Monday and then again at the press conference. Which was *yesterday*. Christ.

He looked away. Shrugged. It was a tense, angry gesture. "I'm … I don't know, to be honest. I'm okay. Do you wanna put some clothes on, by the way?"

Looking down I realised I was standing in my underwear and nothing else.

"Oh, shit." I ran upstairs. "Sorry, gimme two seconds."

In my room, I grabbed some clothes only to notice with horror that I'd not properly shaken off after peeing and had been standing there talking to Simon with a big wet patch on the front of my light blue boxers for all the world to see. "God, I'm a mess," I muttered. But who the fuck turns up pounding on someone's door at 7 a.m. on a Wednesday? Like a … a terrorist.

I threw on a clean pair of underwear, a T-shirt and some shorts that weren't too smelly and checked my breath. Foul. I rubbed the sleep gunk out of my eyes and tried to fix my hair.

Nope, still looked shit. Sheepishly, I left my room and came back downstairs. Simon was at my dining table and had cut up our muffins and laid them out covered in butter, on plates.

"Lovely, thanks." I tried to look anywhere but him.

He made a noise of impatience. "Arden, we've had sex, can you not be embarrassed that I saw you in your pants? You were half asleep. I'm not under the impression you were flaunting yourself at me."

He wasn't wrong there; we did have sex. He had been inside me. I had once come on his chest hair. So, he was right; it pretty much meant any sort of embarrassment was null and void. However, that didn't stop me. God loves a tryer.

"So, um, what brings you to my neck of the woods?" I said, eagerly devouring my muffin. It was nice and moist, and I was starving. Which was not surprising considering I'd been dead to the world for a day.

He exhaled and looked down. For several moments, he said nothing. The only noise was my loud chewing.

"I need your help."

Err … did he need to write a book or something? Did he want advice on dating and breakups? Did he want Polish lessons?

"What kind of help?" I said, aiming for breezy and arriving at something near paranoid.

"God, I said in the texts … do you ever look at your phone?"

"Oh, I turned it off before my nap."

"Your … day-long nap?"

"Yes," I said. Keeping my chin up.

"Is that a common occurrence?" he asked, his brow creasing. "Are you okay, you know …" He gestured at his head. "Mentally?"

I glared at him and took a long time to respond. "Yes, I'm fine, *mentally*," I said through gritted teeth. I tried to tell myself he was in the military, which meant he was probably a Neanderthal at anything involving the psychological, so his lack of tact was surely not his fault. This explained all those soldiers going around with PTSD, but hey, that was the army's problem and not mine.

"Okay …" he said, clearly not believing me. Well, I was. I was fine. Except for the ex who tried to kill me, and the tripping over dead bodies wherever I went. Fine. Totally fine.

"So." I brushed off my muffin crumbs and eyed a second in the Tupperware container. "What do you need my help with?" *Please don't say funerals, please don't say funerals.*

Simon played with the strap of his watch and took a long time to respond. I watched him intently, the crease between his brow, the trickle of sweat running down behind his ear from the heat that was already building up outside, the sun-kissed freckles along the back of his neck. It wasn't long before my eyes slinked down to his large shoulders, which were straining the T-shirt he was wearing, or his arms that stretched the seams on the sleeves. He was only average height, but there was a definite built-like-a-brick-shithouse air to his physique.

But then he spoke, and my attention snapped back.

"I want you to help me find who killed Riz."

Chapter 14

There was a long silence.

"I'm sorry," I said after I'd found my jaw somewhere on my un-hoovered floor and picked it up again. "Did you say—"

"The cops are fucking useless; the intelligence services are even worse. They've both convinced the others that it was a random mugging gone wrong."

"But—"

"It's like they want it to be that way, Arden!" He slammed his fist down on the table, which caused Kennedy to whine and disappear underneath it. "They don't want it to be political, or a hate crime, or, God forbid, terrorism. So, they've decided it's much easier for the UK's reputation to take a hit as some lawless hellhole where gangs of street kids go around with pistols shooting people in cars rather than find out what happened."

"Which was—"

"I haven't got a fucking clue!" he yelled and stood up, knocking his chair down. Kennedy whined again and burrowed into my leg under the table.

Simon paced my tiny dining room, running his hands through his hair.

"They … they're going in with their minds made up. They want some tearaway kid from an estate to pin this on."

"Simon, calm down."

"Don't you see, Arden?" He turned to me, his arms wide. "This is exactly the stunt they pulled with Tarquin! Only you saw it for what it was; they wanted a quick arrest to clean up their stats. They couldn't care less about who killed Arabella. They'd have happily let Tarquin keep wandering about outside and put Pawel away if it was easier. I bet you that they're going to do the same with Riz's killer!"

"Simon—"

"So, help me catch them! C'mon." He got down beside me, right in my face. "How did you do it? How did you figure it all out and decide it was Tarquin that did it? What do we need to do?"

Before I could answer, he was pacing again. "We need a list of suspects. Marina. All the other candidates. I'll have to be on it too—"

He continued to work himself up, pacing backwards and forwards and ignoring me calling his name. "Simon!" I said loudly, which made Kenny whine even more. He couldn't trust me either now, so instead hid under another chair.

"Would you please calm down?" I yelled at him, ducking under the table as I shouted, so it wasn't to his face.

"C'mere, mate," I said to Kenny, who was cowering. "I'm sorry I yelled, c'mere, mate. It's okay, I promise." I patted my thigh, and slowly he wagged his tail and came back towards me. I stroked his head and gave him a kiss. "And you scared Kenny." More than a bit of annoyance filled my voice.

Simon's legs were at a standstill. I couldn't see anything above mid-thigh from my spot on the floor. His jeans and desert boots were rooted to the spot.

"Isn't he a guard dog?" he asked eventually.

"He's had a tough life," I said, stroking him behind his ears. "Come sit with us." I pushed a chair out of the way.

There was a long pause. Then a huff, and slowly Simon sat down on the floor beside me and reached out to touch Kenny. "I'm not sure we're going to be friends; he didn't seem to like me very much when I let him out earlier. Even feeding him didn't seem to win him over."

"Luckily, Kennedy is forgiving. For whatever reason you upset him earlier, he'll let it slide. Won't you, boy?" I said and gave the enormous mane of fur around his neck a ruffle. His tongue fell out of his mouth, and he lolled over me with joy.

Simon delicately put his hand on Kenny's head and gave him a quick scratch before pulling it away again. "Oh, for God's sake," I said and grabbed his hand – his big, strong, pale, freckly hands that had cupped my arse perfectly – ahem – and guided it back towards Kenny's neck. "Give him a proper scratch. Come on, it's calming to play with dogs, there are studies and shit about it and everything."

"Is that why you got him?"

I shrugged. "I got him for lots of reasons."

Simon paused, waiting for me to continue.

With a sigh, I spoke: "Guard dog, companionship, someone to come home to at the end of the day who is always pleased to see me."

"You work from home," he said with a crick in his brow.

"Fine, someone who's pleased to see me no matter where I've been or what time it is."

Simon's hands reached forward, and he tentatively placed them on Kenny's mane. He let his fingers sift through his fur and smiled slightly. "Soft."

"You're damn right it is; I spend a fortune on this mutt's fur. He goes to the groomer every month, and I brush him as often as I can get him to sit still long enough to do it. I get enough to fill an armchair in a single sitting."

Simon snorted.

He looked up at me and we locked eyes.

"Simon—" I started, but then noticed the wetness rolling down his cheeks.

"Sorry," he said, brushing his face. "I don't know what to do. Mum and Dad mean well but they're suffocating me. I … I can't go back to work. They've told me to keep away until this is all … I don't even know, what they think."

His phone buzzed in his pocket. "That'll be Mum. She'll have seen I'm gone and will want to know where I am." His phone buzzed a few more times. "Yup. She's convinced I'm going to top myself."

"So, finding you gone at 7 a.m.?"

He sighed and pulled out his phone. "Am fine," he narrated as he texted a response. "Have gone for a walk …" He looked up at me. "With Arden and his dog. Might be a few hours."

He put his phone back in his pocket. "There. Now, can you please listen to me about this?"

I resisted the urge to pinch the bridge of my nose.

"Fine. Okay, whatever. I need a shower and to brush my teeth. While I'm in the shower …" I stood up and grabbed a notepad that I kept to scribble ideas in while I was writing and ripped off the page I'd been brainstorming on the other day. I gave Simon the pad with a fresh page on top. "Write down everything that happened between you and Riz the last" – I thought for a second – "seventy-two hours before he was killed. Every text, every phone call, and everyone he met. Timelines, everything. You have until I get out of the shower."

I departed without looking back because I knew Simon was middle class and would try to say thank you or something. Instead, I went up to the bathroom and took an epically long shower. Apparently, sleeping for that long gave me an ache in my shoulders and chest. I seemed to have creases from my pillowcases permanently tattooed on my cheek.

I would have taken up acrobatics and Chinese lessons if it meant staying in the bathroom longer and not having to face what was downstairs. Namely, a heartbroken man thinking I had some magical answers to, what, exactly – bringing back Riz? Getting him justice?

Even if that wasn't the case, then the fact that it was Simon would still be an issue. Prickly, judgemental Simon, who made it abundantly clear he didn't like me. Who regretted our one-night stand, who thought I was some floozy who collected men like supermarket coupons and, what was it that he'd said a few days ago, oh yeah, that I'd been trying to pick up men in a police station toilet. I mean, really.

I did that once when I was twenty. And it was in Soho. It's practically encouraged.

So why I was putting on a nice shirt and jeans that sculpted themselves around my arse instead of shorts was neither here nor there. I hesitated over my phone. It was switched off. After several seconds of lip chewing over whether to turn it on and bring it downstairs with me, I decided to leave it up in my room.

I came downstairs to find that Simon had … oh, sweet Jesus and all the serial-killing-saints. My living room walls were now covered in pages from the notepad like a madman's lair. Kenny, that traitor, had abandoned his usual spot outside the bathroom door whenever I was in there and was following Simon about the place like he was a god. If only I'd known that was all it took. There had been some awkward moments when I was busy trying to take care of nature as quickly as possible before he clawed the door down.

"Do you have a printer?" Simon asked before I could even open my mouth to ascertain why he'd turned my home into Dexter's workshop.

"Um, yes, it's in the dining room under the window," I said.

"Great, I'll email you some stuff and you can print it. I think it'll give you some clues."

"Clues?"

"Yes, clues. Should I send it to the same email you gave me when I was working on the kitchen?"

"Ah, yes, that'd be fine. Um …" I looked at my fireplace, which was where Simon seemed to have put most of the paper that formed a timeline of Riz's last few days.

"Right, shall we get started?" He clapped his hands together and came to stand beside me, radiating warmth and a pleasant musky scent that spoke of man, and sweat, and more … man. God, I wanted to jump his bones.

I inwardly groaned. What. Was. Wrong. With. Me? Why, why, did I let my dick control my life? Just once could I get through a social interaction with a semi-attractive man without becoming a slave to what was between my legs?

"Okay, um." I pinched the bridge of my nose again. This was going to be harder than I thought. How could I let him down gently? "Er, why don't we go through Riz's last movements? I got the feeling there was a lot they weren't telling us at the press conference," I said and then berated myself for letting that slip. Don't feed his fantasy.

Simon got some papers together and stuck his tongue out as he concentrated. I sat on the sofa and leaned forward to try and give an air of interest and enthusiasm.

"Right, okay, so you know what the cops said in the conference?" He began taping up a long sheet of A4 he'd Blu-Tacked together over the mirror on my mantlepiece. "More or less accurate, bar a few things."

"Such as?"

"That the number he was calling obsessively wasn't registered. It was a burner phone."

I cocked my head. "So, they …"

"Have no idea? Yes. Which leads me to believe it was something bad. I thought originally it was some political intrigue." He played with the hem of his T-shirt, lifting it slightly and giving me a glimpse of that lovely body underneath. "I confronted him about it on Saturday night. We'd argued before we came to Honningtons."

I perked up. "Did you tell the police?"

He nodded. "Yes, I was honest about it. I told them I … I didn't think he was completely above board on the campaign. I had …" He looked around the room at basically any direction but me. "I wondered if he had something to do with Guy's photos being leaked."

I cocked my head. "How would he know about that? Were he and Guy acquainted?"

"No." Simon shook his head. "Riz had heard of him, but they'd never met before the campaign. He had a lot of questions when we" – he averted his gaze – "got back together. All of a sudden, he was quite intrigued by him, but I put it down to rubbernecking over Arabella's death."

And yet you proposed to him. What taste.

"Okay, so you thought he was up to no good …" A suspicion formed in my mind for a second, but I tried to push it down. It was a terrible idea to bring up. Simon was pacing my living room, all but tearing his hair out with his family worried he was about to hurt himself. I couldn't.

But he was looking at me now. "What? Have you had an idea?"

Jesus, I'm not fucking Sherlock Holmes. "It's nothing." *And you'll kick off if I say it.*

"No, say it. No thought too stupid or small." He offered a slight smile.

Noticing the knees of my jeans were beginning to fray, I played with the material for several seconds and mouthed at the air, trying to think of an excuse to keep my gob shut. But Simon's big blue eyes were imploring me.

"Have you considered the possibility that maybe he was with someone else, another man?" I asked in a high-pitched voice. "I only say because of the phone calls, all the secrets …" My voice trailed off as I took in the expression on Simon's face.

"Of course I had," he said. "It was my first thought. He begins acting weird and taking phone calls at all hours. And not from Marina like he claimed they were from at the beginning. Because I could tell he was getting the calls from a private number, and then that changed to being under Marina's name. Except he had Marina in his phone already as Marina with a capital 'M'. Then her name changed to being spelt with a lowercase letter. I don't think he'd picked up he'd done it, or he'd done it to keep the people separate in his head so he knew who was actually calling and was hoping I wouldn't notice."

"Did you confront him about your suspicions?"

"The cheating? Yes, that was the day I proposed."

A factoid to pocket for later. "And about the names?"

"Yes, when we came back from Honningtons. That's why he left. We had a blazing row. Marina almost had to referee. I told him I wasn't going to let him treat me like a fool. I didn't know what was happening, but I wasn't going to be a part of it."

"So, the police are aware of this?"

"Oh, yes," he said, sneering. "Neuberger was very interested."

I felt a headache coming on as I listened. "Okay" – I was pinching the bridge of my nose again – "you were convinced Riz was doing something dodgy? I mean, I don't want to sound mean, but you were marrying the guy. You're not painting the prettiest of pictures to me."

Simon stopped his pacing for a second and looked at me squarely. I thought I'd offended him again, which was something I had a talent for with Mr Anson. Eventually, though, he looked away and sat down in the armchair opposite me.

Kenny rushed to put his head on a thigh and get himself some snout scratches. He huffed slightly when Simon didn't instantly comply. "You need to—" I gestured at the dog to tell Simon so he didn't get barked at, which was what I could tell Kenny was working up to. There had been upwards of seven seconds of him not being adored, and he frankly couldn't take it any longer. Kenny shot me a look, as if saying *But why has he forsaken me? Teach him, teach him the ways!* But I refused to be drawn. Traitorous mutt was finding out his mistress wasn't as attentive as the one he had at home.

Simon got the picture and put his hand around Kenny's mane to scoop him in closer to cuddle against his leg. Instantly, Kenny's tongue fell out of the corner of his mouth, and he took on a serene expression, all prior ignoring forgiven. The slut.

"He was a difficult man," Simon said eventually. "A good man. At least I thought. An interesting man. Like, really interesting. Full of ideas and passions. He wanted to change the world. Had all sorts of plans for ways the country could be run better. Our first date" – Simon grinned to himself as he remembered the event – "we were in this pub, and he had all these beermats he used to build a model. He was trying to explain ideas he had for redoing operating theatres using techniques he'd seen during a junket to the States he'd gone on. I remember thinking how handsome he was when he was passionate about something."

"You were in love with him," I said quietly. I hoped the envy in my voice didn't make itself known. Maybe that's why he hadn't wanted more than one night with me; my face didn't light up when I discussed proofreading.

"Not really." He shook his head.

"What?"

"The whole thing was a charade. Marina dreamt it up."

"Wait—"

"We were together, yes. And we got back together – but the engagement? Pure theatre. I was never going to marry him. The more I saw him twisting himself into this awful person who wanted to win no matter what, the more I wanted to be out of there as soon as possible."

He paused for a second and puffed out his cheeks as if he'd had to breathe hard to say that. He held Kenny close, and I kept still, trying not to interrupt. "He … he wasn't close to anyone. His parents – he hadn't spoken to them in months. I thought it was because they were old-fashioned, you know, they were disapproving of him being gay, but the longer I knew him … He distanced himself from his parents, not the other way around. I'd only met them once before yesterday. But they seemed … not scared of him, but wary."

I couldn't think of anything to say, so was glad when Simon's phone started buzzing. He took it out of his pocket and rolled his eyes. "It's mum. She will not be put off. I best go." He stood up.

His abruptness took me by surprise, but I saw a flicker of doubt on his face, and he wasn't meeting my eye. "I'm glad you told me those things," I said eventually. Perhaps his doubt was from revealing his emotions. I know how he felt.

He came over to me, and I found myself holding him, ever so lightly and briefly. But as we pulled away, he clung to the back of my arms, gripping on to the tender flesh there.

"We can do this, right?" He looked at me intently. His bright eyes were glassy with unshed tears.

I lied. "Yes."

He hesitated for a second and then gave me a bro-y backslap. "I'll see you tomorrow. Hopefully, we can make some progress."

I tried to disagree, but before I knew it, he was gone.

The house echoed around its newfound silence. Kennedy was giving me mournful looks and seemed to be already missing his new friend.

I paced around the house for half an hour, full of nervous energy, while I contemplated everything that he'd just told me. It all made sense, but none of it pointed to a reason for Riz being killed. The only logical option did look to be what the police – and, gulp, whoever the hell in the intelligence services that Simon worked for exactly – were saying. That Riz was killed in some sort of bizarre mugging gone wrong.

But those phone calls. They were the only thing that stood out. If I did go through with this ridiculous idea, then maybe our first port of call should be Marina Holt.

I shook my head. This was absurd. I was no detective. It was blind luck I'd found out anything about Tarquin. Instead, I grabbed Kennedy's lead, and we went for a long walk across the hills. We passed the Parkinsons in a field, and I waved enthusiastically but ignored Rita's beckoning hail in return and pretended not to hear her calling my name as she invited me for lunch. The last thing I needed was to be 'on' for more people.

We returned home, one of us more fatigued than the other. I ate another muffin and slumped on the sofa at lunchtime. I had put off the inevitable long enough. My phone was in my hand. I grimaced and switched it on. As soon as it was loaded up, it vibrated for what seemed like an eternity as messages came through. Gritting my teeth, I opened them after they'd all been received.

Several were from Simon, as he had said. A couple of texts from yesterday and later a voicemail, and then this morning a curt message asking if I was dead.

A voicemail from Nigella with an update on Jed, asking me to call her back.

Ollie had rung late in the evening yesterday and then sent me a text telling me he had found a lawyer for me and to ring him back.

There were several messages from Verity. I didn't have the energy or the patience to listen to or read any of them.

Instead, I grabbed Kennedy's lead and headed outside. As we reached the door, a familiar tiny pink car pulled up in my driveway, and Sonia stepped out.

She took off her sunglasses and looked up at me. "Have you got a minute?"

"I was just off to call on Nigella." I looked down at her from my doorstep. "Is everything okay?"

Her normally immaculate hair was a bit skew-whiff. She scrunched her face up and fiddled with the strap of her designer (knock-off) handbag. "Um, not really."

I felt a frown form on my face. It must be bad for sunny Sonia to be feeling it. "Can you get over grass in those? Let's walk and talk," I said and took her elbow, giving a brief glimpse at her shoes. As usual, they were heels, five inches high and precarious. Sonia basically wore heels to bed, so she was not about to let a dirt track tell her that her life choices weren't compatible.

She scurried along beside me and gamely climbed the stile. "So, what's up?" I said and held her handbag while she righted her skirt.

"It's …" She paused. "It's hard to explain, Arden, but I thought you'd know more than I would. You know, cos you're all wise."

Am I?

"It's, well, it's Trev and Dhaps. I think they're stealing from the company."

Chapter 15

"Say what now?" was my reaction.

She grabbed my arm and, exhaling a huffy sigh, dragged me along the path. "God, it's already boiling, this heatwave is a killer. But, yeah, you 'eard. I think they're ripping off the company. Embossing—"

"Embezzling."

"Yeah, that one."

"Wait, why? What evidence do you have?" I leaned into her. "What's brought all this on?"

She chewed her lip as we walked, Kennedy dancing in the fields around us. "Start from the beginning," I said, trying to placate her.

She took a second to collect her thoughts and then launched into her story. "You know how Dad retired last year? He's handed over the company to Trevor and me, fifty-fifty. Dhapinder was already a senior manager, and her being married to Trevor, what's his is hers and all that."

"Right," I said. "Have they been freezing you out?" Sonia had always been anxious about her place in the firm. She outranked several much older and established estate agents there, who thought little of her abilities, and from what I could tell, Trevor and Dhapinder didn't exactly have her back during these spats.

She nodded. "Always have done, nothing new. I know the areas of the business to focus on, and what I want to achieve. They have plans and the vision, so I let them get on with it mostly. But I'm not a dummy, I know the books as well as Dhapinder does, even though she doesn't know I do. Mum used to do the books in the early days, and I learned from her. I know all the ins and outs and what everything means. I'm really good at it."

"Good for you, Son," I said genuinely.

She blushed. "I've been doing classes online. No one knows except Mum." She frowned again. "Since the whole … Arabella thing, Trevor has been acting well weird. Like, I know he was …"

"We don't need to say it."

"Screwing her," she said with a grimace. "Ugh, the bastard. Anyway, since then, he and Dhapinder have barely said two words to me, always off with their heads together in the corner. At first, I thought it was because they were having problems. But then I did some digging. Not on purpose, you know, by accident. I needed some numbers and went to the books. Well, I know what I'm looking for now."

"What did you find?" I asked. We were about halfway down the hill now; I glanced over at Simon's street and held in a wistful sigh.

"Do you know how VAT works?"

"Er … let's assume that I don't," I said.

"Okay, well, VAT payments are separate from main transactions and are kept on their own ledger. It's quite easy to lose track of. If you hear about a business in trouble with the taxman, well, they likely cocked up their VAT payments."

"Right."

"It's also the easiest to fiddle."

"Oh."

We came to a stop. I put my face up to the baking sun and felt it warm my skin. "So … they've been skimming off the top?"

Sonia nodded. "It looks it. Money going missing here and there. Payment amounts that don't quite match up. But …"

"But?"

"I can't be sure."

"How could you find out?"

"Go through the books with a fine-toothed comb."

"Can you do that without raising suspicion?" I asked.

She shook her head and yanked a piece of grass from the side of the path and fiddled with it between her fingers.

I looked out and watched Kennedy chasing bugs in the long grass. "Okay, well, a) you need definitive evidence of what is happening and b) that they're the ones who are doing it."

She nodded. "I know."

"Do you want my help?"

She nodded again. "It's been going on for months, Arden. I don't think they're planning on stopping anytime soon. And it's small amounts. Small enough that the business isn't noticing it – I mean, business is good, the company is doing well."

It was my turn to nod. "In a way, that's better. Gives us time to plan."

She gave me a smile. "I knew you'd help." She gripped my arm, and we started walking again. "Why are we going to Nigella's?"

"Oh, you know, just a catch-up."

"Her and her fella are having problems, innit?"

"Yeah— wait, what, how'd you know?"

"I'm very intuitive, I am."

I glared. "Okay, but in reality, how do you know? Also, I don't think she particularly wants it broadcasted."

"I haven't told a soul! Arden, how little you think of me. They've kids, for God's sake. I wouldn't go around blabbing about her private life. It's against the code of ethics for a responsible estate agent. But, yeah, I read between the lines when she was giving updates about you when you was all AWOL. I thought to myself, there's a woman with a lot of free time in the evenings for drinking wine and sitting in her big kitchen sending very long texts."

"Bloody hell," I said.

"I'll pretend to be ignorant to her marital strife. Like I am with Dhaps and Trev."

I pursed my lips and said nothing. We entered the village and walked to Nigella's house in time to see her emerging from her car outside.

"Hello! Aren't you two a sight for sore eyes. You'll never guess where I've been?"

"A branch of LK Bennett?" I said.

"Yoga for the over sixties?" Sonia said.

Nigella glared. "I am not over sixty," she hissed. Her smile returned. "No, I've been to see Jed. His mum rang last night and said he could have visitors, so I popped over first thing this morning and spoke to him."

I perked right up. "Really? How is he?"

Nigella beckoned us into her house and walked as she talked. "Groggy. Confused, but improving every day. He's spoken to the police and said he can't remember much, but between you and me, his doctors have said it's likely he'll remember more as he starts to improve."

That was going to be my next question, so, instead, I nodded sagely. Not that I needed to say anything; Sonia and Nigella kept up a verbal volley that was, frankly, staggering to behold, as the two of them could talk for England. We'd been there twenty minutes before Nigella had finished telling us about Jed, and Sonia had gushed about Ade and asked for more details about how Guy was.

"This Ade chap of yours, I must say, a definite improvement on the last one," Nigella said, pouring us tea.

I rubbed the spot on my head where I had a scar from being knocked into the road by The Last One and grumbled.

Sonia rolled her eyes. "One concussion and he thinks he's Joan of Arc." She paused. "Is that who I mean? One of 'em, whatchamacallit, Martians?"

"Martyr?" I offered.
"That's the one." She glared at me. "Yeah, that's what you are."
"I was assaulted."
"You were milking it."
"Oh, charming. Well, I take back my offer."
"What offer?" Nigella asked.
"My brother and his missus are stealing from the company." She gasped. "Oh my God, I can't believe I said it out loud!" She clasped her hand over her mouth.
"Really? I can," I muttered at the ceiling. Of course, instead of being shocked, Nigella wanted details and for the next hour pumped Sonia for every facet of information she had. There were flow-charts. The twins' art supplies were raided so they could start making columns. Sonia was reading out figures from emails on her phone when I eventually recovered.
"Don't you have to get back to work? Your lunch break is heading for the two-hour mark," I said.
Sonia looked at the time. "You're right. I must dash. Bloody hell, I've got to walk up that hill in these heels." She was running about getting her things when she noticed that I was sitting. "Coming?"
"Umm, got to talk to Nigella about … a thing. It's boring, you won't be interested."
"What is it?" Sonia asked.
Nigella raised an eyebrow at me. "A book. About the Tudor period. I lent it to Arden. Oh, it's fascinating. They describe the architecture. There are three chapters alone on gables."
I saw Sonia's eyes glaze over as she spoke. "Yeah, no, I'm not sticking around for that." She gave us each a kiss on the cheek – even Kenny – and made her departure.
Nigella waited for the door to click. "Right, so what do you want to discuss? I mean, I am reading a book about the Tudors if you want to borrow it. Well, it's a bodice

ripper. But, from my online research, most accurate in the descriptions of the men's jerkins."

Sonia's comment about having far too much time on her hands came flooding back into my mind.

I gripped my mug. "Simon visited me this morning."

She put her teacup down. "No, Arden, please tell me you didn't find more rooms in your house to sleep with him in. Where now? The bathtub?"

"What? No. I didn't shag him. I wanted to, but that's nothing new."

"Good, because your house isn't that big."

"Are you listening? Anyway, he wants me to help him solve Riz's murder."

Nigella's face fell.

"That was pretty much my reaction. What do I do, Gella? I can't … encourage him, can I? And I haven't got a clue what I'm doing. If the police can't find the killer, how will I?"

"This is serious," she said and tapped her finger on her teacup. "How did he seem?"

"Er, a mess. Like a guy whose fiancé was just deaded."

She thought for a moment, tapping her cup again, then got up and walked around the room for a few seconds, seeming to work things out in her head. At least I hoped she was.

"Okay, here's what you do." She made eye contact. I leaned in expectantly. "String him along."

"What?"

"I know. But it's what we do for now. The grief … mania, I suppose, will pass eventually. He'll go back to work; he'll calm himself down. In the meantime, we hope the police make some headway. But you – you keep going, softly-softly, nothing major, nothing earth-shattering. Just little things."

"Feed the crazy?"

"Ahhh, let's not call it that."

"This is a terrible idea."
"Of course it is," she snapped. "Our friend's fiancé was just murdered. No one has any good ideas right now. Arden" – she sat back down and took my hand – "your job here is to keep him centred. You can let him work it all through in his mind. Let him process it in his own way."
I nodded. That made a bit more sense.
"Every time he suggests going to … I don't know, break into someone's house to find evidence, you suggest maybe a nice walk instead to carefully plan it all out."
I scoffed. Break into someone's house, me? Never.
"And what do I do if that doesn't work?"
"We'll come up with some other plans to, sort of, fill his days."
"I was hoping you'd have more suggestions," I said.
"This isn't exactly my forte. And I don't see you having any ideas."
"Well—" Oh. Actually. Maybe I did have one?

The next morning, I woke up bright and early and felt mildly better. Seeing friends, leaving the house, and long walks with Kenny. Maybe that was the key.
So, when Simon knocked on the door at around 9 a.m. I was ready for him.
In he walked without even waiting to say hello and began talking ten to the dozen about an idea he'd had.
"Okay, so how often do terrible things happen in Lilbury? Answer – not often."
I gave him a look.
"So … semi-not often," he said and walked around my kitchen fixing himself breakfast, while Kenny followed him. "Coffee?"
"That cupboard."
"So, my idea was … well, several very bad things have happened here recently, right?"

"Like …"

"The Guy thing. And your article."

"I'm not involved in this."

"You are a little bit. Do you only have oat milk?" His head was in my fridge.

"I get bloated from cow's milk."

He sighed. "It'll do, I suppose. Do you want some of this crumble, by the way? Someone brought it and it's really good. I don't suppose you have any cream?"

I shook my head as he cut me a slice of Mrs Bliss' crumble. "There might be vanilla ice cream in the freezer."

His eyes lit up like a kid's. "I'm going to be the size of a house from all this," he told me. I sat at the breakfast bar, trying to look calm as he foisted food on me and acted like a man possessed.

"As I was saying, what if all these bad things were connected?"

I blinked. Well, I can't deny that I'd had that thought myself. But I didn't believe it.

"One small problem. Riz wasn't killed in Lilbury."

"Yes, but he was a politician. As was Guy."

"But I'm not a politician."

He ate his crumble. "It's a theory. I think there's a link."

I ate more crumble. Mrs Bliss was a talented woman.

"Need to ask Mum who dropped this off and see if we can get more," Simon said, licking his spoon. I definitely didn't watch that with my beady little eyes. He was wearing a tan T-shirt today in a muscle fit and a pair of light blue skinny jeans that were so old and faded they were almost white.

And they clung. God, they clung.

"I do have an idea of what we could do …" I said, stirring my ice cream around the bowl so it'd melt faster. Not that it needed much help. I swear it was getting hotter every day. And the dust. The ground was bone dry after so long with no rain. England was a different colour. My runs with Kenny saw me coming back so covered in dust that I was worried I was going to get accosted for doing blackface.

I watched as Simon cocked his head at me like Kenny did when he wanted food. He lifted his arm, and even the sweat stain on his armpit was doing things for me today.

"Tell me."

I stuttered. "Nigella went to see JedRev yesterday. He's up for visitors. We should go. It'd be good to get out of the village, and he's your friend."

"But he's not involved."

"No, maybe not."

His eyes went wide. "You think he could've been a target. Holy hell. I suppose he was known to be mates with Guy. And there are other connections …"

I was about to ask what he meant when the sound of a car nearby set Kenny off barking.

"Now you're a guard dog?" I asked him as he shot off to the front door and woofed himself stupid at it.

"Hush now, hush!" I told the mad mutt as I followed him to the door. I clapped for Simon's attention – he'd been staring into space. "Can you?" I gestured to Kenny..

"Yup." Simon loped over and took Kenny in his arms like he weighed nothing and carried him to the living room.

I opened the door in time to see a car pull up outside. My heart sank. Oh, no, what did they want?

"Good morning, Mr Forrest," called Neuberger as he surveyed my overgrown garden.

Simon closed the living room door with Kenny inside and came to stand beside me, but I tried to push him back in.

"Morning, detective," I called and then out the corner of my mouth: "Go upstairs or something. Hide."

"Why?" asked Simon.

"Do you want them to know you're here?"

Simon rolled his eyes but sank back into the living room. "You alone?" Neuberger called. "Can we come in?

"Please, do," I said, ignoring the first question. I scrambled to move Simon's bowl as they entered a few seconds later. "Sorry, haven't done the dishes. Place is a tip, do forgive me."

Neuberger came in and couldn't hide his disdain. Maslin followed him, looking a bit less displeased.

The DI went towards the living room door, already snooping. "Oh, my dog is in there, please don't let him out with the front door open." Maslin had the good sense to close that door. "He's not good with strangers; it'll be a racket if he's out here." Neuberger narrowed his eyes, still poised for the living room.

As if on cue, Kenny started barking loudly. Neuberger grimaced and turned away.

"Your garden is looking very overgrown," he said. "Even in this weather, it needs a mow."

"I've been meaning to put up a sign in the village to hire someone to look after it."

"Not keen on getting your hands dirty yourself?" he asked.

I shrugged. "Why would I?"

"It's cheaper to do it yourself."

"I'm rich," I said.

They both stared at me and then gave each other a look.

"How can I help you two gents?" Play nice, play nice.

"Just routine, Mr Forrest. We had a few loose ends to clean up."

I smiled as best I could.

"We were hoping you might be able to tell us more about your previous interactions with Mr Patel?"

I cocked my head. Trying not to let the panic get to me. I was sweating now. My armpits wouldn't be as interesting to me as Simon's. Did I have a new fetish for men's armpits? Oh no, this was going to involve having to look at some very weird porn sites to find out if it was a thing I was into. I didn't have the time.

"Mr Forrest?" Maslin asked.

"Sorry, right. Um, I first met him a week or two ago at a hustings. Only for a minute. After that, I think … at the vigil for Jed Fulford. I never spoke to him, just saw him. Er, I think it was that night at Honningtons that I spoke to him again."

Neuberger looked at me. "And no other interaction?"

I smiled sweetly. "Such as?"

"Never came across him on a dating app?" Neuberger checked his notepad. "Mr Patel had accounts with several. And several subscriptions to websites that made for interesting viewing for one of our constables."

The smile was still in place. "I don't use any of the dating apps, I'm afraid. I've no stomach for it." Smile sweetly, Arden.

"I see. You're sure your interactions with Mr Patel were that limited? You are friends with his fiancé, aren't you? We understand you visited him the other day."

"Not really, I barely know him. The fiancé that is."

Neuberger pursed his lips at this. "So, you and Mr Anson aren't friends?"

Were they back on the Simon-did-it bandwagon? "We know each other, obviously, but we're not close."

"Right," said Neuberger. "And, you couldn't give us an insight into his temperament?"

Was that not what I did in the car the other day? I gave Maslin a look. He looked back as if butter wouldn't melt. "I only really know him in a professional sense. As in, he worked for me a few months back. Reliable, punctual. Hard worker. People in the village assure me he's a nice guy."

"Assure you?" Neuberger asked. "Because you barely socialise, is that correct? It's what you told my colleague the other day." He gestured to Maslin, who was staring at me. His vast body took up a large chunk of my dining room.

Sweat was running down my back. Simon was three metres away, and I was acting as if I'd barely met him. "We know each other," I corrected myself. "But we're hardly bosom buddies, is all." Saying too much again. First, they ask if I'm hooking up with Riz, now they want me to dob Simon in.

Kennedy started barking again. I could hear him whining against the door and scratching.

Maslin turned around. "That dog okay? Seems agitated."

"He's fine, I need to take him for a run."

There was the sound of a crash from the living room and a human voice saying "Fuck" very distinctly.

Neuberger narrowed his eyes. "I thought you said you were alone."

I kept my gaze steady. "No. I didn't."

Neuberger got up and went to the door at the same time Simon opened it, and Kennedy took flight at being let out again. Rather a lot of Alsatian/Dobermann met middle-aged detective at full speed, and Neuberger became well acquainted with my floor.

Pandemonium ensued as Neuberger screamed blue murder while Simon and Maslin tried to sort out the kerfuffle.

"Kenny, bad dog. No, get off him. Very bad dog," I said, blithely checking my nails.

Simon pulled Kenny off the detective before he licked him to death.

"Do you want a cloth? You've got dog slobber all over your gilet," I asked.

Maslin helped his boss up and then stood back, trying – I swear – not to laugh.

Neuberger patted himself down. He was bright red and seeking to remain calm. Simon held on to Kenny's collar with a firm grip.

Kenny panted loudly and strained at the bit, his tongue all the way out, clearly thinking he was playing a fun new game. "Mr Anson, how nice to see you. What an interesting place to find you. Mr Forrest's company must be such a balm in your time of need."

Great. Now he thought we were shagging.

"I hope you're okay?" he continued, though his expression informed us all he couldn't give a toss about Simon's well-being. "Rest assured; we're doing everything we can to find your fiancé's killer." He gave me a look.

Seriously? He thought I did it?

Neuberger turned to me fully. "Oh, and Mr Forrest. You'll be glad to hear that we spoke to Mr Mottley. He confirmed your alibi. That you'd been together all night in his room at the Cock and Feather." Neuberger smiled at me. I gulped and kept my eyes averted from Simon. Neuberger turned to him.

"Did you know about them? I wasn't aware Mr Forrest and Mr Mottley had been dating. We were assured by both men that it was a one-time thing. But with Mr Forrest's previous boyfriend, it makes sense to check."

He nodded at both of us. "Thank you for your time. If we need anything else from you, we'll call. Maslin," he snapped.

They departed and I watched them go. Giving a big hearty wave as they left, though I wanted to give the *bras d'honneur*, but decided it wasn't worth the aggro.

Their car drove off. I closed the door and turned to Simon. "At least they didn't go in the living room and see all the bloody serial killer scribblings you put up yesterday."

Simon stared into the middle distance, clenched his jaw. "I should go."

"No, don't," I said. "We were talking about—"

Simon let go of Kenny, who instantly bounded around the house in an excited daze trying to jump on furniture and look out the window to catch a parting glance at his new friend.

He was avoiding my eye and shuffling his foot. "We should go see JedRev," I blurted out.

"I don't think that's a good idea."

"Why not?" I demanded. "Because of Neuberger and his crackpot theories?" Simon said nothing. "Or because I fucked Errol? Really? You're upset about that?"

"No!" He glared at me. "No!" he repeated even more vehemently. "Because this is stupid and you're right about my serial killer scribbles. I've got myself all muddled up."

He was looking everywhere but me. I sighed and rubbed my face.

"Then this has nothing to do with the police finding you here and trying to rile you? They were insinuating shit to try and get a reaction."

"They don't really have to insinuate with you," Simon muttered.

"Excuse me?"

He flushed bright red. "Sorry, that was … uncalled for. Actually, no, it wasn't. You found Riz on your way back from getting ploughed all night by Errol? Errol, really? He … he's so smarmy. We were all desperately worried about you, but you went off and decided the best way to deal with your problems was to bend over for him."

Wow. Okay. People really had opinions on how I spent my time, didn't they?

"First things first, I already said *I* screwed Errol, Simon, not the other way around – not that either way diminishes anyone. It's called being vers, and it makes sex a lot more fun. You should try it sometime rather than being too scared you'll be one of 'those gays' if you take it up the arse. It might help you be less of a grumpy bastard. Second, how I process my private life …" My voice cracked and – dammit – Simon noticed. I cleared my throat. "How I process my private life being splashed all over the fucking papers is my business."

I didn't mean to sound churlish, but not all of us were blessed with a George and Marion as our parents, so Simon could fuck off if he thought he could shame me for this. Happy, middle-class Simon, with his – no doubt – nice four-bedroom family house, two cars, parents who knew his teachers' names and holidays to France every summer, could go all the way to fuck if he wanted to judge me on how I coped with things.

The reality might have been different. But until I had tales of childhood trauma confirmed to me, I was going to internally assign him all the trimmings of a happy adolescence.

"And one more thing, you burst into my house and start spouting off ideas about this all being connected," I said, getting to the crux of the matter. "Okay, you may be onto something. If you can put aside your disgust that, yes, Simon, I have sex from time to time, we can get back to the matter at hand." I thought of what Nigella had said yesterday. It seemed to be the only thing to occupy him at the moment. And, while I thought it was extremely unhealthy, it was better than stewing in his anger and sadness.

There was a very long silence.

He eventually cleared his throat. "God, I hate Neuberger." He gave me a look – almost shyly – and a tiny flicker moved at the corner of his mouth. The hint of a smile.

"Oh my God, he is such an arsewipe," I said. "What the hell was he trying to do? Insinuate that I put some kind of hit out on Riz or something?"

"Right?" Simon said, leaning down to stroke Kennedy, who had come to stand beside him. "Me being here probably played into some fantasy he's concocted of us being accomplices."

"It was all an inside job, with me and Suzy Rabbit, to get the Lib Dems a victory."

At this, he snorted.

"Let's go see Jed," I said. "We can take our minds off this and remind ourselves there's other shit in the world."

He nodded. "That's a nice idea. I've been ignoring Jed, and I feel terrible. He's been good to me. He was the first friend I made when I moved to Lilbury."

We began to get ready, and Simon continued to talk. "He was the one who told me about the rugby team in Compney that I joined, where I met Trevor and made a few other friends. He and I were drinking buddies for quite a while. It was through him that I became friends with Guy, too."

"You didn't receive the full Nigella when you arrived?" I asked as we headed out for my car, with Kennedy having a full meltdown in the background about being left at home. Oh, the howling, oh, the sulking. He would be in such a mood when I got home. But hospitals weren't dog-friendly environments.

"No, the twins were toddlers when I arrived. It's only the last couple of years that Nigella has had the free time to start being so sociable again."

I can imagine twins in one's late forties took it out of you. My heart hurt for her. She'd finally got the family she'd always wanted later in life, but it had helped drive her and Matteo apart.

We lapsed into silence as I started towards Bournemouth. I was self-conscious about my driving.

"You can go a bit faster," Simon said. "You're barely doing sixty."

"I'd prefer not to end up in the hospital next to Jed, thank you."

He gave me a look and muttered something under his breath about 'an old woman' that I didn't catch.

We fell into silence again, but this time less tense.

"Is that what you meant about the connection – earlier, you mentioned that JedRev and Guy were friends," I asked. "Is that how you think this could all be linked? What, people are attacking all the pillars of the establishment? Westminster, the C of E, and the landed gentry. Will we have to form a protective barrier around the Women's Institute next to make sure no one tries to kill Margo Cadbury-Smythe?"

Simon pursed his lips. "Would anyone miss Margo?"

"What? Simon! She's my best friend."

He chuckled. "I've already had to warn that new lady who moved into Arabella's house to stay clear," he said.

"Katrina? She's really nice."

Simon looked like he was going to say something, but then thought better of it.

Conversation was over after that until we reached the hospital. Simon had been texting Nigella on the way there for details of where to locate Jed.

We made our way to his ward and found a reception desk. The bored woman waved us through to a different section where there were only a few beds per room. "I love the NHS," I muttered. "But thank God I can afford to go private."

"Yeah, how rich are you?" Simon asked as we looked into various rooms. "Were you making fun of Neuberger earlier?"

"Er, Mr Anson, I thought that it was very un-British to ask about money."

He shrugged. "I've lived abroad. Go on, what are we talking? Well-to-do middle-class, tech start-up entrepreneur, City banker, or children's wizard book writer?"

I remembered the situation with my contract, and my chest tightened involuntarily. "Somewhere in between the two middle ones. If I lived frugally, I could survive off my savings, until, well, a pretty long time and never work again. Maybe. It depends."

Simon whistled. "You're a bit of a catch then."

We came to the last room in the corridor, and I saw a couple in their seventies talking at the foot of a bed. "Let's say that, if I wanted to, I could afford to have paid for everything Neuberger thinks I did have done for me without getting my hands dirty."

Simon didn't respond to that.

"I think this is his room," I said. The couple were pottering around a man lying in the bed, slightly raised. "They seem like the sort of people who would have a vicar for a son." I looked at Simon. "Have you met his parents before?"

"Once," he said. "A couple of Christmases ago, when they stayed in the village. Not sure they'll remember me."

He cleared his throat and knocked on the door. It was then that I realised neither of us had thought to bring a gift of any sort. Simon entered, and I meekly followed, feeling self-conscious.

The woman, who had a kind face, rose to greet us. "Not sure if you remember me …" Simon said.

"Simon, Jed's friend from the village. Of course, we do." She held out a hand.

He gave it a hearty shake. "This is Arden, from the village as well and a friend of Jed's."

"Alice Fulford," she said. "And this is Jed's father, Harold."

"Pleasure to meet you both," I said. "So sorry about the circumstances."

We both followed Alice over to Jed's bed, where Harold was fussing around his son.

Jed was up and blinking. He looked gaunt, with reddy-brown stubble across his face, heavily mixed with grey. His skin was red and raw, and his lips were being dutifully attended to but were still chapped.

"Simon," he said quietly, with the smallest of smiles.

"Hello, mate." Simon came up to his bed and gently squeezed his arm. "Look at the state of you."

"I know, I know," he wheezed. "I'm a drama queen."

I hung back. Not wanting to be involved in their moment. "Who's that with you?" Jed whispered.

"It's Arden," Simon said.

I waved but stayed a couple of metres back by the wall. "Hi, Jed, good to see you recovering." Jed gave me a smile.

He and Simon made small talk for a few minutes. The pair moved closer to one another, their heads together. I made polite inquiries to Alice and Harold and passed the time.

After several minutes, Jed clutched Simon's arm, and we all started. Jed turned to his parents. "Mum, Dad, can I have a minute with Si and Arden, please?"

They looked worried at the thought of moving away, but Harold nodded and led his wife from the room. I gave my best smile to them as they departed before making my way over to the bed.

"Love them," Jed said in his hoarse voice. "But Christ, they're dull. Dying for a fag and a pint." Simon looked unfazed by Jed's abrupt change in demeanour, so apparently this was par for the course.

"Next, you'll be complaining the hospital's Wi-Fi has all the porn sites blocked," Simon said.

Jed's eyes widened. "I hadn't even thought of that. Why would they do that to a man trying to recover?"

Simon shrugged. "Jed, we need to talk to you," he said, becoming serious. "You need to tell us about that day. Is there anything you can think of that could help?"

Jed went to shake his head but thought better of it. The bandages that were wrapped around it hid his injuries mostly, but God only knows what mess his skull was in underneath them. His eyes were dark. They darted around the room far faster than the rest of his body could move.

He leaned back slightly and looked at the ceiling. "I'm sorry about Riz, Si, I really am. But … I don't know anything else. I was in … I was in the church; I thought I heard Mrs Crocker. Then I woke up here. I can't remember anything else."

"It's alright, mate," said Simon.

"Don't sound so happy," Jed joked. "It's a miracle I'm alive, you know."

"There are many things about you that are miraculous, Jed," Simon said. "But the fact that your skull is so thick that you can't be killed with a blunt instrument is not one of them. Anyone who's tried to explain the offside rule to you could have told the doctors that."

Jed chuckled. But his eyes were wide, and his breathing laboured.

"I think we've tired you out, mate," Simon said. "We'll let you get your rest."

We made to leave, but Jed clutched at Simon's arm as we began to head out. "You know why this happened, don't you?"

I looked at both men, but Simon's expression was unreadable.

"What we did. We were always going to pay for it."

"Okay, okay," Simon said gently. "I think that's enough for today. Don't want to tire you out too much." He removed Jed's hand and gently tucked him back into bed. "I'll come back in a few days and see you again, yeah?"

I hovered, hoping for more. What on earth could it mean? Was Jed delirious? Simon made the briefest of eye contact with me before turning to Jed and hunkering down beside him at the bed, their heads centimetres apart. He whispered something that I couldn't hear.

After he'd finished speaking, Simon stood and ushered me out. In the corridor, I desperately wanted to ask him questions, but the formalities of saying goodbye to Jed's parents took precedence. Several minutes later, we eventually made our way out of the building, and we were able to talk. "What was that all about? What did he mean?"

Simon stared straight ahead as we walked towards my car.

"Simon?"

"Hmm? What do you mean exactly?"

"Er, about the whole '*we knew we'd pay for it*'."

"I have no idea."

"Surely …"

"Do you know how many painkillers Jed's on? His brain is scrambled eggs. Poor guy. Might never be the same again."

"Si—"

His phone buzzed. "Let's get home, Mum's getting worried again." I stood in the car park and watched him. What the hell was going on?

He made it to my car and waited at the passenger door. "Well, come on, are we going?" he asked impatiently.

I fumbled for my keys. "Yes, yes, of course."

We drove home in silence.

When we got to my house, Simon jumped out.

"Do you want to stay for lunch? We could order something and spit ball?"

He shook his head. “This was all a mistake,” he said, not looking at me. “I don’t know what I was thinking. I’m being crazy.”

“Simon,” I whispered.

He slammed the door – the window was open, and he leaned in. “Listen, forget it, yeah? I think I’ll make myself scarce, Arden. This is stupid.” He tapped the car door in a gesture of finality and then made off across the road to the path through the field. I could see him shaking his head as he walked.

“Simon!”

He didn’t answer.

Chapter 16

I didn't see Simon for a few days after that.

In fact, the next several days were eerily quiet. This meant that I managed to get quite a lot of work done. I took Kennedy to a dog obedience class in Sittingston, where the instructor gave him one look and moved us up to their special 'Premium Deluxe' package.

There was no news from Verity. Not a single piece of correspondence passed between us for almost an entire week, which was unheard of in all the years we'd known one another.

Fine. If she wanted to be like that, then I'd show her how the silent treatment was done.

The heat refused to break. The opposite, actually, it kept building. Every day, I opened my curtains to blinding sunshine and perfect, blue, cloudless skies.

I even took to writing in the garden with my top off. Maybe if I tried hard enough, those deep recessive Mediterranean genes that I'd discovered in Valencia all those years ago would come back to the forefront.

One afternoon, the next week after our trip to see Jed, the lawyer that Ollie had found for me rang, and she and I had a productive conversation.

Her name was Constance Cropper. She was apparently the best in the business.

"Can I afford you?" I asked.

"Only some can, so do your sums before you engage," she told me in a crisp RP accent, which gave me all the confidence in the system I needed. "Now that you've told me what you're up against, I think we can handle it, and I don't think I'll need to bankrupt you in fees fighting it."

Oh, well, that's one positive thing.

"Leave it with me, and we'll make them regret this whole action," she said and hung up before I could get a word in edgeways.

Later that week, I arrived home from Kennedy's second obedience training class ("A mild improvement," the instructor said. "Like how there are different strains of the bubonic plague."), when a text from Nigella came through.

Riz's funeral is on TV.

I switched on the news channel to see a reporter outside the Hindu Temple in Bournemouth talking about the delays in releasing the body.

They showed footage of several high-ranking politicians arriving and other dignitaries. There was no sign of Simon.

I rang Nigella. "Haven't you heard?" she said when I asked where he was.

"No," I said. "Clearly not, like I told you, we haven't spoken since that day we went to see Jed."

"He went back up to Scotland with his parents to stay for a while. I don't know how long for. They left at the weekend; I thought you knew."

Oh.

Well. He's under no obligation to tell me where he goes. None of my business.

And if that was the case, why did I go have a long shower and stand under the hot water, feeling sorry for myself?

That night, as I lay under a single sheet, sweltering in the heat, I gave myself my first real opportunity to think things through.

So, Riz was an extremely ambitious man. He was a doctor who'd risen through the ranks of his chosen career and the local Labour Party to be put forward as a candidate. Even if he was cannon fodder in an unwinnable seat, it was a big deal to get nominated.

Was his ambition what drove him away from his family?

And, then there was Simon, apparently, he was willing to play the game enough to get back together with an ex purely for political reasons. I thought back to the other day when Neuberger had mentioned Riz's accounts on dating apps. Were he and Simon even together properly? Was that why Simon hadn't seemed that fazed by the idea the phone calls meant he was carrying on with another man?

Were they open? They had only been broken up for a couple of months, and yet Riz had amassed a fair collection of profiles and subscriptions all tailored to discreetly getting his end away.

Open relationships, polyamory, and all that jazz was something that had never really appealed to me. Some of the guys I'd dated in my early twenties … well, I was very aware that I was far from the only person warming their bed, and a few of them, I knew, had someone more long-term waiting for them at home, which was why I was happy to be nothing more than casual.

I'd like to think I was fairly live and let live, but if Simon were someone who thought monogamy was a social construct … then I'd keep my opinions to myself and purse my lips in private.

Okay, so back to Riz. He was ambitious. What did that mean? Had he leaked the photos of Guy and Tarquin? It would have been in his interest to do so, but he had been investigated to an extent, and no one suspected him.

What about Marina Holt?

Now, there was someone I'd have been interested in as the leaker. But how? Did she know someone from Guy's past? Had they paid someone? Who would know about some photos of Guy and Tarquin? It's not like they'd have ever been spread about. Presumably, they had sat on a USB stick or, maybe, a folder on Guy's hard drive for all these years … maybe he'd been hacked?

Then what happened … she and Riz fought? Maybe Riz felt bad as the photo leak led to a national crisis. He got cold feet and wanted to come clean, and Marina couldn't take that …

I turned this over. In my head, I slowly convinced myself that Riz must have leaked the photos. But how? Was he working with someone? Marina? Another candidate. Who else stood to gain …

The snoring dog next to me on the bed fidgeted in his sleep, but it didn't stop my mind from whirring. Riz was expected to come third after Guy and … Suzy Rabbit. And whose campaign manager had been very cosy to a certain someone from Tarquin's past – me.

Neither of the last two remaining candidates had a chance of winning, and neither had a prior relationship with Riz. Suzy did, through both of them working in healthcare.

Errol could have helped her. My blood ran cold at the thought. Apparently, I was destined to sleep with every murderer going. It would have been easy for him to slip out early that morning. Maybe he'd expected me to sleep the night through and …

I shook my head. It was logistically impossible for Errol to have been involved. He was beside me for upwards of nine hours that night and only left my sight in the pub to use the loo and then in the room to shower. If he was involved, his role had been to – I gulped – keep me out of the way.

But what if all the photos were a double bluff? I'd been fooled by one murderer before; why not a second?

Had Guy suspected Riz as the leaker? Had he attacked Riz after figuring out that the man who swore he was there to help him was really out to get him? I thought back to that interview with Riz that I'd watched the week before his death. The smug smile, the cool demeanour as he, well, kinda, threw Guy under the bus.

But wait. Had Guy released his own photos? Could there be some devilish plot? Maybe an attention grabber that backfired? I found it easier to believe that Guy would murder someone than to leak his own nude photos.

So – Suzy and possibly Errol. Marina Holt. Guy. And the last person on my list.

Simon.

The ex-boyfriend who had become a fiancé. Who had argued with him that night. And who was no fan of the spotlight that being engaged to a politician would bring.

I didn't even know what Simon did for a living. Was he a spy? Why had he been working as a handyman in Lilbury if that was what he really did?

Ollie had told me when I looked into Arabella's death that the majority of murders were committed by a person known to the victim. That partners were more often than not involved, which I knew Maslin at least entertained the idea of. The police seemed to suspect Simon, but not enough that they stopped him from going to Scotland. The very public, orchestrated, manner in which Riz was killed must have dampened their suspicions.

Eventually, with these horrible thoughts swirling, I drifted off. But it wasn't a long sleep, and it definitely wasn't restful.

The next day was, you guessed it, boiling hot and still. Perfect blue skies. It was a Friday. I hadn't seen Simon in over a week. It was two weeks this weekend since Riz's murder.

The papers had quietened down on it. The world had kept moving. No arrest, despite huge resources.

The police gave updates. The gun was brought into the country illegally, and the police were chasing leads of criminal gangs who imported weapons in the hope of finding who did it. But even then, they needed to discover who it had been sold to, and then maybe who they sold it to, and who they sold it to …

There were no cars on the CCTV coming into the car park.

There was no DNA from the killer left at the scene.

For such a brazen murder, the perpetrator had been very clever in their planning.

I was sitting in my garden, topless, with my laptop on my stomach as I typed away in the mid-afternoon sun when my phone rang.

"Sonia," I said. "What a lovely surprise."

"I need a drink."

"Right. Abrupt. Now?"

"Preferably. I'm finishing up in about twenty minutes, fancy meeting in a pub in Sittingston?"

I checked my watch. It was a little after four o'clock. "Sure. Is everything okay?"

She started laughing at that, which I took as a bad sign.

An hour later, my taxi pulled up outside a pub in Sittingston where Sonia had suggested we meet. It was already thrumming with people. The Lucky Feather, Sonia had once told me, was the closest around these parts to a proper club, though she assured me that up until 8 p.m. on a Friday it remained a typical, if noisy, pub.

The driver gave me a wave as he tore off, and I sighed at the thought of having to use that taxi company on the way home. I made my way in through groups of teenagers who didn't look old enough to tie their shoelaces, let alone drink, and searched for Son. I found her off to the side, bopping to the music at a table while sucking her drink down through a straw and texting with her other hand. She noticed me and waved heartily.

"Sorry, I'm late," I said, coming over and getting a kiss on the cheek. "That taxi firm is bloody useless." Sonia was dressed nicely in a summery wrap dress of light blue and orange. I felt a tad overdressed in a short-sleeved black shirt, which was ever so slightly transparent. A tiny bit. But its capped sleeves made my arms look bigger and went well with black skinny jeans.

She nodded in agreement. "Always have been. One of the girls from work who doesn't hate me gave me a ride from Compney on her way home. Maybe I'll get Ade to give me a lift later on."

I grinned at her. "Going well between you two, is it?"

She smiled coyly and sucked on her straw.

"I see. You okay for a drink? I'm going to head to the bar."

"You have loads of money, so yes, I'll have another," she said.

Now I regretted my kind offer. The bar wasn't too crowded yet, despite the pub being busy. There was a stream of people heading back and forth to the gardens, where most of the patrons had grabbed tables. It meant that the side of the bar for customers sitting indoors was a little quieter, and I was served quickly.

Once back with Sonia, I got her to talk about Ade.

"My Ade's lovely. Honestly, Arden, I think we have a real future. Mum thinks he's dead handsome and clever. He says all the right things to Dad about football."

"And he's a great shag, too," I said, knowing it'd embarrass her.

"Arden!" she squealed. "But, yeah, he's fabulous at all that."

She lapsed into silence with a contented sigh. I cocked an eyebrow.

"Not to ruin your good mood, but what was the need for a drink about then?"

Her face fell. "Guess," she said and then downed her cocktail.

"Your brother and Dhapinder?"

"Ding ding ding." She used her straw to stir the ice in her drink for any leftover liquid. "They suspect something."

My eyes shot to hers. "You've not said anything that could warrant them being suspicious, have you?"

"No, no. I'm playing it very cool. But I think they suspect that someone suspects them, not me, but someone in the company suspects. Or they suspect that we suspect that they suspect … that … I suspect … wow, how many of these have I had?"

"You were on your third when I got here."

"That'd explain it. Let's have another."

"Okay," I said, getting off my seat, knowing that meant I needed to buy them. I wasn't annoyed – I really was quite rich. Even if my best friend, who kept calling me manic, was about to try and screw me out of my money to appease fucking Donal Callous. Wow, okay, I really wanted another drink too now. "But Son" – I turned back to her – "you're being careful, yeah? No silly buggers with this. You need to make sure you play this smart. Only try and access the books when you know it's safe, no risks."

She nodded. "I know, I know."

I gave her another look and then went to get the drinks. We'd been there a while now, and the bar was starting to fill up. Tables and chairs were being moved out of the way, and not long after, the lights were dimmed and voilà, the Lucky Feather was now a club.

Some horrendous David Guetta song came on, and Sonia squealed. "Let's dance!" she said and grabbed my hand, pulling me along.

"No, please, no. Come on, Son. I'm, like, ten years older than everyone else in here."

"Yeah, but you've got all them fancy London moisturisers so you look dewy, my love, dewy."

I gave in – begrudgingly – and let Sonia drag me onto the dancefloor surrounded by twenty-year-olds in outfits so cheap a single open flame near them could have the whole place ablaze. Ah, provincial nightclubs. I remembered them well. Actually, not at all. I never went to a single one in the shithole town I grew up in, as my mum needed me peeling potatoes in the kitchens of the pub, but I had heard of them.

We danced for several songs, and I hated to admit, I was having a great time. Sonia threw herself around to whichever Top 40 track came on, and I shimmied behind her, trying not to be the campest man on the dancefloor. Second campest was fine.

Eventually, a half-decent song that I quite liked came on. Sonia pulled a face. "Nipping to the loo while they play this rubbish," she whisper-yelled in my ear and disappeared off in the direction of the ladies.

I made my way to the side of the floor. No one wants to be the guy dancing on his own in a place like this. As I leaned against the wall, toying with my phone, I looked around and saw a familiar shape.

Errol Mottley was cosying up to a very attractive young blond guy with muscles bigger than his head. Errol had his arms around the roid-rage twink's neck and was pulling him close.

He must've been near twice the lad's age, as there was no way the farm boy could have been older than twenty-one. Unfortunately, Errol saw me at exactly the same time, I realised I'd been staring and made to avert my eyes and disappear into the … well, nothing in this part of the world was technically a crowd, but near enough.

The scowl on his face was enough to tell me he wasn't going to be asking for a repeat performance.

I did what any sane coward would do, and I skedaddled. I made it to the terrace outside, where it was crowded with groups sitting at every table, but slightly quieter after the ruckus inside. Errol was right behind me.

"Forrest!"

"Oh, hello, Errol. Didn't see you there," I said innocently, turning to look at him.

He came up to me. "What the hell are you playing at?"

I hesitated. "I'm here with my friend … she's in the loo. I live around here, remember? I do go out. Occasionally."

"Stop being obtuse," he snapped. He looked around and then grabbed my arm and took me further down the terrace so he could presumably argue with me in semi-privacy. Or kill me. Or leak my nude photos. Did I have any nudes on my phone? I must do.

He got in my face and waved his finger. "Telling the detectives we were together that night was a big mistake."

I was confused. He wasn't thinking I'd been stalking him? Oh, that was a bonus … oh, no wait. "Excuse me? Of course I told them. They asked me who I'd been with."

"Yeah, and dropped me right in it. They came knocking that afternoon when I was at a campaign event with Suzy. She was furious when she found out that we'd fucked. I got warnings and reprimands from higher-ups. A whole shebang."

"That's not my fault!" I snapped back. "What did you want me to do? Say, no officer, I have no alibi. Because that wouldn't have been weird or suspicious. Especially when they eventually found out the truth. Besides, you're not a candidate – what does it matter who you let screw you at weekends?"

Errol looked at me like I was a moron. Perhaps I was. I'd thought he was charming that night. He was anything but.

"Because … you're you. You weirdo. With your" – he gestured at me – "fucked up life. The guy with the paedo brother and the killer ex."

"Fine." I paused. "I'm sorry that telling the police the truth was so inconvenient for you and that you got in trouble for having such poor taste in hook ups. And I'm sorry your rather unremarkable performance in bed has been such a headache. So you can go back to the little farmhand you've picked up and let him do you at a bus stop until you forget all about it."

Errol sneered. "You fucking prick. Do you have any idea what people say about you?"

"Is it like what I've said about you? Big dick, no idea how to use it, and uses way too much teeth when he gives head?"

I walked off. It's not often I get the last word.

Of course, I didn't. Errol grabbed my arm. His finger was back in my face. "You watch yourself, yeah. I'm not above taking care of you if you get in my way." He stormed off.

I gulped and tried to make my legs work. Sonia was waiting for me at the other end of the terrace when I eventually arrived. "What was all that about?" she asked.

"Errol has buyer's remorse," I snapped. "And he only rented for the evening."

Sonia narrowed her eyes and thought for a second. "Oh, I get it now. You're the thing what he bought. He was renting you."

"It was a joke, Sonia. Please don't start telling people he actually rented me." Not with what he was already saying about me.

She nodded. "I'm quite drunk. I should call Ade."

I agreed. She spent several minutes trying to call Ade, but seemed to be ringing everyone else in her phone instead.

Eventually, I called a taxi, which miraculously turned up on time. I poured her in. "45 Summer Breeze Gardens, Compney," I told the driver and handed him a £20 note as I took my seat beside Son, who promptly leaned on my shoulder.

Sonia yelled at the driver to turn the radio up as she loved that song. I frowned. The radio wasn't on.

We arrived at her house ten minutes later, and she woozily walked up the path to her front door. I made the driver wait until I saw the door close before I let him drive off.

Once home, I stripped off, made a fuss of Kennedy for half an hour, then showered and ate cereal in my boxers. As I ate, sitting on the kitchen floor, I threw a ball for Kenny.

People said things about me? I was the weirdo?

How?

The next morning, my head had a construction crew living in it, and they were on a deadline.

Work harder, and louder seemed to be their motto. I stumbled into the kitchen in a fog of regret and let Kennedy out for his morning run around the garden. Then I tried to decide on a course of action. A cat miaowed at me from near my foot.

"Hush, beast of an animal," I whispered.

It miaowed again. "Cruel villain," I snapped and poured some biscuits into its already overflowing bowl.

I looked up. There was a man at my kitchen window.

I gave a deep exhale and steadied my nerves.

"Give me five minutes," I said to him and went back upstairs. I threw on last night's jeans and found a T-shirt from my floor and put it on. It smelled, but it wasn't as bad as the shirt I'd worn out to the club.

When I got downstairs, after another deep breath, I opened the door. Simon was standing in my garden. He was in a bright red running shirt that someone must've bought him for a joke and a pair of tiny, tiny shorts.

"Okay, my phone is on this time, so what's your excuse for turning up unannounced?"

He shrugged. "Trying to see you in your pants again."

I glared.

Kennedy came up to him and demanded his crotch to sniff, and while Simon was distracted, I opened the door wide and let him decide if he wanted to come in. I went back to my hunt for ways to pacify the men in my head.

I was downing paracetamol like it was going out of fashion when dog and man came inside. Simon stood awkwardly in the doorway, looking me up and down. His eyes seemed to be taking me in and assessing me. *You saw me a week ago, I don't age that fast*, I was tempted to say, but didn't.

"You went home," I said instead.

He nodded. Once again like the act was painful. "I hadn't been in some time. It was nice to be there. See people from the past. It … grounds you."

I pretended I could empathise with that, but I'd never been back, so I had to imagine it.

"You left without saying goodbye." I cringed as I said it. I turned to face the other way and drank a pint of water.

"Were you annoyed with me?" he asked. His voice was closer to me, but I hadn't heard him move.

"Concerned." I tried to keep my voice even. I turned back and there he was, six inches from me. I could feel the heat pulsating off his body. His face red from being in the sun, the sweat running down his neck onto the hem of his shirt. Those blue eyes.

He ran his fingers ever so lightly over my arm. "I could take you with me next time I go home. My parents loved you; Mum would be happy to have someone to fatten up with her cooking."

"I've never been to Aberdeen."

He turned his hand around, brushing the back of his knuckles over the curve in my arm at the inside of the elbow. The hairs there were standing up, and every time his hand swept across them, I felt a zing in my body jolt from my chest to my toes.

"It's a nice place, but the countryside around it is much more beautiful, you'd like it." His eyes were on me, maybe searching for something. Whatever it was, I wanted to shout the answer was yes. Yes, Simon, I want you. Yes, let's go to my bedroom and lock the door and not come out for days. Yes, move in and let's get married and adopt some dyslexic Azerbaijani orphans. You can be Daddy, and I'll be Papa; you can teach them how to fish, and I'll teach them Polish folksongs while we make pierogi. At night, we'll make love until we pass out in each other's arms.

"Arden," he whispered so quietly I could barely hear him, even as close as he was.

My phone started to buzz.

Simon jerked back like he'd been given a shock. He was on the other side of the room in a blink. "You should get that. I'll feed Kennedy for you." He grabbed a tin of dog food and avoided my eye.

He moved around my kitchen like he really lived here. I watched him and tried to steady myself. "Ah, yeah, thanks."

I grabbed my phone from the counter and took it outside.

"Hi," I said when I eventually calmed myself down enough to answer.

"Are you okay?" Ollie asked.

I took a deep, shaky breath to try and stay calm and held the phone as far from me as I could. "Peachy keen," I answered. "Just hungover. I went to a club last night.

Terrible mistake, those places are not for people in their thirties."

Ollie laughed. "Who did you go with?" he asked. A man?

"Sonia, my friend." I didn't want any complications.

"I haven't heard from you in a few days," he said.

I looked in my kitchen window and saw Simon on the floor with Kenny all over him. The pair of them were as thick as thieves.

"Busy. And also, not much to report."

"Have – have you thought any more about me? About that night?"

I held the phone away from my face and breathed deeply.

"Arden, please, I hoped … it meant something."

"It did."

"But not enough?"

I let it hang in the air.

"I spoke to Constance," I said. "She's great. So, thank you for finding her for me."

"Not a problem. Glad I could help."

I could hear the regret in his voice. The catch in his throat with every word. This conversation was costing him. Picking up the phone to ring me was emotional turmoil. For me to give these answers was a dagger to his chest.

We lapsed into silence. "Ollie," I said softly.

"I miss you," he said.

"I miss you too," I blurted without thinking. I looked up. Simon stood in the doorway. His face impassive.

"I, uh, I've got to go. Kennedy's set fire to the kitchen."

"What if I came down to visit you? Next weekend? I could stay in your spare room," he said in a hurry. "We could talk things through properly, no distractions."

"Let me think about it," I said and hung up.

Shit shit shit.

I went back inside and found Simon at the breakfast bar, with Kennedy beside him, like he was his dog and not mine. Like I was the interloper in this charming domestic scene.

We both stood in silence. I decided to change the subject. "How well do you know Suzy Rabbit? She and Riz were friends, yeah?"

"Yes. She's … Riz was not exactly friends with her. He had—" Simon struggled for words. "There seemed to be something going on there that I didn't understand."

"Last night Errol threatened me."

Simon's head shot up.

"He was at the Lucky Feather. I went with Sonia."

He stood.

"I was thinking about it properly when you were gone. If anyone knew who Riz's killer was, then who really benefitted? Suzy."

"Do you want to help me?" he asked.

"I …" Instead of answering, I pulled up Suzy's website on my phone. It had a link to her Twitter. "She's judging the Bogford Sheldon village fete at lunchtime according to this tweet from last night." I looked at Simon. "Go home and get changed, and I'll pick you up in an hour."

Simon left without a word.

I showered, ate, and dressed quickly. I put Kennedy on his lead and at ten thirty made my way to the car and drove down to Simon's house. Bogford Sheldon was about ten miles to the west of here. It was a smaller village than Lilbury but had a new housing development being built, so was key for younger voters who might be wooed away from the Tory replacement candidate.

Simon's street was busy with the old dears going about their mornings. I pulled up outside his flat. I texted him instead of honking my horn, in case the shock killed half of the oldies. He emerged twenty seconds later in jeans and a white T-shirt.

"Ready?" I asked.
"Let's go get some answers."

Chapter 17

Of course, it isn't quite that easy to run up to a prospective MP in a race when one of their fellow candidates has been killed.

But we gave it a shot. "Follow my lead," Simon said as we parked up on a side street in Bogford twenty minutes later.

We made our way to the village green, where the fete had been set up. It was a fairly chintzy-looking state of affairs that reflected Bogford's status as the rather déclassé incomer of the local villages.

Suzy was easy to spot. The Lib Dems had set up a booth with a table. There were around a dozen volunteers, all clad in various hues of orange and yellow. We began to make our way over. Halfway across, Simon tapped my arm and gave a tiny inclination of his head. Over to his left was a cop car, with two familiar police officers standing beside it, enjoying an ice cream in the sun. Ade and Lauren looked like friendly local coppers, but they'd probably be less than happy to see us.

"Let's not let them know we're here," I said quietly. That plan had a good chance of lasting, oh, about forty-five seconds.

Because as we got closer to the stand, Errol Mottley turned from where he'd been barking orders at a volunteer, and his eyes found me. His face turned to thunder.

"Oh, shit."

"Yeah," Simon said.

"You know what you said about taking the lead. Could you do that now, please?" I asked.

Errol made his way over and looked like he was about to punch me.

"What the hell are you doing here?"

"We're not here for you, Mottley; we want to speak to Suzy," Simon said.

"She's not available." He was dripping with smarm.

Simon smiled politely. "Unfortunately, I'm not taking no for an answer."

Errol's eyes danced over to Ade and Lauren, but Simon shook his head. "Uh-uh-uh. Not unless you want to explain to them how you violently threatened Arden last night in the Lucky Feather and how he should have lied to cover up for you. Not sure your bosses would be glad to hear about that. So, why don't you lead us over to Suzy so we can all have a nice chat?"

Errol looked like he wanted to kill us both. But after a long few moments where he considered all his possible plans of action, he acquiesced. "Fine, come around to the cars." He led the way, and we were soon at the back of a hideous orange van with Suzy's face plastered over it. The woman herself sat on a lawn chair beside the door of the van. She made notes on her papers as she nodded along to whoever she was talking to on her phone.

Simon gave me a look that I took to indicate *do nothing*. So, we waited. Errol became flustered as we continued to stand there silently. He tried to get Suzy's attention for several seconds. Eventually, he burst into her conversation. "Errol, what is it?" she snapped. He jerked his head. Her face turned from a scowl to shock and back to a scowl as she saw Simon and me.

Up close, she was a brassier woman than I'd expected. The blonde hair was a little yellower from lack of toner. The make-up a bit thicker, the eyes a little shrewder. She was more of a politician than she pretended.

She hung up her call. "Simon, good to see you. So sorry about what's happened. God, I can hardly believe it."

We remained silent. "What can I help you with?" she asked. Errol was at her side, about to burst from anxiety.

"I was interested in your history with Riz," Simon said eventually, but without looking at her.

"I don't know what you mean," she replied, painting on a smile.

Simon and I glanced at each other, and I shrugged. "Well," Simon said, dragging out the word. "You two were old friends. Both in the race together, now he's dead, and no one knows why. And you stand the most to gain."

"Are you— Are you seriously … I can't believe this, Errol, get rid of them," she said and turned away. Dismissing us with the flick of a hand.

"You're saying the leaked photos had nothing to do with you?" I said. "Because Guy was the front-runner, and all of a sudden, he's out, and then Riz, who was your only other competition, is a goner. Bizarre that – the path to your seat opening up so quickly."

Suzy stiffened. "How dare you! I'll sue you for that, I'll—"

"I haven't said anything slanderous, merely that you're a lucky woman, all your rivals are out of the way. It makes one wonder how that came to be."

"Maybe Riz knew you were ambitious," Simon said, taking in the van. The doors were open, and a plethora of campaign materials, all with Suzy's face emblazoned on them and only a tiny logo of the party, filled the space. "And you may have buried your history, but it's there if you want to find it. You were a Tory up until a couple of years ago. You had a falling out with Macauley Sheridan and so decided to jump ship."

I couldn't help it; my jaw fell open with shock. Now that was a surprise. She scoffed at him. "I think it's time you leave, Mr Anson."

"You can't get far as a Lib Dem in this country," Simon carried on, ignoring her completely. I wasn't sure if it was a spy thing, but every comment he gave came after an excruciatingly long pause, which only he seemed to be immune to the awkwardness of. He didn't make eye contact either, preferring to make his statements to the middle distance. "But what if you jumped back once you were ensconced in Parliament? All that publicity, all that backslapping. All that experience in the NHS. They'd be stupid not to promote you.

"I wonder what the falling out was," he continued, as Suzy's face went redder and redder. "Was it that he was a bit of a sexist, was it that he was a snob, that he liked pretty young men, like, say, Guy Frobisher?" Simon took his time saying the rest. "Posh, handsome, male. Guy caught the eye of our lecherous old MP, and capable, mumsy Suzy was not who he wanted to pass the baton to."

Suzy was so red I thought she might be about to explode.

"You listen here, you little meddling prick," she said, her tongue slithering about her mouth. "Riz was a nasty piece of work, and even worse, he was stupid. He knew what he wanted like I did, but the trouble was that he wasn't willing to work for it and bide his time."

"Suzy," Errol whispered.

"Shut up, Errol, you fool," she spat. She never took her eyes off us. "I worked my way up to this position. Your Riz, well, he got here by doing what he did best. Blackmail. He sold his soul to the devil to get his shot at Parliament, and it came back to bite him in the arse."

She shook her hair and returned to her paperwork. "And now, gentlemen, I suggest you leave. Before I call those lovely officers over and tell them about this … harassment."

Simon smiled. "Of course, thank you for your time, Suzy."

I glanced at Errol. He looked ashen-faced. He'd been as shocked as I was at Suzy's past. Good.

He gulped a little and wouldn't make eye contact as Simon and I slowly turned and took our leave.

As we walked back to the car, I was buzzing. "Holy shit! That was amazing," I said, dragging Kennedy away from the cake stall he was desperate to investigate.

Simon said nothing and kept looking straight ahead.

"How did you know all that stuff about her?" I asked.

He frowned. "Because I researched her. Isn't that how you found out everything about Tarquin? I thought you would have known all of that. It's in my notes at your house."

"Ahhhhh," I said. This was awkward. "I've been a bit … distracted."

"Well, I've had a week to stew on it and think things through. Certain comments Riz made about Suzy over the past few months led me to believe she wasn't the loving mum and hospital administrator she was presenting to the world."

We arrived back at my car, and I unlocked it. We both sat with the doors open to let it cool down in the baking sunshine.

"It's like the Sahara," I commented. "Speaking of hotter than hell. What was that she said about deals with the devil?"

Simon scrunched up his face.

"No idea. But I know who to ask."

The election was five days away, this coming Thursday, and here we were on a Saturday afternoon, trailing candidates for answers.

"I'll pull in up here," Simon said, as we came to a stop near the extremely picturesque house a few miles to the east of Dorchester. It was an hour later, and after a spirit-rallying sandwich and iced coffee, we'd traversed through several laneways and exceedingly narrow roads to a village called Forstenmitre.

We'd stopped off at my house on the way here and collected Simon's notes. Hence why he was driving. And pulling faces at everything my car did. While I sat in the passenger seat and read through his dossier.

I finished reading what he'd said about Suzy – only a bit late – and felt a fool. If I hadn't been busy swanning about the place, feeling sorry for myself since Riz's death, I might have been able to help.

Simon parked my car on a tiny verge near an intersection. The fields around us were overgrown, and trees hung over the road. The stone walls that lined the laneway were crumbling. With the sunshine blaring down on us, it was almost too perfect an English idyll. If I got out of the car and there were butterflies in the wildflowers, then I'd know we were in a dream.

"This village is forgotten about," Simon said. "Long ago, there were more people here. Half the houses are boarded up."

That seemed unusual in southern England, where every spare scrap of land was accounted for and marked up at a huge profit as we tried to cram in more houses. Because heaven forbid the English learned to live in mid-rise apartment blocks like their continental cousins.

Forstenmitre might be nearly deserted, but its – I loathe to use the word – aura was that of somewhere much more important. Because there are places like this. There are patches of England, so ancient, and so long settled by humans, that the energy is different.

It's like a point that wants you to forget it, for you to avert your eyes. And when you try to look straight at it, your subconscious says no for reasons you don't quite understand.

My mother believed in this stuff. Rural, paganist energy.

Magic.

Magic of fertility. Solstices and harvests. Countryside magic. Women's magic. When we moved to England, the first village we'd lived in had been involved in a scandal in the 1950s of women holding bonfires and chanting. My mother had laughed and gone out looking for them.

"*Who put Bella in the Wych Elm?*" I muttered under my breath. Forstenmitre was silent. "You doing the talking again?" I asked as we got out of the car.

"It worked well last time," he said. I frowned. "That came out wrong. I meant, me opening, you do the follow-up, it worked well with Suzy and Errol."

As we crossed the road to the tumbledown – yet absolutely charming – cottage, the front door to it opened. A little girl with red hair stood shyly in the doorway, sucking on the ear of the stuffed toy rabbit that she held.

"Hello, Matilda," Simon said in a voice I'd never heard him use before. "Do you remember me? Is your mummy in?"

"She's in the garden," the girl – Matilda – said.

Simon thanked her, and we went around the side – the lawn needed mowing, but the plants were thriving. *All* the plants in the village were thriving. Lush and green. Unlike the rest of the parched county.

Around the house, I could hear a man's voice and the splashing of water. We emerged into the back garden to see a little boy playing naked in a paddling pool, while a woman with her back to us was on her knees pulling weeds out from a flowerbed. A small portable radio was next to her with Radio 4 playing.

"Hello, Marina," Simon said to the woman's back. She froze, her hands staying encased in the dirt. Slowly, ever so slowly, she stood and turned. Marina Holt was actually younger than I previously pegged her for. I had thought her mid-forties on our first meet, but she was closer to mine – well, maybe Simon's – age.

She had her curly auburn hair, which, unfortunately for her, fell naturally like it had been freshly crimped, in a severe ponytail. She must usually straighten it, I realised, which was probably why it always looked darker. Her face was make-up free, and her plucked eyebrows were hunched together in a frown.

She had a thin mouth and a square jaw. She wasn't unpretty, but nor was she conventionally attractive. Her face was interesting, one might say, rather than beautiful.

The three of us stood there in silence. "What a charming house you have," I said eventually. The little boy had stopped splashing in the pool and was staring at us.

"I'm not here to cause any problems, Marina," Simon said. "I need answers."

She huffed. "Don't we all?"

Matilda came out of the house, still sucking on that rabbit's ear, and walked to her mum. She hid behind her legs and peeked out at us.

"It isn't appropriate for you to turn up at my house like this," she said.

"And it wasn't appropriate for you to do it to me all those times," Simon replied without any feeling.

She inhaled sharply. "Fine."

She gestured to a table and chairs, which had seen better days, on the small patio by the French doors that led inside. "I'll bring us some tea. Tilly, Matty, come with me."

The two children did as they were told. "Oh, no, it's fine, we can watch them," I said without thinking. Little Matty seemed most annoyed at having to get out of his paddling pool. I didn't blame him; it was scorching.

She narrowed her eyes but eventually nodded. "Fine, kids, stay with Mr Anson and his … friend."

I beamed. She went inside, and Tilly came over to me and held out her rabbit. "Oh," I said, as Simon looked at me like I'd grown an extra head. I got down on my knees to be at Tilly's level. "Nice to meet you," I said, shaking the rabbit's paw. "I'm Arden, how do you do?"

Tilly giggled. "This is Mr Bunny," she told me. I gave a mock bow in solemnity.

"Mr Bunny, an honour, indeed. I have heard about you on my travels." This made Tilly laugh again, and out the corner of my eye, I could see Matty coming towards me. He was holding a toy truck. When he reached us, it was presented for my inspection.

"Goodness, this is a fine vehicle. Do you partake in Formula One with it?" I asked. Both children descended into giggles.

Simon was still staring as if he'd never seen a creature such as me before. I heard the rattle of a tea tray and looked up to see Marina staring at me, too.

"Do you want to see me race my trucks?" Matty asked me, jumping with excitement.

I gave my finest Shakespearean gasp. "Could I? What do you think, Tilly? I think we should, don't you?"

They both seemed to enjoy that, and before I knew it, I was being led to the French doors where a large number of toy vehicles were laid out for my assessment. "Ah, yes, the red fire truck, a classic," I said, stroking my chin. "And this wooden police car on a string. A fine vehicle for apprehending criminals."

"Children, why don't you go and watch TV? I need to talk to these men for a moment," Marina's voice was tight. Both kids looked annoyed and gave me beseeching stares. I pouted as hard as I could.

"Adults are no fun," I whispered to Tilly and set her off giggling again.

"Kids," Marina said in a warning tone, and both Matty and Tilly ran inside.

I took a seat at the patio table beside Simon. Both he and Marina were eyeing me strangely.

Eventually, Simon turned to Marina. "We've been to see Suzy Rabbit."

Marina's hands were shaking as she poured the tea. "That bitch," she said with more than a little intensity.

"She told us a number of interesting things," Simon said. Had she? "About you," he continued. "About what you and Riz were up to."

"We weren't up to anything. I was trying to stop Riz!" she said, clearly without thinking.

She pursed her lips together and put the teapot down. "Milk? Sugar?"

"Yes, please," I said at the same time Simon said "No."

"She doesn't much like you either," I said to Marina. "Why is that?"

"Because she's a snake. She spread rumours about me." Marina rubbed at her neck. She was pink from the sun, but this seemed to be more of a nervous habit.

"Were these rumours that you and Riz had been up to something?" I asked.

Simon was quiet, watching.

"No! Yes, well, look, I told the police all this. That she wasn't to be trusted. They laughed at me."

"Do you think she leaked the pictures of Guy?"

Marina went quiet for a long time after I asked her that. "No, I know she didn't. Because Riz did."

Oh.

"How do you know that?" I asked Marina. She was staring at the ground. I could see Simon's hand on the armrest of his chair; he was gripping it so hard his knuckles were white. As subtly as I could, I rested my hand on his. Lest he do something stupid.

I could feel his weight shift as I did so, his arm losing some of its tension.

"After Riz's death" – Marina was looking in our direction as she spoke, but not at us exactly, more somewhere off in the distance, over the fields – "Suzy came to me a few days later, she said Riz had told her everything, that the pictures had fallen into his lap, that he … he felt he had no choice to do it. She accused me of getting them. I had no idea where she thought I got them from! I didn't know Guy Frobisher from Adam before the campaign. And I've only heard about this Tarquin Scott chap from the news."

"So why did Suzy think that you had provided them?"

"Your husband," Simon said.

Marina looked away. Eventually, she mumbled, "*Ex*-husband."

"Currently serving eighteen months for blackmail and extortion," Simon said to no one in particular. "All very hush-hush, what with who it was that he'd been blackmailing. Using his position in the party to gain access to senior figures and then threatening to spill their secrets."

"I had nothing to do with it!" Marina snapped. Her eyes were wet. "I was disgusted when I found out what Peter had done. He said he did it for us, for the children, but it was all for him. I should never have married him. And now …" Her voice broke as she stifled a sob. "Now, I'm stuck in this house that I can't afford to sell and I can't afford to make liveable, drowning in his lawyer's bills, and this was my last shot."

She shook her head. "The moment I met Riz, I could see it in his eyes, the same hunger that Peter had. The desire to win no matter what the cost, no matter what it did to you or anyone else. I could see it like a freight train coming towards us all, and I couldn't do anything to stop it."

"Instead, you let him carry on."

"No, I tried, again and again, to warn him off. I tried everything."

"Where did he get the pictures?" Simon asked tersely.

"I don't know. He didn't give me any warning. I only found out afterwards, and he wouldn't tell me."

"You could have stopped him!" Simon snarled. "You could have told me that he'd leaked the photos, you could have done anything apart from the route you took!"

"I know!" she cried. "Don't you think I know that? But Riz, he had, I don't know, there was someone he was working with. I don't know where he was getting all this information from, but someone was helping him. Someone who had intel, money, I don't know. I thought it was someone from within the party, or a Tory who wanted to sabotage Guy. That's why I reached out to Suzy; in case she knows someone from Macauley Sheridan's inner cabal who might be against him."

"Inner cabal?" I scoffed.

"Sheridan had a lot of enemies," Marina said, her eyes flashing. "That man had been in Parliament a long time; he knew a lot of secrets. Isn't that right, Simon?"

Simon's face remained impassive.

There was a long silence. "You let Riz dig his own grave," Simon said through gritted teeth.

"I didn't want him to die!" Marina shouted. "God, Simon. Yes, Riz was no innocent, but no one deserves that. To be tricked, to be left dead in a bloody car park with a bullet hole—" She broke off and squeezed her eyes shut.

No, Riz wasn't innocent. He was far from it. But the image of him in that car, slumped over, his eyes open, his hair spilling over his face. I couldn't not see it. The smell of the blood. The … the bits of his brain and skull over the passenger seat. I felt bile in my throat. Riz may have been a shit, but no one deserved to die that way. Not alone, not by someone else's hand.

Riz, like everyone, was complicated. He was flawed and ambitious. He lied, and he was petty. But he was also a doctor who helped people, who deep down probably loved Simon, and was loved by him. Who, once upon a time, had been a boy with a mum and dad who loved him very much and had clapped at his graduation, so proud of their son, the doctor.

Now he was ashes in the wind, his body cremated, and his killer free.

"Let me get this straight," I said, pinching the gap between my eyebrows. "Riz got the photos from someone, you have no idea who?"

Marina nodded.

"He was in contact with this person after the photos came out?"

She nodded again. "I think so. But after the photos, well, he was shaken. I don't think he knew what it would kick off."

"You mean everyone and their mum leaking photos of MPs and every dirty little secret habit they had, which cost us three cabinet members?" I asked.

"Not to mention that Welsh MP who tried to hang himself when his internet history got leaked," Simon muttered.

"Exactly," Marina said. "It was only ever supposed to be about knocking Guy off his perch. Riz hadn't intended to shake the whole bloody system."

"And you have no idea who this person was?" Simon asked.

"Not a clue. I tried to get him to tell me. I really did, Simon, you have to believe me!" Her eyes fell downwards. "I thought he'd got them from you for a few days."

"From me?" He sounded shocked.

She shrugged. "Your name was mentioned in a few meetings. I was told—" She shifted uneasily in her seat. "To stay clear of you and to tell higher-ups in the party immediately if you offered any information or if I felt something was off."

"And did you?" I asked.
She shook her head. "Simon can confirm that he and I barely spoke two words to one another the whole time."
I looked at Simon. His scowl – if it was possible – was even deeper than usual.
"Let's clear this up, once and for all," I said. My head was hurting from the sun and the hangover. "You say you knew Riz leaked the photos – after?"
"Yes, when Suzy told me that Riz had come clean to her."
"You had no idea beforehand?"
She nodded. "He'd mentioned some underhand tactics might come into play. That's why I didn't tell the police … I thought … well, you know, I should have stopped him earlier."
"Who was the other Marina in his phone?" Simon asked.
"I have no idea," she said after a long pause. "I wasn't aware … wait, no, I remember once. He got a phone call from someone when we were in the same room a few days before the photos were leaked, and the caller ID was Marina. I thought it was strange at the time, and I even asked if he had a friend called Marina. He said he used to work with her."
"Convenient." I turned to Simon. "Did Riz only work at the hospital in Salisbury? Do you know where else he'd been employed?"
Simon shook his head. "He did his med school in Edinburgh," he said. "I think he worked around there for a few years before moving back nearer his parents once he was all trained up."
"So, this other Marina is the person who had the photos?" I asked out loud. I turned to her. "What about Jed Fulford?"
She shook her head. "The vicar? What about him?"
Simon was rigid.

"Did Riz ever mention him?" She shook her head again at my question.

"No, just that day when the news broke about him being attacked."

"He was with me that day," Simon said stiffly. "I got a call, which was the first he knew about it. He didn't even know who Jed was until then."

"You never introduced them?" I asked, confused. "Jed and you are friends."

Simon kept his eyes firmly in that middle distance. "Jed isn't quite as tolerant about the men who like men stuff as he pretends to be. He likes it kept at a distance."

I pursed my lips at this. I'd take Simon's word for it, but that didn't sound like the man who was happy to be included in dinner parties to set me and Guy Frobisher up, like he had been when I first moved here. Then again, he'd been a no-show that night on account of an upset stomach, so God only knows.

"Look," Marina said. "I know I screwed up monumentally. I should've told the police about the photos. I will do so – tomorrow. I'll go in and make a statement."

A thought occurred to me. "Wait until Monday."

They both looked at me.

"I need to check on my children," she said. It was time to go. Marina, with her last bit of confidence, was politely telling us to fuck off.

She ushered us out to the front of the run-down house with its flaking paint on the window frames and weeds in its guttering. I'd lived in houses like this. Simon made for the car, but I held back.

"This." I gestured to her house. "This isn't your fault. Riz screwed you over. If you need anything. Anything for the children – don't be proud, I can help." I pulled out the receipt for my iced coffee from my pocket. "Have you got a pen?"

She looked surprised but went inside and came back a moment later with one. I scribbled my number on the receipt.

I left her and walked back to the car. Simon was glaring at me. “What were you saying?” he asked.

Inside the car, it was hotter than the fucking sun. “I was offering a hand if she needed help with the kids, if she was hard up.”

“It’s not your problem what mess she’s got herself into,” he said, starting the engine. All of a sudden, the idea of him driving my car annoyed me.

It was okay for Simon, who’d probably never had to worry about money in his life, to say it wasn’t my problem to look out for anyone else’s kids. But I’d been those kids, with parents too stupid and feckless to figure out how to put a roof over our heads and food on the table. Whatever the sins of the parents, those kids didn’t deserve to suffer for it.

Apparently, I was glaring at Simon pretty hard because he gave me a sheepish smile. “Okay, I didn’t mean to sound quite so heartless. It’s a nice thing to do.”

He shook his head. “This village gives me the creeps.”

I said nothing. I didn’t feel quite the same way. Forstenmitre felt welcoming to me. Like I could almost hear it laughing, like it wanted me to stay and play.

Simon began to drive in the direction of home. After a couple of minutes, he tried again with conversation. “I didn’t know you were so good with kids,” he said and gave me a cheery look. “They loved you.”

I shrugged. “Little kids always like me; I don’t know why. Babies as well. I pull a silly face, and they stop crying.” My mother used to say it was because my dark hair and big brown eyes were easy for the baby to focus on, and they got distracted. Whatever it was, she used me as a baby pacifier whenever a noisy one came into the pub. "She teething, is she? Let me get my son from the back. Arek, come pull face for baby!"

"When you come up to Aberdeen, you should meet my sister's boy. He isn't very impressed with me, but apparently, he'd think you're the bee's knees."

Oh, now I'm all but coming to live in Scotland, am I? I didn't know how to feel about that. I changed tack.

"What's your sister's name?"

"Mhairi," he said. "She got the traditional name. She's a teacher like Mum was. Her little boy is four now, and she and her husband, Duncan, have a place north of town."

"What's your nephew called?"

He grinned. "You promise not to laugh?"

I frowned. "I changed my name to Arden. Do you honestly think I mock other people's names?"

He shrugged. "Good point. I forget it isn't your real name. It's so … you."

"It is my *real* name. I changed it legally."

He looked at me for a second. "That's brave," he said. "You know, you can choose to go by a different name under UK law. There was nothing stopping you from being Arden, without having to sign a single form."

I didn't like this conversation. That was what I had done for several years, but eventually I decided I was Arden Forrest. Arkadiusz Puszcza had been dead for several years at that point, and he wasn't coming back. Goodbye, Arek, hello Arden.

My silence must've been telling because Simon switched topics. "His name is Mungo, by the way. After the patron saint of Glasgow. It's where they met, at uni, and she had to drag Duncan kicking and screaming to the North East."

"Mungo Anson?"

"Er, no, Mungo Campbell."

I rolled my eyes. "Are you the most Scottish people to ever exist?"

He shrugged. We crested a small hill as we headed home and were blinded by the sun on a corner. Simon pulled the shade down. "This car is a heap of junk. No offence."

"This car saved my life!"

"Then reward it by putting it out of its misery."

What is it with men and taking against my trusty Green Mobile? It came back from the dead after I had to slam it into a wall to get away from Tarquin. It deserved respect.

"The only way I'd get rid of it is for one of those nice new electric hybrid thingies," I said. "But good luck finding a charging station around here."

Simon scoffed and then pulled a face. "Riz was passionate about installing those."

"He drove a gas-guzzling SUV."

"He was complicated."

Ain't that the truth? I mulled over the idea that had occurred to me earlier. I decided to go for it. "We should search his house."

Chapter 18

Honestly, he was such a drama queen.

The way he carried on. It was like I'd said we should sacrifice Mungo to the gods to find the killer.

"It's illegal," he said, spitting feathers he was so outraged.

"I take it that you don't have a key?"

More feather spitting. "So, you *do* have a key?"

"The police have already looked at everything there," he said as he pulled up outside my house. This conversation had already been going around in circles for fifteen minutes. Honestly, reader, be glad I skipped ahead.

He got out of the car and, without even stopping to ask if he could, unlocked my front door and let himself in. "Just move in, why don't you?" I muttered.

He was already feeding Kennedy – delirious to see us, obviously – when I followed him in. "Can you feed the cats, too?" I asked. He nodded. The cats, it will shock you, had neither the inclination, nor, it seemed, the physical energy, to greet us on our return. I gave their entangled fluff a nudge on the chair they were curled up on and received a chirp of displeasure in response. Good, still alive.

Simon sat on my sofa, Kennedy between his legs, looking again through the papers I'd been reading on the way to Marina's.

"Neuberger searched his house already."

"Neuberger's a dick," I countered. "We know what we're looking for."

"Which is?"

"Mmm, dunno, stuff?"

"Oh my God," he said and put his hands around Kennedy to steady himself. "You're not even taking this seriously. Remember when someone broke into

Arabella's house? They never managed to get Tarquin to admit to it."

I went very quiet.

"Oh my God," he said.

"Yeah …"

"Oh my God!" he said for a third time, really taking the Lord's name in vain, here. "It was you?" His eyes were bulging. I shrugged.

"It worked," I said.

He went silent for a few minutes. And then he paced my living room. And then he went upstairs to the toilet for several minutes, where I heard him pacing in there as well. And then he went out to the garden to pace there too. And then he came back inside.

"If you don't stop fucking pacing, I am going to kneecap you," I said. "And you've seen what I did to Tarquin, you know I can."

He looked at me with an expression of wonderment. Oh yeah, never explained to him how I know how to do that. How a nice guy like me could fire guns like that. Well, that's not a story for right now.

"If you're not keen, I'll do it myself." I put my hand out. "Give me the keys, and I'll go tonight. I'll have a mosey and report back."

He shook his head. "It's stupid. Unsafe."

"You don't have to come with me."

"I meant for you as well."

"Ehhhhh. Not the first time I've done it. And with keys, it's a cinch."

Simon's eyes narrowed. "What are you expecting to find?"

I shrugged. "Anything about this mysterious other Marina."

This seemed to do the trick "The police showed me his phone records, said the calls were from an unregistered number. That'll be who they are looking for as well," he said.

Nigella's voice was in my head. This was all to distract him until the mania of his grief had passed. But here I was, getting sucked in all over again.

"Fine," he said. "But I don't have the key on me. Come to my place later, and I'll get it for you." He stood to leave.

I nodded. "I'll be over about midnight then."

He looked pained at this. "You know this stuff is dangerous, right? It's not a game." He looked me up and down.

I jutted my chin out in mock resolution. "I'm a big, brave boy, Simon. I'll be fine."

He nodded slowly. "I'll see you at midnight then." With no warning, he leaned forward and kissed my cheek. "Thank you for your help today." Before I'd quite processed what had happened, he was out the door.

Neither Kennedy nor I knew quite how to deal with that. Instead, Kenny waited downstairs while I took a long shower and, um, worked through some feelings while I was in there.

"Don't look at me like that," I snapped at him when I came back downstairs almost an hour later. I wandered around the house in a towel and grazed at various things in my fridge. I was ravenous but too jittery to cook. In the space of a few weeks, I'd gone from an insomniac who never ate to someone who slept twenty hours and ate constantly without even realising I was doing it.

After a snack, I took a long nap and awoke when it was starting to get dark. I read through Simon's notes again – he had the handwriting of a teenage boy. He pressed into the page too hard with the pen, and his letters were bunched up in thin shapes.

"I thought a spy would have nicer penmanship," I told Kenny. It was at least legible, unlike my loping scrawl.

That evening, I parked my car at the top of Simon's street and then walked around the back to where I'd entered with Nigella that day. Several trips in the dark and a very bruised shin later, I knocked at Simon's door.

He answered in the most circumspect manner.

"Key?" I asked, hand out.

"This is such a stupid idea," he told me.

"Uh-huh. Key?"

"Can you at least take Kenny with you?"

"Take my anxious dog, who gets scared of the sound of a packet of bacon being opened? Who whines if he can't see me for five minutes, so I can't even take a dump in peace? Yeah, that sounds like a good idea. I'm sure he won't make any noise."

Simon looked heavenward with a pained expression on his face. Something I was sure he would claim I was the frequent cause of.

"I'll come with you."

I rolled my eyes. "So benevolent. I'll be fine, I don't need protection."

"Yeah, well, I'm coming with you. Give me two minutes."

"Fine, meet me at the car. I'm parked around by the house with the ugly rose bushes on the corner."

"Mildred's house? God, she'll be watching you through the curtains." He sighed.

Five minutes later – hey, who was counting – a hulking great beast of a man, all clad in black, slipped silently into my car. Which was impressive, considering his size. Simon said nothing, so neither did I.

We'd been driving about fifteen minutes when the silence became too much for me, and something that had been burning a hole in my head since I'd heard it came tumbling out.

"Riz had profiles on a bunch of dating apps then."

Simon said nothing, but the air changed.

"He had several … it was a lot to sign up to in the couple of months you guys were broken up. Were you two … were you guys open?"

Oh, the longest of silences.

"We had certain understandings." It now made sense why Riz's mysterious phone calls potentially being another man hadn't been that worrisome for Simon.

"Right," I said.

"You don't approve."

I flexed my hands on the steering wheel. "It's not my place to comment."

"You're judging."

I swallowed. "No. It's just not my thing. Open relationships and me. It's not my cup of tea, but I don't have any negative opinions on those who do like them." That was a lie. I hated the idea of it. The thought of someone I loved coming home smelling of another man. It made me angry to imagine it. But plenty of people had happy, healthy, open relationships, so my job was to shut my mouth.

"Bullshit," Simon said. "You are a one-hundred-per-cent-monogamy type of guy, and anything else is less than in your eyes."

I could have argued. I should have argued. Should have said anything. But I didn't. I let a silence emerge, and then I let it grow.

I could sense Simon getting more and more tense.

"It's none of your business," he snapped.

"I know, I'm sorry I asked—"

"And for your information, I've had plenty of monogamous relationships. But sometimes they're not. It depends on me, on them, on the situation. Riz and I started exclusive, but then we opened up, okay?"

I held up my hands in defeat. "Sorry that I asked. I wasn't trying to offend."

He sneered. "I suppose in your world it's boy meets boy and then if one of you even looks at someone else it's tears and handbags at dawn."

It was my turn to be offended. "I think this conversation has run its course." *You don't fucking know me, you prick.* "Like I said, sorry I asked."

After forty minutes of driving, we passed signs for Salisbury. The mid-sized town, which, due to English anachronisms, was a city because it had a cathedral. It was advertised as being pretty, but was a very plain town with a modern centre and a plethora of ugly housing. Riz lived in the southern area near the hospital.

We parked up a few streets away. "Arden," Simon said. He'd been quiet for twenty minutes. "I'm sorry about what I said earlier. I was rude."

"It's fine, don't worry." I closed the car door quietly when, really, I wanted to slam it hard enough to wake the dead.

"Arden," he said again.

"It's fine." I began to walk but then stopped to add more. "We have differing views. Just as well we don't think of each other in that way because we're clearly not compatible." I turned from him and started to walk again. But slow enough to see his face fall.

Good. Don't insult me and then think you're in with a chance.

What Riz and he did or didn't do was their business. But if I could manage the lip service to pretend that it didn't bother me, then he could show me some basic compassion, too.

My self-righteous fury lasted a few streets. If you were imagining Riz lived in some lovely red-brick mansion block or converted Victorian townhouse, then I direct you to my previous comments about Salisbury being overrated in terms of aesthetics. No, Riz lived on a new-build estate with all the charm of a tractor reversing down a motorway. Winding cul-de-sacs paved in a yellow stone, with faux-Victorian three-storey houses jostling for space on sections that surrounded us. Anaemic trees attempted to grow on the verges, and the lawns were too small. Like most new-build estates, it struck me as off somehow, the ratio of street to house to green and the depth of the buildings back from the road didn't work.

Simon walked a few steps behind me. I could feel the aggravation emanating from him. "The back door, we should go through there," he whispered. I was too annoyed to even make a joke about gay men and the rear option.

I grunted in response. We slipped through the gate at the side of the house and into the small back garden. Riz's place was a semi-detached red-brick two-storey property. The house that it joined onto had another floor on top, giving Riz's the look of being a wing to this grander home.

There was a plain white door at the back, which Simon opened with the key. We at least had both remembered to wear gloves, though I was tempted to ask why Simon was bothering, as his prints would already be all over the place.

We slipped into Riz's surprisingly spacious kitchen. The various lights around the neighbourhood cast a slight glow into the room, so you could pick out details among the shadows if you tried.

"You turned off your phone, right?" Simon said, conscious of the location data.

I nodded. "Back in Lilbury."

He pulled out a small torch from his pocket and held it in the air. He waved it across the room, with the beam pointing towards the floor. In one corner were a pile of boxes and assorted household items all piled high.

"His parents have started cleaning the place out then," said Simon.

"Where does he keep his paperwork?"

"There is an office upstairs."

Great. Offices. I had history with those. We made our way to the front of the house and up the stairs. Riz's home had white walls and laminate floorings. His choice in décor was too plain for my taste. Maybe he'd been too busy to decorate. At the top of the stairs, the door to the master bedroom was open. Simon paused for a second and looked in. The king-sized bed had been stripped and the bedding piled in boxes next to it.

Whatever Simon was thinking about, I didn't want to interrupt. The passionate nights with Riz in that bed? Waking up in each other's arms? My judgemental side instantly thought of all the other men Riz had probably had in there as well.

I opened the door to the right of us and could just about make out that I had found the office. I felt for a desk of some sort in the tiny bit of light from the windows.

"Simon," I hissed after a minute. "A little help, please?"

The beam from his torch was over my shoulder a few seconds later. He cleared his throat. It seemed to be a tic he did to calm himself down when he was upset.

"This is stupid, we don't even know what we're looking for."

"Yeah, yeah, you've made that quite known, thank you," I said, trying to ignore him. I opened the bottom drawer. You'd think people would put their most important things in the top drawer. But that's where nosey buggers would look first. That drawer revealed several piles of papers and various keys, old SIM cards, a few photos, and the ephemera one would expect in a home office.

I handed Simon the papers. "Shuffle through."

"What am I looking for?"

I gave him a look. "You can stop playing dumb now. You're a spy, you figure it out."

The glare he gave me was something I felt more than saw. What? We both knew I was right.

He did as he was asked. "There's some paperwork from the hospital. Various forms about taking a leave of absence for the election campaign," he said. "His old hospital in Edinburgh. The Royal Lothian." He scanned the paper for details.

I opened another drawer. And that's when everything fell apart. Every bit of distance I'd tried to keep from this predicament that I'd found myself in. The story I'd told myself was that I was doing this to help Simon. To help Nigella. Because Simon wasn't really my friend, but he was friends with other people in the village, and that's why I needed to do this. Because the people in Lilbury had stood by me when my life fell apart after Tarquin. They'd accepted my pleas that I knew nothing about what he'd done without so much as a second thought.

So, my reticence about Simon, about any feelings that might linger, about how we constantly rubbed each other up the wrong way, was put on the backburner.

But now, I was involved. There was almost irrefutable evidence that someone, somewhere, had me in their plans. Just as much as Riz, Guy, and whoever else was involved – and it was staring at me from a piece of paper.

I grabbed it and stuffed it into the pocket of my jacket.

"You found something?" Simon asked.

"Let's go," I said tersely.

"But we've only just started—"

"I said, let's go," I snapped and left the room. Downstairs, I waited for Simon in the kitchen. As soon as I saw him coming, still confused, I left the house and walked back across the garden towards my car. Simon took a few seconds to lock the back door and then joined me as I walked through the streets.

My head was buzzing. How? How did I know these people? How did this involve anyone from my old life?

There was no connection. I knew no one from Simon's life, or Guy's, but there had to be a connection. A … *connection.*

I spun around as we reached my car.

"What is this connection? The one Jed mentioned."

Simon shook his head. "It's nothing."

"For fuck's sake, Simon, enough! Don't make me go back to Jed and shake him until he tells me. I will. I've had enough. You asked me for my help, and you've been hiding things the entire time."

Simon looked heavenwards.

"It's private, okay? It's nothing to do with this."

My turn to call bullshit. "Fine, I'm going to talk to Jed first thing tomorrow. Maybe you should stay home." I opened the door to the car, climbed in, and started the engine.

"Wait, Arden, no." Simon got in beside me. "Okay." He took a deep breath. "There is something. But it's … it's between me, Jed, and someone else."

"Who?" But I knew the answer. I'd known it since the day in the hospital. Maybe before. Maybe when Simon had shaken his head at me when I'd first moved to Lilbury and told me there was more to certain people than meets the eye.

Simon gulped loudly. "Guy."

Chapter 19

We used to play the drinking game 'I Have Never' when I was at university. I never did very well. Maybe I would do better now. Exhibit A: I'd never banged on an aristocrat's door at two in the morning before. But here we are.

Simon hung back, looking like he was about to cut and run. Or more exactly, like he was desperately trying not to shit his pants.

Frankly, I couldn't care less. He was pissing me off something chronic, and I wanted this over and done with.

There was no answer, so I banged again.

A light went on in the furthest reaches of Guy's 'cottage', which was bigger than Wales.

In about twenty minutes, when whatever staff Guy had reached the front door, we'd be let in. I was glad for the break. It was a hot evening, and even though I'd finally stripped off the jacket and gloves I'd worn to leave no trace at Riz's, I was still boiling, waves of sweat cascading off me.

The door opened, and Guy stood there in a blue silk dressing gown, with not much on underneath. He was rubbing his eyes and looked pretty fucked off at being roused from his dreams.

"Good." I barged past him as he began to say something. Probably some obfuscating comments. More inane pleasantries.

"We need to talk," I snapped.

"It's 2 a.m.," he said as he followed me into whichever room I was going into. "What the hell are you doing … Simon? Why are you hovering outside? What on earth is going on?"

“Come inside, Simon,” I said and walked into … I think it was some sort of living room antechamber. “The three of us need a conflab.”

Simon entered meekly. Well, as meekly as a man with shoulders that broad can. Guy tightened his dressing gown a little more, which was a relief as the sight of his sculpted golden skin was distracting me from my anger. And I wanted the anger. Anger was so much more useful than horniness.

“Right, straight to it. There is something between you two and Jed, something that may or may not have been the cause of Jed landing in hospital with half his skull cracked in, of photos of you getting fucked six ways from Sunday by Tarquin being leaked, and even more possibly, of Simon’s fiancé getting killed. I don’t know what it is, but Jed wants to tell everyone, whereas Simon, here, clams up like a top having his arsehole played with every time we broach the subject. So why don’t you tell us, Guy?”

Guy’s eyes darted around the room. “I … Arden, what the fuck is going on?” Guy hardly swore, even in private, so he must be confused and annoyed.

I didn’t care. “What did you three do?” I yelled.

That got his attention. He and Simon shared a look. Slowly, oh so slowly, Guy morphed from befuddled and half asleep to politician-in-waiting. “Arden, let’s take a seat.”

“Nope!” I yelled. “I don’t know about you, Guy. But I found a dead body a couple of weeks ago, and you bastards know something about what caused it, and yet, no one is coming forward. So, I’m done with being polite.”

Guy took a seat, still looking at Simon. He gestured for me to do so as well. “Let’s not yell, it’s late. You’re clearly emotional.”

“Fuck off,” I snapped.

"Arden," Guy said, using a voice I hadn't heard from him before. "Don't speak like that to me in my own home. Please, take a seat, and let's discuss this like adults." I recognised the voice; it was his public-school voice, his landed gentry voice, his lord of the manor voice. The one that said *No, peasant, you do what I tell you to do. You don't give the orders around here.*

The very idea of it made my skin crawl. Instantly, I hated him. The fact that he'd asked me out twice was laughable right now. We were from different worlds. Actually, I was from a different world from him, Simon, and everyone else in this fucking village. Why did I keep forgetting that?

He and Simon were still sharing a look. I took a seat, but I wasn't happy about it. I was fuming, I was pissed off, and I wanted to punch something.

After a long time, Guy spoke. "A connection between Jed, me, and Simon. Yes, there is one; we are all friends. Simon may not act like it, but he and I are great friends. I know, his demeanour is as confusing to me as it is to everyone else. Sometimes I think I imagine his friendship when I receive one of those scowls – just like now. But we are. And we are friends with Jed. The three of us had a little club."

"A club?" I asked.

"A nicer way of saying we were drinking buddies." Guy waved his hand. "To put it bluntly, Jed and Simon would come over and the three of us would get shitfaced on expensive booze."

"There's more," I said.

"I mean, we got very drunk," Guy said. "We acted like students."

"There's more. So, you guys binge drank every once in a while? Big whoop. That doesn't lead to you all getting your lives ruined."

A flash passed through Guy's eyes. I could tell he was cooking something up.

"Don't lie to me," I warned.

Simon put his hand on Guy's shoulder. "I'll tell him." They shared another glance. "Arden, look, you know Riz and I were open. Guy and I have had an arrangement for a few years."

I cocked my head.

"Since I moved here. It's always been casual. When we needed a release."

Jesus Christ. Was every gay man I slept with part of some endless conga line of dicks?

"And once, on one of those nights, Guy and I got a bit carried away, and Jed saw a bit too much. He put two and two together and got five and thought there was more to it than there was."

"He is a vicar," Guy said. "Despite his foibles, he believes, deep down, that sex should be for couples."

I got up and paced the room. Because it was either that or I started laughing until they sent me to the Funny Farm because I might never stop.

The entire connection was that Jed had once walked in on Guy and Simon going at it because they were friends with benefits?

This was a lie. And I was tired.

The antechamber we sat in was big enough to get a fair bit of speed up while pacing, but my legs felt like lead. I sighed. "Fine, fucking hell, whatever. When you're ready to be honest, let me know. In the meantime, I'm going home." I left without saying anything else. They could lie all they wanted; I wasn't interested. There was more to this, and I wanted nothing to do with it any longer.

Slamming the door of Guy's house, I stalked back to my car. I expected Simon to follow me out so I waited a few seconds. Nothing. No footsteps. He was probably already fucking Guy again.

Was this what dating in your thirties was like – an endless parade of people who had barely finished having sex with someone else trying to have sex with you? If I had known how interconnected Guy, Tarquin, Simon, and God knows who else were, would I have become involved with any of them? Probably not, to be honest.

I started my car and drove home. Kennedy was waiting for me when I got there.

Safely ensconced at my cottage, I switched my phone back on and let any messages come through as I got ready for bed. A voicemail from Sonia.

Despite the heat, I curled up under the covers with Kennedy. I decided I'd listen to the message tomorrow.

That damn piece of paper.

Answers, all this meant that I needed answers.

The next day was thankfully cooler. Several degrees lower than previous days, which was a blessed relief. The weather forecast said the temperature would skyrocket back up over the week. But thankfully for one Sunday, it was overcast and mild. After a day of throwing myself into work to avoid any thoughts of men and their annoying traits, Kennedy made himself known at around 4 p.m.

The sky was darkening, with the prospect of a thunderstorm.

But my dog was carrying his lead around the house.

"Walkies time, is it?" I said and slammed my laptop shut. "Good idea, boy." I gave his fur a ruffle and got a tongue loll.

"You're the only man I could ever love," I told him. Which was completely unhealthy.

We went to the top of the garden and turned right, heading towards the crest of the hill and then along the path to Winterborne Minster, which was my new favourite route. Mostly because it avoided Lilbury.

At the crest of the hill, man, and dog both stood surveying the lie of the land. "I think we should move, Kenny," I told him. "How does the Outer Hebrides sound?"

The tongue loll I received was not a definitive answer.

There's a pretty bit of the lane to Winterborne where trees overhang it on both sides, and it becomes very closed off, forming a canopy. You feel as if you're in a magical pixie kingdom. Some kind of Lilliputian fantasy.

Over the past few weeks, it'd been delightfully cool there compared to other parts of the walk, but today we didn't need the respite. However, force of habit now saw me tramping down the small hill towards it, with Kenny beside me.

There were few cars on this road. Why, all last week, I hadn't seen a single one. There were probably fewer today with the overcast weather giving people an excuse to stay at home for the first time in weeks.

We trotted our way down, and I clicked Kenny back on his lead after we'd climbed the fence. I was whistling a tuneless ditty, and Kenny was exploring some new places he hadn't sniffed. I wasn't thinking about Simon or Guy … ahem, I wasn't thinking about … certain people. I wasn't fixating on whether my career was about to go up in smoke; I wasn't worrying about Ollie. Nope, my brain was empty. And that's where it all went wrong.

The birds were chirping, and the sun was trying to peek out of the clouds as we made our way through the trees. Far in the distance, I heard a car's engine and made a mental note to walk closer to the edge in a minute or so when it got to us.

The car approached quicker than I had predicted, and I dutifully moved us off to the side like a good citizen. I looked behind me to make sure it wasn't some vast SUV that I'd have to clamber halfway up the stone wall that lined the road to avoid. If I hadn't, I'd probably be dead.

The car was barrelling down on me at a million miles an hour. "Oh, shit," I said. My stomach dropped, and instinct kicked in.

"Kenny, run, boy!" I yelled and frantically tried to get away.

Kenny started to bark up a storm as he outpaced me. "Go, boy, go!" I yelled. I'd never forgive myself if he was hurt.

What the hell was happening? The massive black car was now fewer than twenty metres away from us and was veering well over to the side of the lane, one of its wheels on the grass, aiming straight for us.

Ahead, I could see where the trees ended and the verge opened to a few metres wide on each side with space to climb the stone wall and get into a field. I had to make it another hundred or so metres, and we'd be okay. There was no way to jump the fence in the trees; the bank it ran on was steep, and, though dry after several weeks of no rain, it was made of loose dirt that, no matter how gainful you were on your pins, would have you falling backwards as you slipped and slid.

The car was now right behind me as I sprinted as hard as I could in loose summer shoes. It bumped up against the back of my legs, and I nearly went flying. I dared to look back to try and see the driver, but it was all shadows, and the act almost cost me as my legs fumbled and nearly ended up under the wheels. The car pulled alongside us, and just in time, I let go of Kenny's lead, as it blindsided me and I went flying into the bank.

As soon as it had come, the car disappeared. The driver veered back onto the road properly and sped off in a cloud of dust.

I lay there in a heap on the bank. "Ow." I didn't seem to be dead or particularly hurt, but being thrown several feet by a car was, I can tell you now, dearest reader, not exactly a pain-free experience.

It was several minutes before I could stand up. The world was spinning, and my legs were jelly. I couldn't see Kenny anywhere, which was making my chest ache. If they had hurt him, I would rip this fucking county apart to get revenge.

Eventually, I managed to get to my feet and, like a newborn lamb, wobbled my way along the path. The entire outer side of my left leg was covered in dirt and had a graze underneath it from where I'd landed after going flying. My right leg, which had taken the brunt of the whack, was throbbing with pain, as was my elbow, which had taken a portion of the hit too. Everything was going to hurt for days. My limp was a thing of beauty.

I stopped walking as I came to the end of the trees. My heart thundered in my chest so hard I thought it would explode. I was dripping in sweat. My legs were still unsteady.

I leaned over and rested my hands on my lower thighs, sucking in deep breaths. The jingle of metal alerted me. Kenny was coming towards me, with his lead dragging along behind him, the catch on it making the noise.

"Good boy," I said and kissed the top of his head. He licked my leg. I stood up straight, which, oh, ow, that was a mistake. That's when I noticed the car had come back. About a hundred metres further down the hill. Waiting. Its engine running. It had clearly driven down the lane, found somewhere to turn around and then come back to finish the job.

"The killer," I whispered. This was the person who had murdered Riz.

My heart was beating so hard in my chest that I feared I'd vomit. Oh, God, the person who'd shot Riz in cold blood and possibly tried to kill Jed was in that car, and they wanted me dead. Maybe they'd been watching Riz's house. They might know what I knew.

Panic started to fill me. But I didn't have time for it to settle as the car revved, and its wheels squealed. It hurtled towards me.

"Shit." I was standing in the middle of the road. Where could I go? Could I vault the fence in time? What about Kenny?

It all happened so fast. Before I even had time to dive, it was on me. I cringed, flinging my hands over my face, like that would save me. I screwed my eyes shut.

There was an almighty shriek. And then nothing. For several seconds, I stood there, my eyes closed. Then my mind clicked; the sound I had heard was a handbrake stop.

I dared to open an eye. The car was no more than a metre from me. Its engine running. But it hadn't hit me. I opened the other eye.

A car door opening shook me out of my daze

"You couldn't help yourself, could you?" asked a voice that I knew from somewhere.

I looked fully at the person who had emerged. Dhapinder Bliss was standing beside the car. Dark sunglasses covered her face. She wore a black trouser suit with an Emerald green blouse underneath and shiny black heels. Her hair was blown out and full of volume. Honestly, she looked fabulous.

"You … y-you?" I mumbled.

She sighed. "It had nothing to do with you! But I should have known; that day you came around for a nosey. Lying about how you wanted to see Sonia. No one ever wants to see Sonia." She laughed mirthlessly.

"What?" I said.

"Don't fuck with me, Arden!" She pointed a stun gun at me.

"Jesus Christ!" I squealed and jumped back about a metre. My whole body protested.

“I know it was you. Your dirty little fingerprints all over it. The sort of thing you’d do, with your murderer boyfriend, probably. Trying to find a new person to blackmail, were you?”

“What?” I asked again. What the hell was she on about?

She looked exasperated. “Don’t deny it. You. You broke into the office last night. The police are already there. I’m sure they won’t find any evidence. Far too experienced for that, aren’t you? But I know it was you.”

What. The. Fuck? “Wait,” I said. “You think I broke into your office? Me? Why?”

Dhapinder looked like she wanted to kill me. Which, to be fair, I think she actually did.

“I’m sure you weaselled loads of information from Sonia on your little evenings out; she probably told you all about the money in the office. I’m sure you were biding your time.” She pressed a button, and the stun gun crackled, then she lunged at me. I shrieked and jumped back again.

Kenny barked and jumped at her and knocked the stun gun from her hand. It was Dhapinder’s turn to scream, as forty kilograms of dog bowled her over. His lips were pulled back, exposing his teeth. “Kenny, no!” I wasn’t having my dog put down because he attacked someone.

Dhapinder screamed again and sank beside the car, her face going pale. I grabbed Kennedy and tried to pull him back, but he was still barking and snapping at Dhapinder. “Shush, boy, it’s okay, the psycho bitch won’t hurt us,” I whispered into his fur.

“What in the ever-loving name of Jesus Christ is going on here?” came a voice off to my left.

Dhapinder and I both turned to see Katrina Pettigrew standing a few metres away. She was wearing a straw sun hat, with a lightweight white skivvy and a red summer jacket over it. On her bottom half were a pair of waterproof walking trousers and sturdy boots. In one hand, she held a walking stick, similar to those favoured by Nordic walkers. In her other hand, she held the stun gun and looked at it like it was alien technology that had dropped off a spaceship.

I saw, what I assumed was her car, its driver's side door open, idling behind Dhapinder's further down the hill.

"This man!" Dhapinder stuttered, pointing at me. "This man and his dog! He attacked me! His dog is out of control. Thank God you're here, I thought he was going to kill me."

"I see," Katrina said, continuing to look at the stun gun. "But this is yours, is it not?"

Dhapinder's eyes darted between us.

"So, you happened to have – wait, aren't these illegal in the UK?" she asked. "You just happened to have one of these to hand?"

"He was in the middle of the road! I stopped to ask him to move out of the way, and he set his dog on me!" Dhapinder yelled.

"Yes, I saw him in the road. I also saw you jump out with this already in your hand." Katrina looked at me after she said this. "Arden, what happened to you?" She took me in, head to toe and arched an eyebrow. "It looks … like someone ran you off the road."

Katrina turned her head slowly to Dhapinder. "Which would put you firmly in the wrong, then," she said.

Dhapinder began to say something. "Quiet!" Katrina barked with a force of will I hadn't expected from a sixty-year-old widow. "Why don't you get back in your car and go back to wherever it is you need to be?"

I kept a hold of Kenny, whose growling had largely subsided, but he was still in attack mode. Dhapinder looked like she wanted to spit tacks. After several seconds of mulling Katrina's words over, while I stood rock still, Dhapinder held out her hand.

"I'll take my property back, then, please!"

"The hell you will," Katrina said, holding up the stun gun to the sun and admiring it. "No, I don't think you need this, deary."

She gave Dhapinder a withering look when the latter opened her mouth to complain. "In you get," Katrina said, cocking her head at the car. "Drive away."

Dhapinder threw me a vicious look and then righted herself. Clearly fuming. "This isn't over, Arden," she whispered and then got in her SUV.

With Katrina's car behind her, she had no option but to go forward, and I managed to haul Kenny to the side of the road as she sped off in a squeal of tyres.

"So, it's true," Katrina said once the sound of Dhapinder's vehicle was long gone. "You really do attract trouble like it's going out of fashion."

I collapsed on the grass.

Katrina hadn't redecorated since she'd bought the house from the Sweets.

As I sat in the kitchen of the TARDIS-style cottage, I noted this with surprise. In fact, it was less that she hadn't redecorated and more the absence of any decoration.

The house looked like a small two-or three-bedroom home from the street. But in reality, it was a labyrinth-style warren of rooms on the ground floor with more of the same upstairs and an attic on top of that. There were about five living rooms and endless doors to spaces that probably had no use, and cupboards, and priest-holes, and Christ only knows what else.

There was also a distinct lack of furniture. When Arabella lived here, it had been full of tasteful-slightly-not-quite-shabby-enough-to-be-convincingly-authentic-shabby-chic furniture and knick-knacks. Huge ornate lamps, overstuffed sofas, east Asian ornaments, antique Persian rugs, and umbrella stands that probably cost the same as the rent on a flat in a Glaswegian tower block for a year.

Katrina's limited décor was much more British. Middle class. Little old lady. She had a few plants, some books. A couple of plain tables.

"Still moving in?" I asked as she busied herself, back and forth, checking her first aid kits.

She glanced around. "Oh, aye. Did a clear-out before I left. It's all up in the air. Can't decide what to do with it. My late husband took control of decorating our old house. It was all very … military."

"He was in the army?" I asked.

She nodded. "Forty years." She went to a different room and brought back a silver-framed photo. A man and a much-younger Katrina on their wedding day.

Her husband was a ramrod-straight-backed man with a small moustache and a barrel chest. He didn't exactly look like an easy-going, joyous kind of bloke. "That's my Andrew."

"You look happy together," I said, which seemed the most innocuous thing to offer up.

She smiled tightly.

"You must miss him terribly?"

She nodded a little. And then came towards me. "Right, you've a wee gash on your head, oh and a horrible scar, goodness, what's that from?"

I jerked away. "Ah, an old accident."

"Looks recent— oh. Gosh, my apologies. I just realised."

It was my turn to smile tightly. "I have these kinds of run-ins semi-regularly," I said, trying for a joke.

"I hope not," she said. "Right, I'll get the antiseptic. This is going to sting."

I gripped the chair underneath as she went to work. From the spot he'd taken at the doorway, Kenny panted at me happily.

"He's a lovely dog," Katrina offered breezily as she poured acid onto my head and dug about with a blunt ice-pick.

I winced and clenched my teeth. "Yup," I said, trying to open my jaw so I could form words. "Ghhhhh" was about as much as I could do. After Dhapinder had driven off, Katrina had taken one look at me and demanded I get in her car, and she'd driven me to hers for a check-up.

"I have a full first aid cupboard," she'd said when I demurred. "No, you need to have those grazes looked at."

So, we bundled in because Katrina wouldn't take no for an answer.

"Do I want to know what that was really about?" she'd asked as we'd driven back to the village.

"Um, once I figure it out, I'll let you know."

"Will you go to the police?" she asked. I hadn't given her an answer.

Now in her kitchen, she was busy getting leaves out of my hair and dabbing at me with cotton wool. "She really tried to run you off the road?"

"I think it was a case of mistaken identity," I said. "She seemed to think I'd done …" It clicked. "Sorry, one second, I need to check something."

I took my phone out and played the voicemail that Sonia had left me yesterday, which I'd never got around to listening to.

"Arden!" came Sonia's disembodied voice. She sounded panicked. "I've done something stupid. Holy shit, what was I thinking? I thought it would be easy. Oh God, they're totally gonna know it was me. Call me, I'm freaking out!"

The message ended. I banged my phone on my forehead, thinking hard.

"Friend of yours?" Katrina asked.

I nodded. Ow. "Who apparently doesn't listen and doesn't have a single shred of self-preservation."

"Oh, dear."

"Innit?"

"I'm glad that I passed by when I did," she said. She looked down at the stun gun on the kitchen table and shuddered. "No idea what that woman would have done if she'd been left to her own devices."

"Yes, thank you. And sorry to interrupt your day out … walking?"

She smiled. "I'd been to the beach, a nice ramble along the cliffs, really brushes away the cobwebs."

"Lovely. I should give it a try," I said.

I caught her looking at the photo again. "Can I ask you a question?"

She nodded as she moved from my head to my arm. She had a bowl of warm water and was washing off the dirt and crud to reveal that the skin on my arm was grazed. It stung like hell.

"If you could do it all over again, would you get married and do it the same?"

She thought for a second. "Yes, yes, I would," she said. "My Andrew, he wasn't the easiest man, but he was a good man. I … how do I put this, well, it was the nineteen-eighties, and you may think, oh, modern times. But, well, it wasn't, not really. Anyway, my first husband" – I gasped, and she nodded – "we married straight out of school. He was a squaddie. Anyway, it wasn't a great marriage. He liked a drink. We tried for a baby for many years and then eventually, when I was already in my thirties, over the hill in those days, I got pregnant with my Rabbie."

"Your son?"

"Aye, my Rab – well, we named him after his dad, but I always called him Rabbie, his middle name, after my father. And there are some things I'd do differently there. But, you know, in the beginning, my ex loved being a dad, up until he didn't. And then it was time for us to leave."

I nodded in sympathy. "My mum had to do the same." As much as I never wanted to see my mother again, I couldn't blame her for her actions in those early days. She had three young kids and a drunk husband. It was eat or be eaten, in her view, and she chose to be the hunter.

"So, you left your ex and found Andrew?"

"Yes, and Andrew was older than me, already in his forties. Never married. But a bright career. An officer. Very senior. Oh, for a girl like me with a wean and no man, it was a godsend. He was a good provider. We lived in a lovely big house; I never worried about bills again. Yes, it could have been a better marriage, and no, we weren't some great love story. But he was all I needed."

"So Rabbie followed his stepdad into the army?"

She nodded. "Dad. Andrew adopted him. But, yes, straight into the officers, oh, so proud of him." She blinked back tears.

"I'm so sorry, Katrina. I didn't mean to dig up painful memories."

She waved away my concern. "It's good to talk. It helps, actually. You're a lot easier to talk to than Odette bloody Douglas, who is always around trying to get every detail of my life out of me."

I shuddered.

She left the room again and came back with a different picture. "This is my Rabbie."

She showed me a handsome young lad in full army uniform posing for a picture. "Well, hello," I said.

Rabbie had been very striking looking with incredibly high cheekbones and almost Asiatic eyes. Chestnut curls were visible under his beret. "He modelled in his teens, you know? His father was Chinese-Malay."

"He must have had them lining up down the street."

"Oh, of course." She gave another of her sad smiles.

"Thank you for telling me that, Katrina," I said sincerely. "I hope the fresh start in Lilbury will be helpful for you. For all its quirks, I decided to stay here after Tarquin and all that, and I'm glad that I did."

"Yes," she said. "Lilbury's been just what I needed." She smiled. "I like you, Arden. You're one of the good ones. I'm glad you haven't got too mixed up in all this nasty business. Best you keep it that way."

She put the photo of her son back down, and his eyes looked up at me as his mother fussed, tending to my wounds.

Chapter 20

Have you ever been knocked off your feet by a speeding car? No? Well, I can tell you now, it fucking hurts. In fact, it hurts more the next day. So much so that the very thought of getting out of bed is too much for you. Especially when you haven't trained your dog yet to bring you food and painkillers.

Kennedy dropped the cat he'd carried up the stairs in his mouth at my feet and looked proud of himself. Roosevelt hissed and fled back downstairs.

"Ugh" was my answer to that situation.

Both my arms were bruised and swollen. My right elbow hurt too much to bend, and the grazes on my left arm and leg seemed to catch on everything and feel like the skin was being ripped off.

I gave up on being conscious and decided Tuesday would be better. I should have known.

Bang bang bang.

"Oh, come on," I begged the gods in heaven above. "You have got to be kidding me?" I rolled over in bed and was glad that it mostly didn't hurt anymore.

"FUCK OFF!" I yelled in the direction of the front of my house. Whoever was knocking, I didn't want to see them.

My bedroom window was open, and I heard my name being called. "Arden? Are you awake?" came Simon's voice.

Oh, no. He was the absolute last person I wanted to speak to. He wasn't going away, though, was he? I harrumphed and threw back the covers. It was late, already well into mid-morning, and I was in no mood for visitors or for doing things. I took my time opening the door. I went to the loo, brushed my teeth, and kept him waiting. If the prick was going to turn up at my house every fucking day with no bloody warning, he could learn to be patient.

Eventually, I deigned to open the door. No running gear today. He was back in those clingy skinny jeans and a blue polo shirt, which had capped sleeves and – goddammit – emphasised how huge his upper arms were.

"I don't want to see you or talk to you or … see you, did I say that already? Anyway, whatever, we're not speaking." I went to close the door.

Simon, being much stronger than I was, stopped me from doing that and peered in at me. "It's all over the village that you got hit by a car. Katrina told Roz at the shop, and now everyone knows. I had three people tell me about it this morning on my run. Odette thinks you were dogging."

I rolled my eyes. "It was a case of mistaken identity."

He frowned. "It … it was on purpose?"

"I'm an enigma wrapped in a riddle, wrapped in … something else, Parma ham? I don't know. I forget that quote," I snapped.

"Are you okay, though?"

I shrugged. "Nothing to worry about." I went to shut the door again. Simon kept himself in the way. "Fine, come in, why don't you?"

I walked off and left him to it. I needed coffee.

"You're limping."

"I got hit by a car," I reminded him through gritted teeth. "It's fine, as soon as I'm fully awake, it'll probably subside."

"We need to talk about the other night."

"Oh, do we?" I answered in a sneery tone. "What, so I can hear more lies? Frankly, Simon, I'm not in the mood. You asked me for my help. I gave you my help. When push came to shove, you weren't interested in telling me what was going on."

"I went to see Jed yesterday."

The kettle was boiling. I threw my coffee cup down and shrugged.

"I didn't want to tell you everything, because it doesn't just affect me," he said.

Still ignoring him, I spooned the instant coffee in – Simon grimaced – and then the sugar. Kennedy sat at my feet, hoping that if I made toast, he might get some.

"You found something at Riz's house," Simon said after a lengthy silence. "Didn't you?"

I looked anywhere but him. I drank my coffee and ate my toast. Kennedy ate his toast. We munched along quite contentedly. "Arden, stop sulking and talk to me! Jesus Christ, you are the most infuriating man on the planet! I leave you alone for two fucking seconds and you get hit by a car! You want to break into houses! You run around screaming at Guy at two in the morning! Your life is a fucking soap opera!"

"You have no idea," I muttered.

"What?" he snapped.

"I said you have no idea," I yelled. "Fine, you wanna know what I found?" I stalked around to where the jacket that I'd worn to Riz's house was hung up and searched in the pocket for the piece of paper. "Here." I threw it at Simon and stalked back to my coffee.

He picked it up from where it had fluttered to the ground.

"What's this?"

"Use your spy-sense and tell me."

"It's a letter. From a barrister … from. Oh."

"From Oliver Ross. Yes, my ex-boyfriend. I don't recognise the name he's sending it to, but it's Riz's address. And it was in Riz's things. Riz knew Ollie, how? Why? What the fuck does my ex have to do with whatever crazy plan your fiancé was cooking up? How is he involved, Simon? Does this mean I'm involved?"

Simon stared at the paper. "I had no idea."

"*Noooo*, because why would you? Why would you have a clue that the man you were going to marry was a fucking psychopath stalker?"

I slammed my cup down and paced my kitchen (now *I* was doing it, apparently). Simon continued to stare at the note. "I have some ideas of what this could mean. Have you spoken to Oliver about it?"

"No. No, I fucking haven't," I snapped. "Too busy being lied to and hit by cars," I added churlishly. Whatever. I was in a mood.

"We need to find out the truth behind this," he said, flourishing the letter at me. "We need to figure out if Riz or … or this secret second Marina knew about this. It could mean the person was gunning for you, too. It could mean that the newspaper article wasn't only because your name had been trending on Twitter."

"Ollie doesn't know Riz," I said. "He'd never heard of him before the photos leaked. He's never even been to Salisbury, as far as I know. And he definitely doesn't hang around with Labour Party apparatchiks."

"As far as you know," Simon said.

I glared at him. "I'll ring him," I said. "Right now. I'll put him on speaker."

Simon shook his head. "It's a piece of piss to lie convincingly down the phone. And if Ollie's been tricked, then he won't even know he's doing it. Best to do it in person."

"What? We can't. He's in London. Well, he might come down this weekend."

He huffed at this. "No, that's too late. The by-election is two days away. What if it's connected?"

"You think this has all been some grand scheme to get Suzy Rabbit elected? Give over."

"I don't know," he said. He took over pacing. Kennedy instantly got up and followed him.

"Fine. We go to London to see him." He checked his watch. "If we leave now, we can be there by 2 p.m."

I rolled my eyes. "I'm not dropping everything to go to London. I have shit to do. I have a book to finish. I have emails from my editor piling up. I've been ignoring them to chase murderers around the countryside."

"Arden, please," Simon said. "Please, do this for me, and I promise I won't ask anything else."

My resistance failed. Judgey Simon was gone. Heartbroken, grief-stricken Simon was back. Mad with pain and anguish. The Simon who needed answers. It happened so quickly – maybe he was acting. I didn't want to imagine that Simon had been manipulating me this entire time.

I shook my head. "Stupid, stupid, stupid." I was still glaring at him. "Fine, but we can't take Kenny, it's not fair for him to spend six hours in a car with us on a hot day. I'm going for a shower. You ring Nigella and ask if she'll take him for the afternoon."

He nodded, and I departed upstairs. I took a long shower, trying to calm my nerves. Stupid Simon bloody Anson and his stupid bloody … arms. And his stupid hair that I wanted to run my fingers through, and his stupid crooked bottom tooth that made me want to put my fingers in his mouth, and his thighs like tree trunks that I wanted gripped around my waist while he …

There was a knock on the door. "You ready? You've been in there for ages."

I absolutely did not lose my footing and fall spreadeagled on the shower floor. "Yup, just a minute, thanks."

Simon went and picked up his truck while I dropped off Kenny at Gella's house.

"Why can't we take my car?"

"Will that thing even get us to London?" he'd asked, giving the tyre a kick.

"Rude," I told him.

Nigella was waiting at her door for me when I arrived. "Where exactly are you and Simon off to?" she asked as I walked up her path.

"London," I said, my voice strangled. "It's a long story. I'm doing what you told me to do. Trying to keep him from doing anything stupid."

"And what about you doing anything stupid?" She touched the graze on my arm and grimaced. "Have you spoken to Sonia? Poor thing has been out of her mind. I don't know what's going on, but she's all over the show."

I shook my head. "Could you look out for her? I'll see her tonight when I'm back or tomorrow. But make sure she's okay?"

Nigella narrowed her eyes. "Of course, though I may need to hear the full story about what's going on."

I kissed her on the cheek and handed her Kenny's lead. "Trust me, you don't want to know. Anyway, thanks for looking after him. You sure it's not too much trouble?"

She crouched to give Kenny a stroke. "Not at all, the boys will be over the moon to play with him. If I end up having to get them a dog, I'm blaming you."

Simon pulled up at the end of her garden in his ridiculous pickup truck. Which was a blessing as it stopped me from telling Nigella that if she wanted to blame me for things, she needed to join a very long line.

I gave Kenny a kiss. "Have fun," Nigella said with a wink and took him inside, stopping to give Simon a wave.

"Can I make a quick call?" I asked as I got in the truck.

He glared. It had already been well over an hour since we'd agreed to this, we now wouldn't reach London until mid-afternoon at the absolute earliest. He held up his hands in defeat.

"Thanks." I rang Sonia.

At that moment, my absolution came in the shape of Odette Douglas. She leaned in the truck. "Oh, Simon. I saw Nigella, but she mustn't have heard me calling as she slammed her door quickish. Probably trying to contain Arden's vicious, brutish mutt. But how are you, darling? Me? I'm so fatigued. Gosh, pregnancy is tiring. Lucky you, gay men don't have families, so you'll never have children and won't ever have to worry about anything like that."

Sonia finally answered.

"Arden, thank God. You're alive."

"Were you worried I might not be?" Wish I wasn't having this conversation next to an employee of the British Government.

"Well, after I— ahem, was told about the break-in on Sunday, I was so worried. Dhapinder and Trevor were spitting tacks. Even Dad had to tell them to calm down or leave. Dhaps looked like she wanted to kill someone."

"Yeah, about that …"

"Oh my God!"

"Yeah."

"That's it. I can't work there any longer. I have to quit. I have to get out. They're crazy."

"Uh, no, don't do that. Wait a few weeks, maybe a month. Take some time off, say the break-in shook you up. And then wait a bit, and then quit. Okay?"

Sonia blubbed for five minutes, telling me how sorry she was. "I had to lie to Adebayo!" she cried. Simon drummed his fingers on the dashboard.

"Uh-huh, listen, I gotta go. But ring Nigella. She's waiting on your call and has a shoulder ready to cry on."

Eventually, Sonia hung up, and I turned to Simon. "Right, ready." He wound the window up even as Odette was still talking.

"What was all that about?" he asked.

I made a face. "Just another aspect of my life that's spiralling out of control."

Simon said nothing. He started the engine, and we set sail for London.

It wasn't long after we started driving that the inevitable silence overtook us. Simon cleared his throat. I looked at him. He said nothing.

As we made our way past Sittingston, he cleared his throat again. This time, he tried to say something. Eventually, words left his mouth. "Sorry if I've been a bit judgemental to you. Especially that time I woke you up."

I frowned. "When exactly?"

"When I turned up at your house, and you'd been asleep all day. I didn't mean to make you feel … I understand how horrible the situation with Tarquin was; I shouldn't have judged you for going through things."

"It's okay."

"No, it's not. You're entitled to have emotions, and I acted like a wanker." He exhaled. This was costing him. "I know you're angry with me, but I … do care, Arden. If you need to talk, I'm happy to listen. That's what I was trying to say that day."

He steadfastly focused on the road.

It was me who cleared my throat this time. "Thank you. If I'm honest, no, I'm not okay."

He looked at me, finally.

"I haven't spoken to anyone about everything … I hoped it'd go away. But – I'm not struggling per se, or—" I tried to find the right words. "I feel … I feel like I'm in a fog. Like, I've woken up from a nap and no matter what I do – however many showers I take, or how many coffees I drink or walks in the fresh air I go on – I can't seem to shake this feeling. Like, I'm looking at my life happening through a window. Like, there's a pane of glass up between me and everything else in the world. I'm one step removed from it all."

"Arden," Simon said firmly. "I'm not a doctor or anything, so please take this with the biggest grain of salt, but I'm pretty sure that's a sign of clinical depression."

"Oh."

I screwed my face up. "I don't feel depressed. Okay, I'm not jumping out of bed in the morning, and …"

I felt his hand touch mine.

"It's okay."

"I don't want pills and doctors prodding about in my life," I whispered.

"Maybe talking about it will help?"

"What, with you?"

Simon frowned. "I have … friends who have had similar things. Been through similar bouts. I know my role is to be a mate and listen, ask how they're doing."

"Okay."

"So, how are you doing?" he said, flashing me a grin.

"Pretty shit, to be honest. My career is in the toilet, I found a dead body a few weeks ago, my ex tried to kill me, someone else tried to run me over, and now I have to go visit my other ex who cheated on me but wants to get back together, and you're mad at me because I slept with Errol Mottley—"

"No, I'm not," he said too quickly.

"Yes, you are."

"Arden." He paused, took a deep breath. "Your sex life is your own. We've discovered that we have very different viewpoints on sex. I just wish you made better decisions for yourself."

"I make perfectly good decisions. It's not like I intend for them to keep blowing up in my face."

"Maybe I've been a bit too casual over the years. But you, you're not like that. Everything leaves a mark on you."

He didn't need to act like he knew me. Or cared. "I've had my share of poor choices that ended up being perfectly enjoyable. I haven't shattered at them." I said.

"Right," he said firmly. He put his hand into a karate chop shape and began tapping the dashboard as he laid out his points. "But I want you to look after yourself. You're a good-looking guy. People are going to be drawn to you, and some of them aren't going to have your best interests at heart."

I scoffed. "I'm average looking."

He stared at me – for several seconds. "Eyes on the road, please. You're doing seventy-five," I said.

He made a choking sound. After a few seconds, he shook his head. "Jesus Christ, you have no idea, do you?" He shook his head again. "You're not faking it? All this time, I thought you were playing coy and innocent."

"What on earth are you talking about?"

"Arden," he said, in a tone of voice that made me think this was physically painful for him. "Why do you think men are constantly throwing themselves at you?"

He stopped talking. There was a silence for several seconds, where I tried to work out whether he was pulling my leg or not. Oh my God, he wasn't.

My reaction was instinctive: I laughed. Oh, how I laughed. I kept laughing. Several minutes later, I was still laughing. Clutching-at-my-sides laughing. "You cannot be serious."

He shrugged. "You are the best-looking person I've ever slept with. I've seen some of the men Tarquin hooked up with – he's had models and dated Eurotrash party boys. You are better looking than them. Guy isn't exactly a slouch either; he's had a couple of boyfriends I've met over the years who were real head-turners, and yet, he couldn't wait five minutes to ask you out."

I made small stuttering noises. "I'm … okay looking," I said eventually.

"I'm not trying to give you an ego. Actually, maybe you could use it. Your self-esteem needs some work." He grinned.

I was silent for a few minutes, watching the countryside go past. I knew I was okay looking … my mother used to tell me I was her Angel-Faced boy. But I was the baby of the family, so of course she would tell me how cute I was.

Loads of men had leered at me in bars. But … huh. Maybe.

I rubbed at a speck of dirt on the window. After a few more minutes, I spoke again. "Did you tell Riz we slept together?"

Simon looked at me and then shook his head. "No, he … Well, I think he worked it out. He must have put the timeline together in his head and gave me a look when you came to Honningtons that night."

I nodded.

"Do you regret sleeping with me?" I asked in a small voice.

"No, not at all," he said. "It was fun, and we both needed it." There was a long, pregnant pause. "I'm sorry that it got in the way of us becoming friends." He paused again. "I'm sorry that *I* let it get in the way of us becoming friends."

I nodded. Simon had no idea that I'd fancied – or still fancied, maybe – him. That I'd been desperately hurt he hadn't wanted to see me again or have anything more from me. The information that Simon thought I was good-looking was churning in my gut. However, it seemed like his good opinion was mirrored by an equal feeling that I was a bit unstable and vacant. And that I invited too many men into my bed. 'I wish you made better decisions.' Hardly a ringing endorsement.

We were quiet again as the countryside whizzed past. It was blazing hot outside, and Simon turned the air con in the car up high, which made conversation harder over the noise.

But I tried, my anxiety gnawing at me. "Do you really think Ollie will be able to help?"

Simon shrugged.

"I don't want you to get your hopes up," I said. "You think I know what I'm doing, but I have no idea."

He rolled his eyes. "Now you tell me."

"Simon, I'm being serious, there's a good chance this is a weird coincidence. Don't build up your hopes; we're not going to walk into Ollie's office and he'll go, *Oh, of course, the man with the smoking gun who was in here two weeks ago. Yes, his name is Bob and here's his address and phone number.*"

"Yes, of course I fucking know," he snapped. "I'm not an idiot."

"I'm just saying, I don't know how things work in spy world, where you pretend to be a handyman or whatever, but it was dumb luck that I found Tarquin—"

"Yeah, I get it, Arden, thank you. You can stop talking now," he said tersely.

"Not trying to belittle—"

"Stop. Talking."

He said it through gritted teeth and then switched on the radio to avoid any further conversation.

I slumped back in my seat and decided to stay silent until we got to London. Old Simon had returned. The veil had lifted for a second but was now firmly back down. Judgey, sensible Simon still thought Arden was suspicious and slutty.

I dared to give him a quick look. He was staring at the road resolutely, his jaw tense. Probably regretted getting in this car with me.

Eventually, London appeared on the horizon, and I spoke up to navigate Simon to Ollie's office. "It's in Temple, so you'll—"

"Yeah, I know where I'm going."

"There's a car park on Bouverie Street that we could—"

"I said, I know where I'm going, thanks."

Okay.

We made it to the east side of Temple. The area is a bizarre, and particularly British, phenomenon. A private world of barristers' chambers enclosed in an ornate green space in central London. The hub of the legal world, where the ordinary public is granted access by express permission.

Simon parked the car, and we walked down – in silence – towards one of the side entrances near the river. "How do you know your way around London?"

"I lived here for four years," he said in a low growl.

"Oh, I didn't know you'd ever … Was it for work?"

He nodded. No more information was forthcoming. "Good chat, good chat," I said more than a little sarcastically.

He sighed. "I worked at the MOD building and lived in north London for a year, then in west London for two years. Then I got my own place for the last year in south London. Kennington."

"So … you moved to Lilbury after this?"

"I moved around a fair bit, did some time here and there. But yes, eventually I ended up in Lilbury."

I ruminated on this as we came up to the entrance. "Kennington. We could have been neighbours." I meant it as a joke and flashed a grin. Simon's grimace told me he wouldn't have liked it.

We came up to the gates. I didn't recognise the security guard on duty. Old Irish Mick must have been off today. His equally as jovial counterpart, Moses, a Nigerian guy who called every man, woman, child, and goat, "my friend" when he spoke to them, was also nowhere to be seen. "Bugger," I said. "I don't know that guard. They won't let us through unless we have an appointment."

"Leave it to me," he said and walked to the gate. After a few minutes, he beckoned me forward, and the security guard waved us through.

"What did you say?"

He shrugged. "That we had a meeting."

Wait, that never worked. I narrowed my eyes. Maybe he'd used some spy jiggery-pokery. That made me gulp. Good God, what exactly did Simon do at the MOD? Images of Russian double agents trussed up in nowt but their Y-fronts begging for mercy flashed through my mind. Wait, come back, was that Russian secret agent filling out those undies better than expected?

I pointed out Ollie's chambers. "It's over here."

We made our way through the main square, where senior barristers were allowed to park their cars, and then off to the side to a smaller, tree-lined part of the grounds. It still looked as it had always done – as if Hollywood had rocked up and spent millions recreating Georgian London with no detail forgotten nor expense spared.

Barristers in gowns and wigs walked past us carrying files and talking on phones.

I was keeping my distance from Simon – something that he seemed to be aware of. I hadn't thought he'd mind, but he kept trying to walk closer to me, and every time I veered away, he would veer too. I gulped. My mind running wild about Russian agents again. Maybe he was suspicious and was trying to keep tabs on me so he could stuff me in a suitcase later? Or poison me with an umbrella tip. Or …

Handyman. Spy. I wondered what the truth was. Actually, no, I didn't. Whatever world Simon inhabited, I wanted to be as far as fucking possible from it. The good thing about parents born under a repressive authoritarian regime: they taught you real quick to stay away from anyone who was gonna lead you down that path.

I tried to think about anything else. It was boiling. Even here, in this green oasis within the concrete jungle of central London, the sun beat down. God, for the cool green fields of Lilbury. I caught myself before I said something along the lines of *Gosh, this weather, eh?* Instead, I pulled my T-shirt from my body and shook it, hoping for a breeze to ease the sweat running down my torso. I looked over and caught Simon averting his eyes a little too slowly to prove he hadn't been peeking.

"It's this way," I said, trying to hide my smug expression.

Ollie's chambers took up a three-storied red-brick building with trees out the front and a main entrance that was up a small staircase. A clerk came out with a box of papers, as we were preparing to knock, and let us in. He didn't give us a second glance, even though my shorts and a T-shirt and Simon's jeans were hardly the normal attire of the clientele that came through here.

It looked the same; it smelled the same. A sea of male heads filled the clerks' room behind the tiny reception desk. Unlike most of London's business world, the majority of administration roles in barrister chambers were occupied by men. Women were few and far between. Which made me glad to see one female among the blokes, especially as she gasped when she spotted me.

"Arden!" she cried from her seat and came up to the desk to gape at me.

"Hello, love," I said and accepted the hug she offered.

"What are you doing here?" she asked in an accent of purest Essex. "We never expected to see you again. Oh, but it's good to see you, though. You're looking …" Her eyes took me in, and she couldn't say 'good' without lying. And then she noticed Simon.

"Simon, this is Natalie, one of the receptionists. Natalie, this is my … neighbour, Simon. We're here to see Ollie."

She smiled. "'Course." She checked the computer for a second and then frowned. "There's no meeting booked …"

I winked. "It's a personal matter, Natalie."

She grinned. "I'll give him a ring." She picked up the phone and punched his extension in and frowned again. "No answer," she said, hanging up and then checking the computer. "He's not scheduled anything."

Huh. I'd been so sure he'd be here; I hadn't even bothered to text him to make sure. Then out of the corner of my eye, I caught a familiar shape. One of the secretaries from upstairs. She saw me as I saw her.

"Arden," she said politely. "Fancy seeing you here."

"Hello, Janet," I said equally politely.

"Arden's looking for Oll— Mr Ross," said Natalie.

Janet smiled serenely. It didn't reach her eyes. "Oh, I'm afraid he's indisposed this afternoon."

"Really? Do you know when he'll be available?" I asked.

"I'm afraid, I don't." Another smile.

"You're his secretary. You know exactly where he is all the time." I smiled as firmly.

Natalie looked at her screen, her eyes not moving.

"Is he at a meeting? With a client? At … Court?" Simon interrupted. "We need to find him. It's urgent."

"Urgent?" both Janet and Natalie said in unison.

"Aye," Simon said in full Scottish. I widened my eyes. "I'm his cousin, from Dumfries. Am afraid there's a family emergency."

Janet faltered. She smiled again. "Well, if it's an emergency. He's working from home this afternoon."

Really? Working from home means 'unavailable'? I glared at her, and I hope she could feel it.

"Brilliant," Simon said, grinning. "Come on, Arden, if we hurry, he can probably speak to Great Aunt Minerva before they switch off the machine. Ladies, thank you." He grabbed my arm, and we left quickly.

He didn't let go until we made our way back out of the grounds and neared the car park. He gave me a look. "What did you do to piss off his secretary?" he asked eventually.

"Nothing," I snapped.

We got in the car. I was putting on my seatbelt when a thought occurred to me. "How did you know Ollie was from Dumfries?"

"Mm," he said, looking at the satnav, ignoring my question. "What's his postcode?"

"How did you know, though?"

He shrugged. "You must've mentioned it. Yeah, I remember now, you mentioned it ages ago."

I was sure I hadn't. He stared at me. "Postcode?"

I typed it in, and we made off. It should have only been a fifteen-minute drive to our – his – flat in Southwark, but it was late afternoon in summer, so the road was packed with taxis, buses, and a million office workers who'd clocked off early and were spilling into the streets as the pubs were already chock-a-block.

This time, Simon did let me give directions – even a shortcut that contradicted his satnav.

We arrived about half an hour later, after I directed him to a place he could park. I was glad, for once, that Ollie had always had a car, even if I'd rolled my eyes when he used to talk about his parking woes. You'd be amazed at the number of people in London who, when asked about parking, looked like you'd demanded they translate the Dead Sea scrolls. I'd been one of them before I'd met Ollie.

We made our way along Borough High Street, and then into the courtyard where you could enter our – his – block of flats.

Our luck was in, because once again, someone was coming out as we were going in. This time, we were acknowledged.

"Arden?" said a voice I recognised. I looked to see a thirty-something woman holding the hand of a toddler and staring at me like I was a ghost.

"Hello, Kasia!" I said in Polish.

"Oh my God, it's been so long. What on earth are you doing here?" she said and grabbed me for a hug. "It's good to see you! I wish I had time to stop and chat, but I have to get this one to the babysitter before my shift starts."

She kissed me on the cheek, gave Simon a quizzical look, and then stopped as she was about to head off – "Are you and Oliver getting back together?"

"Um, it's complicated," I said, glad we were still speaking Polish. Simon was following our conversation but, thankfully, couldn't understand.

She raised an eyebrow and then leaned back in. "He's been a wreck. I made him soup. He never ate it. But I think you did the right thing. Or maybe not … maybe you should come back." She shrugged.

"Thanks, Kasia. Edifying as ever." I rolled my eyes. She grinned.

She gave me a wave and then hurried off, dragging poor wee … I wanna say … Philip behind her? No, Marcin. Kamil?

"Friend?" Simon asked.

"My downstairs – my *old* downstairs neighbour. Kasia."

Simon said nothing and held the door open for us instead. Inside, the cloying familiarity was almost too much. I had to stop from turning heel and bolting. The last time I'd been here was to move my stuff out.

I took a deep breath and called the lift. In we got and I pressed the button for the third floor. I felt sick, and that urge to bolt was still there. What would Ollie say about me turning up on his doorstep like this? Oh, God, it was going to give off all the mixed signals, and I had no energy for that. No, it was for Simon. For Riz. We needed info. Would Ollie be able to tell Simon and I had once had sex? Would we act weird? Could he smell it?

I must've been giving off a vibe because Simon spoke up. "Are you okay? You're basically vibrating."

"Yup, fine. Finefinefine."

The doors opened and I walked down the corridor to our – Ollie's – flat and knocked. No answer. "He might've gone out, we should go—"

Simon pounded on the door.

I cringed at the volume.

Footsteps approached from the other side.

The door opened. "Hi, Ollie," I said.

He had been on the phone. "Riiiiiight," he said slowly to either us or the person on the line. "Katharina, I'm going to have to call you back. Yup, yup, great. Bye." He hung up and then looked at me and then at Simon.

He was wearing a pair of linen sleep pants, which I'd never seen him in before, and an old white T-shirt, barefoot and with his hair mussed from running his hands through it.

"Um, what are you doing here?" he said to me. "And who are you?"

Simon scowled. "We need to speak to you."

Ollie gave me a look, and I held up my hands. "Can we come in? It's important, I swear."

He moved out of the way, and I came in, followed by Simon. I took in the familiar scene. The apartment was rectangular. The hallway to the front door was in the middle between the spare bedroom on the right and the bathroom on the left. The hallway opened to a large room, with the kitchen in the corner, and the dining table and living space in an open plan configuration. Double-height windows ran the length of the right-hand side of the room, giving big clues to the building's former life as a factory. A staircase sat snugly in the corner, which led up to the main bedroom and bathroom en suite, with a large mezzanine-style opening over the living room.

It was a big, light, airy apartment with oodles of space and had been a lovely home. I missed it terribly.

Just as Ollie had said when we'd been in Surrey, he'd made a few changes. A couple of pieces of furniture were in different places, and some others were gone completely. A wall was a different colour. A rug was new. I tried to remind myself I didn't live here anymore, and my opinion on this didn't matter.

Ollie was staring at me. Then staring at Simon. Simon was looking blithely at me, like he really couldn't care less.

"Sorry, I wasn't expecting …" Ollie caught my eye and looked down at himself. "I'll go change."

He disappeared up the stairs and a minute later appeared in a nicer shirt and a pair of jeans.

"So, um, right, what's happening?"

"Okay, Ollie, this is Simon. Simon Anson, Ollie Ross."

"Nice to meet you," they said together, neither looking at the other.

Ollie frowned. "You're the handyman, right? The one who did Ard's kitchen?"

"Handyman," I scoffed.

"More or less," Simon said, giving me a look.

"Which means … oh, shit. You're—"

"Yes, he is, and yes, he did, and yes to every other question," I snapped. "Which brings us to why we're here." I flourished the paper. "We've been trying to find out what happened to Riz ourselves."

Ollie's face fell. "Arden, not again."

I ignored that and kept talking. "We found this. We think the murder was linked to the leaking of Guy's sex tape and the attempted murder of JedRev."

"What?" he said, looking confused. "Who or what is a JedRev?"

"The vicar, obviously," Simon said.

I scrubbed my face. "We're not explaining this very well."

"No, not at all." Ollie cocked his head to the side. "Arden, can I speak to you for a second … in private?"

"Um, we're kind of in a hurry—"

"No, this trumps that."

"We don't have time," Simon said.

I groaned. "Fine." I stormed past them both. Ollie made for the staircase up to the main bedroom, but I carried on into the spare room, which doubled up as a study. I had never used it when I lived here, always preferring to work at the dining table, and let Ollie keep it as his office.

He'd been working here this afternoon; his laptop was open with a half-written email, and papers were all over the desk. As well as a nearly empty iced caramel latte frappe thingy from Starbucks.

"Arden, what the hell?" he whisper-snarled, closing the door.

"Sorry to disturb you like this, and you shouldn't worry, I'm not doing anything dangerous—"

"What, no, I don't care about that. I want you here. And that's fine, but we fucked all night two weeks ago, and then I basically can't get a word out of you, and now you turn up in London, what the hell?"

"Could you keep your voice down?"

He gave me a look. "Who is Simon? Why don't you want him to know?"

"Because his fiancé just got murdered, so stop talking about people fucking," I said, scrambling for a reason.

"Is that why you've disappeared? I have debated getting in the car and driving down to you every night since I came back. I was sure we could have a chance. I was thinking you'd be upset, but instead, you've thrown yourself into this shit again, honestly, Arden, just because of what happened doesn't mean you have to get involved every time!"

"Get involved? What— oh. Oh, yeah, that's what happened."

He glared. "What do you mean?"

I grimaced. "I found Riz's body. I've been involved – inadvertently – since the beginning."

Ollie's face fell. "Oh, Jesus, Ard. Fucking hell, that's heavy. Are you okay?" He came up to me and hugged me. "Why didn't you say? Bloody hell, I knew I should have come down to see you. You could've told me; I would have dropped everything."

"It's fine, it's *fine*. I'm fine, the cops were fine, everything was fine."

He was giving me another look. "Why were the cops 'fine'?" He sighed. "Oh, God, what have you got yourself mixed up in?"

I played for time, but Ollie was giving me his best barrister look, and I was crumbling. "I … I have history with the cops who are running the case; it is the same team who investigated Arabella's murder."

"So, they hate you."

"No! Well, actually, yes."

"And why do they think you're involved?"

"They don't, well, they did, a little bit, but I have an alibi and everything for who I was with at the time of the murder."

"Which was?"

I didn't answer. Ollie's nostrils flared. "Him?" he yelled. "Simon?"

"What, no!" I stumbled for words. "No, anyway, that isn't the point. The point is, we found something, and it involves you."

"What?" He was going red. "Who was he then?"

I groaned. Why? Why was this my life? "Some guy. It doesn't matter. What matters is that we think you might be connected to someone who orchestrated this, and we need to know if they contacted you on purpose."

"Who was the man you were with? Not Guy? Because we've all seen what he's packing." He sniffed. "I'm bigger."

"Oh my God – fine, it was a guy called Errol! He worked on the campaign, okay? He seemed nice enough at the time, but it was nothing special."

Ollie went quiet for a second. Then his face darkened. "Wait, you were with him the night Riz was killed. The Saturday night? So, two nights after we slept together? Wow, Arden, classy. You just jump from man to man now." He paced the room.

"Ollie …"

"I thought that night meant something!" he yelled.

"Of course it did!"

"But you went and found someone else five minutes later."

"Excuse me? You're one to talk. And for your information, I slept with Errol because he … kind of saved me from a bunch of reporters when that article about my brother came out. I was upset, Ollie. He stayed with me and stopped me from making a huge mess of things, and one thing led to another," my voice choked. "Like I said, I was upset, and I wanted to forget about everything."

Ollie was looking everywhere else but me. After several moments of silence, he spoke again. "If you were upset, then I'm right here. I was ringing you all night. But you never answered."

I blinked back tears. Every time we spoke, I ended up feeling worse.

"This was a terrible mistake. I shouldn't have come here. I'll go."

I left and walked out to the living room, where Simon was still standing in the same spot. "I assume you heard all of that?"

He shrugged. "I mean, you were both yelling."

"Christ, this day just gets worse." I turned on my heel and made for the door. Ollie walked out in front of me.

"Wait," he said. "Talk to me about what you need."

Chapter 21

We all took seats at the dining table. Ollie sat across from me and Simon.

"Right, well, there's this letter," I said.

"Start from the beginning," Ollie interrupted.

I inhaled through my nose. "Okay, fine. Right, um. Right, so Riz and Simon" – I gestured at Simon, and both men rolled their eyes – "got back together in February. They're engaged. But it was set up by Riz's campaign manager, Marina."

"Okaaaaay," Ollie said. "Already not liking this."

"Oh, it gets so much worse," I said. "So, the campaign starts. Riz is twenty points behind Guy and the Lib Dem candidate, Suzy. But that's to be expected because it's Dorset."

Ollie nodded. "Can I get either of you a drink?"

"No, please pay attention – Arden, show him the letter."

I sighed. "Fine." I grabbed it out of my pocket. It had become crumpled. "Long story short, we found this in Riz's possessions the other day."

I slid it across to him. Ollie read it. "This is from my office," he said.

We both nodded.

"We'd gathered that," Simon said. Ollie glared at him.

"Be nice," I whispered. Simon rolled his eyes.

"This is taking too long. Look, did Riz come to visit you or not? He may have wanted information about Arden."

Ollie was puzzled. "Why would he want information on Arden?" He looked at me. "You're not in danger, are you? And what happened to your arm?"

"Oh, that. I fell over on a run."

"We don't know why he wanted info on Arden," Simon interrupted. "We think he may have been looking for dirt to smear him with."

"So, he came to me?" Ollie asked. "Hm. I don't remember writing this letter. It's a fairly generic response, so I probably would have asked Janet to draft it. I don't recognise the name."

"Yes, it's addressed to a Mrs S Murray."

"And we don't know who that is. Do you have any clients called that?"

Ollie shook his head. "Ard, babe, you know I can't tell you that."

Simon glared at this answer. "Can't or won't?"

"Excuse me?" Ollie turned to me. "Can you call off your ginger hound, please?"

I pinched the bridge of my nose. "Can we focus and not snipe at each other?" I could feel the worst tension headache coming on.

"I'll get us all a drink of something to cool down," Ollie said and left the table.

"God, is he always this obtuse?" Simon muttered.

I was tempted to remind him that Ollie was a lawyer and got paid by the hour.

Ollie returned with three glasses of water. He put mine down in front of me and rubbed my shoulder. "You cut your head when you fell, as well? Ouch." He reached up and ran his fingers through my hair to look at it.

I could feel Simon trying not to fly into a rage next to me. I smiled at Ollie and removed his hand. "We've not much time. Could you … Could you check with Janet? Maybe she knows the name?"

"Sure, but I'm limited to what I can tell you. Honestly, Arden, you know they can disbar me for this sort of stuff."

I pulled a face. "You once said the Bar Standards Board would let Charles Manson practise, whereas solicitors get struck off if they so much as blow their nose on the wrong side of the road."

"Yes, well, that was before my chambers realised about my digging into Miles Sweet. They sacked poor Tim even though he hadn't done anything wrong."

I shivered. That man's name.

Ollie sighed but then grabbed his phone. "I'll give Janet a ring." He went into the study.

Simon was silent. I pushed his glass towards him. "London tap water. Drink it all up, it's the yummiest in the world."

"You let him call you 'babe' still."

I shrugged. "Force of habit."

"You slept with him after the photos were leaked. But you won't tell him about where you got your bruises."

"I …" I didn't want to talk about this. "It's private. Ollie and I are complicated. We were basically married and … we're detangling ourselves. Slowly."

"What does that make Tarquin then?"

"Ollie and I are broken up, okay?" I growled. My temper was close to snapping. "It was a relapse."

It was a million degrees, my entire body ached, I was lying to Ollie, and Simon was being a prick. Today could, quite frankly, sit on it and swivel.

Ollie came back into the room, and I prayed he hadn't heard what I'd said. "It's the weirdest bloody thing. Janet has never heard of S Murray. Nor do we have any record of them on file as a client."

"But … how?" I asked.

"She has to be lying," Simon said. I shook my head. Nope, Janet was painfully loyal to Ollie. That I knew all too well. Simon stood up and started pacing. Christ, the man must wear out carpets.

Ollie was staring at his phone as if the answer would magically jump out at him. "Janet is the only person at the chambers who is allowed to sign letters in my name. It'd be their job instantly if anyone else did so. Everyone knows it, and we've never had cases of people doing it.

At other chambers, it crops up sometimes, but the partners at mine are so strict they'd never stand for it." He shook his head. "But even the wording used here, it's Janet's voice. This is the exact phrase she uses in all her generic *hi, chasing this up for you, sir* letters. She sends ten per day."

Simon paced harder.

"This doesn't make any sense," Ollie said. "Why was Riz looking for dirt on you in the first place? You said you only met him that one time at the village hall."

Simon stopped pacing, and we looked at each other. I took a deep breath. "Riz was the person who leaked the photos of Guy Frobisher."

Ollie's reactions were going to be seared into my brain for all time. At first, he went bug-eyed and made a choking noise, then he took a long gulp of water. Then he went slightly red and put his head between his knees. Then he joined Simon in pacing, and then he sat down again very suddenly and was quite pale.

"This full story," he said.

"Yes?"

"I think you should tell me."

"I thought you didn't need to know?"

"That was before I knew you were connected to the biggest fucking story to hit British politics since the Profumo Affair! Jesus, Arden, that Birmingham MP got caught trying to flee the country after the photos of her dogging got leaked!"

"We don't have time to give him the whole story!" Simon snapped. "It's already gone five o'clock. Look." He held up his phone. "Do you recognise this man?"

He had Riz's photo on his screen.

"Yes, that's Riz Patel. The chap who was murdered."

"Did you ever meet him, or did he come to your office?"

"No, I only saw him on TV."

"Right." He pressed buttons frantically. "What about this woman?" He held up Marina Holt's photo. Ollie shook his head.

Suzy Rabbit? A head shake.

Errol Mottley? A head shake.

"What about this man?" he said, holding up another photo.

"Who's that?" I asked.

"Peter Holt. Marina's husband."

"Isn't he in prison?"

"It's worth a shot. That letter could be old."

I held it up. "It's dated last month."

Simon slammed his fist down on the table, and both Ollie and I jumped. "I meant, fuck, that the person could have had an appointment with Ollie months and months ago – years ago – and they only asked the letter to be sent now."

There was a long silence. Simon crossed the room and stood by the window, his hands resting on the panes of glass, his head bowed. I didn't dare move a muscle. Ollie shifted the paper out of the way of the water that had spilt from his glass when Simon banged the table. I could hear Simon breathing heavily from the window. Counting backwards from one hundred, maybe, so he didn't kill both of us.

"In two days," Simon said after the silence had dragged on for longer than any of us were comfortable with, "Suzy Rabbit is going to get elected to Parliament, and I need to know she was not part of this. I cannot let that happen. I will not have a murderer sitting in the House of Commons."

Spies. Deep down, they're patriots, really.

Ollie gave a large exhale. He grabbed his phone. "Janet, me again. Look, massive favour. I need a list of every client and matter I've handled since joining chambers couriered over to my place. Yes, I know it's five thirty.

Look, I— yes, I know, I wouldn't ask if it wasn't super important. Yes, thank you, yes, grab whoever you can, promise everyone in the office a bottle of their favourite tipple on me if they help you. Thank you."

He hung up. "So, who wants a takeaway?"

Reader, if anyone ever says, "Hey, you know what'd be fun?", the answer they are not looking for is: "Digging through your ex-boyfriend's near-ten-year-long list of clients spanning almost the length of his career, and cross-referencing every name and address searching for people who may or may not have been plotting to kill someone."

At midnight, we took a break.

I moved the rice in my bowl of chicken korma around. Simon was on the sofa swigging a beer, while Ollie and I sat on the floor around the coffee table, munching on the last dregs of our curries.

"This isn't as good as normal." I let the rice fall off my fork.

"Yeah," Ollie said. "Spice Palace closed last year. I'm trying, slowly but surely, all the other Indian places nearby. This is from Punjabi Dreams."

I pulled a face. "With the terrible neon elephant in the window next to the Nigerian weave shop? God."

"I know. But they're better than Taj Ma-hungry. Their jalfrezi and I were not the best of friends."

"How many more boxes do we have?" Simon asked. It was the first time he'd spoken in an hour or so.

"A lot," Ollie said. "But those are all years old. Unless your ex was plotting this back in 2010, I don't think he'll be in there."

"He's not my ex," Simon muttered. He reached forward and then paused.

Ollie pulled an awkward face at me. "Sorry," he mouthed.

Simon was still frowning at the takeaway boxes. "Who ate all the poppadoms?" he asked.

Ollie burst out laughing. "Oh, my friend, you are in the presence of the world's premier Indian side dish fiend. Put a samosa, an onion bhaji, or a poppadom near him and it's gone in a second. Those poppadoms were as good as eaten the second I brought them into the flat."

I blushed. I mean, he was right. God, I loved poppadoms.

Ollie was laughing but Simon was giving me the strangest look. He wasn't angry, he was … interested. A new fascinating fact about Arden.

"I like Indian food," I muttered into my files of names.

After we'd told Ollie the full story, which had taken the best part of an hour, he'd been on board to search the files. He'd given me plenty of looks over the past six hours, he'd muttered asides, and there had been several moments where I was concerned he was going to start asking awkward questions, but mostly he'd been well behaved.

When the boxes had arrived, Simon had turned into a different person. Gone was sullen, emotional Simon and in was workhorse, detail-orientated Simon. I realised I knew so little about him. I didn't even know what he actually did. What was a spy anyway? Somewhere between James Bond and *Spooks*?

Did he go on missions, with a gun and a licence to kill? Did he sit behind a computer all day and analyse text messages from bored Muslim teenage boys in east London in case they googled Syria one too many times?

I had no idea. What I did know was that he was probably quite good at it. He'd spent six hours going through filing without so much as a back stretch, whereas my pampered, work-shy hands were blistered, darling, blistered from having to touch all this coarse paper.

"Can I get anyone another drink?" Ollie said. He stood, stretched, let his T-shirt roll up a bit to show his flat stomach and then walked past me on the way to the kitchen. As he did, his fingers glided over my shoulder. It wasn't sexual, just affectionate. A long-standing habit of his, from the moment we'd got together. I nearly closed my eyes in the comfort of it.

Of course, Simon saw all of this and glared.

Needing a break, I too stood up and went into the bathroom for a piss. I splashed water on my face and tried to rub the tension from my temples. My head ached. My body ached even worse. Ollie had asked for more details on my alleged accident. I had demurred but eventually said, "You know what Kenny's like. He saw a squirrel. I'm lucky he didn't yank my arm out of my socket." He hadn't believed me.

So far, at least, Ollie and Simon had been somewhat civil to one another. Which was a bonus.

When I'd rung Nigella to tell her that it was likely our trip to London was an all-nighter, I'd left them alone for nearly ten minutes. I had come back to the living room with no one missing any teeth, so I assumed they had behaved.

Nigella had, of course, wanted information as to why she was now a dog-sitting service. "We might have a lead," I said. "Actually, we don't have a lead. Which is a lead in itself."

"Good God," she said. "This is like *House of Cards*, please tell me that none of you are playing the Kevin Spacey role?"

I left the bathroom and came into the living room, where it was just Simon. "Ollie's upstairs peeing as well," he said and took a gulp of his beer.

Ollie had set out a new bottle for me. I took a swig.

"You two still seem very close," Simon said. He fiddled with the label on his beer.

I shrugged. "As I said, we were practically married."

"He's still in love with you," he said in a voice devoid of expression. "He's devoted to you. You could turn up here covered in blood with a severed head in your bag and he wouldn't hesitate to get the bleach out."

I frowned at the mental image. "Very death-orientated, aren't you, Simon?"

He shrugged. "It must be nice," he said after a few seconds. "To have someone love you like that."

I flopped down on the floor again. "It didn't stop him from screwing the intern, so no, it wasn't really that nice."

The door to the bathroom upstairs opened, and Ollie made his way back down. I took another swig of my beer to make sure I kept my mouth shut.

We worked for a few more hours. At 3 a.m. I called time. "This is useless, and we're no closer to any clues."

"You're right," Simon said, which surprised me. "Let's call it a night." He took out his phone. "I'll see if I can find a hotel for a few hours' kip. I don't think I can drive." Simon had only drunk two beers over the course of the evening.

"Don't be stupid," Ollie said. "There's a spare room you can have." He stretched and then turned to me. "I put the fan on earlier in our room," he said. "It'll be nice and cool by now."

Our room.

"Um, I'll take the sofa," I said.

Ollie's face fell. "Oh, but … that's silly. You know that sofa is horrible to sleep on."

"I think it's the best idea. Simon can take the spare room, and I'll take the sofa." I was going to stay firm on this.

Simon watched both of us as we talked. "Sounds good to me," he said eventually. He stood and offered his hand to Ollie. "Thank you for all your help."

Ollie didn't take his eyes off me even as he reached to shake Simon's hand. His eyes were beseeching me. *Please come to bed with me. Please lie with me in the dark, and let's hold each other.*

I broke eye contact. No, no, no. It had to be done. The other week had been fun, but it was clearly a mistake to let anything like that happen between Ollie and me. My emotions for Ollie were still TBC in the long run, but he had made it obvious that his feelings for me were as strong as they ever had been. To do that to him again was cruel. For his own sake, I had to keep a distance.

Simon gave us a look over his shoulder as he departed for the bathroom before turning in.

I began to clear detritus from around the sofa. "I'll get you a blanket and some pillows," Ollie said, his voice thick with emotion.

In a moment of madness, I watched him go up the stairs to our old room and then followed. He was in front of the large linen cupboard in the corner of the room, finding me a blanket. I walked in, and he turned to stare at me. I hadn't been in here since the day I took my stuff.

It was the same. My side of the bed was emptier and a bit tidier, but a few things I'd left on the bedside table were still there. Ollie's pile of non-fiction political memoirs and pop science paperbacks were still piled up on his side. Some clothes strewn about. The print I'd chosen to go above the headboard was still there. I'd seen it in an art gallery in central London and knew it was perfect. It was a map of the clans of Scotland in the style of a London tube map. Simple, not particularly original, but it represented our lives and who we were. After we'd put it up, Ollie put his arm around me and gave me a kiss on the forehead. "We need to find one for Poland."

"We absolutely do not," I'd said and shrugged off his arm, but grinned.

I stared at it now. I cleared my throat. "Thank you for doing this. You didn't have to…" words failed. I sat down on the bed and stroked the duvet cover.

Ollie sat down next to me and took my hand in his own. "You know I'd do anything for you," he whispered.

I sighed. But then I lowered my head onto his shoulder and nuzzled. "I'm sorry I slept with Errol. If it makes you feel better, he turned out to be a bit of a bastard."

He chuckled. "Not really."

"I … I do appreciate you calling me. I do, I promise. It's … there's so much between us, Ollie. Sometimes it overwhelms me, and I can't face it. Every conversation between us feels like some momentous thing. That's why it was so nice in Surrey. It was just us again."

"I understand," he said quietly. "know if you changed your mind about getting back together, I'd be there in an instant. I'd move to Dorset. It could be us again. And Kenny."

"You'd be bored stupid in days. You think anything further out than Clapham is provincial."

"I mean, have you been to Streatham? Dear God."

I laughed, and he gave me a peck on the cheek. "I'm glad you came to me with this. I liked helping," he said.

"And you did help. Well, truly, not at all. Now it all makes even less sense."

The sound of a toilet flushing and the door to the main bathroom downstairs opening roused me from my little holiday of self-induced angst. I stood up and took the blankets and pillows that Ollie had dug out for me.

I ran my hands through his hair as I stood above where he sat on the bed. I leaned down and kissed the top of his head. "Goodnight, Ollie," I said and left the room.

When I got downstairs, I looked up and saw the light from underneath his bedroom door go out. Simon was leaning on the hallway wall. His hands in his pockets.

"I thought you'd changed your mind," he said quietly.

"What do you mean?" I whispered.

"About sleeping on the couch."

I shook my head. "Simon, don't."

He looked like he wanted to say something. The same expression appeared on his face that he'd had in the car when he'd been trying to apologise. But I was exhausted. I switched off the lights. "Goodnight," I said.

He turned and went into the bedroom.

Chapter 22

Of course, I didn't sleep a wink.

My mind was racing. Thoughts of the men in both bedrooms were in my mind. Thoughts of being chased by Dhapinder Bliss. Thoughts of Riz's face. The one time I got close to sleeping, his glassy open eyes appeared in my mind, and I jerked awake.

We were no closer to finding out who killed him, and the election was twenty-four hours away.

Not more than an hour after I turned in, it was bright sunshine outside. Because northern Europe and our 4 a.m. sunrises in summer.

I gave up on sleep and sat on my phone, hoping that Instagram would cure my ills. Like most things related to my phone, it made everything worse.

By 5 a.m., I'd put my clothes back on and dozed on the sofa as best I could. Ollie wouldn't be up for hours; he usually went into the office for 10 a.m., as barristers started a little later than most. The benefits of being self-employed.

At around 8 a.m., the door to the spare room opened, and an angry red-haired bastard emerged. He was wearing nothing but his boxers and looked dishevelled. He took one look at me, walked into the bathroom, and closed the door.

A few minutes later, I heard Ollie get up and turn on the shower in the en suite. I lay there in my sweaty T-shirt and wondered where my life was going.

Simon came out of the bathroom a few minutes later, freshly towelled off and once again in his boxers. A tight white pair.

"Good morning," I offered diplomatically.

He nodded. "I'll get dressed."

I hopped up and took his place in the bathroom. I spent too long under the shower, wanting the world outside to disappear.

Eventually, feeling somewhat refreshed, I turned the water off and dressed. I made do with the meagre toiletries in the bathroom – luckily, there was always toothpaste in here for people who stayed over – usually Ollie's friends or his parents or one of his annoying brothers. So, with some vigorous brushing, I was able to get rid of the dead animal that had crawled into my mouth in the night.

The living room I emerged into was very different from the one I had left twenty minutes earlier. Ollie, freshly showered and wearing one of his dark blue suits, was pouring cafetière coffee for Simon as they each munched on toast. Simon stood at the counter, fully dressed, with his shoes on and ready to leave at a moment's notice. The pair were laughing and joking and getting along. Why did that make me annoyed?

"Good morning, sleepy head," Ollie said. "Have you left any hot water for the rest of London?"

"Not intentionally," I said. He pushed a cup of coffee towards me.

"Made the way you like it. So, stultifying sweet and milky that you can't even tell it's coffee." He gestured to Simon. "I've been asking for more details on some of the aspects of this that don't make sense. It kept me up all night."

"None of it makes any bloody sense," I said, sipping my coffee as I sat to put my shoes on. "There's the whole Jed aspect we didn't even get to last night."

"The vicar?" Ollie asked. "What about him? Wait, the chap who got attacked?"

Simon's demeanour had completely changed in seconds. "Don't think I've forgotten," I told him. "Whatever it is, you need to tell us."

Ollie looked between us. "Wait, there's a whole other part of this you still haven't told me?" He glared at Simon. "Are you fucking joking, mate?"

"Oh, yes, there's some secret between Simon, Jed, and Guy Frobisher, which they've already lied to me about once." I was quite enjoying Simon's furious expression. His scowling and judgements had taken their toll on me, and well, I wanted answers. His endless moods be damned.

"Go on, tell us," Ollie said.

Simon hesitated. "There's more to it than that. Arden, you know the job I do, you know what could happen if I started talking about this stuff."

"No, I don't, Simon. I have no idea what you do. So don't try and fob me off with spy bullshit."

"Spy?" Ollie said, dribbling a bit of his coffee down his chin as he choked in surprise. He wiped it away before trying to ask more questions.

"I can't say anything in front of him," Simon said, jerking his head at Ollie.

"What's that mean?" Ollie asked. And the entente was gone. We'd lasted, oh, about fifteen minutes before it all went tits up. Ollie and Simon were both now yelling at each other. In the back of my mind, I was aware that this was mostly my fault.

"Pissing contest," I muttered under my breath. Honestly, if they wanted to know which of them had the bigger dick, I could tell them.

"It's none of your business!" yelled Simon.

"If it involves Arden, it is my business," Ollie yelled back.

In the middle of this, there was a knock at the door. A sudden silence descended. Ollie's eyes widened, and I could tell he was desperately trying not to look in the direction of the front door.

But all three of us did. "Are you going to get that?" I asked.

"Ignore it. They'll go away," he said.

Simon raised an eyebrow. "It might be your downstairs neighbour with more soup." I blanched – he'd understood our conversation yesterday? Wait, could Simon speak Polish?

I looked over at Ollie. He was flustered. He kept looking at the door out of the corner of his eye but trying to stay focused on me. There was another knock. I spun on my heel and walked to it.

Simon watched me go even as he resumed trading insults with Ollie.

I opened the door and had the breath taken out of my chest.

In front of me, standing proud, was a handsome man. He was younger than me by several years and several inches taller. He was wearing an immaculate charcoal grey suit and a crisp white shirt. His black ringlets were cut close to his head. His mouth was wide, his teeth straight and white, and his skin was olive and perfect. The hands that gripped his work bag were large and led to muscles on his arm that were sculpted from hours in the gym.

And he looked pissed off as hell.

"You," he snarled at me.

"Jamie," I said. My stomach dropped to the floor. He stormed past me into the flat, and I was left standing too dumbstruck to move.

He reached the kitchen. I could hear him behind me start to yell at Ollie, and Ollie yell back, but I couldn't bring myself to turn around. My feet were rooted to the spot. I couldn't breathe.

Did this mean … yes, Arden, it meant that. That was the only thing it could mean. Slowly, I closed the door and turned to face what was coming.

Jamie was yelling at Ollie, who was desperately trying to get past him, towards me. But Jamie waved his hands and tried to crowd him. Simon stood off to the side, watching the scene with his perpetual scowl. He saw me and looked concerned. "Arden?"

At my name, Ollie managed to push past Jamie and made to come towards me.

"Arden," he breathed.

"What is he doing here?" Jamie hissed before I could say anything.

"We were in the area," Simon said amiably.

"I didn't ask you; I don't even know who the fuck you are," Jamie spat out at him. "Ollie, did you invite him here?"

"Arden, I can explain," Ollie said, his voice strained. "This isn't what it looks like."

"You cancelled on me last night for him?" Jamie asked.

Ollie opened his mouth to speak, but I beat him to it. "Are you two together?" I demanded. Before Ollie could even answer, I turned to Simon: "Where are my manners? Simon, this is Jamie, with whom Ollie had an affair last year. Who he swore blind to me he hadn't seen in months."

"Excuse me?" Jamie yelled. "Just because he chose me—"

"We're not together," Ollie said, his eyes bearing down on me. He tried to move towards me, but I put my hand out to stop him. "It's just – it's casual, him and me. It's just an arrangement."

"Does he know that?" Simon muttered.

"Casual? We've been back together since Christmas," Jamie snapped.

I felt the last little part of my love for Ollie drain away. Everything had been a lie. Again.

"Since Christmas? Five months," I said to no one in particular. "All the begging and pleading to get back together was … what? An act. If I'd said yes, you'd have kept him on the side like before?"

"Of course not. Look, Jamie, you know we're just casual," he said, giving him a serious look. He turned back to me. "We were just passing the time—"

"Excuse me?" Jamie yelled again. Louder this time.

I stood for a few seconds and took a deep breath. I felt like I was going to be sick. "So … the one person I begged you to never see again. The one man I couldn't even stomach being in the same room as" – I threw Jamie a look at this, but he didn't even flinch – "is who you ran back to for a comfort fuck the moment I collected the last of my stuff? Jesus, Christmastime, I had clothes in the wardrobe here and you were still begging me to come back."

"Always the victim," Jamie muttered and rolled his eyes.

"I know, I know, it was stupid, but I was lonely and—"

"Anyone but him!" I yelled, my temper snapping and flying to opposite ends of the room. I picked up one of the stupid ornaments on the console table that I stood beside and threw it on the ground. "ANYONE ELSE! But. Him." Spit was forming at the corner of my mouth. I must look demented, and I didn't care. "You humiliated me for months with him, you invited me to that stupid summer barbecue with your chambers and introduced me to him." I pointed at Jamie, and this time he did flinch. "Half your fucking colleagues already knew; your secretary was already lying for you about it. We all stood there laughing, while you two had probably just finished fucking before I got there! And after all that, you couldn't find *anyone else*, out of all the thousands and thousands of gay men in London, that you could go with instead."

"Arden," he said again.

I whirled on Jamie. I hated him. I hated him more than anyone else in my entire life, and I always would. I hated his privilege. His degree from Cambridge. His RP accent. I hated that he was perfect for Ollie in every way I never would be. "You're a deceitful, nasty, little piece of shit, and I hope you die. You homewrecking slut." He jutted his chin out. "Remember the old saying: when a man marries his mistress, it creates a job opportunity."

I turned to Ollie, full of self-righteous rage. "As for you!" But I looked at him, his lip wobbling, his watery eyes and just felt … nothing. I paused. I took a deep breath. "You're not worth it. You're nothing to me."

I felt, rather than saw, something out of the corner of my eye, and Simon's arm arrived on mine. He gently chided me along to the door. "Come on, Arden. I've got our stuff. Let's go home."

"Arden!" Ollie called back to me. His footsteps followed us down the hall.

I turned to see him approach us, but Simon's hand flew out and landed on Ollie's chest, keeping him at a distance. "Not going to happen, mate."

"Fuck off," Ollie snapped and tried to surge forward, but Simon held him back. I walked out to the stairs and took them two at a time. After a few floors, I heard Simon's footsteps behind me, and then we came to the main entrance, where I exploded through the doors into the baking sunshine. The sky was a perfect blue, and already, London was hot enough to feel like your energy was being sapped from your body. But of course, Jamie had probably walked several streets in this heat and still looked perfect when he'd arrived, whereas I'd have looked like a dishevelled mole rat.

As I'd gone down the stairs, I'd been too shocked to think, but the fresh air jump-started my brain, and before I knew it, I was calling Ollie Ross every name under the sun that I could think of. "Fucking … piece of shit … lying … wanking … fucking tosspot … arsehole … cheating … two-faced … limp-dicked … wanker …

arsemonger … bastard … fucking stupid, ugly, waste of space, cunty, narcissistic, shit-eating, fuckface, prima donna, wankstain, little, bollocking evil, hateful, Scottish, cock-sucking, miserly, micro-dicked, weak-chinned, knobhead, string of piss, dumbarse, fucking *cunt*." I kept marching towards the car – or at least where I vaguely remembered Simon had parked the car – all the while my diatribe kept going. I ran out of words in English, so reverted to Polish. I reached a crescendo as I took a corner onto the street where I was ninety-nine per cent sure we'd parked – and scaring a mother with a child – I called Ollie a "horse-fucking cabbage sniffer" (it sounds better in Polish).

I reached Simon's car as my anger hit boiling point and my muttering burst out of me. I swung my fist down on the bonnet of his truck as hard as I could.

"KURWWWWWWWWWWWWWWWWA!" I screamed.

There was a long silence. I was panting – quite loudly.

"I'll admit you lost me when you switched to Polish. I knew a couple of them, but that last one, well, that's become universal," Simon said.

I was still panting.

Simon nodded and put the bags inside. "In you get." He opened the door, and after a few more seconds of huffing, I eventually slid into the seat and curled up in the corner. I didn't want to look at Simon, I didn't want to interact, and I definitely did not want to talk.

He seemed to understand this because, after a brief look at me, he put his sunglasses on and made his way out into the morning traffic. He switched on a playlist from his phone, and an upbeat techno song started playing.

We drove for about forty-five minutes. Simon began to slow down and took the exit to the motorway services.

"Why are we stopping?"

He looked at me. "Because we didn't finish breakfast. All your histrionics got in the way, and I'm a growing boy." He pulled into a parking space and got out. "Come on." He jerked his head to the building that promised all sorts of delicious carbs. I shook my head. I wanted to wallow. Wallowing was good.

"Suit yourself, I'll bring you back something."

I sat in the car and – as was my wont so often – felt ruinously sorry for myself. My phone buzzed in my hand. Another message from … him. I looked at the screen but didn't open the message. I deleted it unread.

Simon was gone a long time. After twenty-five minutes, I started to wonder if he was coming back. He'd taken the keys. I shrugged. Oh, well, the only way to make my day worse was to lock myself out of the car, so I did just that. There was a pretty-ish copse of trees off to the side of the car park with a few ducks around. Some picnic tables were scattered about, and all of them were empty. I sat. I stared into the middle distance.

Eventually, I saw a red-haired man make his way out to the car holding a selection of baked goods in little white bags with blue logos on them. He looked around when he saw the car was empty and seemed slightly panicked for a second. I raised my hand and gave a wave, so he'd see me. Odd to think about Simon being worried about me.

He came over to the table and laid his wares out in front of us. "I bring sustenance." He opened a bag and bit into a sausage roll. After a few seconds of chewing, he looked in my direction and slid a cup of coffee towards me. "Food and drink is good. It'll make you feel better."

I did what I always did whenever someone was nice to me and burst into tears.

The wretchedness in me took over, and I sat there blubbing, sniffing, snot everywhere, and whining. "I thought he loved me. But he-he never r-really loved me, did he?" I put my head in my hands and fell apart. I was so tired of it all. I wanted a quiet life with a nice man. Why couldn't I get that?

A shadow passed over me, and I felt a weight next to me on the seat. Simon's arm came around my shoulders. "It's okay, it's okay," he whispered.

"I'm such an idiot," I said, trying to wipe my nose.

"No, you're not. You loved him and he let you down," Simon said. "If it makes you feel better, I think he's a twat. Who has you and goes looking elsewhere?"

"It's not like I'm any better. I slept with you, with Tarquin, with Errol. I'm as bad as he is, but I pretend I'm not." The tears began to subside after a while, and I was able to eventually breathe and talk normally again. Simon offered me a napkin covered in sausage roll crumbs.

"First of all, that's utter nonsense," he said, shaking his head. "You haven't cheated on anyone. You're single and can do what you like. And secondly, we've all been there. If I had a fiver for every time that I've bawled into my pillow about some bloke who'd done me over, I'd … well, I'd be as rich as you are."

I laughed because I couldn't imagine Simon having his heart broken. I looked up at him. He was so close. I could see the ginger stubble on his chin, the bags under his eyes and his greasy hair. Those deep blue eyes. That were staring straight at me. "You look like shit," I mumbled.

"So do you. Except you're working with a higher quality canvas than me, so you're still better off," he said. He reached up and pushed a piece of my fringe off my face. "I know you still love him, Arden, and maybe you always will. I wish I could wave a magic wand and make you get over him for good, I really do."

I gulped. And sniffled some more. "You'll meet a nice guy, Arden. I promise you. And all the Ollies and Tarquins of the world will fade to the back of your mind. You'll be happy, and eventually, you'll have to stop and think to remember what their faces looked like."

"You promise?"
"Promise." He smiled and clapped me on my shoulder. "C'mon, eat. Stop letting that twat control your life and let's get home."
I know what you're thinking, reader. That I'm a hypocrite. And, why couldn't Ollie sleep with whoever he felt like? I had dumped him. He was single. He could do what he wanted.
But why had he made so many efforts to win me back if he was still seeing that … that piece of shit, Jamie.
"Maybe Jamie sent the letter," I muttered to myself as I got back in the truck.
"That's the spirit, mate. Let's frame the little wanker for murder," Simon said, joking.
"Why can't you be like this all the time?" I blurted out.
Simon frowned. "What do you mean?"
"Nice! Why can't you always be nice to me? Why do we always have to wind each other up? Why can't we get along – we do when we try. We could be really good friends. But we … no, you said my self-esteem was too low, so fuck it, *you* – it's you who always makes it awkward. You always get in a huff with me about something. But then you go and do nice things, and I don't know where I am with you. It's exhausting. Either hate me or be my friend."
Simon was very quiet for a long time. And then he reached over and took my face in his big hands and kissed me.

Nigella gave me an odd look when I came to pick up Kennedy. Like she could tell I wasn't quite all there. Was she like Verity and concerned I was acting manic? I ignored it.
"Was he well behaved?" I asked.

"An angel. Oh, and Sonia stayed over last night, too. Poor thing was a wreck. We concocted some plans to put her back together."

I cocked an eyebrow. "Full debrief over gin and tonics when I've had some sleep?" I asked.

"I've got a bottle of Tanqueray waiting for whenever you're ready. Bring some lemons."

Kennedy and I walked – slowly – home, and I fell into bed. I slept for hours and hours.

Correction. I slept for about four hours. I woke up in the late afternoon. It was blisteringly hot outside and even hotter in my room. I was drenched in sweat.

After a long shower, I listened to the news on the radio, which was full of predictions for tomorrow's election. Suzy's victory was all but a foregone conclusion. She was believed to be a few points ahead of the replacement Tory candidate, who had made underwhelming impressions in local radio and TV interviews over the past several days. In my trip to London, I had missed several high-profile cabinet ministers and even the Prime Minister visiting the area to curry up support for a seat that three weeks ago they would never have thought they could lose.

I finished eating, made a fuss of the cats, who hadn't even noticed I'd been gone, and told Kennedy to stay. I marched down to the village. It was crunch time. And I needed answers.

Simon was already there, like he said he would be.

Guy's cottage looked even larger in daylight. It was a beautiful, whitewashed building with a thatched roof and latticed windows. Ivy, climbing roses, and wisteria grew all over its frontage. The white gravel outside made the satisfying crunch of money spent on good renovations and upkeep. The lawn around it was a sumptuous shade of green, with nary a weed, and the large shrubs and trees that separated it from Honningtons' grounds were all healthy and well maintained. The great house was visible through a gap in the trees, shimmering in the heat haze.

Simon was nervous. He was sweaty and fidgeting. "He's home?" I asked, not bothering with pleasantries as I walked up to where he stood.

"I've texted him. He's in."

I knocked on his door. A few seconds later, Guy answered it. "Arden, Simon, what a … pleasant surprise."

He was in his riding gear. Clearly, he had been out on one of his horses, as his hair was slicked back by sweat and his shirt clung to his muscular frame.

"Can we come in, Guy?" I asked.

Guy gave Simon a worried glance. "I've spoken to Jed," Simon said. "He said it's okay. It's time we told Arden the truth."

Guy looked at me. "Please don't hate us," he said eventually.

He led Simon and me into the house, and this time we went fully through to its heart. A beautiful, informal living room, at the back, which looked like something from a gentleman's club.

There was a grand fireplace, a liquor cabinet, an antique globe, and even a chessboard set out on a side table.

"Take a seat. Do you want a drink? I know I bloody well do," he said. "It's supposed to thunder in a while." He peered out the window. "Should be soonish."

"Maybe the heatwave is finally breaking," Simon said.

"Can you both stop procrastinating and get on with it?"

Guy ignored me and poured himself a drink. Simon took a seat on one of the sofas and looked as if he was trying his hardest not to squirm. "Guy, could you pour me one too?" he asked.

I tried to control my breathing, but it was increasingly difficult with these two acting like they had all the time in the world. I was basically sitting on my hands to stop myself from ripping the drinks out of their hands and yelling for them to get on with it.

Finally, they both had drinks, and Guy took a seat. Somewhere, far away, thunder clapped.

"And it begins," Guy said.

Simon gulped down half his drink. "I should start."

"Yes, please, do."

He took a steadying breath. "I suppose one thing to tell you is that what we said the other night was untrue, but also not completely untrue." He looked at Guy. "We do have some history."

I exhaled and stared at the carpet. I was going to hear a lot of this sentiment in the story, whatever it contained.

"I moved to Lilbury about four years ago," Simon said. "I took a job, well, I was posted to a research unit nearby in Wiltshire. About forty-five minutes from here. There's a special operations centre there. I can't tell you more about what I do. It's at RAF Kesset; I'm not RAF, I'm Royal Naval Intelligence. Well, I was – anyway, it's a long story. Arden, I can't tell you what I do. I can't."

My eyebrows must have gone sky high and betrayed me because Simon stopped talking and nodded solemnly. "I'm not trying to be obtuse. It is illegal for you to know this stuff. We could all go to prison if some aspects of my job become revealed."

"But Guy knows?" I asked.

"I know what I'm allowed to know," he said calmly. Guy seemed so much older in these situations. He was looking at me in the most queer manner. He seemed out of sorts, but nowhere as nervous as Simon. Maybe boarding school taught you to hide it better.

"There are people I work with, Arden. Men in grey suits who look like mild-mannered commuters on the train who … I can't stress to you enough to stay as far from them as you can. If you ever get approached by someone who acts like they want information from you. If they mention my name or anything about you, about me, or about any connection we might have. Please, run in the opposite direction. These men I work with, they aren't going to be coming to find you because of something good."

"Who do you work for?" I asked after a long silence.

"I can't tell you that," Simon said. "I'm sorry." He gave me a look that I think was trying to show me he was being sincere. *I know this is hard, and I know I'm asking a lot*, it said, *but believe me.*

"No one knows where I work or what I do, except a handful of people. Not my parents, not my sister, not anyone I've ever dated. Guy is one of very few."

I nodded.

Simon turned to Guy for a second and took a deep breath. "Just after I moved here, there was a lad at the base. Risen through the ranks quickly. Hand-picked. He was drafted on to our team. Very clever, spoke Chinese, an analytical brain. He was perfect for us."

The hairs on the back of my arms were standing on end. I knew where this was going. Thunder clapped again. The sky outside was black.

"He was also … he was good-looking. He introduced himself to me. Very flirty. Young, confident. He wouldn't take no for an answer. I'd just moved here; I didn't know anyone. I was single. One day, he sidled over and asked me for a drink. It's not technically allowed, but it's also not expressly forbidden. So, I went for it."

"This lad already had a reputation. Already on thin ice. He was wild, he drank too much, he stayed out all night, and he took a lot of drugs. Neither of us were looking for much more than casual, so it worked for a while. One night, he came over and, well, it was a freezing winter's night, we decided to head down to the Fox and Lamprey.

He was charming, kind, lovely. He had everyone eating out of his hand. We ran into Guy."

"I could tell straight away what he was after," Guy said. "I'm embarrassed to admit we both fell into his game. I'd seen Simon around a bit but hadn't got to know him very well. That night, the three of us sat at a table. He was, as Simon said, good-looking. Very charming. Flattery, drinks pouring. He had his hand on my leg from the moment we all sat down. I freely admit that I wanted it to happen. He rubbed his hand up and down my thigh, making eye contact with Simon, daring him to join in or to rebuff him. If we didn't want it, he wanted us to make a scene."

"But we didn't." Simon gulped the rest of his drink. "Good-looking men are a curse," he said with some bitterness. "They take and take and always expect to get more. He was the same. We came back here. And we … well, we didn't know what he'd taken until he offered it to us. I'd never had it before or again. I didn't enjoy it."

"What was it?" I asked.

"G," Guy said. "GHB, liquid ecstasy. It was his drug of choice. You see it on the chemsex scene."

I raised my eyebrows again. "Oh, fuck off, Arden. We all have histories," he snapped.

Tarquin once described Guy as so stuffy that he thanked his lovers after some half-hearted missionary. I held up my hands in apology and then beckoned for them to carry on.

"That night was wild," Simon said. "There, we admit it. Yes, Guy and I had a threesome with some bloke while all of us were totally off our heads on whatever drugs he had on him. It was stupid, but it was fun. We weren't ashamed."

"And then what happened?" I asked, dreading the answer.

Simon shrugged. "He and I fizzled out. We stopped seeing each other. He moved on to the next."

"That's it?" I asked.

He shook his head. "His behaviour began to get worse. He was reprimanded. They worried he was a liability. He was too young for the job, maybe. I don't know. I know they were looking at ways of moving him out again."

"One night, a few days before Christmas, he turned up here again," Guy said. "He was off his head. I'd say I was surprised he knew how to find me again, but obviously, in that job, they have their ways."

"I was here with Jed," he said. "The pair of us were drunk. Well, I was drunk. Jed was shitfaced. He was passed out in front of the fire. Then in this guy comes, all gorgeous and young. He wants a repeat performance."

"And you said?"

"Yes, obviously," Guy said as if any other answer would have been lunacy.

I was in a parallel universe. "I invited Simon over. He was less than convinced but came anyway. Jed barely knew what was happening. He was so drunk. I think he was dimly aware Simon was here. It wasn't until much later that he realised. Anyway, the three of us went upstairs. Did the deed. Simon and I came back downstairs for a drink and left him up there. He was a bit out of it, so I told him to have a lie-down, and that he could stay the night if he needed to. But he was determined to leave later, said there was a party back on base he wanted to go to."

"We were down here, drinking," Simon said. "After a few hours, it was getting late. Jed had recovered and toddled off for a piss and opened the door to Guy's room. Saw him on the bed."

There was a very long pause.

"He'd mixed it with alcohol," Guy said. "Lethal."

Holy shit.

"Jed freaked out, as one would. There was some naked man upstairs with no pulse on my bed, and where the hell had he even come from, because he wasn't there when Jed arrived." Guy took a long sip of his drink. "We're not proud of what we did next."

I stood up and began to pace. The room felt close and hot. The thunder was near. Every thirty seconds, the booming claps came.

"It would have ruined us all," Guy said.

My heel hovered an inch above the ground as I went to take my next step. "You covered it up?" I spat at them.

Both looked like small boys reprimanded by teachers. Their shoulders were slumped. Guy bit his lip. Simon wouldn't meet my eyes.

"We called one of my bosses," Simon said. "Asked them what to do. A vicar, and someone of Guy's status, on the grounds of a stately manor with some dead twink? A scandal."

"Some dead twink?" I whispered. I couldn't bear to look at him. I felt sick.

"They advised us to bring him back to the base. I was the most sober," Simon said. "So, it was my job to do it, while Guy and Jed cleaned up any evidence of him being here. We … had to do things to the body so people wouldn't know what we'd been up to."

I screwed my face up. "You washed off all the" – I wrinkled my nose – "evidence that he'd been having sex?"

The thunder boomed. Neither of them would look at me now.

"We had to make it convincing. Death by overdose," Simon said. "I drove his body back to the base. I snuck into where he lived and … left him in his bed to be found the next morning."

Silence.

"And then what?" I asked.

"We went back to our lives," Guy said. "It was the truth, he overdosed. We had nothing to do with that. He took those drugs. It wasn't our responsibility to know what a grown adult had taken."

"You took turns fucking him and then disposed of his body?" I said, my anger spilling over. I couldn't bear to know this.

"We didn't do that!" Simon protested.

"Really?" I yelled, slamming my hands down on a table. "Because it sounds like you two were high-fiving while you Eiffel Towered him!"

There was silence.

"Look, he died of an overdose!" Simon shouted at me. "The coroner's report confirmed it. There was nothing we could've done."

"What happened afterwards?" I asked.

Simon fidgeted. "My superiors knew. I was reprimanded. I was essentially fired from the service, but it was more of a suspension. I couldn't be part of the organisation for a while. They told me it was temporary. So, I became a handyman."

I scoffed. I needed to throw something. "That's why you weren't a spy when I arrived? Because someone in the British intelligence services, somewhere, at least had a bit of a conscience?"

He was silent. Just the thunder.

"And what about now? You're back in?"

"The project I was working on. It's nearly at fruition. I was allowed back. But – I'm out of it again until Riz – until this all blows over. I'm a liability. Again."

"My heart bleeds."

"Arden, please! We … we did nothing wrong. He took those drugs; no one forced him to. No one forced him to have sex with us. He wanted it. He initiated everything that night."

"And covering it up and moving his body?" I asked. "Was that his final wish?"

"We're not proud of what we did," Guy said.

I fumed. I paced. I kicked a chair – Guy winced. I paced the room some more. The thunder boomed again. I put my head in my hands and scrubbed my face, hoping it would all make sense.

"Why are you telling me this now? What makes you think this is relevant?"

"How could it not be?" Simon asked. "Jed's attacked, Guy's career is ruined, my fiancé is killed. It must be someone who knows what we did."

"But you didn't do anything wrong," I said in a mocking tone under my breath. Out loud, though, I asked, "Who could know? His family?"

Simon shook his head. "They were estranged. Homophobes, from what he told me."

"A friend?"

"He was close to a lad on the base, platonic, he was straight. His name was Jeremy. He's stationed in Qatar now and has been for a couple of years. I've … asked around. He's not been back to the UK in over a year."

"What about other guys he was with?"

Simon shook his head again. "I haven't got a clue. I've tried to piece things together, but I've got nowhere."

All the while he was running around with me, he'd been doing his own, much more important, investigations. I was only ever to tie up some loose ends. I pursed my lips.

"So, any number of disgruntled ex-boyfriends could have done it?"

He nodded. I resumed pacing. After a few seconds, a thought occurred. "Who else knows? The whole story, I mean? You three, me now, and your superiors?"

They both looked at each other. Guy coughed. "I told Tarquin everything."

"Oh, Jesus Christ," I said. It was endless. The tendrils kept on growing and reaching out to find more nooks and crannies to burrow into.

My head was back in my hands. I was so tired.

The thunder boomed. The air was dry and full of a tangy, metallic taste. Maybe we'd get lucky, a lightning bolt would hit Guy's house, and we'd all go up in flames.

I may have enjoyed that little thought for too long as Guy and Simon were looking at me with concerned expressions. "What was his name?" I asked.

Simon swallowed. "See, that's the thing. His name was Stuart. Stuart Murray."

S Murray.

Simon caught up to me as I walked as fast as I could away from that fucking cottage. Lying, manipulative …

"Arden, please, wait, I'm sorry!"

I kept walking.

"Please, I didn't lie on purpose. Please."

I spun around. "But you lied. You lied to me again and again and a-fucking-gain! It's all you do, Simon. From the moment this all started, you've played me like a fucking puppet on a string. Just dangling half-truths and twisted facts at me, trying to make me jump."

Simon stood a few metres from me. The thunder crashed. The wind had picked up. For the first time in weeks, I was cold in just a T-shirt. Simon's face was wretched in agony. His eyes were wet, his skin was red and blotchy from, I don't know, holding back tears. Self-pity probably.

"No, Arden, I would never do that to you. Everything was genuine. I desperately wanted your help. Everything I kept from you was to protect you."

"You kept me in the dark!" I screamed at him. "Someone is pretending to be your dead ex to murder your other ex! And you don't tell me shit, Simon!"

Tears were rolling down his face. He yelled in frustration and swore at the sky. "I am stuck, Arden. I can't … if I tell you things, we could both go to prison."

"Who do you work for?" I yelled as loud as I could, my voice breaking.

"I can't tell you!" he shouted back.

Tears streaming down my face too. "You are a liar, and you manipulated me and played me for a fool. I – I don't ever want to speak to you again. For God's sake, you kissed me this morning. Was that another ploy that I'm not allowed to know about?"

"You know it wasn't!" he yelled. But he was already talking to my back.

I walked as fast as I could down that path. I'd keep walking. Maybe I'd walk to France.

"Wish I'd never moved to this fucking village," I said, my voice cut through with sobs. Behind me, I heard him shout my name.

"I wish I'd never met you," I said, but the thunder drowned my voice out.

Chapter 23

So that was it. As far as I was concerned. There. Solved. Someone pretending to be Stuart Murray was doing this. They had contacted Ollie's law firm using that name. Then they had sidled up to Riz and concocted a story of how they could guarantee him a place in Parliament at Guy's expense. They had attacked Jed.

And then … they had killed Riz. One of Stuart's ex-boyfriends whom we would never know.

Correction: I would never know. Because I was fucking done with it all.

I switched on the news on Thursday morning after coming in from my run. "It is going to be positively scorching today. But not as hot as tomorrow, when it could be the hottest day in England since records began," the presenter said. "But, right now, all eyes are on Central Dorset, for the by-election that has gripped the country. Voting opened at 7 a.m. and by around midnight, we should know who will win this race, which has seen so many dramatic moments over the past month."

The TV went off. My phone started buzzing. It was Verity.

Two weeks of silence. I … I needed to answer this. It was for work. It was my career. It was important. I stared at the phone and let it go to voicemail. I couldn't. I just couldn't.

Slumping down on my sofa, I admitted it to myself. I was exhausted. Emotionally, mentally, physically, spiritually, financially (unlikely, but I'll throw it in there), fucking exi-bloody-stentially. The only kind of exhausted that I wasn't right now was sexually. Frankly, the first man who turned up on my doorstep would get jumped on.

Eventually, I stood and got dressed. I had put off the inevitable long enough. Time to go be a good citizen.

St Candida Church was probably the prettiest place that I'd ever cast a vote. It was also definitely the most media-focused. Of course, since British laws meant that you couldn't report about an election on the day of it, I'm not sure what they were doing here, but there were several journalists asking people questions as they politely filed in and out of the church to vote.

Across the road, watching like a Greek chorus were three women. Technically, they were an Irish, Polish, and French chorus. Rita Parkinson, Ewa, and Cytrine all greeted me warmly.

"I've just voted," Rita said. Irish citizens were allowed to vote, but Cytrine and Ewa couldn't.

"We came to gawp," Cytrine said.

Ewa gestured to the sky. "It is nice day for gawping."

"Anyone that I need to avoid in there?" I asked Rita quietly.

"No," she said. "Guy voted by post; he told us. There's going to be a bit of a scene around midday when Suzy and all the other candidates are going to lay a wreath in Sittingston. But that's it."

I nodded and left the ladies to get on with their double toils and troubles and joined the queue. "Hello, love," Roz Staines, proprietress of the village shop, said as I sidled up behind her in the line. In one hand, she held an apple she was eating and in the other a celeb gossip magazine. Using her time effectively.

"Morning, Roz."

"Gosh, I can't wait for this all to be over, don't you agree?"

"You have no idea."

Nigella came up behind me and placed a hand on my shoulder. "Are we discussing tactical voting strategies? I say we all write in the Monster Raving Loony Party."

Roz chortled.

Nigella put her arm through mine. "How are you?" she asked.

"I feel a hundred years old."

Nigella looked at me for a few seconds then she patted my arm. "I think you need a holiday."

"Oof, don't we all?" Roz said. "Wait, is that bloody Odette talking to the reporters?"

We shuffled closer just in time to hear Odette's views. "It makes one wonder if we should even have democracy. I was reading a fascinating column in the *Daily Mail* the other day about whether we should have tests before people can vote. Especially people on benefits."

"Dear Lord," Nigella said. She turned to me. "Have you heard from Sonia today?"

"Not a peep."

Nigella looked as if she was going to say something. But then she frowned. "What on earth is he doing here?"

I turned to look in the direction her eyes were focused. The car that had driven me to Sittingston a few weeks ago was now pulling up beside the church. Out of it got Errol Mottley. He was unshaven, his tie was loose, his shirt was crumpled, and his immaculate suit looked like he'd slept in it.

"Christ," I said. "Hide me."

"Arden!" He was coming over.

"Not now, Errol, I'm voting," I said, trying to look anywhere but him. Of course, Odette had directed the reporter to watch me.

"Not even sure Arden's allowed to vote. My husband said he was an illegal immigrant who probably had to stow away in a cargo hold of a plane to get here, but that's not true, is it, Arden … is it?"

Errol grabbed my arm. "I need to talk to you."

I looked at Nigella for help. "Please," he said. "Five minutes."

"Anything you want to say, you can say it here, my love," Roz said, eating her apple, with a glint in her eye.

He looked so desperate. I sighed. "C'mon," I said and shook off his hand. "Nigella, if I'm not back in two minutes, please come save me." I took Errol by the elbow and dragged him around the corner out of sight of the queue – and the journalists – into a very pretty laneway that ran around the south of the church.

Once we got there, I could see how bad Errol looked. "What happened to you?"

He stared at me. "Have you found anything else out?" he asked.

"About?"

"Suzy, you idiot!" he yelled. His face caved in. "I'm sorry, I'm sorry. It's … our internal polling. She's going to win. I need to know I've not helped elect a murderer."

Now he had a conscience. "Where was all this concern the other night when you threatened me?"

He gripped my arm again. "Please, Arden. Do you know of anything she may have done? She's a snake, I know. She's going to betray the party, and no one will listen to me. They're all so excited she's going to snatch the seat. All the press coverage."

I did feel genuinely sorry for him. But also, I was done with being poked and prodded. "Your only concern is that you got tricked by her," I said. "When you hadn't realised she'd turn on you all the moment she got elected, you were fine with her antics." I shrugged.

"Arden!" He grabbed my other arm and dug his fingers in. "Tell me!"

"Get your fucking hands off him," Simon said.

Oh, good. Because this day needed to get worse.

Simon stood at the end of the lane. He was as dishevelled as Errol. His face contorted in anger.

My ire rising, I shrugged off Errol's grip. "I can fight my own battles," I snapped at Simon. "Listen," I said, turning back to Errol. "Suzy's a snake. That's on you. Deal with it and put on a clean shirt." I left him to it.

He called my name as I walked away, but I was so very done.

"Are you okay?" Simon asked as I pushed past him. He put his hand out, but my facial expression must have warned him not to touch me, and he retracted it sharpish.

"What do you think?" I said and kept going.

Nigella had saved my place in the queue. She waved me towards her, but I couldn't face it; Margo Cadbury-Smythe and Lady F had emerged from the church hall and were going over to greet Nigella and Roz. Katrina had joined the end of the line, and I fell in behind her.

"You look like the thunder we had last night," she said.

"I'm beginning to agree with Odette Douglas about democracy."

Katrina laughed. "Nearly over, deary. It's all nearly over."

Nigella beckoned me forward while Margo was in full flow on some topic, but I shook my head. I didn't have the energy for patience.

My phone rang again. We were about to go in. I looked at it. Verity. She was persistent today.

I ignored it. A second later, it pinged with a message.

Verity: If you won't answer me I'm coming to see you.

Our turn to go inside and vote had arrived. Katrina and I both sidled up to the desk to get our papers. Behind us, Simon had joined the line, and his eyes never left me as he waited to grab his own forms.

I took my sheet and went to the tiny desk, partitioned off from other voters. It was busy, with almost every table occupied. The only other station free was obviously the one across from me. Naturally, that's where Simon stood. He watched me like a hawk.

I looked at my voting papers, my hands shaking.

~~PATEL, RIZ – Labour and Co-Operative Party~~
POTSDAM, MARJORIE – Green Party of England and Wales
THRALL, ROBERT – UKIP
RABBIT, SUZANNE – Liberal Democrats

And the last candidate – Michael Cadbury-Smythe. Yup, the replacement Tory candidate was Margo's brother-in-law.

The red line through Riz's name had *WITHDRAWN* written by it.

I ticked the box next to Marjorie's name. Her passion for saving the bees was the only policy position I could remember after everything else that had happened. I left the desk before Simon could start begging me to talk to him and stuffed my ballot in the box. Democratic duty done.

I stalked out of the church hall. Have you ever had several people calling your name before? All asking you to stop and speak? Neither had I until this day. I looked up but kept on walking. Guy had joined his aunt. Several men were around him, one with a bright blue rosette on his chest. Nigella, Roz, and even Katrina were around them too.

I couldn't face it. I walked home as fast as I could. To distract myself, I decided to take Kennedy for a walk. I needed to think of something else. I needed to blow off steam. I needed to hit something. Actually, what I needed was to be anywhere but this village.

"C'mon, lad," I told Kennedy. "Let's get the fuck out of here." Instead of a walk, we piled into the car, and I drove off too fast, heading towards Compney. Nigella had said that Sonia was a mess, so maybe she wanted some company. At least Sonia never lied to me.

Compney High Street was busy in the blistering sunshine. Tables and chairs from several cafés spilt out onto the pavement. Happy, chatting, laughing people enjoyed the early summer day.

The estate agency was closed. Huh. That was unusual. I took out my phone and rang Sonia's number.

A voice answered. But it wasn't Son. It was Dhapinder. "Ah, Arden. How good of you to call." Through the glass, I saw her appear in the shop. "As you can see, we're closed today, but why don't you come on in?"

She walked towards the door and opened it for me with a smile. "What a beautiful day." She let me pass as if the last time we'd met, she hadn't threatened me with a stun gun. "Why do you have Sonia's phone?" I asked. Something was very, very wrong.

I came inside, knowing it was the wrong choice. She bolted the door after me. That's when I saw the knife.

"Why don't you leave that dog of yours in the toilet?" she asked, gesturing her head towards a door. Kenny whimpered and backed away.

"Okay, easy, easy," I said as she flicked the knife in the toilet's direction. With her other hand, she grabbed my phone from me and put it in her pocket. I dragged Kenny to the bathrooms. "C'mon, boy, it'll be okay." I led him into the small room and then gave him a kiss atop his snout. "Good boy, stay calm, and this will all be over soon," I told him. He whimpered again. My hands were shaking.

I backed out of the room. Instantly, Kennedy launched himself at the closed door and started howling for me.

Dhapinder still had the knife aimed at me. Could I take her? She was small, only a few inches above five feet. I'm no giant, but I was still male and bigger. However, that knife looked very sharp. It was a normal kitchen knife, the kind everyone makes as an investment purchase. The 'good' knife. I was glad that at least it wasn't bloody and looking like it had already been used.

“Where’s Sonia?” I asked, hating the tremor in my voice. Dhapinder was sweating; the hairspray she’d used liberally to keep her estate agent helmet in place was clinging on by its fingernails. Her ’do was beginning to droop. She had scuff marks on her legs and shoes.

“She’s in the staff kitchen. Why don’t you go and join her?” She gestured with the knife, and I walked slowly, edging against the wall towards the kitchen. Kennedy was still howling in the bathroom.

So, this was how I died. In an estate agent’s. At the hands of a crazy woman. Oh, well, I had got to live for a few more months after Tarquin had tried it. At least no one was framing me for murder this time.

My heart thundering, I eventually made it to the kitchen under Dhapinder’s gaze. She had lost it. I opened the door and fell into the room.

Sonia was on a chair in the middle of it. Her wrists were tied to the chair legs. She was conscious but gagged at the mouth. Searching the room for help. When she saw me, her eyes went wide, and she strained against her ties. At least she was unhurt. For now.

Beside her, on the floor, his head in his hands, was Trevor Bliss. He looked up at me as we came in. His eyes were red, his face tear-stained, and a big glob of snot hung from his nose. “It was never supposed to be like this,” he told me.

“Oh, Trevor, what have you done?” I asked.

“Be quiet,” said Dhapinder, and the knife prodded me in the back, a tiny nip, but it was enough to make me yelp and jump forward.

“Tie him up,” she barked at her husband.

Trevor fell into a new barrage of sobs.

“Dhapinder, this is madness,” I told her.

“He’s right, babe.” Trevor ran a piece of rope through his hands. “We’re going to prison for so long. This is all crazy.”

"DO IT!" she yelled. Sonia looked at me desperately. Her eyes wide with terror.

Trevor shuffled over, still sobbing and weeping. "Sorry, Arden," he whispered as he manhandled me over to another chair and plonked me down.

"Why are you doing this?" I asked. "How are you going to explain it? There's no way all of this is worth it for whatever amount of money you've stolen."

Trevor looked dazed. "How did you know about …"

"Stop talking, Trevor, and tie him up," Dhapinder yelled. "Let me think."

He did as he was told. "This has all gotten out of hand, hasn't it, Dhapinder?" I asked. Kennedy was still making a racket. Maybe someone in one of the shops next door would hear him and come to investigate? "Let me get this straight. You kidnapped Sonia and held her at knifepoint, and now a second person, also at knifepoint, which, by the way, is like an automatic custodial sentence in this country, without a plan?"

I looked at Trevor. "Custodial means prison, if you didn't know." He gulped, but I kept going. Dhapinder was pacing. People and their fucking pacing.

"You know, prison, like where Tarquin ended up after he killed Arabella. You know about that, cos you were fucking her, so the police suspected you, like all the other guys who had a go." I turned to Dhapinder. "Is that what started this off? When you found out that Trevor had been dipping his candle in other wicks? Humiliating you, and all the while, you weren't even given your share of the business when Daddy Bliss retired?"

"Shut up!" she snarled.

"Listen, Dhapinder, I know how it feels. When someone you love betrays you like that. It hurts so much, but this is stupid."

"Love?" she spat out. She turned to Trevor, the sobbing, slumped wreck of a man beside her, who had been a walking wet dream but now looked too pathetic to elicit as much as a passing tingle.

"I don't love him!" she said, pointing at Trevor. "He used me and only wanted me because that blonde whore turned him down!" She paced some more. "Getting the money was the least he could do after treating me as second best."

Trevor wept some more. She shook her head at him. "Pathetic," she whispered.

"So, you don't love him? Do you hear that, Trevor – she hates you," I said. Sonia's eyes were going so wide. Kennedy was still howling.

There was a banging at the front door. Oh, thank God. A voice came through the room. It was muffled but sounded like it was filled with urgency. Trevor's head shot up. "Mum?" he called.

Dhapinder whipped around. "Gag him or something," she ordered Trevor, meaning me. "I'll go deal with them and that bloody dog."

Deal with my dog? Deal? Did-did she … Oh, hell no.

"Are you gonna let her talk to you like that, Trevor? You're the man here. This harpy wants your family's money. She doesn't even like you. She thinks you're stupid. She'd have divorced you after she found out about Arabella, but she wanted that money more. Are you going to let her destroy your family like this?"

Dhapinder whirled at me. "Shut up!" she screamed. At that moment, another voice came from the door at the back end of the room. It sounded male and authoritative. "Is anyone in there?" he asked. "Sonia? Trev?"

Sonia had managed to get the gag out of her mouth.

"Dad?" she called out. "Dad, is that you – help, Dhapinder and Trevor have gone nuts—"

Dhapinder pushed Sonia's chair back. She toppled onto the floor and let out a scream.

"Sonia!" I yelled. "Trevor, you worthless dumb shit, do something!" My strategy was changing by the second. Dhapinder's eyes flew to her man-child husband. His tear-stained face was now white with anger.

"She hates you, Trevor! She thinks you're weak and stupid."

Trevor's fists clenched. The pounding on the door continued. "What's happening? I've called the police!" Mr Bliss yelled.

"Have you met him?" Dhapinder said – to me – defending herself in the middle of all this. "He is weak and stupid! He's a fucking moron."

I mean, she had a point. The Brain of Britain, Trevor was not.

But he did act now and again. He grabbed his wife's hand and twisted her arm until she yelped. "Drop the knife, Dhapinder," he growled.

Her face twisted in anger. "Weak!" she hissed and slashed at him with the knife. It sunk into his arm, and a crimson streak instantly seeped through his shirt. But it was only superficial. Trevor grabbed her other wrist with his injured arm and crushed her hand until she dropped the knife. "It's over," he said. He took the knife and opened the door to his father.

Mr Bliss took in the scene, and his jaw dropped. Dhapinder collapsed onto the floor and put her head in her hands. Trevor approached his father.

Sonia was lying prostrate on the floor, her hair over her face. She was sobbing. Still, Kennedy howled.

"Dad, I'm sorry," he mumbled, his sobs starting again. Mr Bliss pushed him away as he approached us. "Trevor, what have you done?"

Adebayo and Lauren arrived two minutes later, along with Mrs Bliss, who took Sonia in her arms and sobbed.

Mr Bliss handed the knife he'd taken from Trevor to the police. Adebayo tried his best to act professionally, but his eyes were only for Sonia, and eventually, he stopped pretending he could do his job at this moment and flew to her side. Desperately checking her arms and face for any wounds. "Are you really okay?" he asked her for the millionth time.

Ade kissed her head and held her as tightly as he could, rocking her back and forth in his arms. "It's alright, baby, it's alright."

More police arrived. Dhapinder and Trevor were cuffed and led away. A surprisingly strong Sonia had a blanket put over her and was led outside. I was allowed to grab Kennedy, who was delirious with joy at being let out. "Oh, my good boy, I am so glad she didn't hurt you," I said as I kneeled on the floor and let him lick me. At least no one could say my face was wet because I'd been crying now.

We made our way onto the street where the entire village had seemingly congregated to find out why several police cars had arrived, and the respectable estate agents (pah!) were being led out by the cops.

An SUV pulled up, and a person I hadn't expected to see came running towards us as we were led to the cop cars. Nigella's black hair shone in the sun as she bundled Sonia up in a hug, and then me. "This is all my fault!" she whispered in my ear. "I really am a stupid old gossipy woman like Matteo said."

"What? No, what nonsense," I said. "How is this your fault?"

She cringed. "The night Sonia stayed over. She seemed so wretched. I told her, well, I told her to confront Dhapinder and Trevor if she couldn't take it in any longer."

My face fell. Oh, okay. So, a little bit her fault. "Arden, please don't be mad. Please! I'm so sorry!"

The police took us to Sittingston station. As usual, all I could see was how ugly it was. And as usual, it took hours. However, Kennedy was a hit with the officers, so at least the goodwill from that got me a cup of tea and biscuits. Also, the station had blessed air conditioning. By mid-afternoon, when my phone told me that the temperature outside was in the high thirties, I was surprisingly comfortable on my leather chair in the waiting room.

Eventually, Lauren brought me through, and I gave my statement. After I'd finished, she sighed. "Thank God," she said. "Dhapinder and Trevor have admitted everything. They've stolen nearly £50,000 over the past year. Their plan was to announce they were leaving soon for Spain to set up a new agency, essentially bankrupt the business, let Sonia take the blame as an incompetent owner, and then buy it outright at a fraction of its original value."

I shook my head. "But Trevor's wandering eye put paid to that."

"Yup," she said. "I can't believe it. I go to Zumba with Dhapinder's mum." She sighed. "You're free to go, Mr Forrest. DS Maslin said he'll drive you back to your car in Compney."

"Oh, thanks," I said, confused.

I looked over and saw Jack Maslin waiting for me at the door. I nervously came towards him. He bent down and gave Kennedy a scratch behind the ears. "What is he?" he asked in thick cockney.

"Black Alsatian/Dobermann cross," I answered. "Supposedly fearsome, but he's scared of his own shadow."

Maslin – Jack – scoffed. "Come on, the car's out back." He led the way, and we piled in. It was hotter than hell, and he turned up the AC.

He began his questions before we'd even left the car park. Kennedy, in the back, poked his head through the space between the seats and panted happily in our ears.

"You and Anson have been digging, I hear?"

I froze.

"Don't worry, I couldn't care less," he said. "Frankly, you might have got further than us. Whoever killed Riz knew what they were doing and buried every piece of paper trail behind a wall of shell corporations and overseas bank accounts."

"Though," he added. "Errol Mottley coming to us last night and saying it was Suzy Rabbit who killed Riz was an interesting development."

"What?" I squawked.

"Yeah, I don't think he's right."

"Who do you think did it?" I asked as we left the village.

He shrugged. His shoulders were so broad that I could almost feel the movement as his bulk took up most of the car. "You know the stats on it being the partner?"

"You think it was Simon?"

Another shrug. "You know him better than me."

"I don't know him at all," I said bitterly.

He gave a laugh. "I don't think that's true. I think you and Mr Anson know each other inside and out, even if you act like you hate each other."

I glared at him. "Jealous?" I asked petulantly.

"Little bit," he said, taking his eyes off the road and giving me a once-over.

Oh my God. Simon was right. Jesus, what a horrible thought. "Listen," he said. "Whatever happens, you still have my number. If you find something, call me. This is my first big case outside of the Met. I want to nail them."

"I have some theories," I said after a while.

He stared at me as we waited for a tractor at a give way sign. "Go on."

"I can't say much. I don't know much. But what I do know is that Simon didn't do it. And if he did, he's laid a very convincing path of breadcrumbs to someone else."

"Who is this person?"

Hesitation ran through me. But fuck it. "Stuart Murray. He was an ex-boyfriend of Simon's. I don't know anything more about him. But he OD'd several years back and, well, it's the only thing I can think of. His name keeps cropping up. I don't know who is putting it out there."

"You think that someone – wait, someone killed Riz to get revenge on Simon?" his voice was strained. Kennedy yawned loudly in our ears.

"Maybe," I said, unsure. My brain was so foggy. Adrenaline was receding, and now I needed to sleep for a million hours. "A family member, another ex-boyfriend."

Jack frowned. "I've left some ex-boyfriends pretty irate over the years, but none of them have shot anyone to get back at me."

Oh. Pocket that information for later. "So, family?"

"Let me do some digging. But Riz's killing was so carefully covered up. That breadcrumb trail was well hidden." He gazed off into the distance as we turned the corner into Compney. "Give me a day or two. Then I need to speak to Simon. There'll be more."

"About that," I said as we came onto the high street. "Don't think you'll get far. Simon's job."

Jack furrowed his enormous brow. "We've been shut down at every turn with information about Simon's employment. Politely– and less than politely – told to drop it."

Sounds like the same thing I'd been getting.

We pulled up near where I had parked my car several hours earlier. "Thanks," I said, collecting Kennedy from the back seat.

"I'll go back to the station and investigate this Stuart Murray. I'll let you know what I find. It seems you have the ear of the right people, in this case. Something Neuberger doesn't understand or like."

"Small town politics," I said.

"I wouldn't know. I'm from Canning Town." He grinned and then turned serious again. "But remember," he said, leaning over to talk to me through the passenger-side window. "I only care about who did it. Nothing else."

He drove off.

That night, they called Suzy's victory at 1 a.m., with one of the biggest landslides in recent history. She was going to Parliament.

Chapter 24

That fucking phone. I was going to throw it in a field. Or smash it with a hammer. Who was possibly ringing me at this ungodly hour?

I looked over. Oh, it was nine thirty. Not actually that early. And it was Nigella. I didn't have the energy, but I answered anyway.

Kennedy was most put out that I was moving around and huffed.

"Hello?"

"Good, you're awake. I never know what hours you keep. Anyway!" she said, changing her tone to bright and breezy. "You might want to get dressed and come down to my place. Put on a clean T-shirt and brush your hair. I've a full spread for breakfast."

"Are you throwing a brunch?" I asked.

"An intimate one, yes, just you, me and … er, Verity."

I was fully awake. "What?"

"She'll be here by ten, so chop-chop," she said. "Now, don't be mad. She rang me yesterday morning, before that whole … incident. She wanted to know what was going on. Oh, Arden, you hadn't told her anything about Riz; she had no idea. The pair of you need your heads knocking together. As my last act as a gossipy old woman, before I hang up my meddling hat, I shall do just that. And she said she has some big news for you."

Probably that I was having my contract cancelled. Or that I owed Donal and Ffion money.

"Fine," I said. "But I intend to sulk the entire time."

"That's the spirit, love. See you in a bit."

I stood up. Hated the world. Showered. Was furious with myself. Combed my hair. Muttered under my breath about who the fuck these people thought they were. I looked in the mirror and mushed up my fringe again because my hair, when combed, made me look like a seventies-pornstar-slash-twelve-year-old-boy. And then I cursed out Nigella. And Verity. And Guy. And Simon. And Ollie. And fuck it, Sonia, too. And Maslin. And God. And the fates and my mother and everyone I'd ever seen naked or had seen me naked and the weather and …

"I think I do need a holiday," I told Kennedy. "Shall we go to the seaside next week?"

He wagged his tail at that. "Good, we'll go somewhere miles away, and my phone will be left here. We'll go on nice long walks, and no one will bother us. No one." At the word *walk* his tail started wagging harder.

Feeling slightly less annoyed, but frankly, still thoroughly pissed off with the world, I left the house, with Kennedy following me.

After reaching the village, I walked down the street towards Nigella's place. Too dazed from the previous few days to realise what was going on around me. It all reverberated in my mind. Suzy was our new MP. Verity was in Lilbury. Simon and Guy had been having threesomes with squaddies from Simon's military base for years. One of them died in Guy's house, and they covered it up.

It was all too much. My head was pounding. On top of this, it really was going to be the hottest day on record. Already, I was sweating profusely from the sun beating down on the ground.

My phone rang. I took it out of my pocket, even though I wanted to ignore it. An unknown number. I answered.

"Arden?" came a now familiar cockney accent. "Listen, I've found something. I'm not sure what it means. But you need to be careful. If this is correct, then you were right, Stuart Murray's family killed Riz …" His voice crackled out. The reception was terrible.

"Jack? Jack, I can't hear you." The line was gone. I tried to call him back.

A car drove down the street beside me too fast and distracted me from my phone. I looked up to scowl at whatever prick couldn't follow speed limits and saw a shape I recognised instantly. "Oh, shit."

I began walking the other way back towards the cut-through by the pub.

The car came to a screeching halt about twenty metres in front of me. Shit, shit, shit.

"Arden!" I heard him call. The car door slammed, and I began to pick up the pace. Kennedy bounded along beside me.

Ollie was still following me and still calling my name. "Arden!" he yelled again. "Please, wait!" I kept walking.

"Arek!"

I stopped dead in my tracks at the corner of Nigella's street. She was in her front garden. We made eye contact, and she lifted her head in a *what gives?* gesture.

Ignoring her, I turned and stalked back over to Ollie. "Don't you ever call me that. Ever again! You hear me? You. Don't. Call. Me. That." I punctuated every word with a prod to his chest.

"You said I could—"

"Yeah, in private. Before."

"Arden, please, I need to talk to you. I can't—"

"You turned up where I live to tell me more lies?"

"No." His voice sounded raw. "It's not like that. God, why do I fuck everything up with you?"

"Excuse me?"

"Please, can we go to your house and talk? I need to explain things."

Nigella called out, "Arden, are you coming? Oh, hello, Ollie."

He gave a quick wave. The act seemed to cause him physical pain.

"Just a minute!" I replied to Nigella and turned back to Ollie: "I'm busy right now. This isn't a good time."

He gave me a begging look. "Please."

I groaned in frustration and grabbed his hand – out of instinct more than anything – and dragged him to Nigella's place. "Can I use your back garden for a minute? And can you keep Kenny occupied? Thanks."

Ollie followed me without saying a word. The front door was open, and Nigella's house was delightfully cool. "Go through to the garden and wait for me," I snapped at Ollie, who meekly complied. He headed for the back of the house as someone I had never expected to see here came out of it.

"You made it then," I said to Verity.

There was a noise, and I spun around to see Nigella coming back inside, with an excited Kennedy. She led him into the living room and threw a toy in after him. "Now, let's all be civil, yes? Also, why is Oliver here?"

I ignored all of that.

"Ard," Verity said quietly. "You know I'm on your side, right? I was between a rock and a hard place with Donal and Ffion. They're out for blood, and I was trying to do my best to keep the agency afloat. I never would've let them ditch you or screw you over."

Two weeks of complete silence, and now I had multiple directions pulling me at once. I said nothing.

Ollie was still standing behind her, looking conflicted. "I said to wait in the garden," I yelled at him. I could feel my temper like a rubber band being pulled and pulled and ready to snap.

I turned to Nigella. "Really can't apologise enough for all this. Didn't mean for everyone I've ever met to turn up at your door. If any long-lost relatives arrive, feel free to tell them to wait in the pub."

Aggrieved, I stormed to the end of the hall past Verity. She reached for my arm, and I jerked back. She noticed, and I instantly felt like an arsehole.

"It's okay," I said, feeling rather meek suddenly. "I—" I looked at Ollie. "I need to deal with one thing beforehand."

"I have good news," she offered in a hopeful tone.

"If it's not that we're all going to die tomorrow in an apocalypse, then I'm not interested," I muttered and grabbed Ollie, pulling him into the kitchen, and then sighed.

"Oh, for God's sake."

Inside Nigella's beautiful kitchen were Simon, Guy, and Sonia.

"Hello, everyone," I said.

Ollie noticed Simon. "You."

"You," Simon growled.

"Who are you?" Sonia asked Ollie.

"That's Arden's cheating piece of shit ex," Simon said succinctly.

"I have a name," Ollie said.

"Yeah. Cheating piece of shit." Simon folded his arms. "That's your name."

"You—" Ollie growled and pushed past me. Simon made his way forward, too, only held back by the others. Guy looked half ready to start swinging as well.

"ENOUGH!" I yelled. "Ollie, go out to the garden. You lot" – I gestured to Simon and Guy – "fucking keep it in your pants. The last thing we need is more testosterone."

Nigella slunk in behind me. "Why are they all here too?" I asked.

"Oh, that's actually not my fault. Honestly, they all turned up one by one this morning."

I gave her a look. "I'm very maternal; people flock to me," she said.

Instead of saying anything else, I glared at her as hard as I could. Then I turned and followed Ollie out into the garden and shut the door. Verity and Nigella had joined the others at the kitchen island. They all stood there, facing out towards us, alternately glaring – the men – and looking concerned – the women.

Outside, Ollie was pacing the garden, his hands going through his hair. I never wanted to see anyone pace ever again after the past month. Looking him up and down, he was not the immaculately dressed Ollie who never let the world get the better of him. This Ollie wore running shorts, a pair of plimsolls and an old workout T-shirt that was about two sizes too big for him.

"Did you get dressed in the dark?" I came to stand near him.

"Hmm? Oh, yeah. I took a sick day. Didn't think about an outfit." He cocked his head to the kitchen. "Who the hell are all they? Doesn't anyone have a job in this place?"

I shrugged. "Nigella and Guy? No. Simon, yes, but, you know, dead husband, also, technically no. Verity is her own boss. Sonia … er, that's complicated."

He let out a choked, half-hearted scoff.

"What do you want, Ollie?" I asked.

He stopped pacing, stopped running his hands through his hair. Stopped everything. There was a long, long pause. "I … I need to put this right, Arden. I can't let you be out in the world hating me. Anyone else can hate me all they want, but not you."

Exhaustion washed over me. I had nothing left in the tank. "You don't get to keep coming and doing this to me."

"Give me one more chance. I promise—"

"Promise what, Ollie? That you'll never cheat on me again? That you'll never see Jamie again? Which is it, Ollie?"

"I love you, Arden! I fucked up and I'm sorry!" he yelled, tearing at his hair. "I keep screwing up, and I just want you!"

"You had me! And I wasn't enough for you!" The whole village must be able to hear us. Our voices carried across Nigella's garden. I dared not look inside, but I knew that every word was going through Nigella's double-glazing.

"I'm sorry. Please tell me what to do, Arden. I can't go on like this. I feel sick every day."

"Then why didn't you think of that before?" I asked. I was screaming as loud as I could, but then my voice left me.

After a long silence, I said what I swore I would never admit to. Something I promised myself I'd kept buried deep down in my chest. "You broke me, Ollie. You know what my life had been like up until I met you. You know, because you were the first person that I ever told those things to." I pushed my finger into his tear-stained face.

My voice shook. "I never told anyone about my brother or my dad, I never told anyone, but I told you. I let you use my real name; I gave you everything, but it wasn't enough for you."

"I …"

A year of anger, and rejection poured out of me. The desire to let it all out was too much. "You ruined everything!" I screamed at him. "I never wanted anyone like I wanted you!"

Words failed. But now the anger overwhelmed me. My chest was about to burst. "I wanted to spend the rest of my life with you!"

Ollie was trying not to cry, his hair sticking up and wild from where he'd run his hands through it.

"I wanted to forgive you," I said eventually. My body was exhausted.

"That week in Surrey, I thought I could. I thought when we made love that everything could fall away, and we'd be us again. But we can't."

Silence.

Eventually, Ollie sniffed and looked away. He put his hands on his hips and took some calming breaths.

"Now, isn't that lovely?" said a voice from behind me. "You two are all sorted out then?"

I spun around. Standing at the back gate to Nigella's garden was Katrina Pettigrew. Holding a very large gun. Pointed right at us.

Chapter 25

It took me a few seconds to process it all. But then …

"Of course it was you," I said.

She smiled and swung the gun up at us. "I mean, I didn't try that hard not to get caught. But the police are useless, and everyone else around here was so wrapped up in their own problems that they didn't even notice."

She laughed. "Do you know, I honestly expected to be arrested the very day I shot Riz. But, bloody hell, I'm still here a month later. I'm a bit bored of hiding, actually. I had so many other plans, and I can't do any of them now. Oh, well." She cocked the gun. "Then this morning I get a phone call from DS Maslin asking some interesting questions. And I thought, yes, time to go out in a blaze of glory."

I threw myself at Ollie and pushed him down as the first shot rang out.

"Fuuuuuuck!" he screamed as we fell down the steps towards the doors to Nigella's house.

"Run!" I managed to get the door open and pushed him inside as the second shot rang out. A pane of glass an inch from my hand exploded.

Ollie pushed me to the floor, and we crawled along the ground to get inside, with Katrina's mad laughs following us.

The windows behind us shattered in a hail of bullets. An absolute cacophony of noise descended on us, complete with the sounds of screams from inside. I scrambled along the floor, dragging Ollie.

We made it into the kitchen, and I threw Ollie towards the nearest large object. I scooted behind the kitchen island, where hands clung to me.

Beside me, Nigella and Verity huddled on my right, while Sonia clutched my left arm. On the other side of the room, behind the huge dresser that Nigella used for ornaments, cookbooks, and various accoutrements, were Guy, Simon, and now a shell-shocked Ollie.

"What the fuck is happening?" Ollie screamed.

"Arden, are you okay?" Simon yelled.

Nigella looked at me. "Why is she trying to shoot us?"

"She killed Riz," I said loudly.

Another hail of bullets. "This is no fun," Katrina said. "Come out and play." Her footsteps hung back. Every bullet made my heart stop with fear. They ripped through the room. Deafening. I clenched my jaw against every new noise. So loud, so piercing.

Nigella had her phone out, calling the police. Sonia was texting Ade.

"I don't care if I live or die, as long as I take out some of the men who killed my son." Her voice came out loud and clear.

There was a silence.

"Your … your Rabbie …"

"I told you it was his middle name. His real name was Stuart," she said.

I dared to look over. Guy and Simon were both the palest white.

Ollie breathed out. "S Murray."

"You never said he was bloody Scottish!" I yelled at Simon.

"I didn't know he was." Simon sounded confused.

"Boarding school," Katrina answered. "My husband insisted. Never had a hint of his own accent."

"What the hell is happening?" Nigella whispered.

I shook my head. The dust and fragments of paper from the obliterated kitchen were slowly falling around us like a particularly warped Christmas snowfall in June.

"Yes, why don't you tell us everything, Katrina?" I yelled to her. I heard her footsteps on the concrete outside and the sound of the door opening.

"It's quite simple, you see, my son's death. We were told it was an accidental overdose. We hadn't been close when he died. My husband hated that he was gay. The boy he raised as his own had, in his eyes, rejected him." Her voice was thick with emotion. "Rabbie took it hard. He changed his name back to his father's when he joined the army.

"I was devastated when he died. But I barely had time to grieve; my husband was dying. Long, slow, painful death. Messy and undignified way to go. I had my mind so full of caring for him, that it was only when he died I was able to fully process Rabbie's loss. Fully process how bizarre it had all been."

"What do you mean?" I asked. Everyone looked at me like I was mad. The more she talked, the more time for the police to come. Verity dug her nails into my hand; she was shaking with fear.

"Well, that my boy would die like that. His friend Jeremy told me at his funeral that it seemed odd. I just assumed it was guilt, I knew Jeremy took as many drugs as Rabbie did. Gave them to him. He killed my boy as much as anyone. But he was right. So, I put pressure on my husband's friends. Andrew was very senior in the army. He knew people. They'd had dinner at our house. When I asked questions, they felt obliged to find answers for me."

She paused. The only sound were ragged breaths. "That's how I found out about a man called Simon Anson," she said.

Nigella gasped. "What did you do?" she whispered to the others.

"Katrina, if you want me, I'll come, but let everyone else go," came Simon's voice.

She laughed again. "Why would I do that? Don't try and play your MI6 games with me. I came here to do what I originally intended to. To kill the person that you love the most."

Simon was in MI6? Well, of course, he fucking was. That actually made complete sense.

"You already killed Riz!" Sonia screamed at her.

Katrina continued laughing. "Oh, I know. But Simon hated Riz deep down. They barely tolerated one another. Riz told me, he was so heartbroken, well, he pretended to be, I'm not sure if he was capable of real emotions unless it was about his career. He was always like that."

"So, who does Simon love?" Nigella asked.

"Oh, you know, Gella, it was you who told me. That they were sleeping together."

"Guy?" I asked loudly.

"What?" Sonia yelled. "Them two are doing it?"

Nigella looked shocked. "Really?"

"What? No. You idiots," Katrina yelled. "Arden. Him and Simon."

There was a pause. "You and Simon slept together?" Ollie yelled at me. I cringed and wanted to sink into the ground.

"When the hell was this? You told me there was nothing between you," Ollie continued.

"Yeah, when have you two been shagging?" Guy asked. "When I asked you out again?"

"You asked Arden out again?" Simon yelled.

The gun went off, and a huge chunk of Nigella's kitchen ceiling collapsed onto the ground, with dust and plaster everywhere. There was another chorus of screams – I think most of them were mine. "This isn't *Hollyoaks*!" Katrina yelled. "Can you all shut up?"

"Christ almighty," she continued. "As I was saying. I found out about Simon Anson. I already knew he was responsible from Jeremy. The man my son had been dating, who'd killed him, and my plan was already in motion. But I needed more. And then with some digging, I was able to find the real story."

"How?" Verity breathed.

I closed my eyes and squeezed them tight. "Tarquin."

She laughed again. "Yes, he was incredibly happy to have a visitor in prison. I promised to help get him a better lawyer, and he spilt every secret on Guy Frobisher he had. Told me the full story. Names, dates, he was only too glad to help. And when I asked how I could really, really hurt Simon Anson, his face lit up."

Tarquin. Ruining my life from a ten-by-ten-foot cell.

"So, I enlisted my old friend Riz to get in touch. He had plans to be an MP. And apparently, Guy Frobisher was desperate to run for Parliament. Tarquin had the photos sitting in the inbox of an old email account he'd never got rid of. I logged in and got them."

"And as for Jed," she scoffed. "That idiot. Well, I never meant to kill him. Make him a vegetable, maybe, not that you can really tell the difference."

"You leaked the photos for revenge on Guy?" I said. "And put Jed in hospital, not caring if he lived or died. But why did you kill Riz?"

"Easy," she said. I heard her pulling out a chair from the table and taking a seat. "He wanted to confess everything. He chickened out."

Marina's words came into my head. Riz was in over his head. The photos of Guy were supposed to embarrass him. Not shake the entire establishment.

"But I'd gone too far for him to ruin it. I didn't kill Macauley Sheridan to speed up the election, I didn't destroy every scrap of my old life to make the trail go cold, so he could freeze on me. No, no. Simon, you had to suffer, I'm afraid. And for that to happen Arden had to die. But Riz chickened out. We'd planned it that afternoon after his radio appearance. We'd kill Arden that night. Then when we followed him, he said we couldn't do it while he was with Errol. That he wouldn't do it. We argued. And I shot him." She sounded as if this was the only logical solution.

"You're fucking mad!" Verity screamed. Her nails dug into my hand.

"Yes, well, quite. But you lose a child, my dear, and see how you feel when the men who killed him are wandering about free. You'll discover it's quite easy to stop caring about things like that."

"We didn't kill your son, Katrina!" Guy yelled. "We never laid a finger on him. He died of an overdose! It was his own stupid fault!"

I almost groaned at that. Yup, call the mad woman's son a drug addict who got what he deserved.

"Katrina," I yelled over everything else. "Look, I know you loved Rabbie. I'm so, so, sorry for what happened to him. No one deserves to die like that. I'm sorry you couldn't be with him. I'm sorry your husband created that rift between you, but that's not anyone in this room's fault. They don't know what's going on. Why don't you and I stay in here? Just us. You want me, don't you?"

Far away, I could hear police sirens. Hurry up, hurry up.

Katrina was silent. "Fine. The women can go. They shouldn't suffer for the sins of men."

"Okay," I said. "They're going to go out the door and leave through the front of the house. You'll not harm them, will you?"

"I said I wouldn't," she said in an aggrieved tone. Like, she was offended I'd think she was a liar.

I beckoned for the girls to go. "We can't leave you," Verity said. "She's a nutter. She's going to kill you."

I smiled at her and gripped her hand back. "I'll be fine," I said. She was less than convinced.

"C'mon." Nigella pulled her along as they fled. Verity gripped my hand for as long as she could.

"It'll be alright," I whispered.

The three of them ran from the room. I could hear Kennedy barking and the sirens coming closer.

"Why don't we all sit at the table like civilised folk?" Katrina asked. Sweetness and light.

I dared to look. She was sitting at the table like this was a macabre coffee morning. Across the room, the others were all waiting for me. I nodded.

Standing gingerly, I held my hands in front, where she could see them. "Don't shoot me yet, please, Katrina," I said.

"Course not, love, wouldn't dream of it."

Fucking deranged. I cocked my head for the others to join me. Ollie looked stunned, and when he stood, his legs nearly gave way underneath him. Simon pulled him along and deposited him in a chair.

Guy was shaky but managed on his own. Simon was … well, Simon was scowling.

We sat. There was a silence.

"If it makes any difference, Katrina, I truly am sorry that Stuart died," Simon said. "I enjoyed his company. I never wanted him to get hurt."

She smiled. "Thank you. It changes nothing. But thank you, nonetheless."

"Katrina, if it's me you want, why don't you let them go?" I asked. "It'll be as horrible for them to know I'm dead from outside as it is in here."

She tutted and shook her head. "Oh, no, they deserve to see."

I pointed at Ollie. "He never even met Rabbie. He doesn't know what's going on! Trust me, I'd quite enjoy him to suffer, but not like this."

She shook her head again. "Arden, sweet silly Arden. You remind me a bit of my Rabbie, you know. He was trusting as well. But no, your Oliver is nowhere near as innocent in this as he's made you think." She smiled sweetly as my insides turned to ice. Ollie stared at the ground; a tear fell down his cheek and onto Nigella's plaster-dust-covered table.

"What did you do?" I could barely ask.

"I'm sorry," he whispered. "I never thought it— I didn't know she was insane. I thought it'd help me get you back. I …" His voice choked.

"You knew who S Murray was the entire time?" Simon barked.

He nodded. "I'm sorry. She invited me to a meeting in Bristol. Pretended to be someone else. Told me if I helped her, she'd convince you to take me back. Otherwise, she'd tell you all about Jamie."

"And the letter?" I asked.

"Oh – no, that was me being sneaky," she said. "I gave that to Riz as insurance. If anything happened to me, he was to put it in the police's hands. Oliver knew nothing of that. He did what he was told, so I never needed to use it."

I nodded. Well. That settled that then. I turned to Katrina. "I'm ready. Where should we do this? Outside? I wouldn't want to get my brains all over Nigella's kitchen. Think of her kids. They'll be home from school soon."

Katrina nodded. "Very thoughtful. Outside it is then. You three watch."

She stood, and I followed. As I rose, Simon gripped my hand. Katrina looked pleased with this. He held my hand, his eyes boring into me.

I touched his stubbly cheek and tried to shake my hand free. "It's all going to be okay. Remember, the last time something like this happened? Kennedy burst into the room and knocked over Neuberger? Just remember that." He gripped my hand but eventually let go.

"Guy," I said, giving him a nod. I couldn't bring myself to look at Ollie.

"Let's make a start, shall we?" Katrina said filing us out. "Gents, you can stay seated, or stand and watch.

Except you, Simon. You really must stand at the door. You need to see."

We walked up the short path through the wreckage of Nigella's house and stood in the middle of the garden.

It was scorching hot. The sunshine was blinding. "Nice day for it," she said, loading her gun.

"Quite. You said you burnt every scrap of your old life, that's why there was no trail?"

"Yes. Doesn't matter anymore. I'll hand myself over as soon as this is done."

"So … you don't have any photos of Rabbie?" I asked.

She shook her head. "A painful sacrifice. But the only one I have is the one I showed you."

"Oh."

"Right." She cocked the gun. "Eyes open, please, you need to see it, but aside from that, your choice of pose."

C'mon, c'mon, please. Where were the police?

Please, please, someone protect me. There was no help coming. No one was rushing to save me. My heart was in my mouth. There would be no flashes of inspiration this time. Katrina was not Tarquin with his bumbling attempts to cover up his crimes. No, she wanted me dead and all the world to see.

Nausea rode over me in waves. I fell to my knees. "Katrina, don't do this," I sobbed. Snot and tears rolling down my face. "Please, I never even met Rabbie, I barely know these people. I've only lived here a few months. Please, please!"

She looked at me sympathetically. She swung the gun up.

Death. I was going to die. I tried to stop the sobs that were ripping my chest open. But I couldn't. If you've ever thought you'd be calm and dignified in the face of your executioner, I can tell you now – you won't be. "Do you want me to beg?" I screamed, my voice breaking. "I'll beg, please! I don't want to die!"

"Aw, Arden. No one does."

"I'm only thirty-two. My life's a mess. I want to … please, don't kill me. I want to meet someone and have a family and grow old together," I begged. "Please!"

There was a long pause. She gave me that sweet maternal smile. "You really do remind me of my Rabbie. Anyway, any last words?"

My chest was heaving with painful sobs. I was near hysterical. I looked around me. This was happening. No movie ending for me.

I saw something from the corner of my eye, blurry through the tears and sweat. I nodded at her. "My last words?"

"Yes?" she asked sweetly.

"Good boy," I said.

"What?"

Forty kilograms of Alsatian/Dobermann cross launched himself at her. And this time, Kenny wasn't playing. He was going in for the kill.

Her screams sounded out across the village. She dropped the gun. But I could see she had something else on her.

"No, you fucking don't," I said, launching myself at her, and kicked her hand as hard as I could before she could get to her pocket.

She screamed again. Simon and Guy came running. Guy grabbed Kenny while Simon took the gun she'd been holding and used it to smack her across the face as hard as he could. Blood and a tooth or two flew across the garden. But it was too late. She took her small revolver from her pocket and aimed, and fired. "Simon!" I screamed.

He was lucky. He dived to avoid losing half his skull, but he dropped the other gun, and it scattered across the ground. I lunged for it. My hands were sweaty, but I managed to get it. Katrina and I stood there, weapons pointing at one another.

The others backed off, Guy cradling Kenny. Ollie was standing at the doors of the house, looking stricken. "You know, my husband did four tours in Northern Ireland. It's easy to get guns out of there. This is the one I shot Riz with," she said, shaking her little revolver like it was a cool knick-knack. She pointed it at them wildly. "No one make a move."

We all took a pause. Above us, I could hear a chopper approaching. They'd brought in the big guns. A police siren was still whirring.

"Katrina Pettigrew," came the sound of a voice through a megaphone from the street. "This is DI Neuberger. You are under arrest. Come out with your hands up, and you will not be hurt." Katrina threw back her head and laughed.

None of us spoke for a long time. Just the sound of the helicopter coming closer and the ragged breathing of all involved. "You know that photo of your son," I said. "Looks pretty flammable. It'd be a shame if you never saw your boy's face again.

"You wouldn't dare," she said. I needed to get her away from everyone else. No matter what I did, she had a full cartridge in her gun. I couldn't have much more than one or two bullets in this weapon. I was inching backwards, and she was coming towards me. Further from the others.

I smiled. "Wouldn't I? Well, if you want to know, you gotta catch me first," I said and took off with a jump over Nigella's back fence.

She screamed in frustration. But that was all, I didn't look back; instead, I ran as fast as my skinny little legs could carry me. Down the path to the end of Nigella's street, through overgrown hedges and old rickety fences, rose bushes and thorns ripping at my exposed arms and legs.

I couldn't hear her behind me, but I needed to believe she was.

The crack of a gun. A bullet zinged past my head, and a tree in front of me gave out a shower of bark as the shot lodged itself into the trunk. Yep, definitely behind me. I felt a sharp pain as a splinter punctured my forehead.

"Fuck!" I screamed and hung a left. I emerged onto the street going east through the village. I was sweating and running – literally – on pure adrenaline. My white T-shirt was already soaked through with sweat, plaster, and now stained red from the wound on my forehead, which was pumping out blood at an alarming rate. I took off to the left, heading for Katrina's house.

I reached the corner, sprinting madly. The door to one of the houses on the corner of the street to Katrina's was opening, presumably someone out to look at the helicopter. "Arden, I thought it'd be you involved in this, gosh, it was never like this before you moved here!" She squinted in the bright sunlight. "Oh, look, Katrina is out jogging too. In this heat, and at her age! Hello, Katrina!" she yelled, which turned to a shriek as a huge chunk of Odette's front door took a bullet.

"Fuck off, you annoying cow!" Katrina screamed.

While she tried to kill Odette, I dived onto the tiny path that ran behind the back of this street's houses. The one Sonia and I had used to break into Katrina's house when it was Arabella's. A lifetime ago.

Sprinting along it, I had no idea what I was doing, or what would happen, but as long as Katrina was focused on me, she wouldn't hurt anyone else.

I jumped the fence into her garden and crept along. I couldn't hear her behind me. Clearly, she'd not come this way and instead gone to the front. I moved as quietly as I could.

The garden was overgrown and wild. The plants left to their own devices. Maybe it was because of the heat, causing some to wither, that it was passable at all. I got to the back door and decided, fuck subtlety. I smashed the window and reached through to unlock it.

"Hey, Katrina, I'm in your house, coming to get your son!" I yelled. "Your screwed up druggie son, who let any man who looked at him fuck him because of all his daddy issues!"

I heard a scream of annoyance from the front of the house.

"Dirty addict. He was a stupid little boy!" I kept taunting, a drip-drip of sweat and blood fell off me onto the hardwood floors as I walked. "I bet he was filthy. Addicts always are. Bet he let Simon and Guy do whatever they wanted to him. Bet there were ten guys a night in his bed! None of them probably even knew his name."

A gunshot split through the room. An ornament a few feet from me took the brunt. She was coming through the house. I needed to go forward. Meet in the middle and, hell, I don't know … wrestle her?

My breathing was ragged, and I could barely stop myself from puking, so continuing to yell was not an option for a second. I paused behind a door. My sweaty hands were slipping on the gun.

"You were a terrible mother," I yelled when I could eventually get words out again. "You couldn't keep him safe. You didn't look after him. You let your husband disown him when he came out. Even my mother didn't do that." I heard her scream and come towards me. "I bet he hated you," I yelled as she came through the door. I swung the gun's barrel straight into her head.

She went down. Holy fuck, she hit the ground hard. Her gun scattered along the floor, and I grappled for it. She was down for the count. A huge dent in her head seemed to indicate that I'd done my job. It was over.

Crouching down beside her, I waited for my breathing to get back to normal. "I mean what I said," I spat at her. "People like you don't deserve to be parents. It's supposed to be unconditional love." I took the guns and walked through the front of the house, opened the front door, and went out onto the street.

"Arden!" Jack Maslin yelled. He had a bulletproof jacket on and was pounding the street as he ran towards me.

"I'm putting them down," I shouted, holding the guns. "I'm not going to use them; I will put them down and do whatever you ask."

More police arrived at the end of the street; Jack held up a hand to keep them back. He stopped about twenty metres away from me. The other officers all formed a line behind him. The chopper was right over our heads.

"Okay, Arden, you do exactly that. One at a time, nice and easy, and then I want you to walk two metres to the side of them and put your hands on your head. Understand?"

"I understand," I called out over the distance between us.

Neuberger panted up behind Jack. "Where is Katrina?" he yelled.

"Inside," I shouted back. "She's unarmed. She's … alive," I added, perhaps a bit weakly.

They nodded. I put the guns down. "That's good, Arden. Now move to the side and put your hands on your head and kneel, okay? We'll come towards you slowly," Jack yelled.

I did what he said. I kept my eyes rooted on Jack and Neuberger. They watched me intently. It was going to be okay. I was not going to fuck this up. Everything would be okay. They wouldn't shoot me, thinking I was an accomplice. I was going to get out of this alive.

I had one knee on the ground when Katrina came through the door, screaming madly, and held the stun gun she'd taken off Dhapinder to my throat and pressed it down.

Chapter 26

Ow.

Ouch.

Oh, fuck, ow. Oh, shitting Christing fucking Jesus, everything fucking hurt. Fuck. Oh, God, I was in so much pain.

Why did everything hurt?

Where was I? Was I alive? What was happening? I think my eyes were closed. Or I was dead. Everything was white. Okay, maybe I was in heaven. Heaven sounded … heavenly. Maybe they had air conditioning and iced coffees that were zero calories.

Oof, that sounded good.

"I think he's coming to," said a Welsh voice.

"Thank God," said a second woman's voice in RP.

"Stand back, stand back," said a man's RP accent.

"ARDEN, CAN YOU HEAR US?" came a Dorset twang. Oh, ow, fuck, Jesus.

"Yes, Sonia, I can hear you. Fuck, don't yell," I croaked. My voice was raspy. Talking hurt. Talking hurt so much that I thought I would start crying.

I slowly opened my eyes. Above me were several concerned faces. Nigella, Verity, and Sonia were all peering over me. Guy was there too. Jack Maslin came in and out of focus.

"Wha … where?" I tried to speak, but the burning in my throat was too much. "Water?" I croaked.

Nigella helped me sit up slightly – ow – and a cup of water was pressed to my lips. I blinked and drank, and spent a few seconds taking in my surroundings. I was in a hospital ward.

"Where am I?" I asked eventually.

"A & E, babes," Verity said.

"What happened?"

There was a sharing of looks around the room. Jack came forward. "Katrina hit you with the highest setting on the stun gun. You had a seizure and were knocked out."

Oh. My first thought was the expected. "Did I … did I wet myself?"

"Really, Arden, that's your first question?" Nigella asked. Okay, so not the expected first question. "Not what happened to Katrina?"

"We shot her in the shoulder," Jack said. "She's alive. Under a heavy police guard. And in a different hospital. She's singing like a canary, can't wait to tell anyone who'll listen how she poisoned Macauley Sheridan and shot Riz." He leaned forward. "And no, your dignity was saved."

"Thank God for that."

"He's totally referring to not pissing himself in public," Verity informed us all. "He couldn't care less about Katrina."

"You would too!" I snapped and then coughed. Oh, it burnt.

"Yeah, the throat, not a pleasant place to have it done," Jack said.

I looked around the room. Besides the three women, Jack, and Guy, there was a man in the corner with a dog on his lap. He was stroking the dog's fur and holding on to it tightly.

Simon looked up at me and gave a tired, tight smile. Kennedy wagged his tail and jumped off his lap to come over to me. "He's a hero," Sonia told me. "We heard what he did." She patted his head lovingly.

"He's the best," I told them, as Kenny licked my hand. I looked around again. "Where's Ollie?" I asked.

"He's at the station, answering some questions," Jack said solemnly. There was a silence.

"We don't think he really was involved. Katrina came to him, offering to almost mediate between the two of you. From what he said in the car to the station, he didn't know about anything else. But he'll need to answer a lot of questions."

I nodded. Verity stroked my shoulder. "The doctors want you to stay in overnight."

"I want to sleep."

"You saved our lives, Arden," she sniffled.

"I thought you had your tear ducts fused shut on your eighteenth birthday?" I said.

"I did, but it was a Polish doctor. Couldn't do it right. Too busy thinking about what carb-y stodge to have for lunch." She poked her tongue out at me.

"I think we should give Arden some space, now that we know he's okay," Guy said. He reached down and kissed me on the cheek. "I'm so sorry," he whispered. I nodded and patted his arm.

Nigella gave me a gentle hug and then Sonia did too – much less gingerly.

Jack gripped my hand and told me he'd be in touch. "You did bloody well, Arden," he said and patted my hand. Verity looked between us and raised an eyebrow.

He followed the others out.

Simon stood. "Arden," he whispered.

Verity turned to me. "I can give you a minute?"

"No, that won't be necessary. Simon's leaving now." I didn't look at him. Everything between us had been lies and subterfuge. He didn't respect me. He didn't know me. And I'd almost died because he wouldn't tell me the truth.

"Arden, please!"

"I said leave!" I snapped, my blood boiling. But my energy left as soon as it arrived. "I don't … just go, Simon." My voice was a croak. It was agony to talk.

He set his jaw firm. "I am sorry," he said in an even voice and left.

Then it was me and Verity. She held my hand. "Let it all out, baby. Tell Mama Vee."

I shook my head. Couldn't. I'd never stop.

"How about I tell you my good news then? The news I've been trying to tell you for days." I looked at her. "Donal and Ffion have backed down."

"What?"

"Yup," she said. "I think that lawyer you got scared the shit out of them. But now, well, you know those exploratory meetings we had back in January?"

"With the US TV network?"

She nodded. "I've been in touch with Bryce out in LA. You know his agency has moved mostly into development deals, now? Well, he's your new US representation, if you want him. And you want him. Because your books are going to be adapted into a TV show. And not by the network we were originally thinking – that teen drama bullshit. No, by, um, the biggest network. You know, the one that did the show about the Dragons and that other one about the four racist bitches in New York."

I gaped at her.

"Not only that, but they want you on board to help – what was the phrase – 'craft the world' as an executive producer. Arden, we're talking millions and millions."

Words. I was trying to form words, but none were coming out. "Bryce is waiting for your answer. Honestly, if he didn't want to sit on your face before this, he definitely does now."

"What does this mean?" I managed to ask eventually.

"Er, I just said. It means we're fucking rich, mate. It means Donal and Ffion have crawled back into their cage. The contract renegotiations are off. And that we're flying out to LA next week to put signatures to some very lucrative contracts."

"Oh my God."

"Yeah." She smiled at me and held my hand. "Consider it my apology for being a crap friend. Why didn't you tell me about finding Riz? I would have dropped everything."

"I'm a big boy," I said. "I need to learn to handle my shit."

"You nearly died!"

"So, I'm still learning to handle my shit," I said. Kennedy whined, and I frowned. "Can I take Kennedy to LA? How long are we going for?"

She wrinkled her brow. "Dunno, we can try and pass him off as big hand luggage. They let you do that in first class."

"First class?"

"Babes. We rich. How many times do I have to tell you? You're about to become a multi-gazillionaire."

"God, LA? Wow. I can barely handle the heat here at the moment."

Verity stroked Kennedy's head. "Nah, we don't have to worry about that anymore. Huge thunderstorm appeared around an hour ago. It's pouring rain outside. Like, biblical rain. No more heatwave for us."

"Everything is back to normal then?" I said.

My oldest, dearest friend smiled at me and nodded. My dog rested his head on my hand.

I lay back to finally get some proper sleep.

Acknowledgements

First of all, thank you to you, the reader, for making this happen …

I said in the first acknowledgements that maybe I'd get this one done faster. Well, guess what, Mimi, we did. This one only took five or six years from first keystroke to you reading it. Not eight.

So, in no specific order, thank you to Jehan for being the first friend to read it and saying exciting things such as, "I think you were trying to make a joke here … Anyway."

Specific thanks to Shayna, Jane, and Andy for all their comments, encouraging and otherwise. To Rob, Ellie, and Deanna for the kind words.

Deanna – I will come to New York and do a reading one day. Maybe.

Thank you to Giorgia and Monica for the flowers, and to Cristina for telling me to put more sex in it. Great advice.

Thank you to all my friends, family, colleagues, and everyone else for all the encouragement and attempts at dissuasion.

Thank you to everyone at my husband's work for buying it, even though you've only met me twice.

Thank you to all the people who left reviews on Goodreads and Amazon, saying they enjoyed it. Truly grateful for every one of them. Even the one-star ones.

Thank you to Kirsty Parkinson of Crowberry Editorial for her wonderful copyedit. All typos and subsequent errors are my fault and mine alone.

Thanks to my cat, Sylvester, for having an underactive thyroid, two separate heart problems, and an anxiety disorder, which means he has such eye-wateringly high vet bills that it encourages me to try and try again.

Because, frankly, I need you to buy more copies to pay for him.

Lastly, thank you to my husband, Alasdair, for all of the above and more for the past ten years. You have the patience of a saint.

About the author

James Quentin is a self-published author.

He works as a journalist during the day and has a degree in English Literature.

Away from the world of work, he lives in London with his husband and an extremely needy cat that has multiple expensive health issues (see previous page for more details).

Published by Over It Publishing

eBook ISBN: 978-1-0683290-3-6

Paperback – ISBN: 978-1-0683290-2-9

www.ingramcontent.com/pod-product-compliance
Lightning Source LLC
LaVergne TN
LVHW040825090826
845145LV00001BA/203

* 9 7 8 1 0 6 8 3 2 9 0 2 9 *